HAM   Hamilton, Laurell K,
author.

A shiver of light.

$27.95

DATE			

A SHIVER OF LIGHT

A
SHIVER
OF
LIGHT

LAURELL K. HAMILTON

BERKLEY BOOKS, NEW YORK

THE BERKLEY PUBLISHING GROUP
Published by the Penguin Group
Penguin Group (USA)
375 Hudson Street, New York, New York 10014

USA • Canada • UK • Ireland • Australia • New Zealand • India • South Africa • China

penguin.com

A Penguin Random House Company

This book is an original publication of The Berkley Publishing Group.

Library of Congress Cataloging-in-Publication Data

Hamilton, Laurell K.
A shiver of light / Laurell K. Hamilton. —First edition.
pages cm (A Meredith Gentry novel ; 1)
ISBN 978-0-425-25566-7 (hardback)
1. Gentry, Meredith (Fictitious character)—Fiction.   2. Fairies—Fiction.
3. Los Angeles (Calif.)—Fiction.   I. Title.
PS3558.A443357S54   2014
813'.54—dc23   2014010316

First edition: June 2014

PRINTED IN THE UNITED STATES OF AMERICA

10 9 8 7 6 5 4 3 2 1

Cover art: man © Frank P. Wartenberg/Getty Images; light spatter © Soumen Nath/Thinkstock
Cover design by Judith Lagerman
Interior text design by Kristin del Rosario
Endpaper art: lights © lorenzo104/iStockphoto; wings © thawats/iStockphoto
Endpaper design by Kristin del Rosario

To the fans who let me know
how much they missed Merry and her men.

You finally get to read the next part of the story.

ACKNOWLEDGMENTS

To my husband, Jonathon, partner, friend, lover, who stands by my side and behind the throne. Thank you for holding my coat. To Genevieve, who is both our beautiful maiden and able to grab her own sword and charge into battle. To Shawn, who stood at the battlements when the night was dark and the dragon was fierce. Dragon stew, at last! To Spike, who has entered the fray and proved himself stalwart and true. To Jess, who joined the team this book. To Will, who helped with research on the last book—so nice when friends have expertise that I need. To Pilar, my sister, so glad we're both happy, at last. Welcome to the family, Fran! To Missy, who keeps reminding me of things I've forgotten. To Sherry, Teresa, and Mary, who never give up trying to organize a houseful of artists. And to our dogs, Keiko, Mordor, and Sasquatch, who stayed at my side through all the long nights and early mornings, faithful to me, and their treat drawer.

I feel like one
Who treads alone
Some banquet-hall deserted,
Whose lights are fled,
Whose garlands dead,
And all but he departed!
Thus, in the stilly night,
Ere slumber's chain has bound me,
Sad memory brings the light
Of other days around me.

—THOMAS MOORE

CHAPTER

ONE

woke in the desert, far from home, and knew it was a dream, and that it was also real. I was dreaming, but where I stood was real and whatever happened here tonight, that would be real, too. Stars covered the sky as if electricity had never been invented, so that starlight was enough for me to see my way down the dirt road, with its bomb craters making it almost impossible for anything to drive down it. IEDs had blown the road to hell, partly to kill the soldiers in the armored vehicles that had triggered the bombs, but also to make the road impassable by anyone who came after them. I stood shivering in the cold desert wind, wishing I were wearing something besides the thin silk nightgown that strained over my very pregnant belly. I was only days away from giving birth to twins, and my body was mostly baby now. I moved slowly down the road and found the dirt cool underneath my bare feet. There was a small hut close to the road, and whatever had called me from my bed in Los Angeles was there. How did I know that? Goddess told me, not in words, but in that quiet voice that's almost always in our heads. Goddess and God talk to us all the time, but we are usually being too loud to hear them; in these dreams that "quiet voice" was easier to hear.

I knew my body was still asleep thousands of miles from here, and I'd never been hurt in any of the dream journeys, but I felt the rocks slide under my feet, and as pregnant as I was, my balance wasn't good. I had a moment to wonder what would happen if I fell, but I kept walking toward the hut, because I'd learned that until I'd helped the person calling me, the dream would remain, and I would remain in it.

It was my dream, but it would be someone else's nightmare reality. I was never called unless it was a matter of life and death. Someone who had saved my life, risking their own, and been healed by my hands was nearby and in need; that was always the way it was, who it was. They prayed and I appeared, but only if I was asleep, only in my dreams, so far. I had no idea if some night I would vanish in my real life to be called to someone's side while I was still awake. I hoped not. The dreams were disturbing enough; if it spread to my waking life, I wasn't sure what I'd do.

Soldiers prayed, and collected nails that had been used as shrapnel against me, and rubbed them with blood, and fit them onto leather thongs that they had made, and wore them as others wore a cross. The nails had come from my body, as had the blood, but magic had healed me. The Goddess had given me the ability to heal that night, and the soldiers who had taken the nails and worn them had started healing by touch, as well, in the far-off war. Sometimes their need was great enough to bring me to help them find a way out of an ambush, or shelter from a mountain blizzard.

I am Princess Meredith NicEssus, Princess of Flesh and Blood; I am faerie and only part human, but I am not a goddess, and I didn't like these midnight rambles. I liked helping people, but as I'd gotten more and more pregnant I had worried about the babies, and the men I loved had worried about it, but all they could do was watch over my body until I woke.

Still, the Goddess had work for me, and that was that, so I walked carefully over the smooth dirt and the rough stones, and felt the call, my call, as if I were truly some kind of deity able to answer prayers. Really I thought I might be more like a human saint; there were tales of saints being able to translocate through time and space. I'd done some reading on them, especially the Celtic ones, and there were some really odd stories. Quite a few saints had been Celtic deities that the human Church had adopted. The early Church had preferred to make friends of the local deities, rather than make war; it was so much easier to convert people when they could keep their local saint's day celebrations.

Some saints had appeared in people's dreams, or to lead people to safety, or even to fight in battles, when other witnesses knew they were asleep or wounded. None of the old stories talked about a pregnant faerie princess, but then the Church usually sanitized all the old tales.

The wind spilled my hair around my face in a mass of blinding red curls, though the color must have been more brown than scarlet in the starlit night. I could see nothing but the spill of my own hair for a moment, but when the wind cleared there was a figure in the doorway of the hut.

I didn't recognize her at first, and then the very darkness of her skin let me know that underneath the desert camouflage it was Hayes. She was the only female African American among my soldiers.

I went to her smiling, and she smiled back, as she began to slide down the edge of the doorsill. I wanted to be next to her, and I just was, without having to walk the distance. Dream rules worked sometimes in these journeys; sometimes they didn't.

I knelt beside her, having to grip the doorway to get to my knees. I was heavy enough with child that it was debatable whether I could stand again, but I had to touch Hayes, see what was wrong.

Her hand fell away from her neck and I caught the dull glint of the nail she'd been holding on to with its leather thong necklace. It was my symbol. I took her hand in mine and it was slick with blood. They had to touch the nail with blood to call me; that had been true every time.

"Hayes," I said.

"Meredith, I prayed and here you are. Wow, you're huge. Must really be twins like the news said?"

"It is. Where are you hurt?" I asked.

She patted her side with her other hand. Her armored vest was there, but it was wet, and even as I searched for the wound fresh blood welled out. I knew it was fresh because it was warmer than the stuff that had cooled in the night air.

"It's deep," she said, voice pained, as I tried to find the wound through her clothes and gear.

"What happened?" I asked. I wasn't sure that talking was good for her, but having something to think about while I found the wound and figured out what to do about it was better than just thinking about the fact that she seemed to be bleeding to death. Wasn't it? I'd been answering prayers for only a few months and I still felt out of my depth. I trusted Goddess to know what She was doing, but me, I wasn't so sure about me.

I prayed as I found the wound. It was almost as wide as my palm, and blood was welling out of it. Something that held a lot of blood had been punctured. I'd had human anatomy in college, but for the life of me, or for the life of Hayes, I couldn't seem to think what organ was on this side of the body. I didn't know what had been damaged, but I knew she was going to die if I couldn't help her.

"We were just supposed to take some supplies up to a school, but they ambushed us. The cutest little boy stabbed me, because I hesitated. I couldn't kill a child, or thought I couldn't, but they killed Dickerson, and Breck, and Sunshine, and then he tried to kill me, and suddenly he wasn't a child anymore, he was just another murdering bastard." She started to cry, and that made her groan with pain.

I prayed for guidance. I was trying to hold pressure on the wound, but without a medical kit, or the Goddess granting me the ability to heal with my hands, I couldn't save her. And then I realized that she, Hayes, had healed other wounded with her hands, because she'd told me so when she was on leave last time; had that only been two months ago?

"Heal yourself, Hayes," I said.

She shook her head. "I killed that little boy, Meredith. I killed him. I killed him, and I can't forgive myself. We killed the men before everyone but me died, but the boy . . . he couldn't have been more than ten. My little brother's age. Jesus, Meredith, how could I kill a kid?"

"He tried to kill you, Hayes, and if you don't heal yourself, he will have killed you."

"Maybe I deserve to die."

"No, Hayes, no you don't." I kept pressure on the wound to try to slow the blood loss while I helped her forgive herself, because I knew now that was why I was there.

She cried harder, and that made the wound hurt more and gush hot around my hands. She slipped lower in the doorway. She was going to bleed to death in front of me.

"Goddess, please, help me to help her."

I smelled roses and I knew the Goddess was with me, and then I felt/saw/knew that she would be standing over us. To me she was a cloaked figure, because Goddess comes to us all in different ways, or all ways.

Hayes looked up and said, "Grandma, what you doing here?"

"You let this woman heal you, Angela May Hayes. Don't you fight her."

"You don't know what I did, Grandma."

"I heard, but Angela, if a boy is old enough to pick up a weapon and kill you, then he's not a child anymore, he's a soldier just like you are, and you did what you had to do."

"He was Jeffrey's age."

"Your brother would never hurt anyone."

"Jeffrey was a baby when you died, how do you know?"

I felt the smile like the sun coming through clouds after a storm. You couldn't help but smile when the Goddess smiled. "I keep watch over my babies. I saw you graduate from college. I'm so proud of my angel, and I need you to live, Angela. I need you to go back home and help your mama and Jeffrey and all the rest, do you hear me, Angela?"

"I hear you, Grandma."

"You have to get better; you'll be my angel for real one of these days, but not tonight. You heal and go home to our family."

"Yes, Grandma," she said.

The blood slowed and then stopped pouring out. I hadn't done anything, but Angela Hayes had, and the Goddess had, and Hayes's grandmother had.

"I think I'm better," Hayes said, and grabbed my hand with hers. "Thank you, Meredith, thank you for bringing my grandma to talk to me."

"The Goddess brought your grandmother," I said.

"But you brought the Goddess."

I held her hand tight and said, "The Goddess is always there for you; you don't need me to find Her."

Hayes smiled and then frowned. "I see lights."

I glanced down the road and saw a line of armored vehicles of all kinds coming over the hill, their lights cutting the thick starlight so that the night seemed both more black and less at the same time.

"They talk about a red-haired Madonna that appears when people need her. No one seems to know it's you but us." I knew she meant the other soldiers.

"It's better that way," I said.

She gripped my hand tight. "Then you better go before the trucks get closer."

I touched her face and realized I still had her blood on my hands, so I left the bloody imprints of my fingertips on her skin. "Be well, be safe, come home soon," I said.

She smiled, and this time it was bright and real. "I will, Meredith, I will."

The dream broke while I was still holding her hand. I woke in my bed in Los Angeles with the fathers of my babies on either side of me. My hands and nightgown were covered in blood, and it wasn't mine.

CHAPTER

TWO

Y ou'd think, after a goddess had sent me halfway around the world to save a life and brought me back to my own bed, that my life would be full of magic, and it was, but it was also full of normal things. That's what no one tells you: that even when Deity takes a hand in your life, and you answer their call, your ordinary life doesn't go away. I was still pregnant and it had not been a trouble-free pregnancy. If you are following Deity's plan for you, it isn't always the easy path; sometimes it's the hard one. So why follow? Because to do any less is to betray your own abilities and gifts, and the faith that Deity has in you. Who would do that willingly?

Ultrasound pictures are grainy, black and white and gray, and really not all that clear, but it's a way to get the earliest picture of your unborn child. We had quite a little album of the blurry images at thirty-four weeks into the pregnancy, but the latest one . . . it was the money shot, because it showed something the other ones hadn't: We were having triplets.

The twins, as we'd begun to call them, were still floating in front of the picture, but it was as if they were petals of a flower finally opening up enough to show a third baby, shadowy and much less distinct, but very there. The third baby was visibly smaller than the other two, which wasn't uncommon, Dr. Heelis, my main obstetrician, assured us.

We were all sitting in the conference room at the hospital now, because Dr. Heelis had been joined by Dr. Lee, Dr. Kelly, and Dr. Rodriguez. They each had their specialties in gynecology and delivering babies, or something else needed as a precaution. I hadn't gained most of the extra medical specialists since they spotted the third baby; they'd been my team almost from the beginning of my pregnancy, because I was Princess Meredith NicEssus—legal name Meredith Gentry, because *Princess* looks so pretentious on a driver's license. Dr. Kelly was the new face, but then what was a new doctor compared to a whole new baby?

I was the only faerie princess to be born on American soil, but not for much longer. One of the babies was a girl. My daughter would be Princess Gwenwyfar. We were still negotiating on the rest of her names, since we wouldn't know until DNA testing who her father was; I'd narrowed it down to six.

All six of them sat on either side of the long oval conference table, strung out like strong, handsome beads on the string of my love.

Doyle, Darkness, sat on my left. He was everything his name promised: tall, handsome, and so dark he was black. Not the way people's skin was black, but like a dog's skin and hair could be so black that it had blue and purple highlights in the sun. In the dimmer light of the conference room his skin was just unrelieved blackness, as if the darkest night had been carved into flesh and made real. His ankle-length hair was back in its usual braid so that his pointed ears with their edging of silver earrings showed. If he'd hidden the ears no one would have known he wasn't pure-blooded Unseelie sidhe, but he made sure the one sign that he wasn't pure sidhe showed most of the time in public. I'd never asked him why, but it was a constant slap in the face to every other sidhe who could hide their mixed heritage. He'd stood at the side of the Queen of Air and Darkness for over a thousand years with his less than pure genetics, flaunting them, and the glittering throng had feared him, because he had been the queen's assassin and captain of her guards. No one lived that Doyle was sent to kill. Now he was my Darkness, the Princess's Darkness, but he wasn't my assassin. He was my bodyguard, and he'd guarded my body well enough that I was pregnant with his child. That was some good guarding.

Frost, the Killing Frost, sat on my right. His skin was as white as mine, as though the luster of pearls had been made flesh, but whereas I was five feet even, Frost was six feet of muscle, broad shoulders, long legs, and just one of the most beautiful men in all of faerie. He wore only the upper part of his hair back, leaving the rest of it to fall around his body like a silver veil through which you could glimpse his gray suit, black shirt, and silver tie with black fleur-de-lis done small on the silver. The barrette that held the thickest of his hair back so that if there was a fight it would be out of his eyes was carved bone. It was very old, and he would never tell me what kind of animal it had been carved from. There was always the implication that it had been something that I would have considered a person.

Frost had been Doyle's second-in-command for centuries, and that hadn't changed, but now they were both my lovers, and potential fathers of the babies I carried. The three of us had found love, that true love that they write songs and poems about, but this fairy tale didn't have a happily-ever-after ending, not yet. As I sat there with my hands folded over the round tightness of my belly, I was scared. Scared in the way that women had been for centuries. Would the babies be all right? Would I be all right? Triplets? Really? Really? I didn't know how to feel about it yet, it was too new. I'd been happy about twins, but triplets—how much more complicated had the pregnancy and our lives just become?

I prayed to the Goddess for safety, wisdom, and just a calm center from which to listen to the doctors and the plan. I smelled roses, and I knew she'd heard me, and I knew it was a good sign. I hoped it was a good sign. I knew that sometimes bad things happened for good reasons, but I really, really wanted this to be one of the good things, period, with no caveats.

Doyle squeezed my hand, and a moment later Frost did the same. The men I loved more than anyone in the world were with me; it would be all right. The other men that I loved, but maybe not quite so much, were looking at the doctors and glancing at me, trying to be reassuring and not show that they were worried, too.

Galen was failing to hide his worry, but his face had always been a mirror for his heart. His pale skin had a faint green cast to it to complement the darker green of his short curls. He still had one long, thin braid, which was all that was left of his once-knee-length hair. A cream T-shirt made of silk embraced the lean muscles of his chest and upper body, an apple-green suit jacket that was his only concession to dressing up. The rest of his outfit was jeans, pale blue with holes worn through, giving tantalizing glimpses of bare flesh as he moved. The jeans were tucked seamlessly into brown tooled cowboy boots, which were new, and not his choice. We all represented the high court of faerie and we had to dress accordingly when we were likely to be photographed, and any trip to the hospital had the paparazzi out in droves.

The last of our happy, but tense, sextet of men were Rhys, Mistral, and Sholto. Rhys was mostly shades of white and cream from the waist-length white curls to the cream-colored suit and pale leather loafers hidden underneath the table. His open-necked dress shirt was pale blue and brought out the tricolored blue iris of one eye; the other eye was lost behind a pale blue satiny eye patch. It brought out the wonderful blues of his remaining eye but didn't hide the trailing scars that came from that empty eye socket. Goblins had taken his eye centuries before I was born. At five-six he was woefully short for a purebred sidhe, but still taller than my own humble five feet even. I was the shortest royal in either court.

Sholto was all long, straight white-blond hair in a curtain that almost obscured his black suit and white shirt with its high, round collar so no tie was needed. It wasn't this year's style, but he was King Sholto, Lord of That Which Passes Between, ruler of the sluagh, the dark host of the Unseelie Court, and he didn't really worry about this year's fashions. He wore what he liked, and it usually looked scrumptious on him, or scary, depending on the effect he wanted. The black made his tri-yellow-gold irises very bright, very beautiful, and very alien.

Mistral was the last of my would-be fathers. He was the tallest by a few inches, broadest of shoulders by a fraction, just a very big man, but the bulk of muscle and centuries of warrior training didn't help him be okay inside a man-made building with too much metal and technology for his fey sensibilities. Lesser fey have more trouble with such things, and Mistral was dealing the least well of any of my lovers with this extended stay in the human world. It showed in the hollow look around his eyes, their color that swimming yellow-green that the sky gets just before a tornado sweeps down from the sky and destroys everything in its path. He'd been a storm god once, and his eyes still reflected his moods as if the sky were still his to command. Centuries ago the true sky would have reflected his anxiety. His own black suit made his gray hair look almost charcoal dark, as it fell around his shoulders and swept below the table edge. He wore a white dress shirt half unbuttoned, tucked into his pants, but fanned open to reveal a hand-stitched linen under-shirt. The linen was from his old wardrobe. He'd found that wearing something that felt "normal" against his skin helped him deal better with all this frightening newness.

I sat there surrounded by some of the most beautiful men in all of faerie, feeling like a small, less than beautiful jewel in their midst, but it's hard to feel glamorous when you're eight months pregnant with triplets. I hadn't seen my feet in weeks. My back ached as if someone were trying to saw me in half about a third of the way up. It was the worst my back had hurt, as if now that my body knew it was carrying triplets it didn't have to pretend to be brave anymore.

"How could all the tests and ultrasounds have missed a third baby?" Galen asked.

Dr. Heelis, tall, with white hair cut short, smiled his best professional smile at us. He had to be sixty, but he looked about a decade younger with his handsome square-jawed face and clear gray eyes behind their silver-framed glasses.

"I won't make excuses, except that two large babies in a small space just hid the third. It happens sometimes when you have more than twins."

"Is that why there was that echo with the heartbeats a few weeks ago?" I asked. I shifted in my chair, but there was no true way to be comfortable. If my back had just hurt a little less, or the pressure had let up, I'd have felt better.

"It would seem so," he said.

"So all those tests that Merry and the babies had to go through were because you couldn't figure out there was a third baby?" Galen asked.

"We thought there was a heart issue with the twins, and it is possible that what we were picking up was the third baby's heartbeat."

"How did you miss this?" I asked, finally. Heelis had built up months of confidence, and now I doubted it all. Or maybe it was just the pain? I shut my eyes for a moment; it felt like someone was sawing my back in half and trying to push the pieces apart at the same time.

"Are you all right, Princess?" asked Dr. Lee, the only woman on the team.

I nodded. "My back hurts from all the weight. I'm tired of being pregnant."

"It's normal," she said, smiling. Her face was square and always pleasant somehow. Heelis exuded confidence, but Lee was calm, like the eye of the storm. I liked her for it, but then probably all her patients did.

"Multiple births are always a physical challenge, but for someone as petite as you, Princess Meredith, it can be more uncomfortable. We will do everything to make you as comfortable as possible."

"How about if Dr. Kelly just tells us why he's here?" My voice rose a little as if I were fighting not to yell at someone, and maybe I was. I just hurt, and I was just so tired of it all. One of the babies moved, rolling in their sleep, or maybe playing, I didn't know, but it was still an odd sensation for something to move inside me that wasn't me. It wasn't a bad feeling, but it was . . . odd.

Dr. Kelly was having trouble concentrating because he could see that Mistral's eyes were streaming with storm clouds, and a slight movement of wind, as if his irises were a tiny television set forever to the Weather Channel.

"Would Dr. Kelly be able to concentrate on his job if Mistral put his sunglasses on?" Galen asked.

Dr. Kelly startled, and said, "I'm so sorry, I was staring, I . . . I just . . . I'm terribly sorry."

Doyle said one word in his deep, thick voice: "Mistral."

Mistral fished a pair of expensive sunglasses out of his pocket and slid them on. They were silver, metal frames with mirrored lenses that reflected everything like a silver mirror. They looked incredibly sexy on him, but for right now, more importantly they hid his distracting eyes.

"Better?" Mistral asked.

"I do apologize, Prince . . . Lord . . . Duke Mistral, I just . . . I'm new to the team and . . ."

Mistral had surprised me by having a title of duke in his own right. We'd been told to trot out our titles for humans, so we had, but it threw the Americans who weren't used to titles.

"It's okay, Kelly," Dr. Heelis said, "it took all of us a few visits to adjust to the . . . view."

"Not to be rude, but why do we need yet another doctor?" Doyle asked.

Dr. Heelis folded his arms on the table, his hands very still; I'd come to recognize it as part of his "it will be all right, I'm here to reassure you" pose. It usually meant something was wrong, or might be wrong. So far the pregnancy had been remarkably problem free for twins, but we'd had several meetings where Heelis had reassured us as things happened that could have been scary but turned out not to be. Some potential problems that he'd wanted us to know about had fixed themselves with a combination of modern medicine and luck, or maybe it had something to do with me being descended from five different fertility deities. It meant I'd been able to carry twins with much less difficulty than most women, but it was also probably the reason we were now looking at triplets. That was really a little more fertility than I'd wanted.

"When I informed the other members of our team that Princess Meredith was having triplets, they all agreed that Dr. Kelly would be a good addition to our pool of knowledge."

"Why?" Sholto asked, and he seldom spoke in these meetings.

They all turned and looked at him, and then most looked away, except for Heelis, who managed to hold the weight of everyone's gaze without flinching; there was more than one reason he was in charge.

"King Sholto."

Sholto gave a nod to acknowledge his title, and as a sign for Heelis to proceed, which he did.

"First, I know that you were all hoping for a vaginal birth, and we were willing to try with twins, but triplets means it's a cesarean birth."

I must have looked unhappy, because Heelis looked at me. "I am sorry, I know you felt quite strongly about avoiding surgery, but with triplets we just can't risk it, Princess; I am sorry."

"I figured as much when we saw the third baby," I said. I leaned forward in my chair trying to find a more comfortable position, but there really wasn't one. Doyle changed hands so he could still hold my hand and also rub my back. Frost mirrored him and they rubbed my back as if they were hands from the same man instead of two different ones. They'd been best friends and battle buddies for hundreds of years; it meant they seemed aware of each other physically without having to look. It meant they could rub my aching back without bumping into each other's hands, and when the doctors lifted the moratorium on sex, they'd be able to prove that they mirrored each other there, too, again. The last insult had been the "no sex" rule starting a few months ago.

I held on to their hands tighter; it helped distract me from how uncomfortable I was. I wasn't sure why the idea of a cesarean birth bothered me, but it did.

"You do understand that too much could go wrong as the babies all crowd toward the birth canal," Heelis said.

I nodded.

"Whatever will keep Merry and the babies from harm is what we want," Frost said.

The doctor smiled at him. He liked Frost and Galen best for long eye contact, probably because their eyes were the closest to human-normal, gray and green.

"Of course, that's what everyone here wants." He did that reassuring smile that he must have practiced in the mirror, because it was a good one. It filled his own eyes with warmth, and just seemed to exude calm.

"But my question remains unanswered," Doyle said. "Why is Dr. Kelly here?"

"He has the most experience with birth delay of multiples."

"What is birth delay?" I asked.

"With a cesarean birth we might have the option of delivering the first two babies but leaving the third, smaller one in utero for a week or two. It's not a given, but often smaller size means certain systems might not be as developed, and this would give more time for the baby to grow in the perfect self-sustaining environment of the womb."

I just blinked at him for a few seconds. "Are you actually telling me that the triplets might have different birthdays by weeks?"

He nodded, still smiling.

"And if we can't delay the third baby's birth, what then?"

"Then we'll deal with whatever issues may arise."

"You mean we'll deal with whatever is wrong with the babies, especially the smaller . . . triplet."

"We don't like the word *wrong*, Princess, you know that."

I started to cry. I don't know why, but for some reason the thought of having two babies delivered and leaving the third inside me to cook a little bit longer just seemed wrong, and . . . I wanted it over with; I just wanted our babies to be all right and to be on the outside of me. I was tired of being pregnant. I couldn't see my feet. I couldn't tie my own shoes. I couldn't fit behind the wheel of a car to drive myself anywhere. I felt helpless and bloated like a tiny beached whale, and I just wanted it over. Even though nothing had actually gone wrong, the doctors had still warned us about every awful possibility, so that my life had become a list of nightmares that never happened while the babies grew inside me. I was beginning to think I'd had too many good doctors and too much high tech, because there were always more tests, even though in the end all the tests told us was what wasn't wrong. Or maybe they'd missed something and it was all going to go wrong. They'd missed a whole third baby; how could I trust any of them anymore? All the months of confidence building and trust in my doctors was in ruins. I was having triplets. The nursery was done, but we had only two cribs, two of everything. We weren't ready for triplets. I wasn't ready.

I was screaming quietly into Doyle's shoulder while everyone ran around trying to calm the crazy pregnant woman when my water broke.

THREE

H is name was Alastair, and he fit in my arms as if he'd been carved from a missing piece of my heart. He blinked up at me with huge liquid blue eyes set like shining sapphires in the pale, luminescent skin of his face. His hair was thick and black, and one tiny, slightly pointed ear was as black as his hair. The curled tip was almost lost in the midnight straightness of his hair. The other ear was like a carved seashell, shining mother-of-pearl set in the velvet of his hair.

All the exhaustion, all the pain, the panic of finding that Gwenwyfar was too far into the birth canal for a c-section, and her brother, Alastair, came so close behind her there was no time, and it was all lost on the wonder of tracing that tiny ear down through Alastair's hair to find that the black of the one ear trailed down onto the side of his neck, like a spot on the side of a puppy's ear.

Doyle was still in his surgical scrubs, pink against his shining black skin. He traced the side of Alastair's neck and said, "Do you mind?"

It took me a moment to understand the question, and then I blinked up at him, like I was waking from a dream. "You mean the spot?"

I smiled up at him, and whatever he saw made him smile back. "He's beautiful, Doyle; our son is beautiful."

I got to see what very few had ever seen: The Darkness cried as he turned our tiny son gently in my arms so that he could show me a black star-shaped mark on his tiny back. It was a five-pointed star, almost perfect, taking up the middle of his back.

Alastair made a protesting sound, and I turned him back so I could see his face. The moment he had eye contact again, he quieted and just studied my face with those solemn blue eyes.

"Alastair," I said, softly. "Star, our star."

Doyle kissed me softly, and then kissed his son's forehead. Alastair frowned at him.

"I think he's already competing for Mommy's attention," Galen said from the other side of the bed. He had Gwenwyfar wrapped in a blanket, but she was already pushing at it with all the strength of her small legs and arms.

"She doesn't like being swaddled," Rhys said, and took her from Galen's so-careful arms, and began to unwrap her from the careful swaddling the nurses had done.

"I'm afraid I'll drop her," Galen said.

"You'll get better with practice," Rhys said, and he grinned down at me and helped slide Gwenwyfar into my other arm, but with a baby in each arm I couldn't touch them, look at them like works of art that you wanted to see every inch of, explore, and memorize.

They both stared up at me so seriously. Gwenwyfar was bigger just at a glance, and one pound made a big difference in newborns, but she was longer, too.

"So you were the little troublemaker who couldn't wait to get out," I said, softly.

She blinked deep blue eyes up at me, and there were already darker blue lines in her eyes; in a few days we'd see what her tricolored irises would look like. Right now they were baby blue, but if she took after Rhys maybe it would be three shades of blue? Her hair was a mass of white curls. I wanted to touch her hair, feel the texture of it again, but I was out of hands.

Dr. Heelis was still squatted between my legs, stitching me up. It had all happened too fast. I was numb, not from drugs, but just from abuse of the area. I felt the tugging of what he was doing, but the baby took all my attention—babies.

Gwenwyfar flailed a small fist as if trying to reach my hair, though I knew it was too early for that, but something caught the light on that small arm like gold, or quicksilver.

"What is that on her arm?" I asked.

Rhys lifted her arm out of the blankets and let her wrap one tiny fist around his fingertip, and as he moved her arm we saw a trace of almost metallic lace. It was forked lightning traced like the most delicate gold and silver wire across her arm, almost from shoulder to wrist.

"Mistral, you need to see your daughter," Rhys said.

Mistral had huddled at the edge of the room through everything, terrified and overwhelmed the way some men are, and suffering in the presence of too much technology.

"There is no way to know who belongs to who," he said.

"Come see," Rhys said.

"Come, Mistral, master of storms, and see our daughter," I said.

Doyle kissed me again and lifted Alastair up to make room for me to hold our daughter. She kept Rhys's finger in a tight grip, so Mistral came to the other side of the bed. He looked scared, his big hands clasped together as if he were afraid to touch anything, but when he looked down and saw the lightning pattern on her skin he grinned, and then he laughed a loud, happy chortle of a sound that I'd never heard from him before.

He used one big finger to trace that birthmark of power, and where he touched Gwenwyfar tiny static bolts danced and jumped. She cried, whether because it hurt or scared her I didn't know, but it made him jerk back and look uncertain.

"Hold your daughter, Mistral," I said.

"She didn't like me touching her."

"She'll need to start controlling it; might as well start now, and who better to teach her." Rhys handed Gwenwyfar to Mistral while he was still protesting.

Without a baby to distract me, I was suddenly aware that I was getting more stitches than I'd ever had in my life, in a part of my body where I'd never wanted any stitches.

"How is Bryluen?" I asked, and I looked to the incubator where our smallest baby lay. There were too many doctors, too many nurses huddled around her. I had concentrated on the two babies I had; I'd known that there was a third baby only an hour before it all started, but somehow seeing her, so tiny, with her curly red hair, body almost as red as her hair, as my hair, I wanted to hold her, needed to touch her.

Dr. Lee came with her black hair peeking out of her scrubs, but her face was too serious. "She's five pounds; that's a good weight, but she seems weeks younger than the other two developmentally."

"What does that mean?" Doyle asked.

"She's going need to stay on oxygen for a few days and be fed fluids. She won't be able to go home with the others."

"Can I hold her?" I asked, but I was scared now.

"You can, but don't be alarmed by the tubes and things, okay?" Dr. Lee smiled, and it was totally unconvincing. She was worried. I didn't like that one of the best baby docs in the country was worried.

They wheeled her over, and five pounds might be a good weight, but comparing it to the six and seven that Alastair and Gwenwyfar had made her look tiny. Her arms were like little sticks too delicate to be real. The tubes did look alarming, and the IV in her little leg didn't look like birth, it looked more like death. The aura that blazed around the other two babies was dim in this tiny spark of a baby.

Frost stood on the other side of the tiny incubator with tears shining unshed in his gray eyes. We'd had no third name, so he'd wanted Rose, after a long-lost love and a long-lost daughter. *Bryluen* was Cornish for "rose." It had seemed perfect for our tiny red-haired daughter, but now I watched the fate of those earlier lost roses in Frost's face and it tightened my chest, and made me afraid.

Doyle took my hand in his, and asked, "Dr. Lee, is it just her size that makes you believe she's developmentally behind the other two?"

"No, it's her test scores. She's just not as engaged as the other babies are, very much as if she's simply a few weeks behind them. We'll use the technology to make up for what she didn't get inside you."

"And she'll be all right then?" I asked.

Dr. Lee's face fought between cheerfully blank and something less pleasant. "You know how this works, Princess; I can't say that with absolute certainty."

"Doctors never guarantee things, do they?" I asked.

"Modern doctors do not," Doyle said.

"But then modern doctors aren't likely to be executed for saying they can cure the princess and then failing," Rhys said. He came with a smile to help cheer the gloomy bunch of us. Galen was normally cheerful, but not about our little Rose; Frost was usually the gloomiest man in my life, and Doyle was a serious person. I'd just given birth to triplets. I was allowed to be worried.

Dr. Lee looked at him as if she didn't find his joke funny at all. "Excuse me?"

He grinned at her. "Trying to lighten my partners' moods; they are determined to think the worst."

"Look at her," Galen said, motioning at the tiny, tiny infant.

"Remember what my specialty is," Rhys said. "She doesn't shine as bright as the others, but neither does she have a shade around her. She is not dying. I would see it."

Doyle's hand tightened on mine, and he said, "Swear it, by the Darkness That Eats All Things."

Rhys looked very serious then. "Let me swear it on the love I bear Merry, our children, and the men in this room, the men and women who are waiting for news at the home we have all built. Let me swear on the first true happiness I have known in lo these long, dark centuries, our little Rose will not die here like this; she will grow strong and crawl fast enough to frustrate her brother."

"You see this in the future truly?" Frost asked.

"Yes," Rhys said.

"I don't understand anything you're talking about, but did you threaten our lives if the baby doesn't live?" Dr. Lee asked.

"No," Rhys said. "I just wanted to remind my family here that modern medicine can do wonders that even magic could not do once, and to have faith. The bad old days are past; let us enjoy the new good days."

Doyle and I both held our hands out to Rhys, and he came to take them both. He laid a kiss on mine, then did the same to Doyle. "My queen, my liege, my lover, my friend, let us rejoice and chase despair away from this day, as we chased it from each other this year past."

Galen went around and hugged Rhys from the back, which turned Rhys laughing to hug him back. It made us all laugh a little, and then the nurses were putting the tiniest of babies in my arms. She was so light, birdlike, and dreamlike. It reminded me of holding one of the demi-fey, those of faerie that look like butterflies and moths, but who feel more like the hollow bones of birds when they land and walk upon you.

Bryluen had tubes coming out of her nose trailing to her oxygen, and an IV in her tiny leg, like the one in my arm. Even with Rhys's reassurance, she looked injured. She was loosely wrapped in one of the thin blankets, and everywhere her skin touched mine she burned as if with fever.

Bryluen started to cry, a high-pitched, thin, and piteous sound that only the very youngest infants make. I knew something was wrong just by her cry. I couldn't explain it, but something the doctors were doing wasn't the right thing for this one.

"Doyle, help me unwrap this blanket. She doesn't like it."

He didn't question it, just helped me unwrap Bryluen, and it was as we lifted her gently that my hand crossed her bare back and found something unexpected. I raised her against my shoulder, one hand firm to support her head, and the other her lower body, so that I could see what my hands had felt.

Scales graced almost the entire back of her body, trailing down into the tiny diaper. They weren't the rainbow scales of a snake like Kitto had on his back, but more like the wide, delicate scales on a butterfly or moth wing, except these were impossibly large, bigger than any natural butterfly on the planet.

Doyle traced one big, dark finger down the brilliant pink-and-seashell shine of the scales that trailed like a cape from her thin shoulders to sweep down her miniature waist and be lost underneath the diaper.

"They're wings," he whispered.

Frost was on the other side of the bed, leaning over to draw his own large hand gently down Bryluen's back. "Wings more real than Nicca's. They are raised above her skin, not like a tattoo."

Galen leaned in to touch the miracle of shining proto-wings. "They don't look like any insect I've ever seen," he whispered.

Mistral came close with Gwenwyfar held in his arms as if she'd always been there. Frost moved up beside them, touching a hand to Gwenwyfar's white curls and gazing down at Bryluen. "I have not seen dragon wings on our demi-fey since I was not the Killing Frost, but only little Jackul Frosti."

Sholto came closer and said, "They look almost like the wings of a baby nightflyer, but light and jewel-bright instead of dark and leathery."

It was when I brushed her tight red curls near her forehead and found the buds of antennae that I understood. "Get the plastic out of her, now!" I held her out to the doctor.

"Without extra oxygen and feeding tubes she will not survive."

"Do you see the wings and the antenna buds? She's part demi-fey, part sluagh, a part of faerie that doesn't do well around metal and man-made things. If you keep putting artificial things into her, she will die."

"You mean she's allergic to man-made plastics?"

"Yes," I said, not wanting to waste time to explain the unexplainable.

Dr. Lee didn't argue but took Bryluen, and she and the nurses began to strip out everything they'd put in. The baby cried piteously as soon as they took her from me, and it made my heart ache to hear it. The other two babies started to cry as if in sympathy.

Rhys picked Alastair up from the nurse and seemed to know just how to hold him so that the baby just watched everything with dark solemn eyes, as if he understood more than he could say yet. Gwenwyfar just tried to yell loudest no matter what Mistral did.

"You never mentioned a family allergy this severe," Dr. Heelis said, and he looked angry.

"Give her to me, please; it's important that she just touch natural things," I said.

I think they were sending for different things to use on Bryluen and gave her back to me simply as a delay while they rushed around. They gave her back to me nude, because the diaper was man-made, too. I held my tiny naked daughter and could feel that the wings went almost all the way down the back of her body, and they were raised above her skin, part of her, not just a design.

I didn't think I had any demi-fey in my genetics, but I knew that the demi-fey could die in the city, fade and just die from too much metal, too much plastic, too much garbage. I gave her the only thing I knew was absolutely natural. I turned her so that tiny rosebud of a mouth could nurse.

"She's too small," one of the nurses said, "she'll never latch on enough to feed."

Bryluen did look impossibly small against my swollen breast, but she latched on tight enough for me to almost say *Ow*, but it was a good sign. I felt her begin to feed and it was the most amazing sensation. I watched her delicate throat, almost bird thin, swallow convulsively over and over as if she couldn't get enough. My other breast began to leak in sympathy.

Mistral handed Gwenwyfar to me, though it took him, Frost, and me to get our other girl into the twin football hold that I'd been practicing for months in preparation for twins. I realized as the two girls settled in to nurse that I needed an extra breast. I had triplets; there was no hold for triplets.

As if on cue, Alastair began to cry, wanting his share. I had no idea what to do about it, but as I felt Bryluen drink hungrily, strongly at my breast, I was too relieved to worry that much. Gwenwyfar and he could take turns until Bryluen caught up. A nurse handed Rhys a bottle, and just like he'd practiced in class, he fed our son. Alastair didn't seem to mind that he was sucking on something plastic and man-made. All three babies sank into a happy, satisfied silence, and looking around at the men in my life I knew we might need at least two more fathers to round out my men. I'd had sex with one demi-fey and one snake goblin while I was already pregnant with the twins, so I thought I didn't need protection. I was already pregnant, as safe as a girl could be, but as I felt the first tiny flexing of those wings on Bryluen's back, I knew that I needed two more men to come see their daughter.

I was descended from a handful of fertility deities, but I guess I really hadn't understood what that meant. I mean, there was fertile and then there was being able to get pregnant while you were already pregnant. I started to laugh, and the laughter turned into happy tears. One of my daughters had wings; maybe she would be able to fly?

CHAPTER

FOUR

They say you have no sense of smell when you dream, but I woke to the scent of roses and had a moment of wondering why the dim hospital room smelled like wild roses in the noon warmth of a summer meadow. The room was almost in darkness except for night lights underneath a shelf and one near the only inner door, which led to a bathroom. But I saw a pale, fluffy cloud across the room from where I lay in the bed. Galen was asleep in a chair underneath the cloud, which wasn't a cloud at all, but the massed blossoms of a small fruit tree that had grown behind his chair. I'd seen temporary plants grow like this from too much magic in a place, but to my knowledge we hadn't done magic. Maybe I'd missed something while I slept, or maybe surprise triplets were magic enough. Galen had one hand inside the plastic crib beside him. I couldn't tell in the dim light which of the bigger twins lay inside the blanket, but Galen's hand was resting on the tiny form, as if even in his sleep he had reached out to our child.

It made me smile. Galen might not be the best warrior of my men, and he was a terrible politician, but it didn't surprise me at all that he would be good at this part.

The sound of movement beside me made me turn and find another plastic crib on its tall wheeled legs beside me. There was a woven basket with little handles for carrying inside the plastic so that Bryluen wouldn't touch the man-made things that seemed to hurt her. There were wings softly flexing inside the blanket with her, more than just Royal and his sister Penny, who had come to visit his daughter, and her niece.

I smelled roses even more strongly and looked up to find that there were rose vines growing above my bed, like a living canopy of thorns and pale flowers, starlike in the darkness. I smelled the sweetness of apple blossoms now, and knew what kind of tree grew across the room.

I wondered what the nurses thought of the new decorations. There were moths fluttering in the flowers above me, and I could see the movement of them in the blossoms across the room now, but I knew they only looked like moths. Dozens of demi-fey fluttered in the new garden, but they weren't just sipping nectar and pollen, they were guarding, and they were attracted to this new magic like an ordinary moth drawn to a light.

I glanced to the far side of the room and found Rhys on the couch, asleep on his back with Gwenwyfar across his chest. Her white curls looked so very like his in the dim light. One of her small fists was wrapped around his finger, as if they held each other even in their sleep.

Sholto sat artfully slumping in a chair with his back to the room's only window. He'd changed clothes since last I'd seen him, because his clothes were dark enough that they blended in with the darkness, leaving his long hair to gleam like a pale yellow curtain around the darkness of the rest of him. His eyes were pale, but I wouldn't have wanted to guess at their color in this light. Nothing human had yellow eyes like his; they were just some pale color, but not as pale as his white, white skin, which gleamed like Rhys's and the baby's hair in the near-blackness of the room.

The wall behind him moved. I had to narrow my vision and concentrate to see that it wasn't the wall that was moving, but that there was a solid sheet of nightflyers hanging on the wall like giant bats, though even bats wouldn't be able to hang flat against a smooth modern wall, but then bats didn't have tentacles with suction on them and the nightflyers did. Their fleshy bodies framed the window and clung halfway across the ceiling. Once they'd chased me like the nightmares they appeared to be, but now the nightmares were on my side, and I knew that while they were in the room almost nothing in this world, or the next, dared to attack us.

A tentacle much bigger than anything the flyers could boast waved at the window behind them all. That let me know that more of the sluagh was on guard outside our room. We had powerful enemies, but we hadn't needed this much overt protection since we escaped from faerie and came back to California to have the babies.

I had to fight to keep my voice soft, not wanting to wake anyone, but needing to ask, "What's wrong?"

Sholto blinked at me, and there was a shine to his eyes as if they'd caught what little light there was in a way that human eyes did not reflect. He sat up a little straighter, and I could see the gleam of jewels against the black of his shirt. The necklace covered most of his upper chest. It was a piece that even the Hollywood elite wouldn't have worn. They were jewels meant for a king, which he was, King of the Sluagh. I'd seen him wear the piece in the high courts of faerie when he was reminding other nobles that he wasn't just another lordling, or even princeling. Short of wearing his crown he was declaring himself king; the question was, why? Or rather, why now?

My heart sped at the sight of the jewels, because he might bring the sluagh out to warn enemies not to try us, but to dress as a king. . . . It was a very short list of situations he would do that for.

He smiled almost too faintly for me to see it in the dimness. He spoke quietly, too, the way you do around sleeping people. "Why should anything be wrong, Merry?"

"It shouldn't, but it is," I said.

"We are your bodyguards, sweet Merry; becoming fathers does not change that. I merely watch over your slumber, and that of our children, and my fellow fathers."

"You are wearing court clothes and kingly jewels, something I've only seen you do in the high courts of faerie. You don't waste such finery on the human world, or on me."

"When you are recovered and the doctors free you of restrictions, I would gladly wear all this to your bed."

I glanced up at the clinging nightflyers, which he was totally ignoring, as if I couldn't see them.

"You do know that I see the nightflyers, right?"

He grinned then, and shook his head. "I am not trying to hide them from you."

"Could you, if you wished?"

He seemed to think about it, and then said, "I believe so."

"Could you hide them from the queen herself?"

"I do not want to hide them from her," he said.

I smiled then. "So that is why the show of force. The queen has threatened us."

He sighed, frowned, and fidgeted in his chair, which he didn't do often. "I was told not to worry you."

"Who by?" I asked.

"Doyle—you know it was him, or I wouldn't have tried so hard to obey him. He is technically the captain of your guard, and when in the Unseelie Court my captain."

"You are the Lord of That Which Passes Between in the Unseelie Court, but you sit here now as King Sholto, ruler of the darkest part of the Unseelie host. What did our queen do, or say, to warrant this show of force, Sholto?"

"Doyle will be unhappy with me if I tell you."

"Just Doyle?" I asked.

He smiled again. "No, not just Doyle, but I am not worried about Frost."

"You think you could take my Killing Frost in a duel, but not my Darkness," I said.

"Yes," Sholto said. It was interesting that he didn't try to equivocate or salve his ego. It was just a statement of fact; he feared Doyle's prowess in battle, but not Frost's. "But your using their more fearsome nicknames is also a show of force, my dear Merry."

"Why do you say, 'my dear Merry,' as if it's not true?"

"Because I am no longer certain that any of the babies are mine."

I frowned at him. "Goddess showed me that you were one of the fathers."

"Yes, but She did not show me, and I see none of my father's blood-line in any of the triplets."

His father had been a nightflyer like those that clung in alien layers to the wall and ceiling of the room. He wasn't the product of rape, either, but of a highborn sidhe woman wanting a night of perverted pleasure. To be willing to sleep with the monsters of the sluagh was one of the few things that even the Unseelie Court saw as perverse. As Doyle had been the Queen's Darkness for centuries, and Frost her Killing Frost, so she had nicknamed Sholto her Perverse Creature, but where I could call the other two men by those pet names, I could not do the same for Sholto. He had hated being called her Perverse Creature and feared that someday as Doyle was simply her Darkness, so he would become her Creature, or just Creature.

Sholto looked as handsome and perfect as any of my sidhe lovers, but once he had not. Once, from about midchest to just above a truly beau-tiful groin, had been a nest of tentacles identical to those on the under-side of the nightflyers that clustered around him. Magic and the return of the blessings of Goddess and Her Consort, the Gods that had long withheld their favors from the sidhe, who had been worshipped as deities themselves, had given Sholto the gift of being able to turn the tentacles to a tattoo. Before that he had been able to hide them visually with glam-our, that magic that faerie used to trick the eye of mortals, but it had been an illusion, a trick, and the first time I'd touched him with the mass of tentacles touching me, I hadn't been able to work past it for sex. Now Goddess had given him the body that the rest of him promised, and I'd learned that all those extra bits had pleasures of their own that no more humanlike body could give. I went to his bed joyfully now, and he valued that I loved all of him physically with no squeamishness. I was the only other sidhe lover he'd ever had, because the rest of the courts feared him as proof that the noble blood was wearing thin and we would all be monsters someday, as they feared my mortal blood as proof that their immortality would be the next to vanish.

"I think you're overly sensitive about your father's genetics, and you might want to ask yourself if your new ability to make your wonderful extras into a true tattoo might affect the children, too."

His face grew serious as he thought about my words. He was a serious man as a general rule, and thought about, or even overthought, most things.

"You may be right, but I don't seem to feel the connection to the babes that others of your lovers feel."

"Have you held any of the babies?" I asked.

"All of them," he said. "I felt nothing except that I was afraid I would drop them. They are so small."

Galen's voice came thick with sleep, and soft as if he were whispering to not wake the babe beside him. "I was afraid I'd drop them, too, but I worked through it. Once I got over feeling like I didn't know what I was doing, it was wonderful."

"I did not find it so," Sholto said.

"You didn't stay and take care of them, the way most of us did. I think because they didn't come out of our bodies, fathers have to work harder at feeling connected."

Galen sucked at court politics, and at a lot of stuff that the other men in my life were good at, but most of the men wouldn't have had that insight. It was a good insight.

"I hadn't thought about how hard it might be for all of you to feel connected to the babies," I said.

Galen smiled. "You've felt connected to them for months, but then you have been holding them more intimately than we ever can."

Sholto asked, "Are you saying that you did not feel connected to the babes at first either?"

"Not like I do after having held them, cuddled them, and helped give bottles. There was a moment when Alastair looked up at me with those dark eyes, so like Doyle's eyes, but that was okay, he was suddenly my son, too."

Rhys's voice came even and quiet. I think he was trying not to wake the baby sleeping on his chest. "I had the same moment with Gwenwyfar. She's obviously Mistral's daughter, but now she's mine, too."

"Wait," I said. "I thought we decided to call her Gwennie, when I went to sleep."

"She liked Gwenwyfar better," Rhys said, matter-of-factly.

"Gwennie wouldn't stop fussing, but the moment Rhys called her Gwenwyfar she stopped," Galen said.

I frowned at him. "She's too young to know the difference."

He smiled and gave a small shrug. "She made a tiny bit of lightning when Mistral first touched her, Merry. Is her preferring a name any less amazing than that?"

I couldn't argue with his point, but I wanted to.

"Gwenwyfar has your hair," Sholto said. "None of them have anything of mine."

"We don't know that yet," I said.

"They're too new," Galen said. "Give them a few weeks to find out what they are, who they are."

Sholto shook his head. "I had thought about having an heir to my throne. I have been a good enough king that the host might allow our kingship to become heredity, as well as choice of the people, but not if none of them are descended from the host."

I hadn't thought about the fact that we had more than one throne to sit someone on, and suddenly Sholto's worries about his father's genetics didn't seem so silly.

"You're saying that it was your extra bits that helped make the sluagh comfortable making you their king," I said.

"Yes," he said. "They will not take a completely sidhe king or queen."

"Bryluen is not completely sidhe," Galen said.

"She is demi-fey, and perhaps goblin, but those wings are nothing that flies with my people."

I wondered if he'd meant to make the modern Americanism *It doesn't fly with me*, but I thought it more likely he'd meant it literally.

"Galen is right, Sholto. The babies haven't been here a whole day yet; they'll change how they look and who they look like as they get older."

"They won't change that much," Sholto said.

"You might be surprised how much babies change as they get older," Rhys said.

"That's right," Galen said. "You've had children before."

"Yes," Rhys said. Gwenwyfar moved restlessly on his chest, and he rubbed her back, laid a soft kiss on her curls. It was all done almost automatically. I knew that it had to have been centuries since he'd had other children—did parenting skills stay with you forever once you'd learned them? Or was Rhys just more of a natural father than I'd expected? I wanted to ask him but wasn't certain how to ask it without implying that I hadn't expected him to be this good with the babies.

Doyle had felt instantly bonded with Alastair, but he hadn't helped feed and take care of him as much as Galen had. Maybe it was what Galen had said: He hadn't felt bonded, so he'd worked at it. Doyle had, so he didn't have to work at it. Or maybe Doyle was just too busy trying to keep the Queen of Air and Darkness from doing something bad to be a baby-daddy right now.

"Did the queen threaten us, or the babies?" I asked.

The men shifted uneasily—Galen looking at the floor, not meeting their eyes; Rhys kissing the baby again and again purposefully not looking at the other men. Sholto glanced at both of them and then back at me. His face was very serious, arrogant, unreadable, which let me know that whatever the queen had done was frightening, or would at the very least upset me.

My heartbeat was in my throat now, and I was frightened. What could the queen have said, or done, to make them not want to tell me? I probably didn't want to know. I just wanted to enjoy being a new mom and watch the men I loved be fathers, and just enjoy the moment, but my relatives had been ruining the happy moments of my life for as long as I could remember. Why should this be any different?

"One of you talk to me," I said. My voice was only a little breathy. I gave myself a point for sounding so much calmer than I felt.

It was Royal who rose into the air on black-and-gray moth wings, with a bull's-eye spot on the lower wings of scarlet and yellow. His tiny silken loincloth was red, to echo the red in his wings and make you see it more. His wings beat much faster than those of any actual moth, more like the buzzing wings of a dragonfly or bee. Royal was ten inches tall, bigger than any real moth, so he needed wings that were bigger and moved as no moth or butterfly could. He had short curly black hair with delicate antennae coming out of those curls. Bryluen's hair color was mine, but the antennae were his. But I hadn't had sex with him until after I was supposed to already be pregnant with the twins. Unless there was some unknown demi-fey genetics in my background, or one of the other men's, then she had to be partly Royal's child, but how? I'd accepted it calmly in the moment of wonderment of holding Bryluen, but now I was thinking, not feeling, and it made no sense.

I'd invited Royal and the other demi-fey to the hospital in a fit of postdelivery endorphins and baby intoxication, but now I was sobering up and logic had never been a friend to faerie. We weren't about logic; in fact, most of faerie defied logic and science. We were impossible; that was sort of the point of fairyland.

I was the first of my kind to go to a modern college in the United States, and my degree was in biology. It was like I'd been driven temporarily mad and now sanity had returned, and I didn't understand why I'd been so happily sure about Royal and about Kitto. Poor Kitto was out shopping for all the things we needed to turn our twins' nursery into one for triplets. He'd been so happy, and Bryluen could be his, because he'd been my lover longer than Royal, but . . . she had wings and antennae, so it had to be demi-fey blood, didn't it?

One minute Royal looked like the picture from some child's story-book and the next he stood beside the bed as tall as I was, taller than Kitto, who was only four feet tall, the smallest of my lovers. The moth wings that had been a blur of color when he needed to fly were like some fantastic cape at his back, except this cape flexed and moved with his breath, his thoughts, emotions. Wings could be like the tail on a dog, giving away involuntary things.

He stood unselfconsciously nude, because the little bit of silk he'd worn hadn't survived the shape change. It wasn't like the Incredible Hulk's pants that always magically stayed on; when Royal shifted size, his clothes either shredded or became a mound of cloth for his smaller self to fight free of.

"I will tell you what the queen said."

"Merry looks pale, as if she already knows all our news," Sholto said.

"Are you all right?" Galen asked. He stood up and stopped touching Alastair, who waved tiny fists in the air almost immediately, as if only Galen's touch had kept him still. Maybe he was a cuddly baby and liked skin contact, or maybe it was magic like the tree and the roses?

"I don't know," I said.

"What's wrong, Merry?" Rhys asked. He was sitting up, rubbing Gwenwyfar's back as she rested against his chest. She was moving fitfully even with the touching.

I didn't want to say it in front of Royal. I wanted time to think and to be able to discuss it with the other men. I needed time to think.

"Royal, tell me what my aunt has done to frighten everyone."

"She wants to see her great-nieces and nephew," he said.

"She wants to visit the hospital?"

"She does."

I pictured my aunt, the Queen of Air and Darkness, tall, sidhe slender, with her long, straight black hair tangling around her legs, dressed in her signature black, her eyes circles of black and shades of gray with black lines encircling every color so that it always looked as if she'd outlined the iris with eyeliner. It was always a startling and frightening effect, or maybe that last part was just me? Maybe if she hadn't tried to drown me when I was six, or torment me casually on so many occasions, I would have simply thought her eyes were striking. Perhaps, if I hadn't seen her covered in the blood of her torture victims, or had so many of them flee to us here in California looking for a sort of political asylum with the wounds of her creativity still unhealed in their flesh, I would have thought her beautiful, but I knew too much about my aunt to ever see her as anything but frightening. "Is she still torturing her court nobles on mad whims?" I asked.

"Last we checked," Rhys said.

"Then she's too crazy to be trusted among humans, or near our babies."

"We agree," Rhys said. He was rocking Gwenwyfar, gently, but she was moving more. I thought she was working up to a cry, but I was wrong. It was Bryluen who let out a high, thin wail more like the sound that a small animal makes than a baby; just the cry alone said how tiny she was, and how newborn. My body responded to it with milk seeping out of my breasts and soaking through the nursing bra and the gown I was wearing. Well, at least something was working the way it was meant to. I reached for my smallest daughter. I wasn't sure who her father or fathers were, but I knew she was mine. That was one of the nice things about being the woman: You never had to guess how many kids were yours. Men . . . did they ever really know before genetic testing existed?

CHAPTER

FIVE

I seemed to have enough milk for all three babies but was short a breast, so whichever baby wasn't feeding cried, which made the others fussy. The nurses brought bottles and were thoroughly scandalized that Royal was naked. They brought him a set of surgical scrubs to wear when he was big, after we explained the problem. Rhys took Gwenwyfar to Sholto in his chair with the nightflyers shifting restlessly around him.

"No," Sholto said, holding his hands up as if to keep the baby at bay.

"Yes," Rhys said, and put the baby in the other man's arms so that he had to hold her, or risk having her fall. Sholto held her as if she were made of glass and would break, but he did hold her.

"Hold the bottle like this," Rhys said.

Bryluen and Alastair were content, feeding deeply, and that near-magical endorphin rush came over me so that it was comforting to me to feed them and make them feel comfortable. I wondered if cows felt that way around milking machines, or just around their calves.

Gwenwyfar started to cry, and it was high and told some part of my brain I hadn't even known was there that she was little, but that part of me also knew instinctively that she wasn't as little as Bryluen. How did just the sound of their cries tell me that?

"You're too tense," Rhys said. "She's picking it up."

"See, she doesn't like me."

Galen sighed and came beside my bed. "May I take our boy? He's more easygoing than Gwenwyfar."

"You can tell that already?" I asked.

"Oh, yeah," he said, and there was something about the expression on his face that made me wonder.

"What did I miss while I slept, besides my aunt wanting to visit?"

"We all got to know the babies," Galen said with a smile.

I had a little trouble getting Alastair to let go of his nice, warm meal—me—and he fussed as Galen picked him up, but he didn't cry.

Gwenwyfar was crying full-out. Rhys picked her up and he and Galen passed each other as Gwenwyfar came to feed beside her sister, and Alastair got to be bottle-fed by Sholto.

Gwenwyfar settled onto my other breast across from her sister with a little sigh of contentment. Did babies really come into the world knowing that much of who they were and what they wanted? Gwenwyfar already had a strong preference for Mommy, as opposed to the bottle.

I realized that the room was quiet, full of contented noises, which meant Alastair was taking his bottle. I looked across the room to where Rhys and Galen had both been working with Sholto to help him bottle-feed. Sholto had a little smile on his face, and he had relaxed, so that Alastair fit in the crook of his arm and the bottle was at a good angle. The baby was drinking hard and steady, his tiny curled fist on one side of the bottle as if he were already trying to help hold it. I knew that part was accidental, but it was still amazing to me. I guess everyone thinks their babies are wonderful and precocious.

"Alastair takes the bottle easier," Galen said.

Sholto glanced up. "You had trouble feeding the girl, too?"

"I got her to take the bottle, but she doesn't like it as well, and she let me know that." He turned and grinned back at the bed and his reluctant daughter.

Rhys said, "She has strong preferences, our Gwenwyfar."

"Already?" I asked.

"Some babies come like that," Rhys said with a smile.

I stared down at my two daughters, and I just liked the phrase *my two daughters*, and smiled. I could feel that the smile was silly and almost an "in love" type of smile. I had expected to love the babies, but I hadn't expected to feel like this. I was still sore and aching in places that had never hurt before, but it was okay, and long moments like this made me forget that anything hurt. There is power and magic in love, all kinds of love.

Royal came to the other side of the bed by Bryluen. He was wearing an oversized hospital gown turned so the open back let his wings be free, and a pair of surgical scrub pants. It made him look even daintier than he was, and somehow less like he belonged.

"May I feed one of the babies?"

"Of course," I said.

Rhys was already moving across the room, with the last bottle that the nurses had brought. He didn't apologize but let Royal settle onto the edge of the chair that Galen had used. Royal couldn't sit back too far, because of his wings. I wondered if people with wings got backaches from always having to sit without a back support.

Bryluen didn't look so small in Royal's arms. There was a fit there; was it just that the sizes matched better, or was it the happy smile as he gazed down at the baby?

"She's looking right at me," Royal said in a voice that held wonder.

"She keeps her eyes open more than the other two," Rhys said.

I wasn't sure about the other men, but Rhys and Galen had spent my nap learning the ins and outs of our children. I liked that a lot.

I fitted my bra back over one breast and looked down at Gwenwyfar. "So, you're already demanding what you want?"

The baby didn't even open her eyes, just continued to feed happily. I held her closer and leaned over so I could lay a kiss on her white curls. The top of her head smelled amazing, clean and like baby lotion, even though I was almost certain no one had put lotion on her. Did baby lotion smell like newborn babies, or was that just my imagination?

"They smell so good," Royal said; he'd bent over Bryluen's hair just as I had over Gwenwyfar.

"They do," I said.

I caught movement out of the corner of my eye and saw that Sholto had bent over Alastair. "The smell is clean and somehow calming." He sounded surprised.

"Have you never held a baby before?" Rhys asked.

"Not one that was this . . . human," he said.

"You know these aren't antenna buds," Royal said; he was rubbing his cheek against Bryluen's hair, apparently, over the little black beginnings of her antennae.

"What are they then?" I asked.

"Something harder. I think they're tiny horns," he said.

"Did you say horns?" Sholto asked.

"I think they are," Royal said, "but I'm certain they aren't antennae."

Sholto looked down at the baby in his arms. He smiled down and said, half to the baby and half to Galen, "I hate to disturb you, but can someone else finish feeding him?"

"Happy to," Galen said. He took Alastair out of Sholto's arms like he'd done it forever. I wondered if he'd sit in Sholto's chair, but he didn't. Galen moved to the couch to finish giving Alastair his bottle. Would the nightflyers have cared if Galen had sat where their king had sat, or would it have made Galen uncomfortable to be surrounded by them? Most of the sidhe, of both courts, were afraid of the sluagh. We were meant to be, otherwise they weren't a threat, and they so were that.

Sholto walked over to Royal. He offered, "Do you want to feed her?"

"No," Sholto said, and knelt beside them. His hair pooled around his legs so that he was lost in a cloak of it, except for the black of his boots. I couldn't see what he was doing, but Rhys was watching him closely.

"I think they are horns," Sholto said.

I could see his shoulders moving even through the mask of his hair. He exclaimed, "Blood and fire, it can't be!"

I hugged Gwenwyfar tighter and asked, "It can't be what?"

Sholto turned, still on his knees, so that I got a just a glimpse of that handsome face framed by all that hair. "The wings do not feel like butterfly scales, or moth."

"They're like butterfly wings fresh out of a chrysalis, before blood pumps them into full shape," I said.

"They may look like pink and crystal gossamer, but they feel leathery, more like bat, or reptile," Sholto said.

I frowned. "I don't understand."

He smiled, and it was that rare one that made his face look younger, as if it were a glimpse of what he might have been like if his life had not made him so hard.

"Horns and leathery wings are sluagh, Merry."

In my head I thought, *Goblins have horns*, but I didn't say it out loud. The horns and wings could be his genetics; we really didn't know. If his throne hadn't been potentially on the line, it wouldn't have mattered, but to rule the sluagh you had to be part sluagh, just as to rule the Unseelie and Seelie courts you had to be descended from their bloodline. Every court in faerie was like that; you had to be the type of fey to rule that type of fey. Since I'd thought we'd given up all plans for any of our children to be on any throne, I hadn't worried about it.

Sholto's throne was not normally an inherited one. You were elected to it, chosen by the people. It was the only rulership in all of our lands that was democratic. I hadn't known he would look down at our babies and begin to dream of a royal bloodline for his people. Funny, what fatherhood means to different men.

"If it's sluagh, then it can't be demi-fey," Royal said, and he looked sad.

"We have a geneticist who's going to be testing the babies. We won't really know without that," I said.

The men all did another of those looks, almost looking at each other, and avoiding my eyes.

I hugged Gwenwyfar to me, for my comfort this time. "What were those looks about? You told me my aunt wants to see the babies and we're guarding them and the hospital, because she's still insane and too dangerous to come, but that look just now says there's more you haven't told me."

"Have you always been able to read us this easily, or have you grown more observant?" Sholto asked.

"I love you all in my way; a woman pays attention to the men she loves."

"You love us," Rhys said, "but you're not in love with all of us."

"I said what I meant, Rhys."

He nodded. "It was diplomatically worded." His tone was mild, but his face unhappy.

"Rhys," Galen said.

The two men exchanged a long look, both their faces serious. Rhys looked away first. "You're right, you are so right."

Since Galen hadn't said anything out loud, I wasn't sure what he was so right about. It was as if the men had had a conversation that I hadn't heard and were still saying bits of it. I could ask, or . . .

"I'm sorry that you're unhappy with me, but you aren't going to distract me from my question. What else has gone wrong, besides my aunt?"

"Some of us love you more than you love us; it's an old topic," Rhys said.

"Stop changing the subject, and trying to distract me with emotional issues we've already discussed. It must be something bad for you to bring this back up again, Rhys," I said.

He nodded, and sighed. "Bad enough."

Sholto stood up, brushing the knees of his pants automatically. "I'm not in love with Merry, nor do I expect her to be with me. We care for each other, which is more than you usually get out of a royal marriage."

"Then you tell me what the three of you, four of you, are keeping from me," I said.

Galen held Alastair closer, much as I had with Gwenwyfar. "It's the other side of your family."

"The other side, you mean the Seelie Court?"

He nodded, resting his cheek against the top of the baby's thick black hair.

Sholto came to stand beside the bed and laid a hand over my arm and half cradled Gwenwyfar, because his hand was that big in comparison to the baby. "Your uncle, the King of the Seelie Court, is trying to get permission to see the babies, also."

I stared up at him. "My aunt wants to see the potential heirs to Unseelie thrones and her beloved brother's grandchildren. I understand that, and if she weren't a sexual sadist and serial killer we'd allow it, but what in the name of all that is holy makes Taranis think he has the right to see our children?"

Rhys came nearer the bed. "He's still claiming that one or all of them are his, Merry."

I shook my head. "I was pregnant when he raped me. They are not his."

"But you were only weeks pregnant, not showing at all. He's maintaining that you were with child only after he . . . was with you," Rhys said, but I didn't like the long hesitation before he finished his sentence.

"What is he really saying, Rhys?"

"He's made it a 'he said, she said' sort of thing."

"We knew he'd deny the rape, but we have forensic evidence that he did it. The rape kit came back . . ." I couldn't even say it. Taranis, the King of Light and Illusion, ruler of the Seelie Court, the golden court of faerie, was my uncle. Technically he was my great-uncle, brother of my grandfather, but since the sidhe do not age, he didn't look like a grandfather.

"He's saying that it was consensual, but we all knew he would."

"He's probably come to believe his own lie," I said.

"Taranis will not believe that you refused him in favor of the monsters of the Unseelie Court," Sholto said.

"He's the monster," I said.

Sholto smiled, and bent and laid a gentle kiss on my forehead. "That you mean that, when speaking to me, means a great deal to me, our Merry."

I looked at his face as he stood back upright. "He raped me while I was unconscious, Sholto, and he's my uncle. That was monstrous."

"I'm sorry, Merry, but one of the reasons that Taranis is making a case is that you don't remember. He's saying that you consented and then passed out, but he didn't realize you were unconscious until it was too late," Rhys said.

"Too late to stop? Too late to not have sex with his own niece? Too late for what, Rhys?" I was almost yelling.

Gwenwyfar stopped nursing and started to fuss, as if she hadn't liked me yelling. I spoke in a calmer voice, but I couldn't control how I felt. "Rhys, you said 'make a case'; is he actually trying to get legal visitation with the babies?"

"He was, but our lawyers countered, and now Taranis is pushing for genetic testing of the babies. He's so sure that one or all of them will be his, I think he believes his own delusion now."

"He's always believed his own magic more than he should," Sholto said.

"Once his illusions could become real," Rhys said.

"That was a very long time ago."

"If the genetic tests come back negative for him, then I think his days as King of the Seelie Court are over," Rhys said.

"If we can prove that he knew he was infertile a hundred years ago but didn't step down from the throne, they may execute him," Galen said, and there was a hardness in his voice that I'd never heard before.

I looked past the other men to my green knight. "You want them to kill him, don't you?"

"Don't you?" he asked, and his green eyes held a bleak rage that was so not like him, but truth was truth.

"Yes," I said.

"Good," Galen said, and that one word wasn't good at all. The tone was very bad, very sure of its anger.

"If the ruler of court is infertile, then it condemns the entire court to be childless; no true king would stay on the throne under those circumstances," Rhys said.

"Or queen," Galen said.

We all looked at him.

"That's why she agreed to step down if Merry had a child, because she'd tried all the modern fertility treatments and was still childless."

"She had a son," I said, softly. Holding my own child in my arms made it seem like I should add out loud that I'd killed that only son. He'd been trying to kill me and the men I loved, but I'd still killed him, and his death seemed to have driven the last of her sanity away.

"Cel was hundreds of years old, and her only child. She knew she was infertile long before," Galen said, and again there was a hardness to him that I had never heard or seen in him. People think that becoming a parent will make you soft, more sentimental, and maybe it does for some, but for him it seemed to have helped him find a new strength. I'd wanted him stronger, but I hadn't understood that perhaps with the extra strength, some softness might be lost, that with every gain, there might be a loss.

I studied his face, and the other men were doing the same thing. We were all looking at my gentle knight and realizing that maybe he wasn't that anymore. There were other men in my life that I counted on to be harsh and protective; until that moment I hadn't realized that I'd counted on Galen for softer things. My eyes felt hot, my throat tight; was I going to cry? Not about the rape and the legal mess, but about losing Galen's softness? Or maybe I was going to cry about it all, about both, about all three, or maybe baby hormones made you more emotional, or maybe, just maybe, I would cry because Galen wouldn't anymore.

CHAPTER

SIX

Doyle came back in while I was still crying, which led to him asking what happened and the other men admitting they'd told me.

"The last orders I gave were for Merry not to be upset."

"First, we are all fathers of her children," Rhys said, "so as our captain you can order us, but as just another of Merry's sweethearts you need to give us all room to decide the parameters of our relationship with her and our children."

"Are you saying you deliberately went against my orders?" Doyle stalked farther into the room toward Rhys.

"I'm not stupid," I said. "I could tell something was wrong and I demanded to know what it was."

Doyle didn't look back at me but continued to loom over Rhys. Galen still had Alastair in his arms as he moved toward the other men.

"Merry is our princess and crowned by Goddess as our queen; she outranks her own captain of the guard," Galen said.

Doyle's head turned, ever so slightly, neck and shoulders so tight it looked painful. His deep voice held anger like it was all he could do to contain it. "Are you saying that none of you will obey my orders?"

"Of course we will," Galen said, "but Merry is supposed to lead not just us, but all our people. How can we ignore her when she demands something from us?"

Sholto got up from where he was kneeling by Bryluen. He left her in Royal's arms. The demi-fey looked frightened and didn't try to hide it. Sholto joined the other sidhe in the middle of the room.

"If you were the only king that Goddess and faerie had crowned for Merry, then we would obey you, Darkness, but you are one of many kings."

Doyle turned to face the other man. "I have not forgotten that she was crowned to be queen to your king, Sholto."

Sholto raised his arm and pushed back the sleeve just enough to show the beginnings of the tattoo that he and I shared. It had been real rose vines that night, and had pierced both our arms, entwining like the rope, or thread, that was used for a regular handfasting, but this "rope" had set thorns into our flesh and wedded our hands together more completely than any mere ceremony could have, and the marks of those vines and roses were painted on our arms.

"We were handfasted by Goddess and faerie," Sholto said.

"And I have no such mark; you have pointed that out more than once over these months," Doyle said.

That was news to me. Sholto was the only man to whom Goddess had personally handfasted me, but She had crowned Doyle and me as King and Queen of the Unseelie Court.

"Maybe the reason Goddess bound Merry to you was that you were the only one who is king in his own right," Galen said.

The two men looked at him, as if he'd interrupted a longstanding disagreement. It isn't always wise to get in the middle of two people who are fighting.

Galen smiled at them and shifted the baby in his arms, just enough to remind them the baby was there. I didn't think the movement was accidental; Galen understood that the baby was a free pass from any violence. He was right, but I hoped he didn't push the idea too far, because he wouldn't be holding a baby forever, and both Sholto and Doyle had long memories.

"Merry had to become your queen; the rest of us had to become her kings."

"Why should that matter?" Sholto said.

"Merry had to marry you to become your queen; for the rest of us, we had to father a child to become Merry's kings, or princes. I think for the Unseelie Court, the Goddess and Consort already chose the king."

"I gave up my crown to save Frost," Doyle said.

"Barinthus still hasn't forgiven you, or Merry, for that," Galen said, with a smile.

"He is a Kingmaker, or a Queenmaker," Sholto said. "The two of you gave up what Barinthus had worked for decades to accomplish."

"He dreamed of putting my father on the throne, not me, and certainly not Doyle," I said.

"True," Sholto said.

"Very true," Doyle said.

"I don't believe we would all have lived to see the babies born," Rhys said.

"Too many enemies still left in the darkling court," Doyle agreed.

"Or perhaps the Goddess and God would have protected you," Royal said.

We all looked at the delicate figure still tucked into the chair with a baby who might, or might not, be his daughter.

"What do you mean?" I asked.

"If the Goddess and God crowned the two of you, maybe they would have worked to keep you safe on the throne?"

I thought about it. "Are you saying we needed to have faith, little one?" Doyle asked.

"You still talk as if the power of the Goddess has not returned to bless us all with Her Grace, but she has moved among us these last months even here outside faerie, in the far Western Lands."

I said, "The Goddess told me that if the fey weren't willing to accept Her blessings, then I should take them out among the humans and see if they appreciated them more."

"Humans are always impressed with magic," Sholto said.

"But it's not magic," I said. "It's miracles."

"Aren't miracles just a type of magic?" he asked.

I thought about that, and finally said, "I'm not sure, perhaps."

"What did the queen say when you told her not to come?" I asked.

Doyle met my eyes, but his face was unreadable, as closed and mysterious as he had ever been, but now I understood what the look meant. He was hiding something from me, protecting me, he thought. I saw it as not sharing information that I needed.

"What makes you think I have spoken to the queen?"

"Who else had a chance of persuading her to stay away but the Queen's Darkness?"

"I am no longer her Darkness, but yours."

"Then tell me what she said, and what she wants."

"She wants to see her brother's grandchildren."

"You've told me that she's still torturing random people at court," I said.

"She was the most composed I have seen her since this last madness gripped her."

"And how composed was that?" Rhys asked, and by tone and expression he showed that he didn't believe it would be composed enough.

"She seemed her old self, before Cel's death and our giving up the throne drove her mad."

"You still believe that she was trying to be so insane that some of her court would kill her?"

"I believe that for this space of time she sought death, or didn't care whether she lived or died," Doyle said.

I thought about the broken, bloody bodies of the people that had been brought to us or escaped to find refuge with us. The queen had not tried to hunt down any of the refugees of her court, even though it was well known that her nobles had come to seek asylum with us.

"If positions had been reversed, she would have sent me to kill you months ago," Doyle said.

I nodded, hugging Gwenwyfar a little closer, feeling her deeply asleep in my arms. It helped me stay calm and say, "She would have said, 'Where is my Darkness? Bring me my Darkness,' and you would have come like a shadow and ended my life."

"I would have done the same if you had asked, Meredith."

"I know that, but I would not risk you back in the Unseelie Court by yourself, Doyle."

"If anyone could assassinate the queen and live to tell about it, it is Doyle," Sholto said.

"If anyone could do it, he could, I know that."

"Then why have we hesitated?"

"Because the word *if* is in every conversation we have about this, and I'm not willing to risk Doyle on an *if*."

"You love him and the Killing Frost more than a queen should love anyone," Sholto said.

"Do you say that from experience, King Sholto?" I asked.

"You do not love me as you love Doyle, or Frost. We all know that they are your most beloved, so I am not betraying you if I say that I am not in love with you either."

"Don't you love the babies more than duty, or crown?" Galen asked. I'm not sure I would have asked, not out loud.

Sholto turned and looked at him, so I couldn't see the expression he gave the other man, but I was almost certain it was his arrogant face. The one that made him look model handsome and was his version of a blank face.

"I would give my life to keep them safe, but I do not know if I value them above duty to my people and my kingdom. My throne and crown they could have, but not if it cost my people their independence or their lives. I hope I never have to choose between the children and the duty that I owe my people."

"You are the best king that faerie has had in a very long time," Doyle said.

"You don't hold duty above the lives of our children, do you, Doyle?" I asked.

He turned and smiled at me. "No, Merry, of course not; they are more precious to me than any crown, but then I already proved that I prefer love to a throne. If I would give up being King of the Unseelie Court for love of our Frost, then I would do no less for our children."

And that was the answer I wanted, that no duty or sense of honor outweighed the love to these small new lives. I laid my cheek against the soft curls, breathed in the sweet scent of our daughter, and asked, "Who has persuaded the king to stay inside faerie?"

"The lawyers and the police," Rhys said.

"Human lawyers and human police? How have they persuaded the King of Light and Illusion to do anything?"

"Human law confined him to faerie after he attacked us and the lawyers with us."

"He hadn't left the Seelie Court in years," I said. "It was no hardship for him."

"There's also a court order keeping him five hundred feet away from you and all your lovers and an injunction preventing him from contacting us directly, even by magic."

"That was a fun one to get a judge to sign off on," I said.

"We have set new precedents for human law and magic," Rhys agreed.

"He attacked a room full of some of the most powerful attorneys in California; it helped our case."

"Human police will not be able to arrest him," I said.

"There will be no arresting him, Merry. If Taranis escapes faerie and comes for you, or the babies, he will die."

"He'll slaughter the humans," I said.

"He's not bulletproof," Galen said.

"Human police aren't trained to kill first, but second, and that will be all the time he needs to kill them," I said.

"Soldiers are trained to kill, not save, and that is what is needed," Doyle said.

"Is there still a National Guard unit outside the faerie mounds in Illinois?" I asked.

"You know there is," he said.

"I don't want them dying for me, Doyle."

"They won't die for you, or us, but as I understand it in defense of their country and constitution."

"And what does fighting a king of the sidhe have to do with defending the constitution?"

Rhys said, "Merry, if Taranis could be king of this country, he would be, and he would rule with the same arrogance and cruel carelessness that he has displayed toward the Seelie Court."

"There is no danger of him ruling this country, and you know that."

"I do, but he still needs killing."

"Because he raped me?" I asked, and studied his face as I said it. It had taken me months to say the words that casually.

Rhys nodded. "Oh, for that, definitely for that."

"Definitely," Doyle said.

"Yes," Galen said.

"If it would not cause war between the sluagh and the Seelie Court, yes."

"I am too weak to ever harm anyone so powerful, but if I could kill him for what he did to you, I would," Royal said.

The demi-fey that were still fluttering tiny and fragile-looking among the roses and blossoms in the room rose in a cloud of wings and said in small voices, "Command us, Merry, and we will do what you need."

"Are you saying you would kill Taranis for me?"

"Yes." They said it in unison like birds chirping a word all at once.

"Rid me of this inconvenient man, really?"

"Yes," they sang again.

"No, I would not send so many of the demi-fey to their death. I do not want vengeance so badly that I would sacrifice all of you."

"And that is why we would do it for you," Royal said.

I shook my head. "No, no more deaths of those I value. I've lost too many people and seen too much blood spilled because of the madness of kings and queens."

"Then what do you want us to do about him?" Rhys asked.

"I don't know; if he loses his head and tries to come near me or the babies again, then we kill him. I won't let him hurt me again, and I won't let him near our children."

"We kill him then," Doyle said.

"If we can," Rhys said.

"Oh, we can kill him," Galen said, as if it were a matter of fact and not a nearly impossible feat.

"How can you be so sure?" Rhys asked.

Galen's face wore that new harsher expression as he hugged our son. "Because if he comes for Merry and we don't kill him, he'll hurt her again, and we won't allow that."

"So we'll kill him, because we have to," Rhys said.

Galen nodded. "Yes."

The men all looked at each other and then at me, and I saw the beginnings of a determination that could only end in one way. Taranis, King of Light and Illusion, was going to have to die.

CHAPTER

SEVEN

The triplets were in the nursery with Doyle, Frost, and a handful of other guards watching over them while the nurses and doctors did last-minute things in preparation for going home. Galen, Rhys, and I were in the room trying to figure out how we were going to get everything else home. Flowers and other gifts had come from friends, but most of it was from strangers. The fact that Princess Meredith had had her babies had made the news, and America was thrilled to have their faerie princess have triplets! I appreciated the thought, but we were a little overwhelmed by their generosity.

"We'll need a van just to cart all the flowers and presents home," Rhys said. He stood in the middle of the room with his hands on hips, surveying all the bouquets, balloons, stuffed animals, potted plants, and gift baskets of food that filled most of the room. We'd started turning away some of the well-meaning gifts, because we needed to leave room for us and the medical personnel to use the room. The hospital had been much happier with the florist shop invasion than with the plants that were still growing in the room. The blooming apple tree curled above all of it. The treetop was pushed against the ceiling as if still trying to grow taller, as if it had come up against the sky and been surprised to find it solid and unforgiving. The nurses had asked if the tree was permanent, and I'd given the only answer I had: I didn't know.

They were even less happy with the wild roses around the bed because they had thorns. Two nurses and a doctor had pricked themselves on the thorny vines.

"We've already given away a lot of it to other patients," Galen said.

"Most of the stuffed toys should go to the children's ward," I said. I turned too fast to motion at the toys and had to stop and try a less dramatic turn. I felt good, but if I moved a certain way I could feel the stitches and the abuse my body had suffered to get our little trio on the outside. I was just happy to be in real clothes again. The sundress was designer maternity, one of the many gifts we'd had over the months that came with the words, "Just tell people what you're wearing and it's free." Since we were supporting a small army of fey on not-large-enough salaries, we'd taken most of the gifts. The ones that didn't come with contracts to sign, those we'd let our entertainment lawyers to look over.

We'd been offered a reality show. Did we want cameras following us around everywhere? No. Did we need the money? Yes. Which was why the entertainment lawyers were going over the contracts, but we had to decide today. The producers wanted it to begin with the babies coming home, so that meant that the film crew needed to either come to the hospital to start filming, or film us as we brought the babies into the house. We needed the money, but what would my relatives do on camera?

As if he'd read my mind, Rhys said, "I think the reality show is a bad idea, have I said that yet?"

"You mentioned it," I said, still staring at the stuffed animals, some of which were nearly three feet tall. What would newborn babies do with such a thing? We'd leave them for older children who would love them and needed them more than our tiny ones. Bryluen, Gwenwyfar, and Alastair weren't able to reach for things yet, let alone manage a forest of giant toys. The world was big enough to them right now without that.

"I agree with Rhys, but I know that Merry feels it's wrong to expect Maeve to keep supporting all of us."

"It's an old tradition that when the ruler visited his nobles they were expected to entertain him, or her, and all their traveling court," Rhys said. He picked up one of the potted plants and shook his head. I think he was thinking what I was thinking: We couldn't possibly take all the plants home. It would be a full-time job just to water them all. Though some of the tiny winged demi-fey had picked a few of them to cuddle into; those we'd bring home.

"I've read that Henry the Eighth used that tradition to bankrupt rivals, or nobles he was trying to control," I said.

"People make jokes about fat Henry, but he was a very good politician and understood the power of being king."

"He abused that power," I said.

"He did, but they all did. It's hard to resist absolute power, Merry."

"Is that from personal experience?" Galen asked.

Rhys looked at him, and then down at the piles of gifts. "Being a deity with worshippers does tend to make a person a little high-handed, but I learned my lesson."

"What lesson is that?" I asked, and came up to wrap my arm through his so that I could rest my cheek against his shoulder.

He turned his head enough to smile at me, and said, "That just because people call you a god doesn't make you one."

A tiny and very female voice said, "You were the great god Cromm Cruach, and your followers healed all hurts."

We looked at one of the winged demi-fey; it was Penny, Royal's twin sister. She'd been fluttering among the flowers but now rose so she'd be head height for us. She had her brother's short black curls, pale skin, and black almond-shaped eyes, but her face was even more delicate, her body a little smaller. She was wearing a gauzy red-and-black dress that looked very nice with her wings.

Rhys looked at her, face not happy. "That makes you very old indeed, little one, much older than I thought."

"I had no wings then, because our Princess Merry had not worked her wild magic and made us able to fly. We wingless ones among the demi-fey went even more unnoticed than the rest; at least they were color and beauty, but those of us who had not been so blessed only watched from the grass and the roots of things. It gives a perspective that I might not have had if I'd been on the wing back then."

"What perspective is that?" Rhys asked.

"To know that everyone starts on the ground. Trees, flowers, people, even the mighty sidhe must stand upon the dirt in order to move forward."

"If you have a point, make it," he said.

"You have no illusions about what and who you are now; you can make a life that is real, not some fantasy, but something true and good, just as a tree that puts down deep roots can withstand storms, but one with shallow roots is knocked over by the first strong wind. You have become deep-rooted, Rhys, and that is not a bad thing."

He smiled then, nodding and squeezing my arm where I touched him. "Thank you, Penny, I think I understand. Once I built myself on power that was given to me by the Goddess and Her Consort, but I forgot that it wasn't my power, so when we lost the grace of the Gods, I was lost, but whatever I am now it's real and it's me, and no one can take that from me."

"Yes," she said, hovering near Rhys's face, her wings beating so quickly that the edge of his curls blew softly in the wind of her flight.

"Did I seem like I needed a pep talk to you?" Rhys asked.

"There is often an air of melancholy about you."

I glanced from the tiny fey to Rhys and wondered, would I have thought that? Was that true? He joked a lot and made light comments, but . . . behind all of it, Penny was right. I found it interesting that she had paid that much attention to him. I thought of several motives for a female to pay that much attention to a man—did Penny have a crush on Rhys? Or was she just that wise and observant of all of us, of everything? If the first was true, then I doubted Rhys would realize it, and if the second was true, then hearing her thoughts on other things might be interesting.

"Penny, do you think we should do the reality show?" I asked.

She dipped down, which was a flying demi-fey's way of stumbling. I'd surprised her.

"It is not my place to say."

"I've asked your opinion," I said.

She cocked her head to one side, then moved in the air so she was more in front of my face than Rhys's. "Why ask my opinion, my lady?"

"It will affect you, as it will affect everyone who lives with us, so I am interested in what you think."

She gave me a very serious, searching look. I saw the intelligence in that tiny face that I hadn't seen before; she was as bright as her brother, but maybe a better thinker, deeper anyway.

"Very well. The queen is always very careful to look good in front of the human media, so if you did the reality show, then cameras might keep us all safe from her."

"The queen is insane, she can't help herself," Galen said.

Penny looked at him, then back to me. "If that were true, then she would have lost her control at a press conference decades ago, but she never has; if she can control herself to that degree then she is not truly insane, she is simply cruel. Never mistake someone who cannot control their murderous impulses from someone who simply has no one to tell them, 'Stop, behave yourself.' I find that most cruel people, no matter how awful their actions, once faced with punishment, or someone stronger, behave. Mean is not crazy, it is merely mean."

I thought about what Penny had said, really thought about it. "She's right. My aunt has never lost control of herself in front of the media. If she were truly serial killer crazy, she'd have lost it at least once, but she never has, not that I remember." I looked at Rhys and then at Galen.

They looked at each other, and then back at me. "Well, I'll be damned," Rhys said.

"Penny is right, isn't she?" Galen asked.

I nodded. "I think she is."

"The king also has never lost control in front of the media."

"He attacked our human lawyers and us once before he kidnapped me," I said.

"But there was no media to record it, Princess Merry. It is still a matter of witnesses, but no video or pictures."

"I think that the king was honestly insane during that attack," Rhys said. "His guard had to physically jump him, bury him under their bodies to keep him from continuing the attack."

I shivered and cuddled into Rhys. Taranis had almost killed Doyle in that attack, and my Darkness was not an easy kill.

"If that is true, then a television show may not protect us from the king."

One of the other demi-fey flew upward on tiny white wings with little black spots on them. She was even tinier than Penny's Barbie doll size, as if she were trying harder to ape the butterfly she resembled. It was a Cabbage White, an American butterfly, which meant she'd likely been born here.

Her voice was high and musical, as if a trilling bird's song could be words. "My sister is still in the Seelie Court. She told me that the king was enraged that you had slipped his seduction magic. He'd never had a woman except for the queen of the Unseelie Court escape from his spells."

"Which is why he came for me later," I said, softly.

The little faerie flew closer and laid a hand no bigger than the nail of my little finger on my hand. "But even then his magic did not work; he had to hit you with brute force like any human. He knows now that his magic does not work on you."

"Did your sister hear him say that?" Rhys asked.

She nodded so hard that her pale blond curls bobbed.

"We think the king will not try magic again," Penny said.

"We, you mean the demi-fey?" I said.

"I do," she said.

The little one patted my finger, as I might have patted someone's shoulder. "We are all sorry that he hurt you, Princess Merry."

"That is much appreciated," I said.

The little one flew up higher, her butterfly wings a blur of white as she hovered, but also showing agitation, nerves.

"Tell her, Pansy," Penny said.

"Many speak in front of us as if we are dogs and can neither understand nor report to others," Pansy said.

I nodded. "You are some of the best spies in all of faerie because of it."

She smiled. "The king has decided that it was his magic you found objectionable, and he plans to try to woo you as a regular man might."

"What does that mean?" I asked.

"It might mean that he would behave for the cameras as nicely as the queen," Penny said.

"How long have you known this bit of information?" Rhys asked.

"Pansy only heard from her sister recently, and the gossip came up. Her sister did not realize the importance of it, or the use we might make of the information."

I found the "we" interesting. Penny didn't mean just demi-fey, but us, her, me, all of us fey living at the estate in Holmby Hills. It was rare for one type of fey to include themselves with others not of their kind. But then I'd accepted any fey who came into exile with us, or were already here in California in an exile older than my own. With a few exceptions, everyone was welcome.

There was a knock at the door, and the guard opened the door and peeked in, saying, "The ambassador is back."

I sighed, and said, "Send him in."

Peter Benz walked through the door smiling, his handsome face set in easy lines, his hand already out to shake. His dark blond hair was cut short and neat; his suit was tailored to his five-foot, eight-inch frame so he looked taller, and it showed off that he exercised and ate carefully enough that he was in shape. He was vain enough that he'd paid for his suit to fit, rather than hide his body. The last ambassador had been vain, too, and Taranis had played on that vanity for all he was worth.

I didn't really want to play that game, but I wanted this ambassador to be one who worked for both courts, not just the Seelie, so I made myself smile and walk toward that extended hand.

His even white teeth spread in a Hollywood-worthy smile. Mr. Benz was an ambassador now, but he had the feel of someone who had much bigger goals for his future. Ambition wasn't a bad thing; it could make a person very good at his job.

His handshake was firm, but not too firm. He also didn't have an issue with my hand being small; so many men either engulfed my hand in theirs or barely touched my hand as if afraid they'd crush it.

"Princess Meredith, thank you for seeing me again."

"Mr. Benz, you are the new ambassador to my people; why wouldn't I receive you?"

He raised a well-groomed eyebrow at that, but turned with a smile to shake first Galen's hand and then Rhys's. The cloud of flying demi-fey he didn't really look at; he treated them as if they were the insects they resembled. I would have said, *How very human*, but even among the sidhe, we forgot to count them, or many did.

I glanced at Penny and Pansy as they hovered in the air. They met my look with one of their own; they'd noticed his lack of notice, too. The demi-fey would be wonderful spies on human politicians. To my knowledge no one in faerie was doing that, but it was a thought, a potentially useful one. I filed it away for later, much later. We had a long way to go before spying on human politics was a priority for me.

"I know you must be eager to go home."

I looked at him. "Define *home*," I said.

He smiled again and made a little push-away gesture with his manicured hands. "You've made it very clear that Ms. Reed's mansion is your home for now."

"While my uncle is confined to faerie, I think I will not be safe there."

The smile faded. "I am sorrier than I can say about all the problems you and King Taranis are having."

"Did you know that once upon a time the king could hear any conversation that mentioned his name?" Rhys said.

Benz gave him a skeptical but pleasant look. "I was told that hadn't been true in a very long time, Mr. Rhys."

"No, but then he hadn't been able to use his hand of light through a mirror being used as a magical Skype interview in centuries either."

"We also believe he's reacquired the ability to use the mirrors as a door that he can step through, or pull someone else through," I said.

Again, that eyebrow rose. "Really?"

"Yes," I said, "really."

"No one saw him step through a mirror or pull someone else into one during the unfortunate events in your lawyers' chambers," Benz said.

"But we did see herbs touch the surface of the mirror, and they floated as if on water tension," I said.

"When a mirror runs like water, or even semiliquid, it usually means that the person on the other side can step through," Rhys said.

"Does it really?" This time Benz looked more interested than skeptical.

We both nodded. Galen was sort of ignoring us all as he continued to sort the things we were taking from those we were donating. Oddly, Galen was probably best suited to have charmed the ambassador; it was actual ability for him, a type of glamour magic, which was why we'd decided he would leave the talking to us. We didn't want to be accused of trying to magically influence the new ambassador after what had happened to the last one.

Benz said, "I am learning so much about faerie and its magic. Thank you for being my teachers."

"We are some of your teachers, but not all," I said.

He gave a little self-deprecating head gesture, almost an aw-shucks head bob, like a bashful movement. I wondered if it was the last remnant of an old gesture. Had our so-secure Benz been shy once?

"That is true; I am to be ambassador to all the courts of faerie, not just your lovely part of it, Princess Meredith."

"Have you spoken to all the courts of faerie, then?" I asked.

He nodded, flashing that brilliant smile that would probably look amazing on camera.

"How did you like King Kurag?" I asked.

He looked puzzled, the smile slipping. "King Kurag, you mean the goblin king?"

"Yes, Kurag, the goblin king."

"I haven't actually spoken to him."

"What about Queen Niceven of the demi-fey?"

"Um, no, I have spoken with King . . . the king of the Seelie Court, and your aunt, the Queen of Air and Darkness."

Leaving off Taranis's name because we'd just said something about it was good, but leaving off both their names, just in case, meant he'd made the logical leap. If one sidhe ruler of faerie could hear when his name was spoken, then maybe the other one could, too. I liked him better for being a quick study. Quick and smart was good.

"You have spoken with King Sholto, because we were here for that talk," I said.

He looked uncertain, but only for a second, and then his face was back to smiling and pleasant. "I spoke to him as your royal consort and father of your children, but not specifically as king in his own right."

"Then you plan to be ambassador to the Unseelie and Seelie courts of the sidhe, and not really ambassador to all the courts of faerie," I said.

He fought that puzzled look away and said, "My duties, as described by Washington, are to the sidhe, both Unseelie and Seelie."

"So the other courts are to be ignored?"

"They are smaller courts within the two larger ones, or that's what I was told; was I misinformed?"

I debated, and finally because we aren't allowed to lie, I said, "Yes, and no."

"Please enlighten me; what do you mean by that, Princess?"

"The goblins, sluagh, and Queen Niceven's demi-fey are part of the Unseelie Court. The ruler of the Seelie Court's demi-fey is no longer an official royal, but a duchess."

His smile flashed back to full brightness. "Then I deal with the high king and high queen of faerie as I was told."

I nodded. "It's the way most people in and out of faerie do it."

He cocked his head to one side and studied me for a moment. "And how else might a person deal with the rulers of faerie?"

"I deal with the kings and queens of faerie as leaders with rights and merits of their own."

"Do you encourage me to deal directly with the goblins and the sluagh?"

I laughed a surprised burst of sound.

"Isn't that what you're hinting at, that you want me to treat them as equal to the sidhe courts?"

"Not equal to, but important, but Goddess, please do not try dealing with the goblins by yourself. I would not want to be responsible for the diplomatic disaster that might follow."

He frowned, just a little, as if he were fighting not to frown harder. "I am very good at my job, Princess Meredith; I think I could avoid offending anyone."

"It's not your offending the goblins I'm concerned with, Mr. Benz. I'm more afraid that they might injure you if there was a cultural misunderstanding."

"What kind of cultural misunderstanding?" he asked.

"The goblins revere only strength and power, Mr. Benz. A human without magic or the martial arts training of a Chuck Norris would find himself treated badly."

"Maybe that's why the humans stopped dealing with the goblins directly," Rhys said.

I glanced at him. "You may be right."

"I don't understand," Benz said.

"I would like you to appreciate more of faerie than just our two courts, but culturally we are the closest to human, and the safest for you, so perhaps you should just ignore me for now. If I ever feel safe to return to faerie, perhaps you can accompany me on a visit to some of the lesser courts."

Rhys patted him on the shoulder. "We'd keep you safe."

"Surely they wouldn't harm a representative of the United States government."

We all laughed then, even Galen, and the demi-fey's laughter was like the sweet ringing of chimes, or tiny bells. The sound alone made Benz smile. The demi-fey have some of the most powerful glamour and illusion ability left in all of faerie. It made them so much more dangerous than they looked.

Benz frowned again, looking puzzled, and smoothed his hands down the front of his suit. It was almost as if he knew that something had just affected him in a more than normal way, but he wasn't sure what it had been. I was betting the ambassador was carrying some kind of charm against our magic. He'd need it.

"It is the last country on the planet that would allow your people to immigrate," Benz said.

"That is true, but the goblins would not see it as harming you, but as your proving unworthy to deal with them as a representative of the government."

"Are you saying that an ambassador to the goblin court would have to be a soldier?"

"Unless you're willing to shoot someone when you step through the door, no, not a soldier," I said.

"What then?" he asked.

"A human witch or wizard, though it's a more patriarchal society, so a wizard would be better."

"A wizard with military training would be your best bet," Rhys said. He came closer to the ambassador and raised the eye patch that was covering the smooth scars of his empty eye socket. "The goblins took my eye, Ambassador Benz, and I'm a lot harder to injure than a human."

Benz did a long blink but didn't flinch, which earned him another point. I wondered what he'd think if he saw the goblins. They prided themselves on extra limbs and eyes, so that females that looked like humanoid spiders were the height of beauty among the goblins. For that matter, he hadn't seen Sholto with his extra tentacles visible. Benz was going to have a lot more chances to practice not flinching.

"Are you saying the goblins would attack me?"

I stepped in. "No, it is perfectly possible to visit and negotiate with the goblins in safety, but it requires an understanding of their culture that is rare even among the sidhe. I know of no human who has ever been that successfully intimate with the goblin court."

Rhys snugged his eye patch back into place. "I've learned that my injury came through a lack of cultural understanding." His voice was only a little bitter. He lost his eye hundreds of years ago, but I'd explained the misunderstanding to him only about a year ago. He'd hated the goblins and blamed them for it for a very long time, and had only a short time to get used to the idea that his injury was as much his fault as that of the goblin who took his eye.

"My goal is to be a true ambassador to both of the high courts of faerie, both Unseelie and Seelie, but no one in our government has spoken to me of the goblins, or even of Lord Sholto in his role as king."

"Perhaps if your post as ambassador goes very well, we could escort you through the other courts at some point," I said.

"I would be most grateful for the education in your wider culture," he said, with a very nice smile. Even his brown eyes were shining with pleasure. I still felt we'd presented him with something he wasn't prepared for, but he covered it better than most envoys, human or faerie.

I smiled, and turned carefully away in my designer sundress, not sure I could equal his pleasant falseness. He really was very good.

"Now, Princess Meredith, I had my own security wait outside the room with yours, since those inside the room are fathers and royal consorts, and security stays out. I've acted in accordance with your wishes this time."

"Thank you, Ambassador," I said with a smile.

"But I also have additional diplomatic security for you."

"We discussed this, Ambassador; they are not needed."

"Not meaning any insult to your bodyguards, but you were allegedly kidnapped by the king while under their care."

"We've explained that I told them all to leave me alone, and they had to obey my orders."

"But don't they still have to obey your orders, Princess?"

"We've all agreed that Merry is never to be left alone without guards, and the same is true of the children," Rhys said.

"Even if she orders you to do so?" Benz asked.

Rhys and Galen both nodded. "She will never be left alone again," Galen said, and his voice held that new seriousness. I knew he meant it, and he was well trained as a fighter, but he didn't have the skill level of Rhys, or Doyle, or Frost. I wasn't sure if it was just the difference in years of practice, or if it had been a willingness to do deadly harm. The other men had been in real wars and had learned what it meant to kill and be killed. Galen had never had that; he'd had very few "real" fights. Honestly, I'd always thought that it wasn't just lack of battle hardness, but that his personality, the very gentleness that I loved him for, prevented him from being the warrior he could have been. Now I was no longer sure of Galen, or of many things.

He came to me then, took my hand in his, and smiled down at me, his green eyes filling with that warmth they'd always held. "You look sad, my Merry. I would do anything to chase that look from your eyes."

How could I tell him that it was his new resolution that made me sad? I couldn't; we were all being changed by the events of the last year. We were parents now, and that would change us more.

"Kiss me, my green knight, and it will wipe the sadness from my eyes."

I was rewarded with that brilliant smile of his, the one that had been making my heart skip a beat since I was fourteen, and then he leaned over, bending that six feet of muscle down to lay his mouth upon mine. The kiss was chaste by our standards, but the ambassador finally cleared his throat.

I had to break away from the kiss and explain, "Throat clearing is a human way of expressing awkwardness, or impatience with something sexual, or romantic."

Galen glanced at the ambassador. "That wasn't sexual by court standards, not by Unseelie standards anyway."

"I've been told that sexuality is freer among the sidhe," he said.

"If you try the throat-clearing routine with my aunt, the queen, either it will prompt her to say something scathing, or she will be more vigorous at whatever is bothering you."

"It was not the kiss, but the fact that I think you are changing the subject from the princess having extra security from our government, that made me want to interrupt. I think of myself as fairly bohemian."

"Bohemian," Rhys said, "that's not a term I've heard in a while."

Benz looked at him, and there was intelligence in all the charm, which was good; he'd need it. "Is it the wrong word to use?"

"No, but to thrive at the Unseelie Court, you'll need to be a little bit more than bohemian."

"What would you suggest?"

"Profligate, perverse, but perhaps not." Rhys looked at Galen and me.

"You've thought of something," Galen said.

"I was just thinking that the queen never allows the human media to see her at her most flagrant. I was wondering if a human ambassador to our court might have a . . . calming effect." His eye was full of humor at the very mildness of his word choice. If Queen Andais had to behave for human sensibilities, then torture as dinner entertainment might be over. It was always mild torture, by her standards, and it wasn't common, but her love of true torture might have to be more controlled if Benz was visiting our court—if she could control herself and hadn't gone so far into her own madness that nothing would help her regain herself. That was actually the question that stood in the way of her visiting the babies. Was she truly mad or just aiming her grief at her own court because she could? If she had to find other outlets for her grief, I wondered if I could talk her into grief counseling. She'd gone to human fertility specialists; maybe she'd do therapy.

Rhys came to join Galen, adding his arms to the other man's so he had an arm around both my waist and Galen's. "Now it's you who've thought of something interesting, our Merry."

I nodded. "We'll discuss it later."

"When I'm not here to listen in," Benz said.

I glanced at him. "Yes," I said.

He laughed then, and said, "You know that most humans would have denied it, just to be polite."

"It's too close to a lie, and a lie that you would know was one. Why should I bother?"

"Ah, Princess Meredith, I think I am going find being ambassador to you a very interesting, even educational, experience."

"Which means it could be good, or bad," I said.

He nodded. "I don't know which it will be myself, yet."

"Be careful, Ambassador Benz," Rhys said, "or we'll make you too honest to be a diplomat out among the humans."

He looked surprised then, before he could stop himself, and then he laughed out loud, head back. It was the most unprotected and real expression I'd seen from him.

"Oh, Lord Rhys, a diplomat who cannot lie would be useless indeed out among the humans, but for a time I think a little brutal honesty might be a nice change. Now, about adding some diplomatic security agents to the princess's detail . . ."

We let him talk, and I hoped that the "brutal honesty" wouldn't be too brutal on Ambassador Peter Benz, or on us, for that matter. I couldn't trust my aunt, Queen Andais, to be safe and sane around our babies, but I also wasn't entirely sure we could keep telling her no. How do you tell someone who has been the ultimate power of life and death for more than two thousand years that she can't come visit her great-nieces and nephew? That was always the trouble with dealing with the immortal; they were so used to getting their way.

CHAPTER

EIGHT

Detective Lucy Tate was tall, dark haired, and dressed in the female version of the plainclothes detective pantsuit, black with a white dress shirt this time. It seemed only color varied for the detectives of the homicide bureau. When Lucy had first come through the door I'd thought she had a murder she wanted a fey perspective on, but she'd had a trio of small teddy bears in her hands, and I was pretty certain that made it a friendly visit, not business. I'd been half right.

"Merry, it's reasonable for the local police to be worried that Maeve Reed's estate isn't safe. The bastard kidnapped you from there."

"I can't go into a safe house with the babies," I said. The room was almost empty now. Most of the flowers had gone to other people in the hospital, as had most of the toys. We'd kept flowers and presents from actual friends, or people whose gifts it would be impolitic not to keep, and just that had filled up a second SUV, leaving room only for a driver. Lucy's bears, two pink and one blue, had been newborn safe, and were tucked into the things we were keeping.

Doyle said, "This isn't a homicide issue, Detective; why are you here?"

"She's a friend, Doyle," I said.

"She is, but they sent her because they thought a friend could persuade you where the others had failed, isn't that right, Detective Tate?"

He looked at her with that black-on-black gaze; his face was unreadable, blank so that it was almost threatening in its absolute neutrality. The way a wild animal will look at you: It doesn't want to hurt you, but if you crowd it, it will defend itself. If you don't crowd it, then you can depart in peace, but the warning is there. Back off, or things will go badly.

Lucy reacted to it by taking a half step back, one foot in front of the other in a stance that let her move if she needed to. I doubted she was even fully aware of what she'd done, but the cop in her had seen the implied threat and reacted accordingly. Doyle wouldn't attack and she wouldn't do anything to push that neutrality, but it was still unsettling to watch my friend and my love face off. I didn't want unsettling, I wanted settled. I wanted to just be happy with the babies and the loves of my life, but my family was going to make sure this milestone was as traumatic as they'd made every other important event in my life. My father had protected me from them as much as he could, but once he died it had just been me trying to survive. I was tired of this shit, so tired of it.

"I'm not going into a safe house, Lucy. I appreciate the thought, but human cops would just be cannon fodder if the king attacks us. Read the police report on what his power did to Doyle, and think what that would have done to a human being."

"I've seen the reports," she said.

"That's how they persuaded you to come down," I said.

She nodded. "He can turn light into heat and project it from his hand; that's like crazy."

"He is the King of Light and Illusion; he can do many things with light, especially daylight," Doyle said.

"Like what else can he do with light?" Lucy asked.

Doyle shook his head. "I'm hoping he hasn't regained all his old abilities; if he has, then it could go badly no matter where Merry is."

"Well, aren't you just a bundle of cheer," she said.

"Instead of being able to spend time with Merry and our children, I have spent the last day and night negotiating with one high court of faerie or another. The king's courtiers have assured me that he will wait until the DNA tests come back. If they show that none of the babes are his, then he will acknowledge he has no claim on them, or Merry."

"Merry was already pregnant when he . . ." She stopped as if afraid she'd said too much.

"It's okay, Lucy, but the geneticist has informed us that it may not be that simple. The king is my great-uncle, and the sidhe of both courts have been intermarrying for centuries; we could share a lot of genetics. It's probably not enough to prove paternity, but enough to confuse the issue if my uncle wishes not to give up his claim."

"He won't give up," Doyle said.

"Is it true that if he's not able to have children, then he has to relinquish the throne?" she asked.

I fought to keep my face neutral. I hadn't known that the human police knew that, or any human knew that.

"The blank face from both of you is answer enough," she said.

I cursed softly inside my head—sometimes in trying so hard not to give something away, the very effort screams your answer. The big question was: Did the police know that it wasn't a matter of stepping down from the throne, but execution, for having cursed his court with infertility a century after Taranis knew he was infertile? The old idea that your health, prosperity, and fertility came from your king, or queen, was very true in faerie. Taranis was fighting for his very life. Did Lucy know that?

"What happens if he steps down?" she asked.

"He ceases to be king," Doyle said.

"That part I figured, but is he exiled from faerie?"

"No, why do you ask?" I said.

She shrugged. "Because exile would explain why he's so desperate to prove one of the babies is his."

"I think it's simpler than that, Lucy. I think he just can't stand the thought of not being absolute ruler of the Seelie Court after all these centuries. I think he'd do anything to keep his throne."

"Define *anything*," she said, and I didn't like the very shrewd look in her brown eyes. She was smart and very good at her job.

One of the babies made a sound from the cribs. Lucy had ignored them except for a brief glimpse at the cloth-wrapped bundles. She was here on business, not to see babies, but the noise made us turn to find out which baby was waking up.

It was Bryluen, moving fitfully in her basket like a crib within a crib. Doyle picked her up with his big, dark hands. The baby looked even tinier. Some of the fathers had been awkward holding them, but Doyle held our daughter with the same physical ease and grace with which he did everything. Bryluen's eyes were open enough to gleam in the light like dark jewels.

"May I hold her?" Lucy asked, and the request surprised me.

Doyle looked to me, and I said, "Of course. We're waiting for the nurse to bring the wheelchair; they won't let me walk out, and most of the other men are helping load the gifts."

Lucy didn't seem to hear me as Doyle laid Bryluen in her arms. Lucy didn't know how to hold the baby, which said she'd never really been around them. Doyle helped move her arms into place, and once she had the baby tucked into the crook of her arm she just stared down. Lucy's face got this happy, almost beatific glow to it, as if the world had narrowed down to the baby in her arms.

I hadn't expected Lucy to be that entranced with babies, but maybe she was having that "I'm in my midthirties and the clock is ticking" moment.

"Detective Tate," Doyle said.

She never reacted, just started humming softly and rocking Bryluen gently.

"Detective Tate," he said again, with a little more force to his voice.

When she didn't react this time, I moved closer to her and said, "Lucy, can you hear me?"

She never reacted, as we hadn't spoken.

"Lucy!" I said it sharply this time.

She blinked up at me as if she were waking from a dream. She stared at me, trying to say something, but she had to blink twice more to finally say, "What did you say?"

"I need to get Bryluen ready to go downstairs." I took the baby from her arms, and she was reluctant to let her go, but once she wasn't holding the baby Lucy seemed to recover herself. She shook visibly, like shaking off a nightmare, and said, "Wow, I just had that sensation like someone walked over my grave."

I nodded. "It happens."

She shivered again, and when she looked at me her eyes looked normal. Detective Tate was in there again.

"I'm sorry, Lucy, and I hope it doesn't get you in trouble with the higher-ups in your department, but we need to take more precautions against my uncle, and Maeve Reed's estate is more magically guarded than any safe house would be."

"We'll have police wizards on the detail, Merry."

"The last time you and I worked together, one of the bad guys was one of those wizards," I said.

"That's not fair, Merry."

"Perhaps not, but it's still true."

"You're saying that you don't trust the police?"

"No, I'm saying that no matter how safe you think you are, you're probably wrong."

"That sounds pretty hopeless," she said.

"I thought it sounded realistic."

She smiled, but it wasn't entirely a happy one. "We'll put extra patrols in your neighborhood. Call and we'll be there."

"I know that," I said.

"Promise if anything goes wrong you'll call the police and not try to handle it yourselves."

"I can't promise that."

"Because you're not allowed to lie," she said.

I nodded.

"You'll handle this internally, if you can, won't you?"

I nodded again, cuddling Bryluen to me.

She turned to Doyle. "Don't you or any of the people she loves play hero and get killed when we could have prevented it, okay?"

"We will endeavor not to," he said.

"I mean it. Merry loves you, and I don't want to hold her hand while she mourns you, or Frost, or Galen, or any of you guys. We're the police; it's our job to risk our lives to protect and serve."

"It is our job, as well, where Merry and the babes are concerned."

"Yeah, but Merry won't be devastated if we get hurt, and police dying in the line of duty won't lose the babies their dads."

He gave a small bow from his neck. "I will remember what you said, and thank you for putting our lives above yours for Merry's sake."

"I don't want to die, none of us do, but it's our job to stop this bastard from hurting her again."

"And ours," he said.

She frowned and made a little push-away gesture. "You're going to do what you're going to do; I'll tell them I tried."

"We really do appreciate you coming down, Lucy."

She smiled at me. "I know you do. I just really want to get this guy."

I realized that Lucy had taken my rape more personally, because we were friends. It made me care for her even more, and say with real feeling, "Thank you, Lucy."

She smiled a little wider. "I'll leave you to get the little tykes ready to leave, and go join the cops helping to keep back the crowd."

"I assume the press," I said.

"And just people wanting to see the little prince and princess; it's not every day that America gets newborn royals."

"True," I said, and smiled at her.

She smiled back and then left us with, "I'm not usually into babies, but she's a cute one."

We thanked her, and once the door closed behind her, Doyle and I looked at each other. He came to stand beside me, and we both looked down at Bryluen.

"Mustn't bespell the humans," I said to her.

She blinked those exotic-looking eyes at me. The little knit cap was tucked over most of her red curls and completely hid the horn buds. She was tiny and perfect, and already magical.

"Do you think she understands?" I asked.

"No, but that answers one question."

I looked up at him. "What question?"

"Maeve Reed has a human nanny for her baby, but we cannot risk human caregivers."

"You mean we can't risk the human caregivers being ensorcelled by the babies."

"Yes, that is what I mean."

I looked down at our little bundle of joy. "She's part demi-fey, or part sluagh, one has the best glamour in all faerie, and the other is some of the last of the wild magic left in faerie."

"There is wild magic about, my Merry." He motioned at the tree and the wild rose vines.

I smiled. "True, but I've never seen a baby bespell someone that quickly and that well. Lucy has a strong will, and was likely wearing some protections against faerie glamour just as a precaution. Most police that deal with us do."

"Yet Bryluen clouded her mind and senses as if it were nothing," Doyle said.

"It was very quick and well done. I've known sidhe with centuries of practice who couldn't have done it."

He placed his hand gently on top of her head, so very dark against the multicolored cap. Bryluen blinked up at us. "They are going to be very powerful, Merry."

"How do we teach them to control their powers if they have them this early, Doyle? Bryluen can't understand right from wrong yet."

"We will have to protect the humans from them until they are old enough to learn control."

"How long will that be?"

"I do not know, but we know now that they have come into the world with instinctive magic and there is no waiting until puberty for their powers to manifest."

"It would have been easier if their magic had waited," I said.

"It would, but I do not think our path was ever meant to be easy, my

Merry; wondrous, beautiful, exciting, thrilling, even frightening, but not easy."

I raised Bryluen to lay a kiss upon her cheek. I loved her already; she was mine, ours, but I was a little frightened now. If she could make humans like her, want to hold and rock her, what else could she make them do? Child psychologists say that children are born sociopaths and have to learn to have a conscience. It happens around the age of two, usually, but until then there's no conscience to appeal to, no way to understand that something is wrong or right.

I held our beautiful little sociopath and prayed to the Goddess that she wouldn't hurt anyone before we'd had time to teach her that it was wrong.

The scent of roses filled the room, and it wasn't just the clean sweetness of the wild rose vine, but that richer musk that is more from cultivation than nature. It was a heady scent, and reassurance from the Goddess. Normally, it would have been enough to lay my fears to rest, but this time there was a kernel of unease that stayed inside my heart. How could I doubt her, after all she'd shown me, all she'd awakened around me? But it wasn't the Goddess I doubted, it was more just worry. I was a new mother, and mothers worry.

CHAPTER

NINE

Maeve Reed, the Golden Goddess of Hollywood since about 1950, came to the hospital to escort us home to her house. We'd lived in her guesthouse when we first moved in with her, but as more fey had flocked to us, Maeve had moved us into the main house with her and left the guesthouse to new exiles from faerie who weren't as close to her. She was an exile herself, so she understood the confusion of being cast out from faerie and being thrust into the modern world.

Though very few exiles had succeeded as well as Maeve Reed at adapting to this brave, new world. The guard outside opened the door, and I heard Maeve's voice. "So happy you loved my last movie. Congratulations on your baby, he is adorable." Her voice was warm and utterly sincere, and in part it was the truth, but she had been a great actress for decades and could turn utter sincerity on and off like a well-oiled switch. I doubted I would ever be that skilled at being "on" for the public, and being merely mortal I wouldn't live long enough for the centuries of practice that had helped her get so very good at it.

She came breezing into the room with a casual wave of her hand that was too big a gesture for the room but would have looked great in a photo, as would the brilliant smile on her face. She was dressed in an oyster-white pantsuit that flowed and moved with her; a silk shell in a deep but subdued blue helped her not look quite the six feet that she was, forcing the eye down once it had started up those long legs. She smiled at me and I had a moment of catching the edge of the smile she'd used on the fan outside. It was a good smile, and sincere in its way, because she was genuinely happy that the woman liked her film, and meant the congratulations, but . . . the moment the door closed behind her the smile vanished, and she had a moment where it was as if she laid down some invisible burden across her shoulders. Nothing could make her less than gorgeous with that perfect pale gold tan, the perfect blue eyes in subdued but equally perfect makeup, those cheekbones, those full, kissable lips, but she had a moment of looking tired. Then she straightened up and those high, tight breasts pressed against the blue shell, perky forever without any need for cosmetic surgery.

Her gaze went to the fruit tree that was shedding its blossoms like a pink snow, and the roses on the other side of the room. "Ah, the new wonders. The nurses asked me when the plants would be going away."

"We aren't sure," Doyle said.

"Doyle, Frost, I stopped by the nursery first and the babies are beautiful."

"They are," Doyle said, as if to say, *Of course.*

"Welcome home, Maeve," Frost said.

She wasted a few extra watts of smile on him, but she didn't mean it. He wasn't pure sidhe enough for her; most of my men weren't. She'd made no secret about the fact that she'd have had sex with Rhys or Mistral, if they and I had been okay with it. Among humans it would have been an insult; among the fey if you found someone attractive and didn't let them know, it was an insult. She was afraid of Doyle, not because he'd done anything to her, but because she'd spent too many centuries seeing him as my aunt's assassin. She'd lost people she cared about to him long ago, so she never flirted with him. He was fine with that.

Then she turned to me, and the look on her face was suddenly cautious. She'd actually texted me before she came, asking if I was angry at her for neglecting me. I'd reassured her via text but realized I'd need to do more reassuring in person.

I held my hand out to her, and she came to me smiling, but it was a different smile, less perfect than on film, letting me see the uncertainty in her eyes. I valued that I got to see her when the cameras weren't rolling and she let down her guard.

"I'm so sorry that I couldn't come sooner. I saw the babies in the nursery and they are so beautiful."

"You had to fly back from Europe just to see us."

She took my hand in hers, studying my face. "How are you feeling, honestly?"

Her hand was warm, the bones long and delicate as I rubbed my fingers down them. "What's wrong, Maeve?"

"The media circus is in full swing outside, Merry." A frown showed between those perfect brows and those famous blue eyes. If only her legion of fans were ever allowed to see her eyes when they weren't hidden by faerie glamour to appear more human; as beautiful as she was now, stripped of all illusions she was even more so.

"You say that like the media is entirely your fault. I'm the first American-born faerie princess; I've lived with cameras and reporters all my life."

"That's true, but combine your fame with mine and it's worse than I've seen it, and Merry, I've seen it at its worst." She squeezed my hand in hers. I wasn't sure if it was to reassure me, or herself, or maybe neither; maybe it was just the comfort of another hand to hold.

People say they want to be famous, but there is a level of fame that becomes almost crippling. I'd had the literal weight of the press break a window from trying to get a better view of me with Doyle and Frost once. Some of them had been cut, nothing serious, but they had rained glass down on us and the other customers in the shop.

"You are actually frightened," Doyle said.

She looked up at him and nodded.

Frost came forward to lay his hand on my shoulder. "Is Merry in danger?"

"Police have moved them all back enough that we can exit, and other patients can get into the hospital, but I have never seen so many reporters."

"You have been the reigning Goddess of Hollywood for decades, and you have never seen so many of them." Doyle made it a half-question.

"No, I have not," she said.

"Then it will help boost the money that your newly released film makes, which is what your producers, and all of us, wanted," I said. I raised my hand and laid it over Frost's where he touched me.

"I don't think our publicist could have envisioned this," she said.

"We could send you home and sign the papers for the reality TV show. That would bring in more money," I said.

"No, we don't want cameras in our house, not like that."

"Then you're the major breadwinner for our court in exile, Maeve. It behooves us to do as much as possible to help promote your career. The rest of us couldn't earn what's needed, especially not to live in the style to which you're spoiling us. We could say yes to the reality show and bring in more money than we can from being private detectives," I said.

"I earned thirty million dollars for my last film, Merry; I think I can afford you all, though admittedly the Red Caps eat more than I thought possible," she said with a smile.

Frost didn't hear the joke in her words. "They range from seven to thirteen feet tall and are big enough to fill out such frames. It takes fuel to make a warrior as big as an ogre run."

She raised her smile and aimed it at him, but it wasn't a flirting smile now, more the "isn't he cute not understanding" smile. "I was making a slight joke, Frost."

He frowned. "I did not think it was funny."

"Nor I," Doyle said.

She looked from one to the other of them, and then turned to me, laughing. "They can be so terribly serious sometimes."

"If you want jokes, best turn to Rhys or Galen," I said. I leaned my body back against Frost as I said it, letting him know I valued him, but it was true that humor was not the strong suit for my two main loves.

Frost wrapped his arm across the front of me, pulling me closer. I let Maeve's hand go so that I could grip his arm with both of my hands, holding on and leaning hard against the solidness of him. It was as if the strength of him seeped into me just from him holding me this close. I loved him more and more every day, and took more comfort from his presence in my life. I'd lost him once, or thought I had, and it frightened me that I loved him even more now, because when I thought he was gone forever it had been a near-killing sorrow. I knew if I lost him now it would hurt even more, and that was frightening, but I couldn't hold back from him either, because love can die from being withheld, like a flower that is so beautiful you hide it away from the sun trying to make it last longer; but every flower needs sun, and being in love requires risking yourself. It can require risking everything you are, not just in battle, but emotionally. Sometimes you have to risk it all to gain it all. I basked in the warmth of Frost's love and let him feel mine.

He hugged me tighter and leaned down to place a gentle kiss on the top of my head, resting his cheek against me. "I love you, my Merry," he whispered.

"And I love you, my Killing Frost." I turned my head, rising so we could kiss. I'd purposefully waited to put on lipstick, because we all tended to kiss a lot, and we didn't want to face the cameras with lipstick smeared across our faces like clown makeup.

"Seeing the two of you together makes me hope that I'll find another love of my own life someday," Maeve said.

Frost and I broke the kiss to look at Maeve. She had lost her human husband, the director who had discovered her back in the fifties, to cancer.

"I am sorry we could not save him, Maeve," I said.

"Even the magic of faerie can't heal a human that near death," she said.

I started to go to her to hug her, but Doyle surprised us by moving toward her. He held out his hand. "I know what it is to lose someone you love, and all the magic in the world does not ease the loss."

Maeve hesitated, then put her hand in his dark one. "All those years of seeing you stand beside the Queen of Air and Darkness, you were her Darkness, a bringer of blood and death; you gave no clue that you were actually a romantic."

"And achingly lonely," he said, "but neither was helpful as the right hand of the queen."

"But you helped Merry give me a chance to have a child with my husband, and now I have Liam."

"The magic that helped you grow fertile was Galen and Merry's doing, none of mine."

"You kept her alive long enough to do the spell, and that Galen could not have done," Maeve said.

Doyle acknowledged it with a nod, and then Maeve moved slowly into him and put her arms around him. He was stiff and a little unsure, but he patted her as she hugged him almost as awkwardly.

There was a flash from the window behind us. Doyle moved so fast it was hard to follow, as if the gun had just appeared in his hand and was pointed at the window, as he moved toward it. Frost had shoved me behind him. He had a gun in one hand and a blade in the other.

Maeve yelled, "It's a camera, Doyle; don't shoot them."

"Unless they can fly, it cannot be reporters," he said. There was another flash of light. I couldn't see past Frost's body and knew better than to even peer around him. He was guarding me; I had to let him do his job, but I wanted to see, badly.

Doyle cursed. "Anu's Breasts, they're on window-washing equipment, two of them."

"Well, someone has to work the controls while the other one takes pictures, or film," Maeve said as if it were just an everyday occurrence. Maybe it was for the Golden Goddess of Hollywood, but we'd never had reporters climbing down the windows of a hospital before.

Doyle shut the curtains, cutting out the sunlight with them so the room was suddenly dim.

"Thus it begins," Maeve said.

"I hate paparazzi," Frost said.

We all agreed with him and then called hospital security to let them know they'd been breached.

CHAPTER

TEN

Doyle had negotiated three days for me to recover my strength from giving birth, and then Aunt Andais, the Queen of Air and Darkness, got to speak to me directly. She wasn't going to use the telephone, because she wanted to see me while we spoke. We weren't going to use the computer for a Skype face-to-face either. Aunt Andais didn't even own a cell phone, and computers were for her staff, but for her it was the old-fashioned way: a mirror. The sidhe could speak through reflective surfaces of more than one kind, but mirrors were the easiest and clearest view. We chose the antique mirror in the dining room. One, because it was large and had been as big as one wall of the room once, before wild magic had expanded the room to the size of a small football field. The French doors showed a forest that had never existed in California. The clearing and forest were new lands of faerie, or old lands returned. We'd been so happy when it had happened, and then Taranis had walked into that bit of fairyland, knocked me unconscious, and stolen me away. Now there were locks on the French doors, and two guards posted at all times. If Taranis kidnapped me again, it wouldn't be through this opening.

The mirror was still large enough to act like a huge flat-screen TV, so that the queen would get a good view first of me, and then, if that went well, the babies, but since some of us could use mirrors to travel from one point to another we weren't risking the babies until Aunt Andais had shown herself sane, or at least sane-ish. I'd take the "ish" because asking for more than that would mean I'd never speak with her.

I debated on what color maternity dress to wear. It wasn't a casual concern. Andais was very into fashion, but more than that, she had taken insult from my choice of clothing in the past. Her feeling insulted had led to my being hurt, or even bleeding, so we put serious thought into what I would wear to sit before the queen. Shades of rich, dark green were some of my best colors. They brought out the green in my eyes, but Aunt Andais didn't always like to be reminded that my eyes were the color of the Seelie Court, and not the Unseelie. So, no green, which took out several of my maternity dresses. The red one was almost the color of fresh blood, not something we wanted my torture-loving aunt to think of when looking at me. The purple dress was at the dry cleaner. That left us with a soft floral print, royal blue, or a rich, salmon pink. Pants were a no-go; I was still too sore to want to wear them. We finally decided on the pink, saving the blue in case we had to do television earlier than we'd planned.

I sat facing the mirror, in the same large thronelike chair that I'd used to do business with the goblins months ago, before I started showing. It was the closest thing we had to a throne. The only downside to it was that my feet couldn't touch the floor, so I felt like a child. There was no footstool in the house that wasn't hard plastic and cheap looking. No one made velvet and wood stools for the queen to put her feet on anymore. Funny how things like that had gone out of style.

It was Kitto who came up with a solution. "I'll be your footstool."

He stood there gazing up at me, the only man I'd ever been with who was significantly shorter than my five feet even. He had moonlight skin like mine, like Frost's, white and pale and perfect as a winter's morn. His hair was a black almost as dark as Doyle's, but as Kitto's hair had grown out it had gotten wavy, so that it fell to his shoulders in an artful tangle of waves and curls as if it couldn't quite decide. I'd taught him how to take care of his longer hair, so that it looked artfully tousled, not messy. If he'd been taller he could have passed for pure Unseelie sidhe, except for three things. His eyes were huge, dominating his face, almond-shaped and a wondrous bright blue that swallowed his entire eye, except for the black point of his pupil; the color was sidhe, the shape and form were not. But more than the eyes, the line of shining scaled skin that grew down his back along his entire spine showed him not pure sidhe. The scales were flat, smooth, in colors of pink, gold, ivory, and small flecks of black, but so bright in color that the line of it looked more like a purposeful decoration than the scales of a snake. It was his back scales that made me wonder if Bryluen's wings might be partially from Kitto; goblins didn't have wings, but her wings were almost the same color as his snake skin. We wouldn't know until the tests came back. If Taranis hadn't been pushing we wouldn't have cared so much about who was the biological father or fathers of the babies, but to prove it wasn't Taranis, we had to prove who it was. Kitto's Cupid's-bow mouth hid a forked tongue, and he had to work hard not to slur his *s*'s, and the last bit of difference was two long, retractable fangs that tucked up against the roof of his mouth unless he chose to bring them down. He was one lover that I could never allow to bite me, because snake goblins were venomous, and his father had been one. If Bryluen could possibly be his daughter, I'd want to watch for those when her teeth started coming in, because even baby vipers have venom.

"The queen may try to frighten you, Kitto," I said.

"I am a stool for your feet, Merry. Footstools can't hear, or talk, or interact with anyone. I can ignore her, because I can just be the object I'm acting as."

I wasn't sure how I felt about him being just a piece of furniture for my feet. It must have shown on my face, because Kitto took my hand in his; his hand was the same size as mine, the only man in my life for whom that was true.

"I will be honored to act for you in this, Merry. I remember when the high kings, even among the humans, had virgins who held their feet so they did not touch the ground when the king sat upon the throne. It was an honored position, but you were not allowed to address the women at all. You had to treat them as the footstool for the king, and thus they were a part of the throne. If the queen speaks directly to me at all, it will be breaking protocol. I think she may talk to you about me, but I do not believe she will address me; besides, I am just a small goblin and she has never thought highly of me."

I couldn't argue that. There was some debate about what Kitto would wear, but not about his acting as my footstool. The other men agreed that he would wear the metal and cloth thong that I'd first seen him in; it was a lovely piece of workmanship, and it showed off his scales beautifully. Among the goblins if you had an extra bit of beauty, it was natural to dress to show it off. Though the fewer clothes you wore, the less dominant you were among the goblins; it was a way of showing visually that you were opting out of the near-constant battles for supremacy in the goblin court. By dressing as he had when I first met him, Kitto had been advertising that he was not a leader and didn't want to be. There was no need to fight him, because his scanty clothing was a white flag of sorts. It had also marked him as a potential victim, if someone wanted to claim him as a sort of mistress, or concubine; there really was no good human word for a man in his situation, and among the goblins there was no word that differentiated between male and female for the role. Goblins didn't care what sex you were, only how big, how strong, how tough. If a female was able to beat the shit out of enough other goblins, then she could rise as high in their ranks as a male. It was just rare, because their women, like most human women, had less muscle mass, size, and strength to back up their threat. It put women at a serious disadvantage in their culture, but then that was true among a lot of cultures.

The rest of the men had gone for the elegant warrior look. Doyle was in his signature black, but he'd put in the diamond stud earrings, to go with his usual silver rings that climbed up to the tops of his delicately pointed ears. He stood at my side, behind the throne, like a piece of the night made handsome and dangerous flesh.

Frost was at my other side in white and silver to match his skin, hair, and eyes, so that he was coldly elegant like a man carved of ice and snow. If Goddess could have taken winter and formed it into flesh and beauty, it would be the Killing Frost. His face was set in arrogant lines, the expression he wore when he was hiding his emotions. We would all hide our emotions tonight.

Rhys turned from where he was standing by the mirror and said, "Frost and Doyle look like bookends, light and darkness, balanced at your side, Merry."

I glanced up and back at the two men and could only agree. It was in moments like this that I still marveled that these two men, the ones who had seemed the most remote, untouchable by any emotion I understood, were now my greatest loves and fathers to my children.

Rhys was in white as well, but whereas most of the men had chosen medieval dress or some older fashion, he was in modern dress pants with a pale blue T-shirt loose over them, and his cream-colored trench coat; he'd even added his white fedora pulled down at a rakish angle over his long white curls. He was wearing a new eye patch in a pale blue that complemented his remaining eye and made all three of the different shades of blue brighter and deeper.

"You look good, Rhys," Galen said as he went to take his place beside the chair, "but I can't tell if you're doing Sam Spade in *The Maltese Falcon* or a sexy ice cream man."

Rhys grinned. "Well, I always go for sexy, and who doesn't like ice cream, but film noir is where I get most of my clothing inspirations."

Galen grinned back. "I just wear what I'm told to put on." That wasn't entirely true, because he had colors he preferred, but he was probably one of the least picky beyond that. He'd had less than a hundred years of my aunt choosing clothes for her guards, and he had never been a favorite, or far enough out of favor, for her to pay special attention to his appearance. That had given him freedom that the other guards had not had to find their own personal sense of style. Rhys's style was personal, but he'd only been able to indulge his film noir kick here in California with me; before that the queen had dressed him to show off his muscles, somewhere between a pornographic warrior and disco. I'd always thought she did it to humiliate Rhys, or that she didn't know what to do with him.

Galen was in pale green pants, untucked dress shirt, and a darker green tailored jacket. His pale curls with the one long braid always looked green, but his skin often looked just white; in the colors he'd chosen today his skin, eyes, and hair were all green. Only his soft tan dress shoes spoiled the solidarity of his color. He looked good in the outfit, but he didn't look spectacular. Had he not cared? Had he thought the queen would pay more attention to everyone else, as she always had? Or perhaps he had chosen green defiantly, because it made it impossible not to think "pixie," which was what his father had been—a pixie who had seduced one of the queen's ladies-in-waiting, back before she'd exchanged them for gentlemen-in-waiting.

The queen had executed Galen's father for his audacious seduction. How dare a lesser creature of faerie touch the sidhe of her court—and then the lady had come up pregnant and it turned out the queen had killed half of a fertile couple. Galen had been the only child born into the Unseelie sidhe once they arrived on American soil. She would not have killed Galen's father if she had known in time. Her temper coupled with her absolute power had cheated her court out of more babies, as her temper and power had cheated her out of being welcomed into our home to see our babies like a normal aunt.

Now Galen was the father of royal triplets, and he'd dressed to remind the queen of his father. Galen wanted her to remember what her anger and arrogance had cost her, and him, once. It was both brave and smart of him. Brave because he was rubbing the queen's nose in her mistake, and smart because it might remind her that a mistake here and now might cost her more.

It was very unlike Galen, so much so that I had to ask, "Who chose your clothing tonight?"

He walked toward me, smiling. "I did." But again there was a new look in his eyes, harsher, more sure of itself. I had mourned it earlier, but now I welcomed it. I needed all the help I could get negotiating with the queen.

I raised my hand and Galen took it, raising it to kiss first my hand, and then lowering his tall frame to kiss me gently on the lips. We didn't want to muss my bright red lipstick. He drew back with lipstick on his mouth, like a scarlet shadow of my smaller mouth between his lips.

"You'll want to rub that off," I said.

He shook his head. "I'll wear your lipstick proudly, my Merry. Let her see that I am in your favor, and that I am one of the Greenmen who prophecy said would bring life to the court."

"And remind her that your father might have brought more life to the courts if she hadn't killed him," I said, still holding his hand.

"That, too," he said. He squeezed my hand and stepped back because everyone else was spilling into the room at once. The prearranged time for the call was close, and we needed everyone in place so we could look impressive for our queen.

Mistral came first, looking impatient and tugging at his tunic. It was dark burnished gold with brighter gold and silver thread worked into the puff sleeves and cuffs, and in a more elaborate pattern across the chest. The pants were a color between tan and gold and bloused over the rich dark brown leather of his knee-high boots. The boots and pants he'd worn before, but the tunic had spent many long years put away, because it was a reminder of the power and magic he had lost. As he walked into the room it was as if lightning reflected down his long, unbound hair. Strands of it had turned gold, yellow, silver, a white so bright it nearly glowed. Some of that was a permanent color change, just a single strand here and there among the gray, but the flashing, reflected light that moved through all his hair came and went like lightning does.

His hair had changed in the last twenty-four hours, as if something had returned more of his power to him. He'd been holding Gwenwyfar, rocking her to sleep, when we'd noticed the first flash of light in his hair.

Now he strode into the room tugging at the tunic, and the colors in it brought out the strands of color in his hair, but I didn't really think it showed off the flash of light. I thought solid black clothing might showcase the lightning display more, but we'd think about that for another night when we wanted to be impressive, or frightening.

Kitto came in, wearing his metal thong. He was smiling and said, "Nicca and Biddy are watching the babies." That meant we could concentrate on meeting the queen without worrying that the babies would cry and need us, which was especially good since the pink dress was not a dark color. If the babies cried, any of the babies, sometimes my milk came down and the nursing bra wasn't enough to stop it from staining. It was a mark of the blessing of the Goddess that I could nurse my children, but it was not convenient for looking serious and in charge.

Kitto went down on the floor so that my feet in their purple and pink flats could rest on his bare back. I'd felt that acting as my footstool had been degrading to him, but now that I felt him solid under my feet it just felt right, as if he grounded me, centered me. I felt less of an impostor dressed up to play queen, and more . . . queenly.

Sholto was the last of the fathers to stride in through the door, and he was in black, an outfit almost identical to the one he'd worn in the hospital when he wanted to be certain to be seen as a king. His white-blond hair was unbound around all the blackness and gleaming jewelry, so he looked both beautiful and frightening, which was the effect he wanted.

Behind Sholto came the guards, who were now just guards for me. We had all discussed it and decided that though our customs didn't force me to limit my sexual attentions to the fathers of my children, there were already too many of them and not enough of me. So not every handsome face, beautiful body, dangerously armed guard, male or female, who came through the door was my lover. Honestly, most never had been, but sometimes it's good to finalize the rules of a relationship, even one with a group as large as ours.

They fanned out around the room in their warrior garb, some in actual armor, but most in modern clothing with body armor under or over the clothing. Though in truth if the Queen of Air and Darkness wanted you dead, armor wouldn't save you. Her name was not an idle title but named her two main powers. She could travel through the dark to anywhere else that was dark, and hear her name spoken in the dark. She could see in the dark without any light to aid her. The air she could make heavy, thick, until you could no longer breathe it and it felt as if your chest were being crushed by the weight of her magic. Andais was truly the Queen of Air and Darkness.

What good was armor against such magic? But they wore it all the same, because sometimes it's not about whether it will actually stop the bullet or the blade, but more about drawing a line in the sand at your enemy's feet. We hoped it would show Andais that we meant to fight rather than submit. All of us were exiles from her court, and almost all of us had suffered at her hands, some more than others. There were a handful of guards that Doyle had decided would not stand with us tonight, because he feared that their memories of what Andais had done to them would make them unable even to stand their ground, let alone fight if the need arose.

We had found therapists for the most damaged of our refugees from faerie. They had been diagnosed with post-traumatic stress disorder, or PTSD. I wouldn't have been surprised if most of us had a touch of it. You don't have to be the one being cut up to be traumatized; watching it is enough sometimes. Those who were most fragile were barred from the room and given duties elsewhere. They could help keep the amazing crush of media from climbing the wall around Maeve's estate, or help patrol the grounds looking for each new bit of faerie that appeared. It was as if the old lands were emerging in puzzle pieces in this bit of America where they had never existed, though faerie wasn't a place you could reliably find on a map. It was more an idea, or ideal, of wild magic that had a mind and will of its own. Faerie moved at its own whim, and that of the Goddess and Her Consort. So the grounds were patrolled, searching for each bit of wild magic as it manifested. Already the lands inside the walls were much larger than ordinary senses said the walls could contain, which was wonderful, but Taranis had stepped through on the new lands, and so might the queen. The danger of that meant guards had to be posted, to warn the rest of us if either of them was seen. I think we all felt that we would lose a pitched battle against either the king or the queen, but if the alarm was given first, then even if the guard who discovered the breach died, there would be more warriors coming to defend us. And when I said "us," I didn't mean just my babies and me. Maeve and one other of our female guards had given birth here in this new Western kingdom of faerie. We'd run away from faerie to save our lives, and now faerie was coming to us, building itself around us. Doyle and

I had given up our crowns to the Unseelie Court to save our Killing Frost, but the Goddess and the land of faerie itself wasn't done. If we could not rule the Unseelie, it seemed likely we'd get a chance to rule something else, something new, something here.

I hadn't refused Detective Lucy Tate's offer of a safe house just because I thought it would get the nice policemen killed. I had refused because wild magic was everywhere around me and the fathers of my babies. In a human safe house surrounded by human police, we wouldn't be able to hide just how much of the old powers were returning. What would the police have done if they'd woken up with their safe house growing an extra room overnight, or a new door that led to a forest that had never existed on the West Coast of America?

So we stayed inside Maeve's walled estate and let it grow and become magical. I thought about the tree and roses in my hospital room. It had been miraculous even to the sidhe when such things first began appearing around me. Inside faerie some had faded, but others had remained and grown. Outside faerie they had faded over time in the beginning, but lately not so much. I hoped they faded, because we weren't certain what the humans would do if they found out just how much magic was following me around.

Doyle and Frost's positions at my back to left and right had been easily agreed on, but where the other men would stand had been more of a debate. Sholto had won the right to choose his place, because he was a true king in his own right and the Goddess herself had handfasted us and crowned me as his queen. The only issue had been when he tried to insist on standing higher than Doyle or Frost. I had to put my foot down on that, and he'd let me win with almost no argument, which meant he'd made only a token try. He chose to stand beside Doyle on the right of my chair. Rhys had wanted to mirror him beside Frost, until the others pointed out that because of his being six inches shorter than everyone else, he'd be mostly hidden behind whoever was in front. Mistral stood beside Frost, mirroring Sholto. That left Rhys beside Sholto and Galen beside Mistral. Kitto under my feet would not seem to be one of the fathers, and I'd told Royal he couldn't stand at my side tonight. For one thing, Sholto was convinced that Bryluen's wings were from his father's side of the genetics. Even more importantly, if my third baby had truly been fathered after the twins were conceived, that gave credence to Taranis's paternity claim. I didn't want to help Taranis and his team of lawyers stake a claim to my children. I loved Bryluen already, but there was part of me that stared at her red curls, so like my own, and thought, *So like Taranis's hair.* I prayed to Goddess that it was not so, but when so much wild magic and Deity intervention is everywhere, many things are possible, both good and terrible.

"It's time, Merry," Doyle said, his deep voice soft. He laid a hand on my shoulder as if he felt my nervousness.

I put my hand up to cover his, and said, "Then let us begin. Cathbodua, please let my aunt know we are ready to speak with her."

Cathbodua stepped forward from the guards that stretched in a semicircle behind us. She had been part of my father's guards once, the Prince's Cranes, but when he was assassinated the entire female guard had been given to Prince Cel, the queen's son. It had been against the rules and customs to simply transfer them to Cel. Once his master was dead, a guard was supposed to have a choice of either transferring his loyalty to another royal or going back to "private service" and being just another noble of the Unseelie Court. We had learned only in the last year that none of the women had been allowed a choice, and Prince Cel had made them into his personal harem. Some had become his torture victims, as some of the male guards had been for the queen, but some were not so easily victimized.

Cathbodua moved toward the mirror in a rustle of feathers, her raven cloak spreading out around her like the feathers it had once become. She still couldn't transform into full bird guise, but she could communicate with ravens and crows and a few other birds to help spy out the land and look for danger. Her hair was as black as the feathers, so that it was hard to tell where one began and the other ended. Her skin was moonlight skin like mine, like Frost's, like Rhys's, but somehow when you looked at her you thought bone white, not moonlight. She was beautiful as all the sidhe were beautiful, but there was a coldness to her beauty that did not appeal to me. But then I wasn't dating her; as a guard she was excellent, and that was all I required of her.

She touched the side of the mirror, and I heard the distant cawing of crows, like hearing your own phone ringing in your ear, knowing it's louder on the other end.

We had all bet that Andais would keep us waiting, but we were wrong. The mirror fogged as if some invisible giant breathed along the glass, and when it cleared there she sat.

She sat on the edge of her huge black-silk-and-fur-draped bed. It was rich and sensual, and a little threatening, as if there would be pressure to live up to such a bed, and the price for failing expectations might be harsh, or maybe that was just me knowing my aunt far too well.

She was wearing a black silk robe so that her ankle-length black hair mingled with the robe and the sheets, until it was as if her hair was formed out of all that silk and dark fur. Her skin was whiter than white, framed by all that raven darkness, except for one spill of honey-and-white fur to her left that spoiled the effect and showed her hair black and almost normal across it. It wasn't like her to not notice that one bit of pale that spoiled the intimidating effect of her visual.

Her face was almost free of makeup, and without the black eyeliner she usually wore her triple-gray irises weren't as striking, again leaving her eyes almost ordinary. Her beauty didn't need makeup, though without it she was a cold, distant beauty as if carved of ice and raven's wings. That was a strange thought, with Cathbodua standing beside the mirror in her raven wing cloak, but though both women might have begun as similar battle goddesses, where they had gone from their beginnings had made all the difference. It had made one a queen for a millennium and left the other to diminish until she was barely more than human. It is not where you begin, or what gifts you begin with, but what you do with them that matters in the end.

"Greetings, Aunt Andais, Queen of Air and Darkness, sister of my father, ruler of the Unseelie host."

"Greetings, niece Meredith, Princess of Flesh and Blood, daughter of my beloved younger brother, mother of his grandchildren, and conqueror of hearts."

I had chosen my words carefully to remind her that I was her niece and she might value my bloodline if not the rest of me, but she had given an answer as careful as my own, and as nonthreatening. It wasn't like her.

"Aunt Andais, I'm not quite sure what to say next." She was too far off script for me, and when in doubt truth is not a bad fallback plan.

She smiled, and she seemed tired. "I grow tired of torturing people, my niece."

I fought to keep my face blank, and felt Doyle's hand tense on my shoulder where I touched him. I forced my breathing even, and spoke in a normal voice. "May I be so bold as to say, Aunt Andais, that both surprises and pleases me."

"You may, since you already have, Meredith, and you are not surprised that torture no longer pleases me, you are shocked, are you not?"

"Yes, aunt, quite so."

She laughed then, head back, face shining with it, but it was the kind of laugh that slithered down your spine and tickled goose bumps from every inch of your skin. I'd heard that laugh as she cut people's skin with a blade while they screamed.

I swallowed past my suddenly thudding pulse, and knew in that moment that I never wanted her around my babies. I never wanted them to hear that laughter, not ever.

"I see that look upon your face, Meredith. I know that look."

"I don't know what you mean, Aunt Andais."

"Determination, decision, and not in my favor, am I right?"

"In your moments of clarity, aunt, you see much."

"Yes," she said, face growing somber, "in my moments of clarity, when I do not let my bloodlust have full rein, and carve my unhappiness and lust from the bodies of my courtiers."

"Yes, Aunt Andais, when you're not doing that," I said.

She held her hand out to someone out of sight of the mirror. Eamon, her favorite lover for the last hundred years or so, came to take her hand.

He was as pale of skin, as black of hair, as she; a little taller, broader through the shoulders, six-plus feet of sidhe warrior, but the face he turned to the mirror held that calm, even a kindness, that had often been all that stood between Andais and her worst instincts. He'd grown out a thin, neat Vandyke mustache and goatee, but it was still more facial hair than I'd ever seen my aunt allow at our court. Beards and such were for Taranis and his golden throng. Andais preferred her men clean shaven; many of the men couldn't even grow facial hair.

Eamon sat on the bed beside her, putting his arm across her shoulders, and she leaned into him, as if she needed the reassurance of the touching. It was a show of weakness that I never thought she would allow me to see.

"Greetings, Princess Meredith, wielder of the hands of flesh and blood, niece of my beloved," Eamon said.

In all the years that he had stood by her side in mirror calls to others, I had never heard him greet, or be greeted, by anyone. He had been an extension of Andais, nothing more.

"Greetings, Eamon, wielder of the hand of corrupting flame, consort of my Aunt Andais, holder of her heart."

He smiled at me, and it was a good smile, a real one. "I have never heard myself called that last before, Princess Meredith; I thank you for it."

"It was a title I suspected you deserved long ago, but I had never known for certain until today."

He hugged Andais, and she seemed somehow diminished, smaller, or I just had never appreciated how big a man Eamon was, or perhaps a bit of both.

Eamon raised his eyes a little and spoke. "Greetings, Doyle, wielder of the painful flame, Baron Sweet-Tongue, the Queen's Darkness, consort of Princess Meredith."

"And to you, Eamon, all graces and titles deserved and earned to you, as well."

He smiled. "Now, I do not know whom to greet next, Princess Meredith. Do I give formal acknowledgment to Lord Sholto, who is a king in his own right, or to the Killing Frost, who is dearest to you and the Darkness, or to Rhys, who has regained his own sithen again, and no offense to Galen the Green Knight, but our protocols have nothing to cover so many consorts or princes."

"If it is a formal greeting for all of us, then Sholto should be next," Frost said.

I reached out to touch his hand where it sat on the pommel of the sword at his waist. He always touched his weapons when he was nervous. He rewarded me with a smile, and that was enough.

"I will waive such niceties," Sholto said. "For my fellow consorts to acknowledge my title is enough." He gave a small bow from his neck toward Frost, who acknowledged with a bow as low as Sholto's but no lower. There had been a time when you had to know just how low to bow to each level of noble, and to get it wrong was an insult. I was glad such things were in the past. How had anyone gotten anything done?

"Such calm, civilized behavior," Andais said, in a voice that held distaste, as if it wasn't a compliment at all.

Eamon hugged her, laying his cheek gently against her hair. "Would you rather they fight and demand every title we could paint upon them, my queen?"

She ignored his question and spoke, in a voice that seemed as diminished as the rest of her. "Why have you not come to kill me, Meredith?"

I fought to keep my face neutral, and watched Eamon look startled, and the first unease cross his face. What was worse, then his face went back to that handsome, unreadable mask that had allowed him to live and thrive in Andais's bed for so long. Perhaps that last comment had been over the line even for him, chastising his queen in front of others.

I found my voice and said, "I was pregnant with my father's, your brother's, grandchildren and would not risk them for vengeance."

She nodded and put her arm around Eamon's waist, to be held closer. "I went mad after you killed my son and turned down the crown of my court to save your lover, Meredith. Did you realize that?"

"I was aware that you seemed . . . unwell," I said.

She gave that horrible laugh again, and her eyes were fever bright. "Unwell; yes, I have been unwell."

Eamon held her closer, but his face remained unreadable. Whatever happened here, if she went back to being her usual sadistic self, he would survive. Eamon was not our enemy, but he could not afford to be our friend either.

"Meredith, Meredith, the look on your body, your tight control. Do you not understand that after centuries even the fight for control shows to my eyes?"

"I do know that, Aunt Andais, but control is all I can offer."

"Control is all any of us can offer in the end, and I lost mine," she said.

"You seem better now," I said.

She nodded. "It took me months to realize I was trying to force you to send my Darkness to me. I knew if anyone could slay me, it would be him, but day after long day he did not come. Why did you not send him to me, Meredith?"

We had actually discussed sending Doyle to assassinate her, but I had vetoed it. "Because I didn't want to lose my Darkness," I said.

"Your Darkness, yes, I suppose now he is 'your Darkness.'" Anger showed on her face.

I didn't like the "suppose" in that sentence. "Doyle is one of the fathers of my children, which makes us a committed coupling now."

She sat up a little straighter in the curve of Eamon's arm. "Yes, yes, he is yours as a consort, Meredith. I mean nothing by it, beyond the fact that I thought he would be sent to end my pain, but he did not come, and gradually the madness and grief left me. Eamon risked much to bring me back to myself. I tortured Tyler to death one night. I valued him, and I have missed him since, and that helped me realize how far I had fallen."

Tyler had been a barely legal teenage lover. He'd been a human brought into the Unseelie sithen to be her slave, in the bondage-and-submission sense, not in a bought-and-sold sense. Tyler had been good looking in a vapid sort of way; he had been entirely too much pet and not enough person for my tastes, but he had pleased Andais, met a need that was real for her. Apparently he had been more important to her than even she knew.

"I am sorry for your loss, Aunt Andais."

"You sound as if you mean that."

"I would not have wished death by torture on anyone. I had no quarrel with your slave, Tyler. I simply did not understand him or his interactions with you enough to comment."

"Such careful wording, my niece; you never liked Tyler."

"He disturbed me, because you wanted him to disturb me. I know it was part of your games to control me, or amuse yourself, but I was never afraid of Tyler, and he never harmed me. If I hadn't found some value in him I wouldn't have helped your guards and Eamon protect Tyler the night that you almost whipped him to death."

There had been a night in the private chambers of the queen when she had chained Tyler to the wall of her bedroom, and it had gone from a pain-filled game to a near-death experience for him. Eamon had shielded the human with his own body, trying to bring Andais back to sanity in time to save Tyler and keep her from stripping the flesh even from Eamon's bones.

The other guards had been forced to kneel and watch the torture, but what had begun as forcing her celibate guards to watch her have sex with her pet had turned into true life and death. I had watched Rhys, Doyle, Frost, Galen, Mistral, and so many others bloodied and dreadfully injured trying to come to Eamon's aid. In the end I had stepped forward and hoped only to give them time to gather themselves, to think of a way to stop her, but the Goddess had blessed me, and the queen had been stopped by the blessing of the Goddess through me. It was not my power that had done it; I never had illusion otherwise. The best I could claim was that my faith and courage had been rewarded. That night Aunt Andais had been poisoned deliberately to drive her into her full bloodlust in hopes that she would be painted so mad that her nobles would see that Prince Cel, her son, should come to the throne sooner, but I had interfered, and the plan had backfired.

"But you were not there this time, Meredith. You were not in the court that the Goddess and Consort gave to you and Doyle. If you had been, Tyler might still live."

Was she truly going to make this my fault? It was like her self of old; she took little blame for herself and had seen even less attached to Cel, her late son.

Eamon didn't try to soothe her this time, but sat with his arm almost stiffly around her, as if he wasn't sure whether she still welcomed it.

"Would you not have given up your crown to have the man you loved by your side again?" I asked. I wasn't sure it was the right thing to ask, but it was all I could think of to say.

I smelled roses, and knew the Goddess was with me. She either approved of what I'd said or would aid me if the queen did not. Something brushed my cheek and I looked up to find pink and white rose petals falling from empty air. The petals began to collect in my lap like floral snow.

Andais made a sound between a scream and an inarticulate curse. "Pink and white petals, not red, not the colors of our court, but of that golden throng that thinks themselves so superior to us, why, Meredith, why the Goddess of the Seelie and not the Dark Mother?"

"The Goddess is all women, all things, or that is what She has shown to me." I kept my voice calm, but surrounded by the scent of roses in the summer heat of a meadow, in the midst of the soft-petaled rain of roses, I couldn't be upset. Her blessing was too close to me, and it felt warm, safe, like home is meant to be, but so seldom is.

Andais sat up, moving out from the curve of Eamon's arm. "The gardens that have returned to our sithen are full of bright and happy colors. Your Seelie heritage has contaminated our kingdom. You would reshape us in the form of that other world of lies and illusions. You've seen what Taranis considers truth, Meredith. How can you wish our court to become a fairy-tale land that is not real?"

"I did not wish these changes on your court, Aunt Andais. The Goddess returned and with Her the wild magic, and it goes where it will, changing things as it goes. No one of flesh and blood can control the wild magic of faerie itself."

"Would you have returned us to our former dark glory if you could have chosen, Meredith?"

The fall of petals began to slow, but my lap was full of them already. "I do not know, and that is the truth. I had no affection for the court of my uncle; if I had a home in faerie it was the Unseelie Court, and as you remind me, my uncle has made me dread his court even more. So no, aunt, I would not make the Unseelie Court over into that glittering place of lies."

My pulse had sped, not from Andais being so close, but from the thought of Taranis. I mercifully didn't remember most of the attack, but I remembered enough.

Frost and Doyle both laid a hand on my shoulders at the same time. Sholto and Mistral each laid a hand on mine, and I took their hands. Galen went to one knee beside me, his leg almost brushing Kitto, who had remained motionless and still as the footstool he pretended to be, so still that I had almost forgotten him. He had the gift of being that still even when standing beside me. Galen laid his hands on my knee through the layer of petals. He gazed up at me, giving most of his back to the mirror. It was both an insult and a sign that he didn't see her as a threat, or it would have been if one of the other men had done it, but it was Galen and I doubt he thought beyond comforting me. Rhys had taken a half-step forward, so that his hands were free if she was as rash as Taranis had been when he got angry over a mirror call. Galen seemed oblivious to the danger. He had not changed completely. I was both relieved and afraid of what I would find when I raised my eyes from his sweet face to look at my aunt.

I expected anger, disdain, but what I saw was pain, and the closest I'd ever seen to sympathy except when my father died. "It was not my intent to remind you of what he did to you, niece. Our lawyers have told me of what the Seelie king is trying to do, and for that I am sorry, Meredith. I believe Taranis is madder in his own way than I am, or was. At least I come to my senses. He lives in his delusions."

"I appreciate your sentiments, Aunt Andais, more than I can say."

"I made a bargain with you, Meredith, that if you produced a child I would step down for you. Now you have produced three. It is beyond my wildest hopes. I also know that there are two babes from other couplings in your exiled court; again it is more than I hoped for. Come home, Meredith, and the throne is yours, for I gave my word and I cannot go back upon it."

Galen's hand tensed against my knee; the rest of the men went very still where they touched me. Rhys stayed in his forward position. I felt the guards at our backs shift as if a wind had touched them. Turning down Andais never went well.

I fought to keep my voice even. "I do not believe that I would live long upon your throne, Aunt Andais. There are still too many among our court who see my mortal blood as the doom of them all."

"They would not dare harm you for fear of me, just as they have not harmed me during my madness for fear of worse from me, Meredith."

There was a certain logic to what she was saying, but in the end I believed I was correct. "To rule either court, the nobles must take oath to the new ruler, and bind themselves to her or him. At our court it is a blood oath, and I proved on the dueling grounds that to share my blood made my opponents mortal."

"That was unexpected when you killed Arzhul."

"He certainly did not expect the blood oath to make him killable by bullet, or he would never have allowed me a gun against his sword."

She smiled, and looked satisfied. "You were always ruthless, Meredith; why did I not see your worth sooner?"

"You hated my mixed blood as much as any in court, Aunt Andais."

"You're not going to bring back up the time I tried to drown you when you were six, are you? It's very tiresome to be reminded of it, and I would take it back if I could."

"I appreciate that you would take it back, but your belief that I am not worthy to be an Unseelie noble, let alone rule there, is shared by many at the court. They fear taking oath to me, Aunt Andais, for fear that my mortality will cancel out their immortality permanently. Since I cannot promise them it will not happen just as they fear, I think they will choose my death over theirs, or worse, my death over slowly aging like a human."

"For fertile wombs, Meredith, you might be surprised how many would accept you."

"I think that not all the sidhe at your court are as wedded to having children as you are, aunt."

"Perhaps, but have I proved myself calm enough to be allowed a glimpse of my great-nieces and nephew?"

I fought the urge to look at Doyle for reassurance. Rhys glanced back at me and gave me the look I needed. He thought she had been good enough to see the babies, or at least hadn't done anything bad enough to not have earned a glimpse of them. I gave a small nod and then said, "Yes, we will have the babies brought into the room so you may see them tonight, Aunt Andais."

I worded that last carefully, because if I had said, *You may see the babies,* she could interpret it as being allowed to come visit in person, and that she hadn't earned yet.

I gave the order for the babies to be brought into the room. One of the guards went to fetch our nurses and our children to be paraded before their great-aunt, who had nearly killed me when I was little because she thought me not pure-blooded enough, like a mongrel puppy that your prize-winning bitch had dropped. You didn't keep the mistakes, and Andais had seen me as that, or worse. My father had found us, rescued me, fought with his sister, and taken me and all his courtiers with him into the human world. He had chosen exile to keep me safe. I didn't understand what it had cost him until I spent my own three years alone and exiled, hiding here in Los Angeles. My father had loved me dearly; my aunt . . . didn't love me at all. How could I ever trust her around our babies? The answer was obvious: I couldn't.

CHAPTER

ELEVEN

Bryluen fit in my arms as if she had been made to tuck into the curve of my elbow. I lowered my face over that tiny face; the dark ginger of her eyelashes lay on her alabaster skin like decoration, almost too perfect to be real. I'm told all mothers think their babies are beautiful; how do you know if you're seeing the truth, or it's some illusion made of love and baby hormones? There are types of glamour that have nothing to do with faerie and everything to do with love.

Galen had taken Gwenwyfar in his arms, and then sat back down by my legs, careful not to bump my "footstool" so that Kitto wouldn't move and ruin his safe pass before the queen. Sholto held Alastair, but stayed standing beside my chair. He rocked the baby automatically when Alastair started to fuss. Once he believed that Bryluen was his, he had joined in caring for all the babies, as if, one being his, they were all his.

"You forget how very tiny they are," Andais said, and her voice was softer, gentler than any time I'd ever heard her.

I looked up and realized that I'd forgotten she was there; for just a moment there had been nothing but the baby in my arms and my feeling of utter contentment. I'd discovered that sometimes being around the triplets was like being drugged with something slow and pleasant, but I hadn't expected the effect to continue with my aunt still on the "phone."

"I remember that look from when Cel was little. He always had that effect on me to a certain extent. Looking at you now, I wonder if it was more than just motherly affection."

"What do you mean?" I asked.

"Your eyes are unfocused; you look almost drugged."

"Bryluen did have a very strong effect on a human friend of ours, so much so that we've decided no human nannies or babysitters for her," I said.

"Perhaps my great-niece's glamour affects more than just humans, Meredith. You would not knowingly let yourself become this distracted in front of me."

"No, Aunt Andais, I would not."

She had a thoughtful look on her face, and laid a hand on Eamon's thigh where it was hidden under his own silk robe. "Do I dare attribute some of my worst mistakes to magic? Was my own son able to throw glamour over my eyes as . . . Bryluen just did to you?"

"I do not know, Aunt Andais, I cannot speak to it."

"Nor I with any certainty," she said, but she kept touching Eamon, stroking his thigh not in a sexual way, but more for comfort. I knew that touch helped keep our minds free of glamour from the King of Light and Illusion, Taranis, and I wondered if she was touching Eamon for comfort, or because there was glamour coming through the mirror from Bryluen and me.

Doyle put his hand back on my shoulder, and I could think even more clearly. It was a sharpening of focus that let me know I hadn't been at my best just seconds before, and the fact that I hadn't realized that was not good. We would have serious negotiations today and later with other relatives, allies, and enemies. I couldn't be besotted with baby glamour while dealing with all of it. How powerful was Bryluen's effect on the people around her?

"For the idea that my mother's blindness to my son's machinations was magic, I thank you, Meredith, and Bryluen. It's Cornish for 'rose,' a sweet name for a little girl."

"It was a compromise between the men," I said.

She looked past me to one of the men at my back and said, "So, Killing Frost, you wished to name your new daughter after the love you lost centuries ago, Rose?"

I felt him tense without need of touching him, so his startle reflex must have shown over the mirror to her. Rose had been the name of the woman and her daughter he had loved centuries ago when he was merely Jackul Frosti, Little Jackie Frost. It was love for them, desire to protect them that had made Frost grow from a minor player in the procession of winter into the tall, commanding warrior, because little Jack Frost couldn't protect his Roses. The Killing Frost could, but in the end, time had taken them away from him. They'd been human and mortal and died as all mortal flesh is doomed to do.

Andais laughed, a high, delighted, wicked peal of laughter. Perhaps it was actually a pleasant laugh, but we'd all heard it so many times when she was enjoying cruelty that it could be nothing but unpleasant to our ears.

Doyle reached across with his free hand to touch Frost and steady him. His reaction must have been even worse than I'd thought for Doyle to show such weakness before the queen. It wasn't always wise to show how much you truly cared about anyone in front of her.

"So the rumors are true, my Darkness and my Killing Frost are lovers," she said.

I actually glanced behind me then, to see what was prompting her to say that, and found the men holding hands behind my chair.

Rhys said, "Once a man could hold the hand of his best friend and not be thought his lover."

She looked at Rhys, eyes narrowing; it was a look that typically began something bad, a bad mood, a bad event, an order we would not want to follow.

"Are you saying that they are not lovers?" Andais said.

"I am saying, why does it matter, and you shouldn't believe every rumor the human tabloids put out."

Galen was still sitting at my feet, beside Kitto, who had stayed almost immobile. Galen was holding Gwenwyfar, so as he leaned back against my legs he had to brush against Kitto's curls. The baby's hand brushed the long hair, and though she was too young to do it, Gwenwyfar grabbed a tiny fistful of Kitto's curls.

It couldn't have hurt, because the baby didn't have the strength for it yet, but it was probably the one thing that Kitto would have reacted to. He raised his face enough to gaze up at Gwenwyfar. I couldn't see Kitto's expression, but it was almost certainly a smile.

"So, little goblin, you make yourself useful, so the princess does not send you home."

I felt Kitto's reaction up through the soles of my feet on his back. It was a startle as bad as Frost's had been, but Kitto had always been terrified of the queen. Frost had loved and hated Andais; Kitto simply feared her.

"It is against protocol to speak with the royal's footstool," Rhys said. Once he had hated all goblins because one took his eye, so the fact that he stepped up to distract her from Kitto made me love him more. He had come far to value Kitto enough to risk himself for the goblin.

She gave him a narrow look. "You have grown bold, Rhys. Where does this new bravery in the face of your queen come from?"

Rhys stepped closer to the mirror, drawing her eye and partially blocking her view, so Galen could pry Gwenwyfar's tiny hand from Kitto's hair and the goblin could go back to being an immobile piece of furniture, and hopefully beneath the queen's notice.

"I don't think I'm braver, my queen, just understanding the value of those around me more than I did before."

"What does that mean, Rhys?"

"You know my hatred for the goblins."

"I do, but this one seems to have won your favor; how?"

Eamon was utterly still beside her, as if he would have left if he thought it wouldn't attract her attention. She had played sane, but her nearest and most dear love was acting like a rabbit in the grass hoping the fox won't find it, if only it can be still enough.

"It was Kitto who shopped for an extra crib, blankets, toys, everything, when the news came that we were having triplets and not just twins. He made certain we came home to a house that was ready for all the children, and that Merry had everything she needed."

"Any good servant will do as much," Andais said.

"True, but Kitto helps tend the babies not out of duty, but out of love."

"Love." She made it sound distasteful. "Goblins don't understand love for that which is small and helpless. Newborn sidhe are a delicacy among the goblins, you know that better than anyone standing here except for my Darkness. The others were not with me during the last Great War against the Goblins, but you and he know what they are capable of."

He glanced back at Doyle and then back to the mirror. I couldn't see his face, but his voice was fierce and bitter, "Now, my queen, remember I was at your side. I remember that the atrocities weren't all goblin work."

"We didn't eat their young," she said. Her eyes had darkened and were beginning to have that first hint of shine, her power beginning to rise. It could also be a sign of anger, or even anxiety, but it usually meant magic was on the rise.

"No, most goblin flesh is too bitter to eat," he said, and there was a finality in his voice. He'd left all pretense of placating her behind. It was simply the truth, and my joking Rhys had decided to leave humor for honesty, the kind of honesty that royals do not always welcome.

I was shocked enough myself, because I hadn't known that my people, the sidhe, had tasted goblin flesh enough to know the bitter or sweet of it. I held Bryluen closer to my face, smelling the sweet clean scent of her to hide my face, because in that moment I wasn't certain I could have kept it neutral.

Bryluen opened those huge almond-shaped eyes, all swimming blue, and I had a sensation like falling. I had to literally drag myself back from the brink. I lowered my baby away from my face and avoided direct eye contact with her. It wasn't just glamour, she had power, did our little Cornish Rose. How much, and how did we teach her not to use it willy-nilly? How do you explain to a newborn the concept of abuse of power?

"We vowed never to speak of some things, Rhys," Andais said, in a voice that crawled along the spine and raised the hairs on the back of my neck.

Alastair began to cry, high and piteous. He waved small fists as he did it. He couldn't be hungry—we'd made sure that everyone had nursed or had a bottle before this call, so we wouldn't have to deal with it. Sholto began to rock him side to side. Alastair didn't like to be bounced the way Gwenwyfar did, and Bryluen liked to be held up on the shoulder and have her back rubbed while you rocked her. Three days and the babies were already so different, so individual. I'd been told that multiples were like each other, but I was beginning to wonder if that was just because most of them looked alike, so people expected it.

Sholto began to rock Alastair in wider arcs, so his upper body turned from side to side. The movement began to quiet the baby.

"We vowed, but we did not swear," Rhys said. If he had given his sworn word he couldn't have spoken of it, because to be an oathbreaker was one of the few "sins" among the fey. An oathbreaker could be cast out of faerie forever.

Andais was looking at the crying baby. "I have seen the girls, but not the boy. Would you bring him closer so I might?"

It was Doyle who said, "If you will stop trying to unsettle us, my queen, perhaps, but if your behavior of the last few minutes continues, then what is the point? We do not want our children raised in an atmosphere of fear and uncertainty."

"How dare you question my behavior, Darkness?"

He shrugged with his hand on my shoulder, and the other still holding Frost's hand. "And this is exactly why we do not want the babies raised around you, or your court. I thought Essus a fool when he took Merry and his retinue and left the Unseelie Court, but now I see it for wisdom. Even if Merry could have survived in our court as a child, she would have been a different person now. I do not think that person would have been better, or kinder."

"You cannot be kind and rule the sidhe, or the goblins, or the sluagh, or anyone inside or out of faerie. Kindness is for children and human fairy tales."

"Kindness where possible is not a weakness," Doyle said.

"In a queen it most certainly is," she said.

"You have seen Merry on the battlefield; do you think her kindness made her less ruthless, or less dangerous, my queen?" he asked, and his voice was lower, crawling down into those vibratingly low tones that had frightened me once. Now it made me shiver for a different reason, a much more fun reason, because three things make a man's voice lower, and all are testosterone based—heavy exercise, violence, and sex.

"Do you think it is wise to remind me that I watched her slaughter my son in front of me?"

"Do you think it wise that you reminded Frost of the loss of his first love?"

"Frost cannot punish such impudence as I can," she said.

"And there you go again," Rhys said.

She looked back at him. "What are you talking about?"

Eamon moved beside her and spoke low and clear, in the kind of voice you use to calm wild animals or talk jumpers off ledges. "My queen, my beloved, he means that if you keep threatening punishment they have no reason to share your nieces and nephew with you. Your brother's grandchildren are before you; do you want to be a part of their lives, or do you prefer to be the Queen of Air and Darkness, frightening and unyielding to all insults?"

"I have already offered to give up being the Queen of Air and Darkness if Meredith will but take the throne."

"So you would rather be Aunt Andais to Essus's grandchildren than queen of all?"

She seemed to think about it for a moment or two, and then she nodded. "Yes, to see my bloodline continue, to have three descendants of our line who are already displaying such power, for that I would step down."

It wasn't just descendants, but powerful, magical descendants. She'd already seen the lightning mark on Gwenwyfar's arm and watched it spark at Mistral's touch. Alastair had displayed no overt talent as the girls had done, but she seemed willing to take it for granted that he, too, would be powerful. If any of our children proved without magic, by her standards, she would still see them as useless, as not worthy, as she'd decided with me when I turned six and she tried to drown me.

Eamon laid his hand over hers, cautiously. "But, my beloved, it's more than stepping down from the throne; Meredith and her consorts want to feel safe around you, and at this moment, they do not."

"They should not. I am the Queen of Air and Darkness, ruler of the Unseelie Court. The fact that people fear me is part of the point, Eamon; you know that."

"For ruling our court, perhaps, and for keeping the Golden Court in check, absolutely, but my love, perhaps being frightening is not the best way to be Great-Aunt Andais."

She frowned at him as if she didn't understand the words, The words made sense, she could hear them, but I wasn't certain she could grasp their meaning.

She finally said out loud, "I don't understand what you mean, Eamon."

He tried to pull her into his arms as he said, "I know you do not, my love."

She pushed away from him. "Then explain it to me, so I will understand."

"Aunt Andais," I said.

She looked at me, still frowning, still not understanding.

"Do you regret the loss of Tyler?"

"I said so, didn't I?"

"You did."

"Then what are you talking about, Meredith?"

"Will you regret not being Aunt Andais to our children?"

"I am their aunt, Meredith; you cannot change that."

"Perhaps not, but I can decide whether you are aunt in name only, or whether you actually have a place in their lives so they know who you are in a pleasant way; or will you be on the list of people that we warn them about? Do you want to be a bogeyman to your nieces and nephew? If you see your Aunt Andais, run. If she comes for you, call for help, fight back. Is that the legacy you want in their lives?"

"They could not fight me and win, Meredith; even you could not."

"And that is not the point of what I said; the fact that you think it is means you are not welcome here."

"Do not make me your enemy, Meredith."

"Then apologize, Aunt Andais."

"For what?"

"For reminding Frost of past pain, for trying to frighten Kitto, for every threat, every hint of pain and violence you've spoken since this conversation began."

"A queen does not apologize, Meredith."

"But an aunt does."

She blinked at me. "Ah," she said, "you want me to be some cheerful relative that comes with gifts and smiles."

"Yes," I said.

She smiled, but it was an unpleasant one, as if she'd tasted something bitter. "You want me to be other than I am around your children?"

"If by that you mean pleasant, kind, and just a normal aunt, then yes, Andais, that is what I want."

"It is not their heritage to be any of those things."

"My father, your brother, thought otherwise, and he raised me to be all those things."

"And it was love and kindness that got him killed, Meredith. He hesitated, because he loved his killer."

"And perhaps if you had raised your son, as my father raised me, to be kinder, considerate, happy, then neither of them would be dead right now."

She startled as if I had slapped her. "How dare you . . ."

"Speak the truth," I said.

"So I must be this false self, this fiction of a cheerful, smiling auntie, or you will try to keep me out of the lives of my nieces and nephew?"

"Yes, Aunt Andais, that is exactly what I mean."

"And if I said there is always darkness through which I can step and visit as I will, what would you say?"

Doyle said, "I would say that if it is death you seek, come unasked, unbidden, unannounced, and we will grant that wish."

"You dare threaten me, my own Darkness."

"I am no longer your anything, my queen. You cared for me not at all except as a visible threat by your side—'Where is my Darkness, bring me my Darkness'—and then you would send me to kill on your behalf. I have a life now, and a reason to keep living, beyond just the fact that I do not age, and I will let nothing stand between me and that life."

"Not even your queen," she said, voice soft.

"Not even you, my queen."

"So either I concede to your ridiculous demands or I lose all contact with the babes."

"Yes," I, Doyle, Frost, and Rhys said at the same time. The others nodded.

"Once I would have threatened to send my sluagh to the Western Lands and find you, or the babies, and bring all to me, but now the King of the Sluagh stands by your side and no longer answers to me."

"You sent me to the princess, my queen."

"I sent you to bring her home, not to bed her. You I did not choose for her."

"You gave her the choice of all your Raven guards, and I am that, as well as King of the Sluagh."

She looked at me, and there was threat and anger, and everything I wanted to keep away from our babies in her face. "You have stripped me of most of my threat, Meredith. Even the goblins answer to you now, rather than to me, and that I did not intend. That was your doing, niece of mine."

"Essus, your brother, made certain I understood all the courts of faerie, not just the Unseelie. He wanted me to rule all, if I ruled any."

She nodded and looked thoughtful, the anger gone as if she could not stay enraged and think at the same time, and that was probably truer than was pretty to think about.

"You are right, Meredith; it was you who bargained with the goblins so wisely, and you who seduced the sluagh to your side, and you who won the loyalty of my Darkness, and my Killing Frost. I did not see you as a threat to my power, but only as a pawn to be used and discarded if it did not serve me, and now here we are with you more powerful than I ever envisioned, and that is without a crown upon your head."

"I did not have your magic to protect me, aunt; I had to find power where it was offered for it was not within me."

"You wield the hands of flesh and blood, niece; those are formidable powers on the battlefield."

"But if all I depended on was my magic, then I would not have Doyle, or Frost, or Sholto, or the goblins, or any of what I have won. I have killed only to save my life and the lives of those I love. My ability to kill, no matter in what horrific way, is not where my power lies, aunt."

"And where does your power lie, niece?"

"Love, loyalty, and when forced being utterly ruthless, but it is kindness and love that have won me more power than any death I have dealt."

She made a face, as if she smelled something bad. "Your hands of power may be Unseelie Court magic, but you are so"—and here she rolled her eyes—"the descendant of all those bloody fertility deities in the Seelie Court. Love and kindness will win the day, oh yes, oh my, my ass."

"The truth is in the results, aunt."

"I have ruled for over a thousand years; kindness and love will not see you rule for that long."

"No, because I shall not live that long, Aunt Andais, but my children will and their children."

"I've never liked you, Meredith."

"Nor I you."

"But I am beginning to truly hate you."

"You're late to this party, Aunt Andais; I've feared and hated you most of my life."

"Then it's hatred between us."

"I believe so."

"But you want me to come and pretend otherwise in front of your children."

"If you wish to be their aunt in truth, rather than just by bloodline, yes."

"I do not know if I have that much pretense in me."

"That is for you to decide, aunt."

She patted Eamon's hand. "I understand what you were trying to tell me now. I will never be other than your aunt by bloodline, Meredith."

"Agreed, Aunt Andais."

"But you would give me the chance to be more to your children."

"If you behave yourself, yes."

"Why?"

"Truth, you are powerful enough that I would rather not go from hating each other to trying to kill each other."

She laughed so abruptly it was more of a snort. "Well, that is truth."

"But there is one other reason I'm willing to do this, Aunt Andais."

"And what would that be, niece Meredith?"

"My father told me stories of you and him playing together when you were children."

"He did?"

"Yes, he did. He would tell me of you as a little girl with him a little boy, and his face would soften and the memories gave him joy, and in hopes that my father's sister is still inside you somewhere, I will give you a chance to show Essus's grandchildren the part of you that made my father smile."

Her eyes were shining again, but it wasn't magic; tears glittered in her tricolored eyes. She swallowed hard enough I could hear it, and then she said, "Oh, Meredith, nothing you could have said would have hurt me more than that."

"I did not mean to cause you pain."

"And I know that you mean that, and that is the cruelest blow of all, my niece, my brother's daughter, because you remind me of him. He should have killed me and taken the throne when Barinthus urged him to; so much pain could have been saved."

"You were his sister and he loved you," I said.

The tears began to fall down her face. "I know that, Meredith, and I will miss him forever." She blanked the mirror with a wave of her hand as she began to cry harder.

CHAPTER

TWELVE

W ell, that was unexpected," Rhys said.

"Merry made her cry," Cathbodua said, and came to drop to her knees in front of me, her raven-feathered cloak spilling around her like shiny black water. The cloak always moved as if it were made of different things than it appeared to be, as if it were more liquid than solid sometimes, but then once it had given her the gift of shapeshifting, so maybe that was it.

I felt Galen shift where he sat by my legs. He didn't always like Cathbodua. I felt Kitto flex underneath my slippers; he would have flinched if he'd not still been pretending to be an object. He was afraid of Cathbodua, though she'd not done anything to him to make him afraid; it just seemed to be an on-principle sort of thing for him. It seemed to be the same reason Galen didn't like her.

Cathbodua wasn't that close to either of them. She'd knelt far enough away from me to keep everyone in the room in view. Battle goddesses, even fallen ones, always seem to remember that you never look away from anyone who could hurt you, and that meant everyone in the room.

"I have only seen one other person who could move the queen as you just did, and that was your father, Prince Essus. Him I would have followed forever, and today I see that you are your father's daughter."

"Thank you, Cathbodua; that makes me happy to hear, for I loved and respected my father."

"As well you should have, Princess, but I will offer my oath to you."

"I have not asked an oath of service from anyone," I said.

"No, you have not; it was the queen who forced Prince Essus to take our oath to him. He would have trusted to our loyalty and love of him."

Bryluen fussed in her sleep and I raised her to put her against my shoulder. She liked to be upright sometimes. I said, "Andais doesn't trust love, only fear."

"Essus understood that those who follow out of love are more powerful than those who follow out of fear."

"There is no loyalty in fear, only resentment," I said.

"You have been fair and gentle with those of us who would allow it, and fierce and ruthless with those who would not. I ask that you would take my oath so that I may serve you, Princess Meredith, daughter of Essus."

"Once you give oath you are bound to me forever, or until my death, and I may not be as much my father's daughter as you think."

"You are more ruthless than he was, and if you fight, you kill your enemy. I have never seen you offer mercy to anyone who tried to kill you or those dear to you."

"Shouldn't that give you pause, before you tie yourself to me, Cathbodua?"

"No, because if your father had held your edge of harshness he would have slain his assassin and not let love stay his hand. He would have been forced to kill his sister and become king, and so much pain, death, and useless bloodletting would have been avoided."

"Are you saying my father was weak?"

"Never, but he was softer than you are, Princess."

I laughed. "I think most of the nobles would not agree with you."

"Then they have not been paying attention since your hands of power manifested, Princess Meredith."

"I kill because I am not the warrior my father was, and I never will be. I am too small to fight as he could."

"Does it matter why someone has the will to win?" Cathbodua asked.

"I think it does," I said.

"I agree with Cathbodua," Galen said.

I looked down at him holding Gwenwyfar, sitting close enough to touch Kitto, his long leg close to the edge of the raven cloak as it pooled on the floor. He had that serious look in his eyes again; it was partly tiredness maybe, but his eyes looked older than they had before, as if his near-eighty years of life were catching up with him.

"Results are what matter, Merry, not motives. I think our friend Detective Lucy would say, leave the motives to the lawyers and the psychiatrists."

"We are not police officers, just private detectives who help them out on crime involving our people."

"That's not what I mean, Merry," he said, turning more toward me with the baby nestled and sleeping in his arms.

Doyle said, "I think Galen means that you will not try to win the battle with flair, or by some chivalrous code. If forced, you simply destroy your enemy; there is no mercy in you when lives are at stake, though outside that you are very merciful."

"My father was six feet tall and muscled, and had centuries of training as a warrior, and one of his hands of power was usable over a distance. He could afford mercy in battle; I can't."

Bryluen moved against my shoulder, making a small sound. I started rubbing her upper shoulders in small circles, being careful of her wings lower down, though they seemed remarkably flexible. They were definitely more skin and reptile scales over bone than butterfly scales over exoskeleton. That strengthened Sholto's view that sluagh genetics had given her the wings. I was still reserving judgment until the genetic tests came back.

"But that's it exactly," Cathbodua said.

It made me turn back to her. "What do you mean?"

"Essus thought as of old, when we could afford battles and assassinations, but we are in modern-day America now, and we need a modern ruler to see us through this strange new land of technology and social issues. You are the future, Princess, and for the first time in centuries I think our race has a future."

"You mean the babies," I said.

"Not just yours, Princess, but Maeve's son, and Nicca and Biddy's little girl. We are fertile once more thanks to you."

"And all this because the queen cried," I said.

"No, because you made the queen cry."

"If I were as ruthless as you say, I would have sent Doyle to assassinate the queen months ago."

"You want him alive more than you want her dead; that's love, Princess."

"Doesn't that make me soft?"

"No," Galen said, "because I know I would do anything to keep our babies and you safe, anything. Holding Gwenwyfar in my arms, seeing you there with Bryluen, doesn't make me feel soft. It makes me feel fierce, as if for the first time I have things I'm willing to fight for, to kill for, if I have to, and it's love that's given me this new . . . resolve. I will not fail you again through hesitation, or lack of will; I will be the man you and our children need me to be."

I could see that resolve in his face, so sure, so firm, so . . . resolute. I was happy to see it, because I'd feared for my gentle Galen in this sea of brutal politics, but at the same time it made me a little afraid, because I wasn't sure that deciding to be harsher would automatically give you the skills to be that. I just didn't know.

"Take my oath, Princess; let me give you my vow," Cathbodua said.

"You wish to serve me until either your death or mine?"

"Yes, and if Goddess wills it, the babes in your arms will be as worthy of my oath as you and your father."

"I pray that it is so," Doyle said.

"So do I," Frost and Mistral said together.

Everyone agreed, and I said a silent prayer. "Please, Goddess, let our children be worthy of the loyalty and love of their people."

Rose petals began to fall from the air above my head like a sweet-scented *yes*. Guards moved from behind us to join Cathbodua where she knelt. The rose petals began to spread through the room as if the entire ceiling were raining roses.

I took their oaths, and I prayed to be worthy of them, because in the beginning most leaders mean well; it is later when the best of intentions twist into something darker. I knew that Andais, Taranis, and my grandfather, Uar the Cruel, were as much a part of my genetics as my father, Essus. There was more insanity than sanity in my family tree; I hoped that everyone kneeling in front of me remembered that.

CHAPTER

THIRTEEN

Most of the guards went about their business, because otherwise the hallway outside the dining room wouldn't have been big enough for us to walk from there to the nursery. There were enough people in the house now that sometimes it felt claustrophobic, so I'd made it clear that outside of special circumstances, like impressing the queen or guarding me from her, less was more when it came to my retinue. So it was just me, the triplets, and their fathers, except for Mistral, who had gone off with the other guards to tend to something. He didn't really enjoy the nursery duties and often tried to be somewhere else when diapers, bottles, and the like came up. I'd been debating whether I should make him do more of it or let it go. The other men were more than enough, so he wasn't absolutely needed, but still, he was their father; shouldn't he help?

The door at the far end of the white marble hallway opened, and Liam Reed, all of thirteen months old, saw us and grinned. Suddenly the hallway didn't look stately, or cold, or like people in ball gowns should be gliding down it; it just looked like home.

If you've ever wondered why toddlers are called toddlers, all you had to do was watch one who was new at walking. Liam toddled toward us with one of the human nannies chasing behind. He was still unsteady after a month of walking, but he was getting quicker at it. He came staggering toward us as fast as he could, saying, "Babies, babies, babies!" He had a huge grin on his face and was just so excited. He'd been that way since we brought the triplets home. Kadyi, Nicca and Biddy's daughter, who had just started sitting up last week, was apparently not "baby" enough for Liam anymore, because he was fascinated with the newborns.

Liam was as blond and blue-eyed as his mother, Maeve Reed, pretended to be for the human media, and so far he was just a really pretty baby with straight golden blond hair and big, pretty, very human-looking blue eyes. His skin was the pale constant gold of Maeve's, like a pale but perfect suntan, easily passing for human.

Rhys scooped him up and said, "You want to see the babies?"

"Babies!" Liam said, at the top of his voice.

Gwenwyfar and Bryluen both protested with tiny cries. Galen and I started patting and rocking them automatically. It had been only a few days, but for a chance to sleep I'd learned to do what I could to soothe them. Only Alastair stayed quiet and deeply asleep in Sholto's arms as we walked toward the nursery.

Rhys held Liam up so he could see Gwenwyfar first. "Baby!" Liam said, again at the top of his voice.

Gwenwyfar started to cry.

"Shhh," Rhys said, "remember use your quiet voice."

Liam turned a solemn face to Rhys, then leaned over Bryluen and said much more softly, "Baby."

I smiled and moved her so that Bryluen could look back at Liam. He reached out very gently and touched her curls, tracing the tiny horn buds, which he seemed fascinated with, and almost-whispered, "Pitty." Which meant pretty.

"Yes, Bryluen is very pretty."

"Bree-lu," he said, trying to wrap his toddler words around her name. He'd been trying for three days and that was the closest he'd managed.

I smiled at him. "That's right, Liam. This is Bryluen."

"Bree-lu-non."

"Bryluen," I said.

He screwed his face up into a picture of concentration and then blurted out, "Bree!"

We all laughed, and I said, "Bree will do."

Liam smiled up at all of us, and then gazed back down at Bryluen, and said, happily and still a little too loud, "Bree!"

She stared up at him with those big, solemn eyes. He reached down and tried to pat her cheek but missed and poked her in the eye. Bryluen started to cry.

Liam yelled, "Sorry, baby!".

Alastair finally woke up and joined the girls crying. Liam's nursemaid offered to take him from Rhys, but Liam wrapped his arms around Rhys's neck and started to cry. "No, don't want to go!"

Maeve glided gracefully into the hallway, calling above the crying, "What happened?"

Galen said, "Liam poked Bryluen in the eye, by accident." He had to raise his voice, too.

Maeve went up to Rhys and he started to hand the boy to her, but Liam clung to Rhys, screaming, "No! No!"

Maeve stopped trying to get him from Rhys, and once he settled back into Rhys's arms he stopped yelling, tears still wet on his face as he gave a petulant face to his mother. She had been in Europe filming for most of the last five months and had been home for only three days. Liam called her Mommy, but he didn't always act like she was Mommy.

Maeve couldn't keep the hurt out of her face for a moment, and then she smiled brightly.

Rhys said, "Liam, go to your mommy."

"No, baby room," Liam said, very serious, very certain of what he wanted and what he didn't.

"I think he wants to go to the nursery and watch the babies," I said.

"It's okay," Maeve said. "I flew in for his first birthday and then had to leave again."

"You shouldn't have to support us all, if it means you're apart from your son," Doyle said.

"For centuries we were just like the human nobility; no one saw their own children. They were all raised by nannies and caretakers," Maeve said.

"But you are not content with that," Frost said.

Maeve shook her head, and tears sparkled in her eyes. She shook her head a little more vigorously, and then managed a voice that held nothing but good cheer. "I'll join you in the nursery in a few minutes." Then she walked back out the way she'd come and left us with Liam and the babies. At least they'd quieted, and we weren't listening to high-pitched newborn cries echoing off the marble walls.

"It's not right that she's sacrificing her time with Liam for us," Galen said.

"Agreed," Frost said.

"Yes," Doyle said.

Rhys was drying the tears off Liam's face. "He doesn't mean to hurt her feelings."

"I know," I said. Liam had spent much of the last few months falling asleep across my ever-growing stomach, so that at the end he'd looked like the arch of a rainbow, but his nannies couldn't get him to settle down like I could. He'd put his little hand on my stomach and say, "Babies," as if he'd been waiting for them to finally come outside and be able to play.

I wasn't sure what to do with the fact that Liam had bonded with our little family group while Maeve was away. I wasn't even sure there was anything to be done, but it seemed like a topic for a family discussion. We actually had family meetings to discuss the complicated intricacies of our happy home. Most of the time it really was happy, but with this many people involved it didn't just stay happily-ever-after without a lot of discussion and work. I was learning that happily-ever-after was the beginning of the next chapter, not the end of the story.

CHAPTER

FOURTEEN

That night I dreamed. It seemed to be just a dream, not Goddess-sent or prophetic, but a dream like millions of people everywhere have every night. It began well, with my father getting to meet my babies, his grandchildren, but in the way of dreams, what is comforting begins to disturb. It's nothing you can put a finger upon, but the wonderful begins to unsettle you, and you know something is wrong with what you're seeing, you just don't know what yet . . . but you will.

In all the long years since my father's death I had never once dreamed of him, and yet there he stood, tall and handsome with his fall of black hair loose around his legs like a curtain of black water, flowing and moving as he held Bryluen in his arms. The wind played in his hair but didn't tangle it, the way it did for Doyle and Frost. They'd said the wind liked them, and the wind in my dream liked my father.

It was strange, but I never forgot he was dead, even in a dream with him smiling down at me. He was dead and this wasn't real, could never be real again.

"Meredith," he said, smiling, "she is beautiful, my little girl."

"I wish you were here to hold your grandchildren for real, Father."

He laid a gentle kiss on Bryluen's forehead and then raised his face, frowning slightly. "What is in her hair?"

I came closer, and he lowered the baby enough for me to spread her red curls and show the tiny horn buds. He startled, and if I hadn't been standing close he might have dropped her, but I took Bryluen in my arms and moved back. I thought, *I need to put her in her cradle*, and one appeared.

"I thought she was the one, she looks so like us, but if she has horns she can't be ours."

I laid Bryluen in the cradle and looked up at my raven-haired father with his tricolored eyes, completely different from Bryluen's large blue ones. He looked nothing like me, or the baby. It had saddened me as a child that I hadn't looked more like my father.

"What do you mean she looks like us? She looks nothing like you, Father."

He held Alastair in his arms now. The black hair did look more like my father, and all newborns look slightly unfinished so that people can see what they want to see in their features. I think it's a way of making everyone feel included, like the baby belongs to everyone.

He leaned over Alastair and frowned. "Is he spotted like a puppy?"

"Yes," I said, and went to take my son from his arms. He didn't fight when I took Alastair. I put him in the cradle behind me. Bryluen wasn't there, she was safely away, and even as I thought it, Alastair vanished from the cradle, too.

I knew he would be holding Gwenwyfar when I turned back, and he was; he was unwrapping her from the blanket she was swaddled in, but she hadn't been swaddled when we put her down for the night. She hated to be confined like that, and as if my thinking it had caused it, she started to cry, flailing small sturdy arms, tiny hands in fists as if she would fight the world.

He ran his big fingers through her hair.

"She doesn't have horns, if that's what you're looking for," I said.

He lifted Gwenwyfar free of the blanket and looked at the skin that the onesie left bare. "She looks sidhe," he said.

My pulse was beating too fast as I moved to take my daughter from him. He let me do it, I think because she was crying. She quieted in my arms, and I moved back to lay her in the crib. She vanished, and I knew that they were safe. I didn't think they'd been in the dream for real, but just in case I'd wanted them safely away, because I knew that whoever this man looked like, he wasn't my father.

I thought, *This isn't real, it's just a dream.* That should have been enough to shatter the dream. I waited for it to unravel and to wake up in my bed sandwiched between Frost and Doyle, but the dream held.

I had never tried to break a dream with magic, but now I reached outward, tentatively, and found that I could feel the edges of the dream almost like a plastic film that I could press against. Press against, but not break.

"So it is true, you are able to travel through dream."

"I don't know what you mean," I said, but my pulse was in my throat. Something was terribly wrong.

"You travel in your dreams to help your soldiers," he said.

"I don't know what you mean."

"You cannot lie to me in dream, Meredith. Your soldiers wear your sign."

In the final battle with my cousin, Prince Cel, I had been protected by the National Guard, and all of them who had been wounded, or had been touched by my blood, seemed to be able to call upon me when I slept. If they were in danger of their lives they could call me to them, and the Goddess gave me the means to show them to safety or bring them the help they needed. Some of them wore the nails that had been part of the shrapnel in the bomb my cousin had set to kill me. They had tied leather cords around the nails and wore them like a talisman, and through those nails they could call me. The black coach of faerie that had been a limousine when I was first called home was now in the desert, a black armored vehicle of whatever kind was needed. It traveled without a driver and went where it was needed, because I had told it to help them, and somehow it did. The coach had always been wild magic, never fully understood or fully controlled by anyone, but it had listened to me.

"Who are you?" I asked.

He walked toward me looking as my father would if he had never known pain, never been wounded, never died, but the smile was wrong. It was his face, but it wasn't my father's smile.

I backed away, so that his outstretched hand wouldn't touch me. "Who are you?"

He held out his hand. "Come to me, Meredith, but take my hand, and we can step out of this dream."

"And where will we appear once the dream is finished?" I asked.

"Someplace wonderful."

I shook my head. "Liar."

"We cannot lie outright, Meredith; you know that."

"Drop this guise and show me your true face."

"Take my hand."

"Drop this disguise and perhaps I will."

He stepped closer to me, hand still held out toward me. "Who do you want me to be?" he asked.

"Show yourself as you truly are, and stop tormenting me with my dead father's face."

"I thought the sight of Essus would comfort you," he said, and frowned as if he didn't understand, and maybe he didn't.

"You were wrong; show me your face." My voice was strident, not with anger, but fear.

"If you let me hold you now, it will be as if Essus were here to embrace you one last time. I can give you that, Meredith; my powers have returned. The Goddess has blessed us both again."

"The Goddess gives Her power where She will. I do not question it, but one man's blessing is another's curse; drop this illusion and show me . . ." I stopped, because the moment I said *illusion*, I knew; Goddess and Consort help me, but I knew.

One moment I was staring up into the face of my dead father, and next it was Taranis, the King of Light and Illusion. He was all red and gold of hair, his eyes like green petals of some exotic flower, tall and commanding, and truly one of the most handsome men to ever grace the high courts of faerie.

"Come, Meredith, embrace me as one of the fathers of your children."

I screamed.

CHAPTER

FIFTEEN

He grabbed my wrist and started to pull me to him, but I thought, *I need something to hold on to*, and my other hand found smooth wood to grip, a carved banister leading up to nowhere, but it was a handhold, and I made my choice that I'd let him break my arm before I let go.

"Meredith, I'd never hurt you."

"You raped me!"

"Lies, Meredith, all lies. I saved you from the Unseelie monsters. You have a babe that grows horns, and another spotted like a dog, but our daughter is perfect. They are twisted of body, and it is a miracle you have survived."

His eyes began to glow as if every green petaled layer of his iris were turning to green flame, and I was falling into that flame. I wanted to touch his hair, colored like all the brilliance of a fiery sunset. My hand loosened on the banister behind me, and then a single rose petal fell and landed on the mound of my breast. I was not a victim.

He held my wrist; so be it. I opened my hand and laid my palm against his skin and called one of my hands of power. His skin began to writhe as if it were turning liquid where I touched him.

He yelled and let me go. "What is this?"

"The hand of flesh is my hand of power, as my father carried it before me."

Taranis's arm began to roll up on itself, as the bones and muscle began to spill out to the surface, turning inside out, and spreading up his arm.

"Stop this!" he yelled, but even as I watched, the flowing skin had stopped just short of his shoulder. If he'd laid the arm against other bare skin it would have spread, but he had jerked away quickly enough that it hadn't turned his entire body inside out. The hand of flesh could do that, and had. It had been one of the worst things I'd ever seen, but I was half sorry it hadn't done just that to Taranis.

"This is dream; you don't have this power outside of dream." He was staring at his arm, and the horror on his face as he looked up at me made part of me . . . happy.

"You knocked me unconscious and nearly killed me before you mounted me last time. I was too hurt to fight back."

"This is not real!" He yelled it at me.

"I don't know, uncle dear; perhaps when you wake up your arm will be healed, or perhaps it will be a reminder to you to stay away from me, my babies, and everyone I hold dear, because if you ever touch me by force again, in dream or reality, I will destroy you, Taranis."

"It isn't real," he said, but his voice was uncertain.

"For your sake, I hope not," I said. "Honestly, for my own sake, I hope it is."

"I saved you, Meredith; why do you hate me?"

I wished for a sword, and one was in my hand. The hilt was cool and perfect. You had to look close to see the carved tiny bodies melting into each other as the only warning for what might happen if you touched the sword. It was Aben-dul, once my father's centuries before I was born, and it fit my hand as it had the first time it appeared to me in reality. It had never just appeared in my hand before, but this was a dream—anything was possible.

"Where did that come from?" And now he was afraid, and that made me fiercely happy.

"You can stop me from leaving this dream, but you can't stop me from creating what I need inside it."

"You shouldn't be able to do that," he said.

"You said it yourself, uncle: I have traveled through dream to soldiers who held relics of my blood and pain. The Goddess comes to me in my dreams. I hold my father's hand of power and a sword of Unseelie grace, but I am Seelie as well as Unseelie. I hold the wonders and nightmares of both courts inside me, uncle dearest."

"Stop calling me that; I am the father of your baby."

I wrapped both hands around the sword and only the fact that I carried the hand of flesh kept me safe from the magic of the blade, and got into the stance that I'd learned so long ago. I hadn't kept up my sword practice, because I'd realized as a teenager I was never going to choose a blade as my weapon in a duel, and I was never going to challenge anyone to a duel, and so long as they challenged me I chose the weapons, but I knew how to hold a sword. I knew enough to bleed him unless he killed me first, but I'd blasted the arm that held his hand of light; if I was lucky, I'd crippled his magic. If I'd been certain the sword would work here as it did in the real world, I could have used my hand of flesh without touching him, but I wasn't sure enough to risk using it as anything but a sword.

"I was pregnant when you raped me, you psychotic bastard! Now break us both free of this dream, or I swear by the Summerlands, and the Darkness that Swallows the World, I will do all in my power to kill you, uncle dearest."

"Do not call me that, Meredith; you are my queen and will be my wife."

I started forward, doing a feint with the sword. He jerked back, his wounded arm useless at his side. "Come, uncle, let us embrace and I will finish what I began with your arm."

He vanished from the dream, and a second later I woke in bed with Doyle and Frost looking down at me. Doyle was pinning my arms down across my body, because the sword Aben-dul was still in my hands.

CHAPTER

SIXTEEN

M erry, Merry, do you know who we are?"

"Doyle, Frost," I said, my pulse so hard in my throat that it choked my voice down to a whisper.

Frost smoothed my hair back from my face and asked. "Do you know where you are?"

"We are in Los Angeles, in Maeve's house, in our bedroom."

Frost smiled down at me. "Do you remember that we love you?"

I smiled up at him. "Yes, that I always remember." Just gazing up into his face and answering that question helped slow my frantic heartbeat and chase away the last clinging terror of the nightmare.

Doyle's deeper voice turned me to look at him. "If you remember that, then relax your arms, so that I know you will not strike out with the sword you hold in your hands."

I realized that my arms were tense underneath his, as if I meant to use Aben-dul once I was free of the strength that held me down. I fought to relax my arms, but it was as if the thought of not being ready to strike when the need arose frightened me, as if I expected Taranis to appear in the room once I was unarmed. There was a chance that even accidentally touching someone who did not carry the hand of flesh would turn them inside out. I didn't want to hurt my lovers, but . . . The fear wasn't rational.

Normally, I would have said that with Doyle and Frost beside me I was utterly safe, but Taranis had nearly killed Doyle with his hand of power. If he still had a hand of power. If the damage I had caused in dream had truly happened to him in reality, then he might have lost his greatest weapon, because often when our hands were damaged, the hands of power went with the injury. Or sometimes the magic became so wild that it wasn't safe to use, like a fire that you meant to use to cook your dinner, but that got out of hand and burned down the house instead.

"Some thought has gone through your eyes, our Merry," Doyle said.

"I had a dream," I said.

"It was not a Goddess-sent dream," Frost said, "because when you cried out in your sleep we were both able to wake and watch over you."

"And there are no flower petals raining down from nowhere," Doyle said.

"But though we awoke," Frost said, "we could not rouse you, as if it had been a dream from the Goddess."

"If it was not the Goddess, then what held you so tight to this dream?" Doyle asked.

"My uncle entered my dream and trapped me there."

"You mean Taranis?" Doyle said, and I saw the fear on his face now. Good to know I wasn't the only one.

"Yes."

They both leaned over me, too close, and even though I loved them both it was as if I couldn't get enough air. I started to try to sit up, but Doyle still had my arms pinned with the sword, and suddenly I was panicked. It took everything I had not to struggle and lash out at the two men I loved most in the world, because they were too close and were holding me down, and my rapist had been in my dreams.

"I need room." I managed to choke the words out.

"We are in our room," Doyle said.

"Move away from me, please," I said.

They exchanged a look over me, but Frost moved back as I'd asked. Doyle did not. "You seem not yourself, Merry. We have seen spells placed inside others we loved that turned them against us. I would not risk your using this sword upon anyone you love."

"I need to be armed with his touch still fresh upon me, Doyle," I said, fighting not to strain against the ease with which he held my arms and the sword down, harmless.

Frost slid off the bed and came back with one of his own blades. Normally I would have been more distracted by the nude beauty of him in the silver cloud of his hair, but somehow men and the things that went with them were all confused with images of a very different man, the one in my dreams, but not the man of my dreams. One of the men of my dreams sat on the bed and offered me his blade, hilt first. It would have been a knife to him, but to me it was as big as a short sword. Sometimes I felt very much the hobbit to their elves. That ordinary-world thought helped me push back the panic.

"An exchange, our Merry," Frost said gently.

"It is a fine blade, but not a fair exchange for this one," I said.

"No one but you in this room can touch that blade and keep sanity and life, so let it go and take up Frost's knife, and then tell us what happened in the dream."

I breathed deeply, forcing myself to take even breaths, and then I let it out slow, counting as I did so. *Control your breathing and you control nearly everything else, but first gain control of yourself; always begin there.* Those had been my father's words to me. That helped calm me, too.

I let go of Aben-dul, and it lay heavy across my legs, but my hands were empty enough to wrap around the hilt that Frost was offering. Doyle moved back then, sliding off the bed; after a moment Frost echoed him. I had room to sit up, and some weight that had been trying to make me panic and lash out at them eased. It wasn't a spell put on me by Taranis, but it was his damage. He'd raped me, and there were moments when even the most beloved of my partners had to give me space, and time to work through the issues of that attack. I was happy I didn't remember most of it, didn't remember the sex, only waking afterward with the concussion that almost killed me and my unborn children.

"I wish we did not have to ask, Merry, but what happened in the dream?" Doyle said.

I took in another deep breath and counted it out slowly, then nodded. I told them about the dream, everything that had happened in it.

"Do you believe that the injury to his arm will follow him out of dream?" Doyle asked.

"I do not know."

"That is not possible," Frost whispered.

"Once the king could use dream to seduce and bed a woman, and the children that came from those dreams were real enough," Doyle said.

"Are you saying he was able to get women pregnant from just visiting them in their dreams?" I asked.

They both nodded.

I must have paled, because they moved toward the bed, then hesitated and looked at each other, then back at me. "We would comfort you if you would allow it, Merry, but we do not wish to rush this moment," Doyle said.

I nodded, but I didn't really want to be touched right that second. I gripped the hilt in my hands tighter, so that the leather-wrapped metal dug into my hands a little, helped remind me that I was awake and not trapped.

"I will take comfort in a little while, but right now just explain to me how he could do that in just a dream."

"Once he was the Lord of Dreams, but that was centuries before we came to the Western Lands. I do not believe that he can make dreams as real as he once could," Doyle said.

"Do not tell her that, for we do not know. He should not have been able to use his hand of light through the mirror when he nearly killed you, and that was months ago. The Goddess returns and wild magic follows in Her wake," Frost said.

Doyle nodded. "And the magic is like most of our powers, like nature itself; the storm does not mean to tear down your house, but it still might."

"Which means that we have no way of knowing who will have gained powers from the return of the Goddess," I said.

"Sadly, no," Doyle said. He gave me a very solemn look.

"What?" I asked.

"If you damaged his arm in this reality, then he may seek revenge outside of dream."

Frost said, "Or he will be so terrified of Merry that he will not come near her."

"It could go either way, true," Doyle said.

"I didn't know he had ever been able to enter dreams," I said.

"Once upon a time," Doyle said.

"The queen could enter nightmares, or speak to us through them, as well," Frost said.

"So he was the Lord of Dreams, and she was what, the Lady of Dreams?"

They both shook their heads, and I was feeling better, because I was a bit distracted by them both standing there nude. Sadly, I still had weeks to go before we could have sex. It had been too long.

"Merry, did you hear what we said?" Doyle asked.

I blinked and had to think; had I heard anything that those lovely mouths had been saying in the last few minutes? I finally said, "No, I'm sorry, but your being nude distracted me."

They smiled at each other, and then at me. I would have said, *Don't be conceited*, but it was just truth that the two of them standing there nude, bodies not even ready for such things, had made me think of sex, and longing. I still ached too badly to do anything about it, even if the doctors hadn't warned against it, but that my body was interested again was nice. After being hugely pregnant for so long, and so ill with the triplets, it was nice to feel something close to normal and think that maybe my body could get back to doing something besides having babies.

"You're going to have to repeat everything you just said. I will endeavor not to be distracted, but perhaps if you sat down and put the sheet across your laps, that might help my powers of concentration."

Their smiles turned to mischievous grins, but they did as I suggested and sat down on the sides of the bed that had become theirs, Frost to my left and Doyle to my right. Once they had piled the sheet in place, Doyle said, "She was the Queen of Nightmares, for she was never merely a lady of the nobility, Merry, but always destined to be more."

"But the king was once just a lord?" I asked.

They both nodded, Frost's hair spilling forward around his bare shoulders. His ponytail had come undone in the night, as it often did. Even braiding didn't always hold it, as if the hair itself didn't like to be bound.

"Who was the royal family of the Seelie Court, then?" I asked. It had never occurred to me that Taranis didn't descend from a "royal" line like Andais did, but then he'd been king for over a thousand years. I wasn't thirty-five yet; it was a little before my time.

"They were killed in the last great war between the two main courts," Doyle said.

I stared up at him. "Then why isn't our queen the high queen of everything in faerie?"

"Because the remaining Seelie nobles preferred death to the Golden Court being swallowed into the Court of Nightmares, which was one of the Unseelie names back then."

"Why didn't my aunt just slaughter them until the survivors surrendered? It is one thing to say you would rather die, but if you see enough people die before you, most relent, or so I'm told," I said.

"Not always," Doyle continued, "but though we had won the war, our side was sore hurt, and if we had continued the fighting it might have meant the destruction of all the sidhe."

"So a Pyrrhic victory," I said.

"If the fighting had continued, yes."

"I did not know things were so dire," Frost said.

"What do you mean, you didn't know?" I asked.

"Belief and need did not turn me into the Killing Frost until Taranis was already king. The first battles I fought in were against the goblins when the courts of the sidhe joined forces against common foes."

I knew that once my tall, commanding Frost had been little Jack

Frost, a child-size embodiment of the hoarfrost that he painted on windows and the edges of things as he followed in the train of the Winter King. But people thought his work beautiful and paid attention to it, and once mortals pay attention and begin to believe or tell stories about something, it grows stronger, more alive. Just as love and belief made the toy rabbit in the Velveteen Rabbit story into a real bunny, so, too, had the man beside me gone from something that danced over the snow, barely more than a thought of cold and icy beauty, to the Killing Frost beside me. For my Frost, it had been the love of a mortal girl named Rose. She was long in her grave, but it was for love of her that Frost had been willing to grow tall and strong enough to build a life with her. I owed her a thank-you, and since I could not give it, when we had a second daughter to name and Frost suggested "Rose," no one had argued. We'd just found the prettiest version of it, Bryluen, Cornish for "rose."

I kept one hand on the knife he had given me, but reached out my other hand to touch his thigh where it lay peeking from the covers.

"I forget sometimes that Darkness and the Killing Frost were not always paired beside the queen."

He put his hand over mine and gave me a smile that held everything I wanted to see in that moment: tenderness, love, and a gentleness that harked back to his first form that had skipped across the snow and decorated the world in icy beauty.

"There were small battles between the sidhe courts after that, and in those a very new Frost fought against me."

I turned to look at Doyle. "Are you saying the two of you fought each other directly?"

He smiled. "No, I saw him across the battlefield a time or two. He was a shining thing and hard to miss, but he was new to battle and they had not schooled him to arms as I would have before allowing a newly risen warrior to take the field."

"I believe that the Seelie saw me as an accident. I was the first lesser fey to become sidhe in a long time. You do not train lesser fey the way you train sidhe."

"True enough even among the Unseelie, but I believe they expected you to die in those small battles; no need to waste training on cannon fodder."

Frost started rubbing his thumb over my knuckles where I still touched his thigh. "You are probably right, but I survived and they began to teach me."

"If you were once Seelie, then how did you get exiled from them?"

"A human serving girl spilled hot soup on the king's hand. It would have healed in minutes, but he hit her, and when she didn't fall down and cower, but kept her feet and glared at him, he started to beat her." He rubbed my hand over and over, his eyes staring at nothing, empty with remembering.

"You saved her," I said.

"I stepped between them, because I could not watch him kill her, and I didn't understand the other nobles just watching."

"You hadn't been noble long enough," Doyle said. "You didn't understand the privileges of rulership."

"I still don't, but our queen taught me not to stand between her and her victims." He shivered, his broad shoulders huddling in upon himself as if the Frost could be cold, but some chills go beyond temperature and reach the heart and soul.

Doyle reached across me to touch Frost's shoulder. "We all learned not to risk the queen's mercy." It was a saying among the Unseelie; to be *at the queen's mercy* had come to mean any hopeless situation, and to avoid being at the real queen's mercy you would do much, or not do, as the case may be.

Frost looked up and met the other man's eyes. They looked at each other and there was such pain in Frost's face, and such long sorrow in Doyle's. It was as if I had caught a glimpse of the long centuries that had made them the men they were now, and the friends they were to each other. They had been forged in fires of battle and torment.

In that moment I was so glad they were mine, so glad I could keep them safe. Once Queen Andais had said that any man who wasn't father to my children would be forced back into her Raven guard, there to be celibate again except for servicing her. It showed how distracted her son's death had left her, that she believed she could make that threat and still have me come home to accept the crown, to force all the guards I had come to consider mine back to be tortured by a madwoman for all eternity. Everyone wants to be immortal—even I did—but there were times when living forever and healing most injuries could have serious downsides, and being tortured forever was one of those.

That thought made me say out loud, "Once the genetic tests come back and prove conclusively who the fathers are and aren't, do you think the queen will demand her Raven guards back?"

"She has stated that many times," Doyle said.

"But most of them have taken oath to Merry now," Frost said.

"Does one oath supersede the other?" Doyle asked.

"That's why Cathbodua did it," I said.

"You mean offered her oath?"

"Yes."

We all thought about it for a few moments, and then Doyle said, "The queen has been too busy trying to die to think about living, but if she believes either that she will live and need her guards, or that by demanding that all her Ravens come home we will help her die, then she might call all those who are not father to your children back to the Unseelie Court."

"What would we do?" Frost asked.

"I cannot send them back to death and torment," I said.

"Cathbodua was free to give her oath anew, because all the princes were dead, but the male guards shouldn't have been able to make such a vow to Merry while the queen still lived," Doyle said.

"You mean literally, the words wouldn't have come out their mouths, or that some curse for oathbreaking should have happened?" I asked.

"The latter."

"How do we know it has not?" Frost asked.

"Because Sholto and Merry are the ones who brought the Wild Hunt back to life, and that is what hunts oathbreakers among us, but you felt no sense of wrongness as they made oath to you, did you?"

I thought about it, and then shook my head. "No, nothing felt wrong, and Sholto was with us when it happened."

"How can the oath to the queen be mute?" Doyle asked.

"Did you take your oath willingly?" Frost asked.

Doyle nodded.

"I did not, but it was the only avenue left open to me, the only safety from the king's mad pride."

"You're saying if the oath was coerced, then it's not a true oath," Doyle said.

"Perhaps," Frost said.

"If they're oathed to me for real, then they can't be forced back to the queen."

"The oath can't force them back, but her rage and madness could."

We had a moment of just sitting there thinking about it all. I finally said, "Being held sounds very good right now."

"Then let us put away our weapons and huddle together," Doyle said.

"The Darkness does not huddle," Frost said.

"Nor does the Killing Frost," Doyle said.

"I promise not to tell; just hold me, and tell me how to keep the king out of my dreams."

I placed the relic, Aben-dul, on top of the headboard. We'd put it back in the weapons locker later. It was far too dangerous to leave lying about. Frost took back his knife, and we lay down with the two of them wrapped around me, and their long arms touching each other. The Darkness and the Killing Frost might not huddle, but I did, and unless there was a way to keep Taranis out of my dreams, I'd be doing more cuddling and less sleeping from now on. I'd never suffered from insomnia, but I was willing to learn.

SEVENTEEN

The babies were all asleep in their cribs. Once I calmed down from the dream, I had to see them. I knew in all reason that they were safe, but fear isn't always about reason; maybe fear is never about reason, but some fears are reasonable. I feared my uncle, and my aunt, that was reasonable, but I also feared that my babies had somehow been left inside my nightmare—not reasonable.

Kitto stood beside the crib with me. We held hands as we gazed down at Bryluen. She was curled into a tiny ball, as if she were still asleep inside me, trying to find room between her bigger siblings. We walked to Gwenwyfar, to see her white curls almost gleaming in the glow of the night light. Alastair was flopped on his back, arms and legs akimbo, as if he'd played hard and just collapsed where he was the way Liam did sometimes. Were boys so different from the very beginning than girls? I honestly didn't know; there'd been no babies around me growing up, so my learning was all books and classes, and on-the-job training.

Kitto wrapped his arm around my waist, and I slid my arm across his shoulders. They were broader than when he'd first come to me, from Doyle's insistence that the smaller man hit the weight room and even weapons practice. Kitto wasn't expected to take his place among my guards, but Doyle wanted all of us to be able to defend ourselves. I had even joined the practice until I got too big with babies to move well, and the doctors started worrying that some of the training might cause premature labor. As soon as I healed I'd be back to it, because defending myself sounded awesome after my dream about Taranis. But then I had defended myself, hadn't I?

"I swear to you, Merry, the babes have slept peacefully for hours."

I hugged him. "You need to sleep, too, you know?"

He smiled up at me and then gazed at the babies, our babies. "I never thought I'd belong anywhere. I was tolerated among the goblins as long as I served a stronger warrior or his lady as their submissive toy, but if they tired of me, or one got jealous of me with the other, then they could cast me out, and masterless I was anyone's meat."

I put both my arms around him and held him close, resting my head on the top of his black curls; they were soft in texture, not like pure goblin hair, which ran to coarseness. "You're ours now, Kitto."

He hugged me back. "I have a family like I read about in books."

"The goblins aren't much for reading," I said.

"Most are not, but my first mistress taught me how to read, and after that being able to read was an asset to my other masters and mistresses—as much as the sex sometimes."

"So you read them to sleep?" I asked.

"Or read contracts to them, or modern newspapers."

"I didn't know the goblins cared about what was happening in the outside world."

"Some do."

I held him close, rubbing my cheek in the softness of his hair. I thought about all the long centuries that he had managed to survive in a culture that valued brute strength and power on the battlefield, and sex. It sounded like a desperate and lonely existence.

I tried to lighten the mood, because I needed it, too. "Good that you are learned, and fabulous at sex."

"Sometimes I was too good at the sex," he said.

I moved back enough to look into his face. "What do you mean? It's not possible to be too good at sex." I smiled when I said it, but he didn't smile back.

"Several masters and mistresses became jealous that their lovers preferred me to them, and cast me out because of it."

I gave him wide eyes and tried to think my way through that. I finally said the truth. "I'm amazed the jealous lovers didn't just kill you for it."

"Some tried, but the lovers that valued me stopped them, or even fought them in my defense."

"You are very good in bed," I said.

He smiled up at me. "But not that good, you're thinking, not by goblin standards."

"They like it very rough," I said.

"In public, but in private many of them prefer gentler sex."

I'd experienced that difference myself with Holly and Ash, the other goblins in our lives. If anyone knew they enjoyed gentle sex, their reputation would be damaged, so I said nothing, not even to Kitto.

"And if their secret got out that they'd enjoyed that with you, they would be ruined."

"It would be seen as weakness, and that is always challenged among my people."

"Your mother was sidhe, Kitto; we are your people as much as the goblins."

He smiled, and it was a happier one this time. "I was not raised sidhe, Merry, so I will always think of myself as goblin. The sidhe were these impossibly beautiful, magical beings, and the fact that I carried their skin and hair appealed to the goblins that had a fetish for the touch of sidhe flesh."

"It is a serious fetish among the goblins," I said.

"It's what led to so many rapes in the wars between the two races. The sidhe will not voluntarily share themselves with a goblin."

I leaned over and kissed him softly, gently, but thoroughly. "This is one part-sidhe princess who volunteers eagerly."

His face lit up, filled with happiness. "And I will serve you in any way I can for as long as you will have me."

"Kitto, I'm not planning on casting you out, you know that, don't you?"

His happy looks slipped a little around the edges. "If my goblin king calls me home, Merry, there is nothing you can do but let me go."

"You are sidhe now; I have brought you into your power, which means the goblins can't call you from my side, Kitto."

He cuddled tighter against me, rubbing his cheek against the crook of my neck like a cat cuddling closer. He shivered, and not in a happy way.

I hugged him tight. "What's wrong, Kitto? What are you afraid of?"

"I am a goblin with a sidhe hand of power, but Holly and Ash have hands of power, too, and they have stayed in the goblin kingdom."

"They would be insane to try to join the Unseelie kingdom with the queen so unstable," I said.

"True, but the fact that they didn't try to join the sidhe after coming into their magic means that magic alone may not be enough to keep me at your side."

I buried my face in the softness of his curls. I breathed in the scent of him, felt the gentle strength of him, and thought about him not being here by my side. It was a painful thought.

"Has someone said something to you?"

"Have you asked what Holly and Ash are doing with the new hands of power that you helped give them?"

"No, should I?"

"Yes," he said, with his lips soft against my neck.

"Tell me," I said.

"If they find out that I told on them, they will not like it, and their hands of power are much stronger for combat than mine."

He turned in my arms, so he could cuddle even closer to me. He shivered, and it wasn't from happiness at being held. He was afraid of the twin warriors, and he should have been. It suddenly felt like Kitto wasn't close enough to me; sometimes even a robe and pajamas kept the skin hunger and comfort from being fed.

I let go of him enough to open my robe and reach for his shirt. He helped me take it over his head with a smile I could see from the pale glow of the night light. We wrapped our naked upper bodies around each other, his arms wrapping around my waist inside the thin shelter of my robe. The front of him, still in shorts, pressed against my thigh. I could feel that just that much undressing had made his body start to react, but I knew I didn't have to tell Kitto that there would be no sex tonight; he wouldn't push, but be content that I wanted to touch him so closely.

"Now, tell me," I whispered against his curls.

I felt his smile against my neck, and that made me smile in the dimness of the nursery where the babies lay content and safe, despite my dream.

"They are using their newfound magic to fight duels."

"I thought Holly and Ash were so feared even among the goblins that no one would challenge them."

"They are, but there are some insults that no goblin could allow to stand if he or she wanted to keep their reputation, and to lose your reputation is to sign your death sentence among us."

"You mean they're starting the fights," I whispered.

"I mean, they are goading others into challenging them to duels, for they are not only fierce and ruthless warriors, but much craftier than most give them credit for."

I held him in my arms, feeling the warmth and solidness of him, and was afraid for him. He felt so small, delicate as my own more mortal form, and I knew that I would have died quickly among the goblins if I'd had to defend myself from insults.

"They may be nearly as smart as they are strong," I said.

Kitto's breath was hot against my skin as he whispered, "Ash is; I'm not certain about Holly, but he follows where his brother leads and that is enough to save him from mistakes he would make otherwise."

"Do you think they will challenge Kurag, Goblin King, and win the throne from him?"

"They could," Kitto said.

"I have a treaty with Kurag, but not with the twins," I said.

"Yes," he whispered.

I moved back enough to look into his face. "You think they won't honor the treaty agreement," I said.

"I fear they might not."

"Sex with me awakened their hands of power, gave them the blessing of the Goddess," I said.

"Yes, and they are grateful, but I do not believe that Ash is ever so grateful that he would allow it to interfere with his own ambitions."

I nodded. "I know they mean to seat one of them on the goblin throne."

"Kurag knows it, too," Kitto said.

"Why does he not challenge them and be done with it, then?" I asked.

Kitto studied my face. "You know the answer to that as well as I do."

"He fears he will lose," I said.

Kitto nodded.

I let that thought roll around in my head for a minute, and then said, "He's right to be afraid."

"I believe he will lose if he fights them fairly and openly," Kitto said, voice still low so that we didn't wake the sleeping babes.

"Goblin society allows only fair and open fighting. A king who lets someone else do his killing is soon a dead king," I said.

"We must all fight our own battles, that is true; so a king could not hire an assassin, for to be found out would be a death sentence, and likely a long and painful death."

"So what are you saying, Kitto?"

"I am saying that not all assassinations are paid killings."

I frowned at him. "You're being too obtuse for me, Kitto."

He sighed and said, "Kurag is much smarter than he lets most see, and has used it to his advantage politically for years. I believe he might manipulate others into trying to kill the twins for him, and his hands would look clean of their blood."

"But you say the twins are manipulating people into dueling them already; doesn't that feed into what Kurag wishes?"

"No, for the twins are only finding fights with goblins they believe they can beat. They avoid the handful of warriors that they are unsure of on the battlefield."

"You think Kurag might try to arrange a fight between the twins and someone who might be able to kill them," I said.

Kitto nodded.

"Kurag is my ally only for another few weeks, and then the treaty with him ends," I said.

"Unless you bring over more of the half-sidhe among the goblins, yes," Kitto said.

"I am not allowed sex for six more weeks, according to my doctors," I said.

"And by that time the treaty will be over and Kurag will not have to help you against your uncle, or your aunt, if they decide to attack you and yours."

"Are you saying that I should support Kurag in his effort to get the twins killed, or the twins in killing him?"

"I am saying that Kurag fears your enemies and will escape the treaty as soon as he can, and that the twins may not honor a treaty with you. Two of those that insulted them so they had to stand challenge were also sidhe-sided goblins and had made it known that they wished to bed you and gain their own magic."

"You're saying that now that Ash and Holly have their hands of power, they may not want me to give such power to any other goblins," I said.

He nodded. "They do not fear me, for my hand of power only allows me to bring someone through a mirror call against their will, and close the window at will. It is powerful, so I'm told, but it is mostly useless in a duel. Other sidhe-sided may gain other things that are more battle useful."

I wrapped him closer in the circle of my arms, folding my silk robe over both of us. I think the robe would have tied around both of us, we were both so small.

"It is always a gamble which magic will come to a person," I said.

"I've learned that some powers run in bloodlines, as you have the hand of flesh like your father before you."

"True," I said.

"If you had been able to keep fucking them, I think they would still be tied to you more, but when the doctor told you not to risk it with the babies . . ." I could feel him shrug in the circle of my arms.

"You think they want to be free of me?"

"Holly does," Kitto said. "Ash will do whatever will give them the most power."

"It will be six weeks before I can have sex with anyone, according to the doctors."

"And longer before you would risk such roughness in bed as they or Mistral prefer," Kitto said.

I petted Kitto and tried not to betray with even the stillness of my body the secret I'd been keeping. Holly and Ash were perverted by goblin standards. They actually liked gentle sex, and Ash enjoyed giving oral sex, which was a sign among the goblins that he considered himself subservient to me, or anyone he would go down on. It had taken me weeks to convince Kitto to allow me to go down on him, for he feared that it would hurt my reputation among the goblins, and we still needed their threat to keep our enemies in check, or at least to give them pause about attacking me. If the goblins learned the kind of sex that the brothers enjoyed, their reputations would be ruined. It could cost them their lives, because if you were perceived as weak, the challenges to combat could come so fast and often that eventually you would fail, and there was only one cure for failure in a duel among the goblins—death. I was lucky that the sidhe gave other options, or I would have died long before I escaped to Los Angeles.

Kurag, Goblin King, and Niceven, Queen of the Unseelie Demi-fey, had both agreed to forgo their price of treaty until after the babies were born. The goblins would have to wait until I was cleared for sex and had had it successfully with some of the fathers of my children, but Niceven could ask for her blood price to continue sooner. It was but a bit of blood offered to their tiny mouths, but the wild magic that had returned with my own late-blooming hands of power had given wings to the wingless among them, and given extra powers to some among them who had shared my blood and then my bed. Legend had said that some among the demi-fey could change to human size, but we had thought that lost with so much other magic among the fey, until we'd met demi-fey who could do it. I still thought they would be the perfect assassins, though Niceven said that they had never acted as such. I wasn't sure I believed her.

"You've thought of something that makes you sad, or worried," Kitto said softly.

"The demi-fey can demand their bit of blood again sooner than the goblins can demand their bit of flesh," I said.

He snuggled his face against my shoulder and stroked a hand down my back. "You fear the demi-fey, don't you?"

"Remember the case we helped the police solve? That proved to me that the demi-fey can be just as insane and dangerous as any of us." I shivered at the thought of what had almost happened, when our tiny murderer had tried to cut the babies from my body and destroy what she could not have, a regular life with the human she was in love with. They say lovers want the world to love with them, but love thwarted can turn as ugly and dangerous as any hatred I'd ever seen.

He kissed my shoulder. "I am sorry, our Merry, it was careless of me not to remember."

I shook my head, my longer hair sliding over the silk, which meant I was moving more than I thought, as if I could shake the memory of that evil from my mind, but it was too recent a memory to fade. I had been in my first trimester with the babes then, and it had been the case that made the men veto any other cases for the Grey and Hart Detective Agency until after the babies were born. So many things had been waiting for the babies, and now we stood surrounded by all of them. Triplets, the first ones born to the sidhe in more centuries than anyone could remember.

Now, everything and everyone that had been waiting for the births would be wondering when to approach me, and how, and if they wanted to continue with treaties, alliances, or . . . There were those among Tara-nis's court who had been waiting to see if my children were born deformed monsters, which was what the Golden Court had believed happened to all sidhe who joined the Unseelie Court. It wasn't true, but like all truly ugly rumors it was strongly believed by many.

Now that the babies and their first pictures were disproving the rumor, we would see how serious the Seelie nobles had been about doing anything to have children of their own. If I could truly give them babies they would do much, including perhaps killing Taranis for me. I much preferred his death by his own nobles to risking the men I loved in battle against him, and me battling him . . . it was too ludicrous to think about. He'd kill me. He would just kill me. Of course, what he wanted to do to me was to force me to be his queen, because he thought his rape had gotten me with his child. That he thought that was reasonable was just one more example of his insanity.

I stood there wrapped in the warmth of my robe and Kitto's arms, surrounded by our three children, and I wanted to feel content and happy, but there was still too much work to do, too many deaths to accomplish, because I finally owned that only the deaths of at least one of my relatives would bring safety to me and mine.

One of the babies shifted in their crib, making a small sound like the mewing of a kitten or the soft rustle of a bird. Kitto and I tensed, waiting to see if the noise grew and the baby woke, but the movement quieted and the room was full of that contented sleepiness that babies can give off, so you struggle to stay awake around them like being covered in dogs on the couch.

As if my thoughts had called them, I heard a snuffling at the door. The quiet voice of one of the guards came. "No, pups, you'll wake the babies moving around in there."

I looked toward the door. I could see the vague shapes of larger dogs, and the smaller ones; their eyes shone in the light in a way that those of normal dogs did not, but they were the dogs of faerie, and they did a lot of things that normal dogs didn't do.

I spoke softly. "It's all right, let them in."

"As you will, my lady." And the door was opened so the mass of dogs could spill inside. There were so many of them that their wagging tails made a sound, like wind, or the softest of clapping. I'd never had so many dogs in so quiet a room to understand that wagging tails actually make noise. It made me smile.

My two faerie greyhounds, Mungo and Minnie, pressed close like silk over muscle; the pack of terriers and small lapdogs that seemed to always roam the house and grounds milled around our ankles and calves. The smaller dogs started yipping, and one terrier gave a full bark.

"Hush," I said.

"You'll wake the babies," Kitto said.

The door pushed further open, and two more dogs entered. Two large black shapes, like all black Rottweilers, but they weren't Rotties, they were hellhounds, the black, raw stuff of faerie's wild magic made flesh and blood. Most of the dogs had begun as them, like black placeholders that would shift to a different variety of dog once they were needed, though Doyle said that if they remained in this form for long enough they would simply be hellhounds. They actually had nothing to do with hell and everything to do with being wild magic, powerful guardians, and hunting down those who had betrayed or threatened faerie. If you had a pack of them behind you, you might think Christian demons were chasing you. Doyle's father had been a phouka, a shapeshifting faerie, but his mother had been a hellhound, so he could actually turn into a shape very similar to the pair that strode into the room. The other dogs went silent and gave way as the two came to bump against Kitto and me, only Mungo and Minnie stayed on either side of me, hunched, but touching me from behind. They acknowledged the bigger dogs' dominance, but not their place at my side, which was a fine line to walk in dog politics, but so far they'd managed it without fights. I had no illusions who would win a fight between my two slender sight hounds and the more massive guard dogs. Kitto and I both touched the great black heads.

"Big fellas," Kitto said, affectionately.

But then an even bigger shape pushed his way through the door, and the hellhounds gave way to him, as everyone else had given way before them.

"No," I whispered, "that's the big fella."

Spike was one of the biggest dogs I'd ever seen; he could nearly look me in the eye just standing, as tall as a modern Irish wolfhound with the same wiry coat, but broader, beefier. He was the true figure of the dogs that the Romans said could bring down the horses that pulled their chariots and then, if their masters didn't call them off, could slay the charioteer, too. They'd been so fierce that ransoms had been paid in an exchange of dogs. The great dogs had been pitted against lions in the arena, and the dogs had won enough matches to make it a good sport.

Spike strode into the room with an attitude that wasn't sight hound at all; they tend to be more uncertain, nervous, whereas he carried himself more like a German shepherd, and the way he sized up a room was more Doberman. He just had *working guard dog* in every purposeful pad of those great feet. In good light his coat was a wonderful mix of pale brindle stripes. He had a "sibling" that was short-haired to his wire coat, so that his brother looked like a pale tiger, which was what we'd named him, so it was Tiger and Spike.

"Aye," Kitto said, "he is."

The great dog came to me and I put both my hands on the big head and ruffled him. He gave a big tongue-lolling grin, as goofy and happy to be petted as any of the smallest terriers. I put my forehead against his rough, warm fur and whispered, "Did you hear us up, Spike?"

He snuffled me, as if to say yes, or maybe he was just taking a bigger hit of my scent.

Kitto had moved out of the circle of my arms so I could greet Spike. He wasn't afraid of the smaller dogs, but the wolfhounds seemed to give him and all the goblins pause. I'd learned that the wardogs hadn't just killed Romans, but had actually been used in the great wars between the sidhe and goblins, and they had been one of the few things that could bring true death to the immortals. They looked like dogs, but in effect they were living, breathing manifestations of the wild magic of faerie itself, so in effect they were magic made flesh, and that meant they could kill goblins, sidhe, all of us. I put my face over those gigantic jaws and trusted he wouldn't crush my throat with one bite.

Kitto moved away, and some of the smaller dogs followed him, so that he knelt in a swirl of them, petting them, and the sounds of their happy panting, snuffles, snorts, and quiet dog noises filled the room.

The two big, black dogs walked to the cribs and began to sniff them. Kitto got up and went to them. "Hush, you'll wake the babies."

The big black dog put its nose resolutely against the crib bars and looked back at me. It wasn't a dog look in those dark eyes, and as I gazed into them there was a spark of red and green like Yule fires banked and ready to come to life and fill a room with everything the holiday was meant to be, and so seldom was. I smelled roses, and then I smelled pine, like Christmas trees, and I wasn't surprised when I looked back to find Frost coming through the door. When the wild magic had first come here in L.A. he had sacrificed himself, become a great white stag; for a time we thought we'd lost him forever to that form, not dead, but not human enough to know that I was pregnant with his child, not human enough to hold me or love me.

He came to hold my hand now, and I smiled up at him, so happy that he stood beside me now. He bent and kissed me, whispering, "The God called me to your side."

I nodded.

Kitto came to stand on my other side but didn't try to take my hand. I reached out to him, and the smile that flashed joyful across his face was so worth that small gesture. "What's happening?" he whispered.

"Magic," I said.

The black dog snuffled Bryluen's onesie-covered body. She stared at him, eyes intent, not afraid, and then the big nose touched her bare face. The rush of magic washed over us in a skin-tingling, hair-raising wash of warmth that filled the world with the scent of pine and roses, and the scent of spring like a wash of fresh rain that brings the first flowers.

The black fur ran as if it were water moved by wind, and where that wind touched it the fur turned the green of grass and leaves, fur growing slightly longer, thicker, more wiry-looking. The shaggy green head was bigger than the baby it lay beside, but it raised that head and looked at us. Its tongue lolled out happily, and the overly wide eyes held both happy dog and something else, something more.

"Cu Sith," Frost whispered, and it was, the great watchdogs that used to guard our faerie mounds, our sithens. One had appeared in Illinois and attached itself to the Seelie Court, and a second had appeared here in L.A. when the wild magic created new lands of faerie inside the walled estate. The first one had run away to take up its post among the Seelie and spent a lot of time protecting the servants from King Taranis's rage. Taranis was afraid of their Cu Sith, partly because of what it was, and partly, I thought, because it didn't like him, and a Cu Sith was the heart of any sithen it guarded. It was a way of saying that his faerie mound didn't like him much.

Spike raised his head skyward and gave one long, deep baying howl. The other dogs joined him, one, two at a time, so that it was like a choir, each voice rising and blending with the next, so that we stood in the center of that beautiful, mournful, joyful noise. It reminded me more of the sound of wolves than dogs.

Gwenwyfar began to cry, and the other black dog went to her crib and looked back at us whining, as the howls reverberated and faded in the small room. We lowered the crib and the big black dog sniffed her. She cried harder, striking out with tiny legs and waving small fists. The dog snuffled her harder, rolling her a little with its muzzle; one of her tiny fists must have touched the fur, because white began to spread from its nose backward like a white snow covered the bare earth, except that this snow was shaggy fur, and the dog turned huge saucerlike eyes upward. Its great jaws were full of razor-sharp teeth, and though it looked like a big, white dog, there was just enough different about its eyes and mouth to make you think, *Not quite a dog.* It was one, and it wasn't.

"Galleytrot," Kitto said. He was right, it was known as a ghost dog, something that chased travelers on lonely roads and haunted lonely places. As the Cu Sith was the bright, high court of faerie, so the galleytrot was the scary story told around the winter fire, and a warning to stay in groups, because alone, things that weren't human could find you and steal you away. When the wild magic had come, the only other galleytrot had come to the hands of the goblin twins, Holly and Ash. There was no way for them to be Gwenwyfar's fathers; they had come to my bed too late. Galleytrots weren't exclusive to the goblins, but they were certainly more Unseelie than Seelie Court. Gwenwyfar might look perfectly Seelie, but her true heritage showed in the white dog at her side, as Bryluen's showed in her green dog. If theGalleytrot had come to Bryluen, I'd have wondered more if her possible goblin heritage might come from the twins.

Kitto said, "There's no dog for Alastair."

The door opened, and it was Doyle with another black dog at his side. The dog went to Alastair's crib, and Frost lowered it for him. I took his hand in mine again, and Doyle took his other one, so that Frost stood in the middle of us as the black dog sniffed the baby. Alastair stared into the big face like Bryluen had, and then the dog touched his face, gently. Alastair made a soft sound and then the fur ran with colors, but something was different with this one, because it wasn't just the fur that changed, but the dog began to shrink, as if the big black body were being erased, or condensing down.

"What is it?" Kitto asked.

Doyle bent down and picked it up, ruffling its long ears. "A puppy," he said.

"But a puppy what?" Kitto asked.

I touched the long, trailing ears; they were silky. "Hound of some kind," I said.

The puppy began to whine and wriggle. Doyle put it on the floor, but it began to whimper and cry. Alastair started to cry, too.

Doyle frowned for a moment, then picked the puppy up and set it in the crib. It licked Alastair's face, and the crying stopped. It walked around him and settled on the other side, its white and red puppy body stretched the length of his, Alastair's hand touching its back.

"He's too little to have reached out for the puppy," I said.

"Perhaps," Doyle said.

"We can't leave the puppy in with him, it's not housebroken," I said.

"It's his puppy, Merry."

"Do you know what kind of dog it is?"

"As you said, a hound."

"The other two dogs are guard dogs; what can a puppy do?" Frost asked.

The puppy gave a contented sigh, and Alastair made a similar happy sound. "Maybe every boy needs a dog," Doyle said.

"Did you have one when you were little?" I asked.

He smiled. "I did."

I frowned at him. "What kind of dog?"

He shook his head. "Let's say it was a present from one of my aunts."

Since two of his aunts had been hellhounds, with no human form, I had to ask, "Are you saying that one of your cousins was your puppy?"

He smiled. "Dog was my other form; think of it as more a best friend than a boy's dog."

I looked down at our son and the "puppy." "Are you saying that Alastair will be able to shapeshift?"

"I do not know, but let him keep the puppy, and we'll see. It was once one of my symbols." I knew he was referring to the fact that once he had been the god Nodens, a healing deity known for having dogs at his sanctuary that could lick a wound and heal it, among other things.

"Magical dogs; I assumed the dog was you, but you're saying . . ."

"I was not the only dog in my temples," he said.

We looked back down at our son and the puppy. The Cu Sith had lain down in front of Bryluen's crib, and the galleytrot had done the same to Gwenwyfar's.

My hounds bumped me and I stroked their silky heads. Spike put his head into the crib and sniffed both the baby and the puppy. It opened sleepy eyes and licked his nose. Spike rose back up and "smiled" at us, tongue out, so that he lost all his dignity and looked like the big, goofy hound he could be at times.

"Spike approves," I said.

"He does," Doyle said, smiling.

"He's your son," Frost said, sounding pleased.

Doyle took his hand in his and said, "Our son."

Frost's whole face lit up with the happiness of that shared phrase. "Our son," he said.

I moved so that I could wrap my arms around both their waists, and we hugged my two men and me. There were other men in my life, and I loved them, but these were the two who made my heart sing the most. If I'd been human enough, I might have felt guilty about that, but I wasn't, and I didn't; it was just the truth of my heart.

Kitto petted the puppy and kissed the baby, then put the side of the crib back up. "Good night, little prince."

We left the babies to sleep content with their new protectors, and new best friends, because Doyle was right; every child needs a dog.

CHAPTER

EIGHTEEN

Two mornings later I woke to magic breathing and prickling along my skin. I had a moment of staring into the darkened bedroom and then Frost had me around the waist and was lifting me out of the bed, holding me one-armed behind him, while he pointed a sword at the other side of the bed. I gripped his arm where he held me, but I couldn't see the threat around his body, and where was Doyle? Why wasn't he with us?

Frost said, "Doyle, Doyle, it's me, it's your Killing Frost, and our Merry."

A low, deep growl came from the other side of the room. It was a sound to raise the hair on your neck and tighten your body, ready for fight or flight.

"Doyle, do you know me? I am your lieutenant, your right hand, your Frost, do you not know me?" Frost's voice got lower as he spoke, a gentling voice.

The deep, bass growl came again, and I knew in that moment that Doyle was in the room with us. He was just in his dog form, a black dog the size of a small pony.

"Doyle," I said, softly, hesitantly.

He growled again.

Frost leaned ever so slightly so my feet could touch the floor and he could turn himself full toward the threat that was our dearest love. He spoke very carefully as if he were afraid to even move his mouth too much. "Very slowly, we back to the door. When we reach the door, turn the knob carefully, and open the door slowly."

"No sudden movement," I whispered.

"Yes," he said.

The door started opening behind us, and I hissed, "Stop."

It was Usna's voice that said, "What is that?"

"Doyle," I whispered, because I knew that he would hear me. Usna's mother had been cursed into cat form, and it had left him with a lot of very feline traits, including calico-colored hair and skin and extremely good hearing, especially for higher-pitched noises, like women's voices.

"Why is he threatening you?"

"Hush. Usna, when I say so, open the door and grab Merry through," Frost said carefully as he backed us closer to the now partially opened door. He changed our angle slightly to take advantage of the crack in the door.

"What about you?" I asked.

"I will come with you, but your safety is all."

I wasn't sure I agreed with that, but if Frost was actually going to have to fight Doyle in his hellhound/phouka form I wasn't sure I could bear to watch. Why was Doyle still stalking us, growling? It was like a nightmare, and then I had an idea.

"He's dreaming," I said.

"What?" Frost asked, moving us agonizingly slowly closer to the door.

"Doyle is dreaming. He's not awake."

From the other side of the door, Usna said, "You mean he's sleepwalking?"

"Yes."

"He has never done that before," Frost said, and that meant in centuries of friendship Doyle had never done such a thing, so why now?

"The king trapped me in dream," I said. We were almost to the side of the opening. I touched Frost's bare back gently, changing our angle slightly to leave room for Usna to open the door wide enough for us both to escape.

"You escaped," Frost whispered.

"I had to fight, and my father's sword came to me."

"And we had to prevent you from attacking us with it," he said, slowly.

"Shit," Usna said.

"Yes," Frost said.

That evil, frightening growl echoed along my spine, much closer this time. We had to wake Doyle, but how? What had brought me back to myself?

"You and Doyle touching me brought me back."

"If you're close enough to touch," Usna said, "you'll be too close."

I agreed, but . . . I peeked around Frost's body to see the great black dog. It took a moment for my eyes to distinguish it from the darkness of the room, and then it moved, and I could see the shape of the great beast like a piece of the night formed into something of muscle and skin and fur, and a slow, thundering growl. It stepped one paw closer, and the light from the door fell on it. The paw was bigger than my hand. Its lips curled back and teeth gleamed in the light from the hallway behind us.

I moved slightly out from behind Frost, and said, "Doyle, it's me, your Merry."

"Do not . . ." Frost began, and then the dog rushed toward us from less than four feet away, and there was no time for words.

CHAPTER

NINETEEN

F rost had a naked sword in his hand; he could have run the dog through, but he didn't, and the great black shape smashed into him, driving them both against the door and slamming it shut with us trapped inside.

Usna was yelling and pounding at the door. Other voices were joining his, but they couldn't help us, not in time. Frost's hands were holding the dog's throat, keeping those huge, snapping jaws from his face, but even as I watched, the jaws got closer to him.

If it had been some monster sent by Taranis to kill us, I would have picked up one of the many guns in the room and shot it, but it was Doyle, and lead bullets can kill the fey, all of the fey, even the sidhe. I stood there like some helpless princess from one of those foolish stories, and watched the men I loved most locked in a death struggle.

I cursed under my breath and moved toward the bed and my weapons that were still in their nighttime sheaths on the headboard. Frost had moved me too fast for me to grab either my gun or my sword, and I needed one of them. I could wound Doyle to save Frost; I wasn't sure I could kill him to do the same, but maybe lead would break this evil spell.

I moved slowly, not sure if it would attract the great dog, but he was too intent on killing Frost to notice me. I stopped going slow and bounced onto the bed, crawling toward my weapons.

Every hair on my body stood to attention; I smelled ozone, like before a close lightning strike, and had a second to throw myself flat to the bed before the lightning crashed through the upper part of the door and over my head, missing me by inches and leaving me gasping and stunned.

There was a hand on my back, another stroking my hair. Doyle's voice came like a human version of that deep growl, so low it could make me shiver in happy anticipation, but this time it was relief. He was human again, ours again.

"Merry, are you hurt? Did we hurt you?"

I started to say no, but realized I wasn't sure. I didn't think so, but it wasn't until I propped myself up on my elbows, with his hands still petting me, that I was confident enough to say, "No, I'm fine, just frightened."

"I am so sorry." Mistral crawled onto the bed, coming to my side. He was dressed in modern body armor over a black T-shirt. Leather biker pants with extra padding clung to his lower body, spilling into boots that matched them. Since his powers of lightning had returned he couldn't wear his centuries-old metal armor, not and use his major hand of power. His gray hair spilled over his face like clouds to match the smell of lightning that still clung to him and the room.

Doyle turned on him. "You are all strong enough to break a modern door easily; why didn't you try that before you nearly killed Merry?"

His eyes were the sickly green of tornado skies as he looked at the other man. "Doors were stouter things once; I have been on the wrong side of doors that I could not break open without magic."

"Did you even try?"

The green in Mistral's eyes began to swirl with anxiety like clouds do before a storm. "No," he admitted.

"It's all right, Mistral," I said.

"It is not all right," Doyle growled, and his voice still held the bass growls of the great black dog. It made me look at him, as if I needed my eyes to confirm that he hadn't changed back, but he was still there: tall, dark, handsome, and very human. But I reached out to take his hand in mine; I needed the touch of his skin against mine to be certain what was real.

"I'm not hurt, Doyle," I said, shaking his hand in mine.

Frost came to his knees beside the bed. "Alas, I am."

I kept Doyle's hand, but I sat up to see my other love. The front of his body was covered in blood. I let go of Doyle and slid to the floor beside him. "What happened?"

"I happened," Doyle said.

I glanced up at him, and then down at Frost's bloody body. "But how?"

"People think only cats have claws; dogs will cut you up while you keep them from biting your throat out," Usna said, rubbing one hand down the white, red, and black skin of his arm, as if remembering some old wound. His gray eyes were the most human thing about him and most of his face was as white a skin as Frost's and my own, but the edge of his face and neck were patterned with the same red and black spots, as if he'd been the cat his mother had been at his birth. I'd never asked if Usna had been born a kitten or a baby; it had never occurred to me to wonder until that moment.

I turned back to Frost and realized Usna was right. He'd been ripped in great bloody furrows from midchest to thighs; even his arms were marked up, though the worst was his chest, shoulders, and one leg. It took me a moment to realize he'd thrown a knee and thigh up over his groin to keep the great claws from tearing up such tender bits.

"I've sent for a healer," Usna said.

Doyle knelt on the other side of him. "I am so sorry, Frost."

"What happened to trap you in your dreams?" Frost asked, in a voice that held a hint of pain, which meant it hurt even more than I thought, otherwise he'd have hidden it better.

"Nightmares, and it was the Lord of Dreams . . . I guess, King of Dreams now."

"Taranis," I whispered.

"Yes," Doyle said.

"Two nights ago he attacked Merry, tonight you; we must find a way to keep him out of our dreams," Frost said.

"Agreed," Doyle said.

"But how?" I asked.

No one answered me, but my cell phone went off. I jumped and scrambled to get it from the bedside table, because it was Rhys's ring, and he was in charge of security while we slept tonight.

"Tell Mistral to control his anxiety," Rhys said with no hello.

"What?" I asked.

"There's a funnel cloud forming in the air about half a block away. It came out of a clear California night, so tell the storm god to calm down or our neighbors are really going to hate us."

"Shit," I said.

"Yes, now tell him to control himself, now!"

I told Mistral what Rhys had said, but even as I spoke the sickly storm green of his anxious eyes began to fill with movement, and I heard the first crack of thunder above us.

"Control yourself, Mistral," Doyle ordered.

"I am trying, but it's been centuries since I had the weather react to me. I'm out of practice."

Rhys yelled on the phone, "Tell him to practice fast—the tail of the funnel is reaching for the first house."

"Mistral!" I said.

"I'm trying!" His eyes were full of wind and storm.

CHAPTER

TWENTY

The men were yelling at him, Doyle was ordering him. Mistral stood there, big hands clenched into fists; the effort of controlling his magic showed in the muscles in his arms as if stopping the storm had weight that he needed to lift with his body and not just his mind.

I went to him and touched his arm. It made him startle and look down at me with wide eyes. I could see the storm in his irises like tiny movie screens so that I saw the funnel cloud begin to reach for the earth below.

Someone said, "Let him concentrate, Merry."

"We need fair weather," I said, and went up on tiptoe, touching the side of Mistral's neck, and he bent toward me, hands still in tight fists; as he bent lower I was able to slide my hands around his neck, touch his face, and stare into the wonder of Mistral's eyes.

The terrible tension in his shoulders loosened, and then he raised his arms to hold me. We kissed and his lips were as gentle as any man in my bed for an instant, and then his arms enfolded me, lifted me off my feet, the kiss growing into an eagerness that was almost like feeding, as if his mouth had been hungry for mine. His arms tightened into a near-crushing weight, and he kissed me as if he meant to climb inside me through my mouth, forcing me to open wide for him. One arm held me in that so-tight grip and the other found the back of my hair and tightened until it was nearly painful. He let me know with his hands, his arms, his mouth, how much he wanted me, how much he'd missed me these long weeks, and how great his need was for the way we made love.

I gave myself over to the thrill and strength of that kiss, those arms, this man. He drew back enough to look into my face, his eyes almost wild with need. His eyes were a rich dark blue like the sky at dusk after a storm has blown everything clean.

He pressed his mouth against mine again in that passionate, almost painful kissing, turning with me in his arms to kneel on the bed, and begin to crawl us farther onto it. I managed to turn my lower body to the side, so that when he pinned me to the bed it was only part of me pressed under the solid weight of his upper body.

I fought free of his kisses and managed to say, "I cannot have intercourse yet, Mistral. The Gods know I want to, but the doctor says no, not yet." My voice was breathless, my heart loud in my ears, my body thick with the rush and beat of my own pulse.

He laid his head on the bed and made an inarticulate sound, half groan and half yell. He spoke with his face still pressed to the covers, hair pooling over him so I could see nothing but the gray fall of hair. "I shall go mad soon."

I touched his hair, smoothing it back until I could see the side of his face. "It's only five to six more weeks, and then I can make love again."

He rolled an eye up and the color was his more typical gray now. "Perhaps you should start with someone gentler than I, our Merry."

I smiled and smoothed more of his hair back so I could see that handsome profile. "Perhaps, but believe this, my Storm King, I want you as badly as you want me."

He studied my face and then smiled. "That is good to know."

"Rhys said the sky is clear, and it's a beautiful California night," Usna said.

I leaned and laid a much more gentle kiss on Mistral's lips. "We just needed his mood to lighten; fair mood, fair weather," I said.

"That was good and quick thinking, Merry," Doyle said. "I would not have thought of it in time."

"I don't think you kissing Mistral would have had the same effect," Usna said.

Doyle frowned at him, but Frost collapsing to the carpet made us all move toward him. He said, "I am all right, I just need to lie down," which meant he didn't feel well at all.

Hafwyn came through the door, and I realized that until she appeared I hadn't known if Usna had called a doctor or called someone who could heal with magic. *Healer* could mean either in this house.

Doyle knelt with Frost's head in his lap, smoothing the other man's hair and saying, "I am so sorry, Frost."

I held Frost's hand and felt it tighten as Hafwyn began to explore the wounds.

"You were not in your right mind, Darkness; I know you would never hurt me."

"Not deliberately," Doyle said, touching Frost's face gently.

"This is two attacks in our dreams in almost as many nights; what can we do to protect ourselves?" I asked.

Frost's hand tightened enough that I could feel that crushing strength, and I said, "Easy, my Killing Frost, easy." I touched his face as I said it.

He loosened his grip. "I am sorry, Merry."

"It's all right, it must hurt a great deal for you to react so."

"Nay, it does not." I realized that despite the strength in his hands in my and Doyle's grip his face was stoic, and only the cording in his arms showed the muscles he was using to hold on and not react to the pain. I cursed myself for revealing his pain when he was covering it so well, my brave man.

I leaned down and kissed him. He gave me startled eyes as I leaned back. I couldn't explain why I'd kissed him without compounding the mistake, so I just smiled at him and let him see how much I loved him.

That made him smile even as Hafwyn's slender fingers finished exploring the claw marks.

His body reacted to the kiss, and nude he could not hide it. He was not one of my men who enjoyed pain. Everyone's need had grown over the months of enforced celibacy. I'd even been forbidden oral, or really any sexual contact, once the doctors told me that any orgasm might bring on premature labor. It hadn't been worth the risk, but now that the babies were on the outside, we wouldn't endanger them.

"I can't have intercourse for weeks yet, but I could do oral and hand on some of you," I said. If I'd been human it would have been too bold in the situation, but no one in that room was human.

"That is very generous of you, Princess," Hafwyn said, "but it is not our way to offer sex without hope of pleasure in return." She wasn't chiding me, just stating cultural norms, as people do.

"I can orgasm from touching a man, especially oral."

Hafwyn looked at me, head to one side like a curious bird. Both her graceful eyebrows arched at me in surprise. "Truly?"

I smiled. "Truly."

"I'd forgotten what it meant to be a goddess of fertility."

"What do you mean?" I asked.

"Sex is a much broader pleasure for certain goddesses."

"I am no goddess," I said.

She made a small gesture with her head, almost a shrug. "As my princess wills, so shall it be, but there are some humans who live because a bit of metal that once pierced your flesh touched them, and now they use those objects to heal others."

"It is magic, yes, but it is not deity," I said.

She averted her eyes, laying out fresh bandages. "If you say so, then of course it is true."

"Hafwyn, seriously, there can be no talk of gods and goddesses for any of us."

"I know that if we are worshipped in this country it is grounds for our exile as a people," she said, still not looking at me, "but to not speak of a thing does not make it less true."

I didn't know what to say that, because I'd been thinking it as the soldiers that I'd healed had come back here on their leave, or when their tour of duty was up. They had come to me like a kind of pilgrimage, and those who had natural psychic abilities were growing in power, just as priests and priestesses did of old when the sidhe had been worshipped. We were ignoring it if we could, but eventually someone in the government would come to speak to us. I didn't think they'd kick us out of the country, but they would have to do something—but what? How do you forbid people from worshipping in a country where freedom of religion is one of the rights that people believe helped found the country?

I decided to change the subject back to something more pleasant and less confusing. I kissed Frost's hand. "I can pleasure you again, our Frost."

"I am too injured to do you even that much good, our Merry," Frost said, his voice holding some of the pain.

I squeezed his hand. "And I am sorry for that."

"I am more sorry, and will wait until our Frost can join us," Doyle said.

"No, Doyle, you do not have to wait for me."

"I will wait for you, Frost." Doyle made it sound very final.

"Very noble, Darkness, but will you be happy in your nobility as others take their turns first?" Mistral asked.

"Happy, no, but content to wait until Frost is healed so the three of us can be together, yes."

"You are certain?" Mistral asked, and I was almost sure what he would ask next.

"I am," Doyle said.

"I think Merry should begin with someone gentler than myself," he said.

I turned around so I could see him more clearly, and let him see the surprise on my face.

He smiled. "I want you, but I want rough even with just oral and I would prefer you be with others who are less demanding first. I would not want to be accused of souring you on the whole thing by my violence."

"You know how much I enjoy having sex with you, Mistral."

"I do," and his smile widened, filling his eyes with the unclouded blue of a spring sky. "But I also know that birth is a trauma to a woman's body, and would prefer you healed a bit more before we test if our idea of rough sex is pleasant to you."

I nodded. "It is logical."

"And noble of you, Mistral," Doyle said.

"Perhaps, but it will bother me to see other men have pleasure when I could have put myself first."

"Then it is truly noble," Doyle said.

Mistral gave a nod that was almost a bow.

"There was a time when I would have tried to jump the queue, but Cathbodua is in my bed and that is enough for me," Usna said.

"Then who?" Doyle asked.

"Are you not limiting your affections to the fathers of your babies now?" Hafwyn asked.

I looked at Doyle and said the truth. "Yes, for this, the fathers."

"You won't know for certain who the fathers are until the tests come back," she said.

"The Goddess has shown me for Alastair and Gwenwyfar, and I think I know for Bryluen."

"But the Goddess did not show you for certain," Hafwyn said.

"No," I said.

She nodded and said, "I will be able to heal much of this, but not all today."

"How long?" I asked.

"Three to four days," she said.

"In four days, Merry," Doyle said.

"Four days," Frost said.

The looks on both their faces tightened things low in my body that hadn't been getting used for a while. It felt good, but my body let me know that Frost wasn't the only one who was hurt. The doctors said I was healing remarkably fast, but giving birth was a trauma to the body as much as any wound, so I'd want to be careful.

"In four days, my Darkness, and my Killing Frost."

"In four days," Doyle said, and the heat in his eyes made me shiver happily.

CHAPTER

TWENTY-ONE

There were so many things that needed my attention, but I left Doyle to talk to the queen about how to keep Taranis out of our dreams, then left the other fathers with the babies, and I had the first hours of being just me, just Merry, in months. Being pregnant had been what I was for so long: unescapable, wonderful, terrifying, physically overwhelming. The fact that I was pregnant was the first thing people saw about me, thought about me, and during the second half of the pregnancy it was all I thought about myself. Trapped under the weight of triplets, I had been unable to even get out of bed if I was on my back, though lying on my back hadn't really been an option at the very end; it was like being crushed. So I'd slept on pillows, sitting up, which meant I had slept badly, and been exhausted, and . . . I loved the babies, but I was so glad to have them in our arms instead of being forever pregnant.

Maeve Reed was back in her master suite, which I'd used for most of the last year. We'd moved to one of the larger guest rooms in anticipation of her return. It was still a large room, bigger than my apartment in Los Angeles had been. When I said *we*, I meant Doyle and Frost. None of us had spoken of it out loud, but gradually they had moved in and had no other room to call their own. Some of the other men slept with us occasionally, but most of them were as broad through the shoulders as Frost, and what had fit in the bigger bed upstairs was a tight fit here. Since I was planning sex and not sleep, the bed would have been fine, except that Frost was resting in it, because sleep would help him heal faster, so I went to the extra room.

It was one of the other guest rooms in the palatial mansion that Maeve Reed had owned since the 1950s. It was actually one of the smaller bedrooms, but one wall had a bank of windows that faced east, and two skylights, so the room was almost always light and airy and seemed bigger than it actually was. It also had a bathroom complete with shower, which was important for cleaning up afterward. If the room had been bigger I would have moved the three of us in here when we had to leave the master suite, but the shower was narrow enough that some of the men had trouble not bumping their shoulders against the walls. The bathroom in the bedroom that had become ours was much bigger, as was the entire room, but I liked the smaller bedroom better.

I sat on the edge of the bed in a forest-green silk robe, which had been one of the few pieces of clothing that had fit me until right at the end of the pregnancy, and then even the robe hadn't tied over the babies and me. Now it was laced tight. One of the things hardest to explain is that pregnancy makes your body a stranger in a way. You've known it your whole life and yet at some point in pregnancy it's like some stranger has moved in and your body isn't yours anymore. It doesn't react the same way, feel the same way, and there are movements inside you that you know are not your muscles, your fingers and toes wiggling, but other people with their own brains and wills and personalities growing like little strangers inside you. You hope that you'll be friends and like each other, as well as love each other, but you can't really know, not for certain. I'd seen too many people in my family hate each other, kill each other. When that is part of your family's repeated history it destroys a lot of illusions that most women have about their babies and everyone being perfectly happy and loving. That was for Hallmark holiday commercials, not for any reality I'd ever experienced with my actual blood relatives.

I sat with my robe tied tight around a waist and a body that looked, almost, like me again, and wanted to be just me, just Merry, with some-one, for an hour or two.

There was a knock on the door, not a soft one either. I said, "Come in."

Rhys opened the door, smiling. Galen was behind him, sort of loom-ing with his six inches of extra height. I didn't normally think of Galen as that tall, because he seemed smaller compared to the other guards, but now I realized he was as tall as most; only Rhys was under six feet.

I smiled but fought not to frown. "I thought you were supposed to decide which of you it was going to be."

They glanced at each other as Galen closed the door behind them. "We were," Rhys said, "but we spent months sharing your bed, so we . . . tied."

"Tied?" I asked.

"Rhys tried to pull rank, and I wouldn't let him without a fight."

I looked at Galen and didn't try to keep the surprise off my face. "Really?"

"Really," he said, and his usually good-natured face was set in serious lines.

"Really," Rhys said.

I looked from one to the other of them. "How serious a fight were you willing to have?"

"I wasn't backing down," Galen said, and he said it as if it were simple fact and not a total shock.

"I think he might have requested a duel," Rhys said.

Galen looked uncomfortable then, and more his normal self. "I don't know if I would have taken it that far."

"Now you tell me," Rhys said, smiling.

Galen rolled his eyes, and then the kidding faded, and he turned that serious, handsome face to me. "But short of a duel, I wasn't giving up the first chance to touch you in months."

Rhys turned so that only I could see his face. He raised eyebrows at me, but there was something new in his face as he said, "It was the most angry I've ever seen him, outside of a fight to save your life, or ours."

I looked up at him, and suddenly his face was uncertain. "The only one who could tell me no today is you, Merry. Do you want just Rhys? If you do, then I'll leave."

I shook my head. "No, it's all right, I mean . . . stay, both of you stay, though with no intercourse allowed and not even being able to do oral sex on me, I'm not sure what both of you will be doing." I laughed and held my hands out to them both. "It's an embarrassment of riches to have you both."

Galen grinned, and the two men exchanged a look. They'd had months of literally sharing my bed and my body. They worked almost as well together as Frost and Doyle, though since they didn't love each other, the energy wasn't the same. It was good, but not as good, but then more love makes everything better.

CHAPTER

TWENTY-TWO

The clothes came off in an eager rush of hands and kisses, and left them nude and me wearing only the forest-green panties that matched the robe. I wanted to be as naked as they were, wanted to rub as much of my skin on theirs as possible, but my body wasn't healed enough from giving birth, not yet.

They laid me down between them and covered my body with kisses and caresses. Just that brought small eager sounds from me, making me writhe, body arching up against their hands like a cat, except I was lying on my back and arching things up toward them that cats didn't offer their owners. Rhys's hand slid down the front of my panties at last. I cried out just from that, arching my pelvis upward toward his hand.

Rhys put his other hand on my hip. "Easy, we need to be gentle, remember."

I blinked up at him and had a moment of wanting to argue, but my body was already letting me know that I might have been a little overeager, writhing around. It didn't hurt, but I ached.

"I'm sorry, I do remember, it's just been so long."

"It's been a long time for us, too, Merry," Rhys said, leaning in to kiss me. His hand wasn't down my pants anymore; he'd moved to keep from hurting me while I moved too much.

"We need to be slow, not fast," Galen said with a grin.

"Goddess help me, but I don't feel slow, or gentle; I feel crazed with the need to have you touch me everywhere."

"And we would like nothing better, but if we hurt you we'll never forgive ourselves," Rhys said.

"Not to mention that Doyle, Frost, and the rest will kick our asses," Galen said, smiling.

"They'd try," Rhys said.

"I'd put up a good fight," Galen said, "but eventually they'd win."

Rhys's face closed down; it was beyond serious.

"What?" I asked him.

He shook his head. "Nothing."

"Liar," I said.

He grinned. "Now we're not allowed to actually lie."

"But we're allowed to exaggerate until you'd believe the moon was made out of green cheese," I said.

"But we're allowed to lie by omission," Galen said.

Rhys frowned at him. "Don't help me."

I studied his face. "You think you could win against Doyle and Frost."

"I know I could."

I gave him a look.

He smiled, but it left that one tri-blue eye unhappy. "I could bring death with my touch to non-fey when I was just Rhys. You've seen me do it."

"But you killed the goblin that tormented you and Kitto; that's fey."

"I couldn't have done that before you and the Goddess brought me back into my power," he said.

"I don't think Doyle and Frost would let you get close enough to touch them," Galen said.

"I wouldn't have to touch them now."

"What do you mean?" I asked.

"I was Cromm Cruach; I lived for blood and slaughter, and I was good at it. I have a sithen of my own again, Merry. It's disguised as an abandoned Los Angeles apartment building, but it's a piece of faerie that came into being, because you brought me back to what I was; I don't have to get close enough to touch someone to cause their death."

"How do you know that, for certain, I mean?"

He looked away then, and I had to reach up, touch his face, and turn him back to me. "Rhys?"

"Let's just say that my sithen is in a bad section of L.A. and I'm blond and blue-eyed and don't exactly look like I belong."

"Someone attacked you," I said.

"Someones," he said.

"Who?"

"Let's just say that the gang problem in that section of downtown isn't an issue anymore."

"You didn't do it to defend yourself," Galen said.

I looked from one to the other of them. "What do you mean?"

"They hurt one of the people living near your sithen, didn't they?" Galen asked.

Rhys shrugged. "Don't make it sound all noble."

"I wasn't."

Rhys looked at him. "Don't disapprove either."

"I wasn't."

"If you have a point to make, make it soon," Rhys said, and he didn't sound altogether happy.

"I saw the flowers and gifts they leave by your building," Galen said.

"I would have known if any of you were close to my sithen."

"Apparently not," Galen said.

"You scouted me," Rhys said, and again he wasn't happy.

It was Galen's turn to shrug and give a little smile. He was pleased with himself.

"I'd believe that Darkness visited me, but not you."

"The only one of us better at personal glamour than me is Merry."

"True, you never need a disguise to do undercover work back when we are all working at the Grey Detective Agency. Sholto's pretty good at it, too."

"Good enough that both of you, and Sholto, went inside the Seelie sithen to rescue me with only your glamour to hide you from the king and his nobles." I grabbed Galen's hand and then took Rhys's. "And you in your fake beard and hat. You could have gotten all of you killed."

"But we didn't," Rhys said.

"But now you're telling me that you killed an entire gang. You risked yourself to do it, Rhys; don't tell me you didn't."

"I wasn't in much danger; that whole immortal thing, remember."

"Bullets can hurt you, Rhys, all of you, it's lead; cold iron can kill us, and steel hurts—no, don't give me that immortal crap. You could have died." I sat up. "Did you at least take some of the other guards with you as backup?"

The moment he looked away I knew he hadn't. I grabbed his arm. "Don't ever risk yourself like that again, not alone. We're a court, a court of faerie, Rhys; that means we fight our battles together."

"I was willing to risk my own life, Merry, but no one else's. Let's be honest: If you lost me you'd survive, but if I got Doyle or Frost killed, you'd never forgive me."

"Yes, I love Frost and Doyle the most, I'm more in love with them, but that doesn't mean I don't love you. Don't you ever think that I could lose you and it wouldn't hurt. How dare you think so little of me, Rhys. How dare you believe that my heart isn't big enough to love more than just two men." I was yelling at him.

He held his hands up in front of him. "I'm sorry, truly, but I did what I thought was best."

"If I'm the royal here, the would-be queen, then you don't get to make decisions like that without consulting me, is that clear?" I was yelling again.

"It's clear, I'm clear, checking with the queen before I clean up any more neighborhoods."

"You could have died!" And I burst into tears like some hysterical pregnant woman. Stupid hormones.

CHAPTER

TWENTY-THREE

forgave him when he made me yell for a much more fun reason, and the first orgasm in months filled my body, flowed over my skin, and brought me screaming. I screamed his name while his fingers brought me, and my nails carved my pleasure in red scratches down his arm, and across Galen's back, because that was what was under my fingers when Rhys's hand pushed me over that delicious edge.

My skin had not glowed until that last push of pleasure; only then had my pale skin filled with moonlight glow like the clouds had finally been blown away and the light of a full moon could bathe the world in its luminescence. My skin ran with power and I could see swirls of greens and golds from the corners of my vision and knew it was the colors of my own eyes alight with magic.

My magic brought theirs, and Rhys's skin was an answering shine to mine, so that it was two moons entwined, filling the world with a light so bright it would make mortals shield their eyes for fear of losing sight, or mind, from the beauty of it. His one eye glittered like three jewels, carved sapphires in a range of blues from palest blue, as if the sky could burn with its own color, a blue so rich, as if cornflowers could explode with their own beauty, and then the color of the ocean where it runs shallow and warm, as if the sun truly did rise from the water in a burst of glory.

He leaned over and kissed me with lips that were the soft pink of sunrise to the ruby glow of my own. I saw his hand held above us; there was red shining on his fingers as if the color of my lips had been spread like slick fire across his hand. It was my blood from bringing life into the world, and it glowed like every other part of us, thick with magic and the grace of Goddess.

He lifted away from the kiss and there were afterimages of the colors of our lips like a Doppler effect that you could see with your naked eyes. My hands fell back to the bed, all of me limp; my eyes fluttered back into my head with the pleasure of it, and I could see the light of my own irises inside my nearly closed eyes, so that when I tried to open them the world was edged with emerald and molten gold fire. The term *afterglow* had a whole new meaning for the sidhe.

The bed moved, but I couldn't see past my fluttering eyelids and the radiance of my own eyes and skin, as if my own magic blinded me.

Someone kissed me, and I knew from that first touch that it was Galen, because the sky didn't glow the pale green of spring leaves, but that was the color that joined mine, so that the greens of my eyes and the green of his seemed to blend and flow together as we kissed. Where his hands touched me the light flared. I couldn't see it, I could feel it, so that a thrumming warmth followed at his touch, and when he slid his body cuddling close to mine, that warmth pulsed between us, until I couldn't breathe for a minute, and when I did it was a gasp, as if I were already putting my mouth around things much deeper than his kiss could ever be.

He whispered against my lips, "I want to feel your mouth around me."

I breathed out, "Yes . . . please."

He got up on his knees beside me. The fire was beginning to fade so that he looked less magical and more just Galen, but that had been magical enough to me since I was fourteen. My own glow was fading so that I could see him without the shine of my own eyes clouding my vision. He smiled down at me, and I gazed up the long length of him. The one thin braid spilled down the side of his body, the tip of it curling around his groin, so that I reached for the braid first.

"I miss when all your hair was this long," I said.

"I'd grow it long again for you."

I smiled up at him. "I would like to make love to you just once with all that wavy green hair surrounding us."

He grinned. "Did you have a crush on me, or my hair, when you were young?"

"You, but the hair was beautiful. Why did you keep just the one tiny braid?"

"Because the queen's commandment was worded in such a way that I could cut all the rest, so long as I kept some of it this long."

"It was still a horrible risk, Galen. She could have found a reason to punish you for cutting that long hair that she's so fond of."

"And that proves we are high court sidhe; that's really why we grow our hair out, Merry, and why anyone not of the court is forbidden long hair. It's just another way to say we're better than everyone else."

"The custom didn't even start until after the Unseelie began to lose their powers," Rhys said, as he walked toward the bed, a towel folded in his hand.

"I thought it was older than that," I said, still running Galen's braid through my fingers.

"No, the queen decreed it to make sure that at least visually we would be different from the rest of the Unseelie Court."

"You're all sidhe, tall, elegant, gorgeous, and that's true no matter what hair you have," I said.

"True, but the nobles were afraid, Merry. Our power, our magic was what made the rest of the fey, the ones who called themselves Unseelie, let us rule them. Without that our rule was in jeopardy."

"Forbidding the non-sidhe from growing their hair past their shoulders didn't change that," I said.

"People, even the fey, are very concerned with appearance, Merry. We looked different. We were allowed a privilege that the common folk were not. I believe it did help set us apart."

"Just having long hair doesn't make us sidhe," Galen said.

"No, but it was a visual reminder of power. People are more likely to follow you if you look impressive."

"True leaders can rule if they are in rags, my father always said."

"Essus was always wise, and correct, but since not all nobles of the court were true leaders it helped for all of us to look impressive and powerful."

"Even if we were not," Galen said.

Rhys nodded. "Even if some of us were not."

I noticed he said "some of us." I was betting he didn't consider himself one of the powerless ones. Rhys had been one of the lesser lights in the court during my lifetime, but I was learning that once upon a time he had been very major indeed.

"What's the towel for?" Galen asked.

"In case we want to bring Merry again, while she screams her pleasure around our bodies."

Galen had a look that was almost pain. "In case, why wouldn't we?"

"We don't want to make her sore."

Galen nodded. "Oh, right, sorry, I'm a little distracted."

"A little," I said, and slid my hand over his balls to cup them loosely in my hand.

He went very still and then looked down at me, eyes slightly wide.

"I want you more than a little distracted," I said, and moved in toward his body, letting the braid drop to his side. I leaned in toward the soft, waiting part of him, my eyes rolled upward so I could watch his face. His body was already partially erect before I got a lick along the shaft of him. His body gave that involuntary quiver that I loved, because it was something that they couldn't control, a sign of pure eagerness.

Licking him meant that he was mostly erect by the time I slid my mouth over the ripe head of him and down that long, thick shaft. He wasn't as hard as he could get, but from one spill of my mouth over him, to come up for air, and then down again, he was harder yet—hard and eager.

I slid my mouth over him again, and he flexed inside my mouth, that eager involuntary twitch against the roof of my mouth. It made me tighten my hand around the base of him and make soft, eager sounds around him as I began to drive my mouth harder and faster over him.

"Goddess," Galen said, his eyes closed, and he reached outward, as if searching for something to steady himself with, but there was no headboard to this bed.

Rhys climbed onto the bed and grabbed Galen's hand. Galen turned and looked at him, eyes wide, and managed to gasp out, "Thanks."

"You can return the favor," Rhys said, grinning.

Seeing the two of them on the bed hand in hand both excited me and made me want to make Rhys work for it. I started sucking harder as I slid over Galen, and then taking as much of that delicious hardness into my mouth as I could and still be able to suck on him.

Galen's hand convulsed, and I watched Rhys's arm flex, muscles cording as he held the other man steady on the soft surface of the mattress.

"Now you're just being mean," Rhys said, with another grin.

I couldn't actually smile with Galen in my mouth, but my eyes smiled for me, and Rhys shook his head at me, smiling, too.

Galen began to burn for me as if the spring leaves could swallow the sun and make it shine out through the fresh, pale green of those first fragile leaves. Each green curl was edged with sunlight; the thin braid sparkled as if thin gold wire had been woven in with the green. I'd seen Galen shine before, but never edged in gold, as if sunlight and molten metal were edging the moonlight paleness of him.

Every inch of him was shining and thrumming with energy, including the part that I was going down on, so that it was like a reverse hummer, his body humming with energy inside my mouth and down my throat as I pushed it those last few inches so that it was impossible to suck anymore, or swallow, or breathe. I didn't stay down that far long, but the sensation of that power vibrating across my tongue, between my teeth, and down my throat was incredible. When I had enough air to make sounds they spilled from my mouth in eager, excited whimpering noises. Gods, it felt so . . . good!

My skin began to fill with moonlight again, an answering moon to the sunrise of Galen's power. He made a harsh sound and managed to gasp, "Close, I'm close."

We'd been doing this together often enough that he knew to warn me so I could decide whether I was swallowing or he was finishing by spilling on me. I tasted the first sweet hint that he was very close.

Rhys's skin began to run with shining white light, his arm cording with muscle as Galen's grip on his hand tightened and strained his own muscles to hold on. Then from one minute to the next Galen's body spasmed, and he cried out, and I plunged that vibrating thrumming down my throat as far as I could, burying my mouth against his body so that every delicious inch of him was in my mouth, down my throat, so thick, filling me up, and that was it: I orgasmed with him in my mouth, my body bucking with him as deep inside my mouth as he would have been between my legs. I felt the flexing as he came down my throat in a hot spill of power and grace. I came up off him enough to scream my orgasm around his body. It made him cry out again, back arching, head thrown back, eyes closed, the muscles on his arm etched in bold relief under his skin as he held on to Rhys's hand to hold himself on his knees, upright, as a second orgasm took him.

Rhys's skin shone brighter and I saw the glimmer as his threefold blue eye began to glow. Galen gasped out, "Enough, enough, Consort save us, too sensitive, stop, stop, stop."

I came up off him smiling, trailing an edge of saliva and a bit of him from his body to my lips. He collapsed slowly to his side, letting go of Rhys's hand and half-laughing.

Rhys slid his hand through my hair, and I found myself staring at his body, muscled and lean from all the extra time he spent in the gym. No other guard paid as much attention to weights and diet so that the six-pack of his abdomen was carved into his flesh. He was already thick and ready, held tight in front of those amazing abs.

He used his hand in my hair to direct me toward all that yummy goodness, and just that extra bit of dominance from him sped my pulse, started my eyes glowing; my hair was spun garnets and rubies wrapped around the shining white metal of his hand. He pushed himself between my lips and I had to open up wide enough so he didn't catch himself on my teeth. He began to push himself in and out of my mouth in shallow strokes, nothing that would make me choke, just enough to make me eager for more. I opened my mouth wider, relaxing my throat, and he felt it, because he began to push himself deeper inside me. Now when he thrust deep there was that moment when I couldn't breathe and my body knew it. Whereas with Galen I had been in total control of how deep, how long, all of it, Rhys had changed the rules with his hand in my hair, at the back of my head, and his own thrusting hips. I made eager noises for him, but not for long and not as loud as for Galen, because he thrust too deep for me to breathe, and without breath there is no sound, just my eyes too wide rolled up to stare into his face, as he looked down at me with a look that made me shudder and finally try to scream my pleasure around him. He moved back far enough so I could scream around him, and then thrust himself deep and hard down my throat, and this time he held my head so I couldn't come back up right away.

He let me up, and I gasped, catching my breath in harsh, overeager breaths, and then he thrust himself into my mouth and down my throat again. He found a rhythm that was just hard enough, just fast enough, just deep enough that it was nearly the perfect blend of force and pleasure.

Rhys liked gentler, but he knew I didn't, and he'd learned to adapt himself to what I wanted and needed. I rewarded him by screaming my pleasure around him, and then he thrust one last time, deeper, forcing my mouth tight against his body so that every last inch of him was shoved as deep inside my mouth as he could get, and whereas with Galen it had been my control, my choice, so I hadn't fought, this wasn't, and I started struggling just a little. Rhys stared down at me, holding me in place until my eyes watered, and when he drew me back I coughed and choked. He drew himself completely out of my mouth.

"Is it too much?"

I shook my head, coughed, and said, "No, it's amazing."

"Do you want me to finish that way, or on those beautiful breasts of yours?"

"On," I said.

He tightened his hold in my hair; if it had been Mistral I'd have asked for tighter, but Rhys was already rougher than he preferred and I appreciated that. He forced himself into my mouth and down my throat again, and this time he was harder, faster, deeper, so that I had to fight for breath, fight not to choke too much; if his hold on my hair had been tighter it would have hit that switch and I could have taken more, but he wasn't quite rough enough to make me enjoy all of it.

He noticed and drew back. "Am I hurting you?"

"If you tighten your hold on my hair, take control even more, I'll be able to enjoy it more."

He looked a little skeptical, but he did what I asked, fingers digging into my hair until it was painful, but for me that translated into finally relaxing into it, giving myself over to the hand in my hair, Rhys's strength, the thrust of him plunging down my throat as he held me where he wanted me, and began to use my hair as a lever so that he thrust into my mouth and drove my mouth down on him at the same time. It rolled my eyes back into my head and spilled emerald and gold light inside my closed eyelids, so bright that it was like daylight with my eyes closed.

He pulled me off him, hand painful in my hair. I opened my eyes enough to see him stroking himself with his other hand. He spilled in a hot wave of shining white, as if moonlight could be made solid enough to pour down my breasts and drip across them in glistening lines.

He helped me lie down beside Galen, and then he collapsed on the other side of me. "Give me a minute and I'll get you a washrag." His voice was breathless with effort and orgasm.

"I'll get it," Galen said. "You rest." I tried to focus on him enough to see the smile I could heard in his voice, but I couldn't focus that much yet.

Rhys's hand found mine and we lay there holding hands, relearning how to breathe and letting the fire and light of our bodies began to fade back to something resembling human-normal.

"I so needed that," I managed to say.

"Me, too," he said.

I squeezed his hand. "Thank you for being rougher than you wanted to be."

"I knew that would make it better for you, and if you can't have inter-course, you need to have the best I can give you."

"That was good, bestest," I said.

"I love you, Merry."

I turned enough to smile at him. "I love you, too, Rhys."

"I love you both," Galen said, coming back from the bath with a rag.

"Don't say that where the reporters can hear you. They're already foaming at the mouth about Doyle and Frost."

Galen grinned. "Dude, I love you like a brother. A brother that I get naked with and fuck the same woman silly with, but like a brother, totally."

Rhys and I laughed, and then he said, "Totally."

"Very bromance of you both, but it's starting to run down onto the sheets."

Galen brought the washrag. Rhys cleaned me up; he had made the mess, as he said. I used the towel he'd brought to dry off, and then we curled up on the bed, with Galen's tall frame curled around the back of me and Rhys tight against me in front, so that we spooned perfectly. Galen's long arm came over me and hugged along my arm that was holding around Rhys's waist, because regardless of sexual orientation most fey had no problem with simple touch. We snuggled under the sheet with the sunlight filling the room and started to doze.

"How can I be so tired?"

"You had triplets less than a week ago," Rhys said.

"I'm tired because the babies don't really sleep yet," Galen said, his voice muffled as if he'd plunged his face into the pillow. If he'd been shorter he would have buried his face against my hair, but if he did that we couldn't spoon because it moved his body out of position; we'd tried.

"How much of the baby care is falling on you?" I asked.

"Kitto is always there; he helps a lot."

"What about the rest?"

"Rhys does his share," he said, and hugged us both with the one long arm.

"I find it restful. It always cleared my head to go hold a baby."

"Really?" I asked.

"I did some of my best planning rocking babies to sleep."

"I know you had other children before this, but there are no stories of you as a deity having any."

His body was tense now, and the doze was no longer relaxing. "It was too long ago, and I didn't tell my stories to the bards. Holding my son in my arms while he died didn't feel like something I wanted to be remembered for."

I hugged him tight, and Galen hugged us both. "I'm sorry, Rhys," he said.

"I led him in battle, my son. He was tall like his mother, dark-haired like her, too. He was handsome and strong and brave and everything a father wants in his son. He followed me into a battle and he died there. Killed by one of the human inventions, explosives with iron filling. I hunted down every member of the tribe that had fought against us. I killed them all, down to the last baby. I destroyed them as a race, do you understand that, I killed their entire people, even the children, while their mothers begged for mercy. My grief was . . . terrible, and I tried to quench it in blood and death, and do you know what I discovered?"

"No, I don't," I said, voice soft. We held him while he told the awful things in an almost unemotional voice, the way to tell terrible things when they still hurt too much to feel.

"That killing them didn't bring my son back, and it didn't make the grief any less. I killed an entire race of people, centuries of culture and invention all gone, because they followed a different god than me, and they dared to fight against me. I forbade anyone to mention the name of their tribe. I wiped them from history itself, and when my vengeance was as complete as I could make it, then my rage left me. All that was left was my sorrow, and that was why I destroyed them, not because of what they had done, not really, but so I could focus my grief into vengeance and not feel the pain of his loss."

We held him, because it was all we could do. I made comforting noises, but it was Galen who said, "I would die to protect the babies now; I can't imagine how much I'll love them in a few years. I understand why you did it."

I wanted to look behind and see Galen's face, but I couldn't manage it; of all the men in my life he was the one I thought would be horrified at what Rhys had done, not agree with it.

"I pray to Goddess and God that you never know such grief, but remember this, Galen, it's going to hurt no matter what you do, and vengeance just postpones it. I realized in the end that I was angry with myself, blamed myself, because I had wanted that fight. I led him to his death. I was his father and I failed him, and that was why I killed all of them. Once I understood that, I didn't want the bards to sing of it. I didn't deserve any stories. I had made certain that that tribe of people passed out of all memory, all history, so I did the same for me. It seemed fair."

"But we have the stories of Cromm Cruach," I said.

"Oh, Merry, that wasn't my first name."

"What was your first name?" Galen asked.

Rhys shook his head, his hair tickling against my face. "No, that name, that person, is gone. He died with the last breath of a people that he destroyed for a mistake that was his own. I buried that name with the children I slaughtered, because when they were all dead I understood that they were no more important than my son, but they were no less important either. They could have grown up and been good men, good women, but I stole that chance from them. They were mortal and had only a short time to live anyway, and I stole what few years they had, because my immortal son had managed to die at the hands of human technology. I am deeply ashamed of what I'd done, so I destroyed my name, my stories, my history in a sort of penance, though even that was such hubris, thinking that the dead could be appeased by punishing myself."

We held him close, we murmured what comfort we could think of, but in the end what comfort is there? Then I thought of something, and had to know. "It took me almost fifteen years to find the murderer of my father. Cel was trying to kill me and all of us at the time, so it was self-defense, but I'm still glad I killed him."

"Has it lessened your grief for your father?" Rhys asked.

I thought about it. "Yes, yes it has. I feel like I avenged him."

"If my son had died at the hands of a true enemy, another sidhe worth fighting with all the magic and grace I had back then, maybe it would have been more satisfying, but I attacked people who could not hope to defend against me; I was a truly terrible power to be reckoned with on the battlefield, and I didn't attack most of them in battle. I hunted them down in the streets, the mountains, anywhere they ran to hide; I found them, and I killed them."

"Cel was already your enemy, Merry," Galen said. "We all wanted him dead, because we were afraid the queen might actually give him the throne."

Rhys said, "You didn't kill Cel just to avenge your father, Merry; you killed him to keep all of the Unseelie safe from him, and that is worth killing for."

"You know, most people's pillow talk isn't about battle and killing," I said.

"Boring people," Galen said.

"Very boring," Rhys said.

"I don't know, sometimes I think it might be nice to be a little boring if it would keep us from having to kill people, or keep them from trying to kill us."

To that there was nothing to say, because we all agreed, that would be nice. "'May you live in interesting times.' It sounds so positive, but it's not," I said.

"That's an Arabic curse, you know: 'May you live in interesting times,'" Rhys said.

"I thought it was Chinese," Galen said.

"Either way, Merry's right; a little boring routine might be nice for a lifetime."

"If you want boring and routine, you're in the wrong bed," I said.

He turned in my arms so he could look at me. "Am I? Well, then let's do something that's not boring, or routine, shall we?"

I laughed. "We just did that."

He grinned. "Let's do it again." He looked across me at the other man. "Unless you aren't up to it again this soon."

Galen grinned back. "You're the older man in this bed; I'm a young one, I'll keep up."

"Old, really?"

"Yeah, really."

"If I could have intercourse, you could actually prove who can keep up, but you can't just keep doing me by hand and have me suck you; I'll strain a muscle in my tongue."

That made them look down at me, surprised, and then they laughed, we all laughed, but when the laughter stopped we did one more round of "not boring, and not routine," and lying between the two of them with the radiance of our bodies making colored shadows on the ceiling, so that our magic was brighter than the sunlight itself, I owned that maybe I didn't want boring and routine anything, but safety for me and the babies and the men I loved, that I did want. Can you be safe and live an interesting life? Maybe not.

TWENTY-FOUR

Queen Andais was on the large mirror in the dining room again, but it was a very different call. She was wearing a sleek black pant-suit that covered almost all of her; only the lack of a shirt underneath the vest left more cleavage than Auntie Andais should probably have been flashing around her nephew and nieces, but the outfit was such a concession that I wouldn't have dared complain. This was as much as she dressed for a press conference; it was a big step in the right direction.

Her consort, Eamon, was at her side in a tailored black suit, but he'd added a round-collared white shirt with pencil-thin black stripes under his vest so he was showing far less chest.

Doyle was at my side, along with Mistral, Rhys, and Galen. Kitto was back in his place under my feet as my footstool. I'd let him know that this was an informal conference and he could pass on his role, but he had said, "I still do not believe that I am so lucky as to be one of the fathers of the babes, and I would have a place at your side, Merry, even if it is under your feet." What could I say to that?

Kitto was wearing yoga pants today, shirtless, no shoes, because the men were working out after the call. Doyle had insisted everyone learn how to protect themselves at least a little, no exceptions. Doyle and Galen were in jeans, and it was slacks for Rhys and Mistral, because their weaponry needed a belt and fitted waistband to fit properly. They'd change after the phone call. Doyle's weapons blended in with his all-black clothing, but Galen's blue jeans and green T-shirt showed every weapon he had. Mistral and Rhys were in suits with jackets designed to go over weapons, so it was less obvious. One of the exiled lesser fey here in L.A. had built them all leather holsters that were magically less visible under clothes, but the men had decided they wanted the queen to see that they were armed. Well, except for the pregnant lady. I knew how to use a gun and a sword, but when my doctor approved it I was joining the training. It probably wouldn't have helped me against Taranis, but I wanted more options if there was ever a next time. I was wearing one of the purple dresses that was actually fitted around the waist. It was good to be back in real clothes again, though the strappy black sandals with their stiletto heels were just for show. I so wasn't ready to walk in anything like that yet. We'd learned that Kitto liked feeling heels in his back during sex, so he was very okay with the shoes.

"You must make Taranis afraid of you, Meredith; only fear will hold him in check." She'd requested to see the babies, but we were talking business first.

"He's already attacked Doyle, and we believe that was motivated out of fear. The king would not willingly meet him in a duel," I said.

"Yes, he feared the Queen's Darkness, but he does not fear Doyle in the same way. He feared me, Meredith, and my Darkness as an extension of me, but without my protection and threat he sees Doyle as only your strong right hand; chop that hand off and it makes you even weaker than you are. You must make Taranis fear you, Meredith, you and no other, if you are to rule the Unseelie Court. If he does not fear you, then it is only a matter of time before the Seelie try to take your throne and combine it with theirs."

"He's made it clear that he would welcome me as his queen," I said, and looked carefully at nothing when I said it, because I couldn't keep the emotion out of my eyes and Andais had used my emotion against me for years.

"I thought about using his rape of you as a reason to challenge him to a duel."

That made me look at her again. "I didn't think you cared that much about my fate, Aunt Andais."

"It's not your fate, Meredith, it's the insult of him thinking he could kidnap and attack my heir with no retribution."

"Of course, it's an insult to you," I said, and just shook my head. She didn't understand that she'd just admitted that what happened to me was important only because it showed a lack of respect for her.

Eamon laid a hand on her shoulder and looked at me. His face showed that he at least understood, and understood that she didn't. I tried to tell him with my eyes that I appreciated it. Andais went on talking, oblivious.

She said, "It is, but I believe Taranis is actually insane. He has convinced himself that you went willingly with him and were kidnapped from him by the evil Unseelie. The King of Light and Illusion seems to be truly deluded."

"I agree," I said.

"He babbles of taking you as queen if he can only strip you of the abusive Unseelie that are poisoning your mind against him. If I wanted to strip you of your protection I, too, would begin with the Princess's Darkness. It really doesn't have the same ring as the Queen's Darkness, does it?"

"No, Aunt Andais, it does not."

She looked just past my shoulder to where Doyle stood, as he had once stood by her, though he had his hand on my shoulder, a gesture I don't think I'd ever seen him make to her. I raised my hand to lay it over his.

"No need to remind me that I neglected my Darkness."

"I didn't touch his hand to remind you of anything, Aunt Andais; I did it because I wanted to touch him."

She made a small movement with her mouth that meant she was unhappy, and then smoothed it into a smile. She really was trying, on this first call since I'd laid down my ultimatum that she behave like a sane person or she couldn't see the babies.

"I believe that, though I do not understand it."

What I wanted to say was, *How sad for you*, but my aunt had never taken well to pity. She didn't understand it and always saw it as an insult, and she certainly never gave pity to anyone. She was pitiless in the true meaning of the word.

I looked past her to Eamon with his own hand on her shoulder. I was sorry for him, too, and if he had been mine I would have reached up and touched his hand, as I did Doyle's, but he wasn't mine to worry over, and he loved Andais utterly. I'd never understood why, but I knew it to be truth.

"You are the Queen of Air and Darkness, my aunt; all fear you. How do I make Taranis fear me?"

"You disfigured him in the dream, Meredith; that did frighten him."

I tensed, holding tighter to Doyle's hand, my heels involuntarily digging a little harder into Kitto's back. "I told you that I used my hand of power on him in the dream, but not what hand of power I used. How did you know that?"

"Darkness is not the only one with spies at the Golden Court, Meredith. Taranis's sleep is troubled, for he keeps seeing his arm melted and crippled from your magic. If you would do that in reality to someone that he could see, a constant visible reminder, it would be a good start to his fearing you."

"Are you actually suggesting that I pick some random Seelie sidhe and partially cripple or disfigure him, just as an object lesson to Taranis?"

She nodded.

I saw Eamon's hand tighten on her shoulder, as if to caution her. She patted his hand absentmindedly but did not hold on to it.

"There is no one I hate that much at the Seelie Court," I said.

She frowned at me. "It's not about hate, Meredith, it's about practicality. You asked how to frighten Taranis; well, I'm telling you how to do that. If you don't want my help, then do not ask for it; it is most irritating to suggest things and watch you make that face."

"I wasn't aware I was making a face, Aunt Andais; I will try to school my expression better from now on."

"And there you go again, that tone in your voice, never a word out of place, but your tone says, clearly, 'You are a fucking psycho bitch and I hate you.'"

"I would never say such a thing, Aunt Andais."

"No, you would never say it, but you think it hard enough."

"I don't believe I've ever said, or even thought, those exact words about you, my aunt."

"Then what words would you say aloud, if you dared?"

"Are you simply incapable of having a conversation where you don't threaten me or imply something unpleasant?" I asked.

She startled visibly, and this time she did reach for Eamon's hand. "I . . . I hadn't thought about it, niece of mine. I have spent many centuries where my threat was all that kept me and my court safe. You see what Taranis will do if he does not fear another royal."

I nodded. "I do understand that. So you're saying that it's just habit for you to threaten people?"

She seemed to actually think about it for a moment and then said, "Yes, I believe it is."

I sighed and squeezed Doyle's hand. Mistral moved closer to me and laid his hand on my other shoulder. I reached up and took his hand, too. It helped steady me to touch them, though I knew that Mistral did not understand why such casual touch pleased me so; he was the least affectionate of the fathers outside the bedroom, but once he'd accepted that I liked and needed it, he'd tried to do more. I appreciated his efforts and did my best to tell him so.

"That must be very lonely," Galen said.

We all turned to him slowly, like you do in a horror film, because that was pity and you did not let the queen know you pitied her, ever.

She looked at him, head to one side like a crow about to peck the eye out of a corpse. "What did you say?" Her voice made it plain that she didn't believe he'd repeat himself, and that he certainly shouldn't repeat it.

"If people are afraid of you, how do they love you?" he asked.

"Love," she said, and made it sound like a very different kind of four-letter word.

"Yes," he said, softly.

I wanted to say, *Stop this, don't make her look at herself that closely,* but hadn't I done just that the last time we spoke to her? Had my boldness made him bolder, too?

"I do not need to be loved, Galen. I need to be obeyed. I need my people to follow me unquestionably."

"Everyone needs to be loved, my queen," he said.

"Now you remember I'm your queen; how convenient and how too late."

"Too late for what, Aunt Andais?" I asked. My heart was thudding in my throat, and I had to swallow past it to speak clearly. Galen had been one of her lesser guards; he had no special place in her esteem, which meant he had no cards to play here. What was he trying to accomplish?

"If Merry disfigured members of the Seelie Court, they could go to the human media. They would think her a monster, and they'd be right."

She frowned and gave him a very unfriendly look. "Perhaps being thought a monster is the price a queen must pay to keep her people and those she loves safe."

"Perhaps," he said, "but Meredith must win the media's love, or the Golden Court will win their sympathy and all the good work you've done over the years in America will be undone. Haven't you wished for Taranis and his people to be as reviled and feared as we once were?"

She still didn't look happy, but there was a considering look on her face. He had her thinking, which in this case was good. "Go on," she said, voice still unhappy, but under that was another tone. I couldn't quite interpret it, but it wasn't anger.

"What if we make Taranis the monster in the press? What if we use the modern media to win the hearts and minds of viewers to our side?"

"Viewers? I don't understand."

"We've been offered a television show."

"We had decided not to take it," Doyle said.

Galen turned to Doyle. "But don't you see? Taranis will never be able to control himself forever. If we give him enough on-camera rope, I think he'll hang himself."

"You want him to attack us on camera," I said, staring at him.

"I think I do, yes, I do."

"He could hurt or even kill one of us, not to mention endangering the human camera crew," Rhys said.

"True, it's a risk, but maybe we don't have to make him fear Merry, but fear looking bad on TV. He's the King of Light and Illusion; he prides himself on being desirable, right?"

"He does," Doyle said.

"What would he do if he saw himself on film being monstrous and terrifying?"

"The cameras could capture your deaths on film very nicely," Andais said in a voice thick with disdain.

"Or capture us fighting for our lives and defending ourselves."

"You're planning to kill him on camera," Andais said, and she sounded astonished and almost happy.

Galen nodded. "If he attacks us, yes, why not?"

She laughed, head back, her hand in Eamon's swinging, almost like a child skipping beside you.

"We'd be up on murder charges, for one thing," Rhys said.

"Maybe, but the camera crew would be our witnesses, don't you see?"

"It is possible, but Taranis would have to lose complete control on camera," Doyle said.

"And we would have to have the camera crew in the house with us for weeks, months before the chance might come," Mistral said. His hand was tense in mine.

I turned and looked up at him. His long gray hair had more glittering strands of gold, copper, and silver, as if the "light" were getting stronger with his anxiety.

"The thought of them filming us truly bothers you," I said.

"Yes, do you honestly want them filming everything here?"

"There are things that we do, or that happen around us, that we might not want on camera," Doyle said.

I turned and looked at him. He was right, but . . . "No, Mistral, I don't, and Doyle is right."

"If we just want to kill the king, then let's do it. Why do the television show? Why give the courts proof we did it? We could go back home and simply execute him for what he did to Merry."

"I like this plan," Doyle said, and his deep voice was a little deeper with emotion. I knew he'd wanted to slay Taranis for raping me. It had been tempting to let him do it.

"No," I said, "no, the risk is too great." I squeezed his hand in mine and looked up at him. "I will not lose you to vengeance."

"He's tried to kill me twice, Meredith; if he attacks us on camera my life may still be forfeit."

"Then no," I said, "no. We will not lure him here to help us kill him on camera, and we will not go home and slay him there. We will leave the mad king alone."

"He won't leave us alone, Merry," Galen said.

"The boy is right," Mistral said.

"He's going to hunt us in our dreams, Merry; we can't protect ourselves there, so bring him out here where our power is greater."

"What power do we have that is greater?" I asked.

"You are Princess Meredith NicEssus, the first faerie princess born on American soil, and now you have triplets. You are a media darling, or have you forgotten that the police had to help us drive out through the press and people?"

"I haven't forgotten."

"Merry, you are *the* face of faerie right now. If you take this moment and run with it, really embrace it, you will have the power of the media."

"They're already trying to climb the walls and using telephoto lenses on us, Galen. I'm not sure I want more."

"You asked what power we have that is greater than Taranis; well, that's it. You can be the biggest star, the biggest illusion in all faerie, because we pick and choose what they see. We can take this moment and show the Unseelie as good and loving, and eventually the king will lose it and have to come to us. He won't be able to resist, because above all else he has to be the star, the center of attention."

"He always has been a media slut," Rhys said.

"No," I said, "just no; I just want to enjoy my children and the men I love. I don't want more attention."

"You can do what the queen suggested, and maim someone with your hand of flesh, but then you will be the bad guy. Let's just for once make the Seelie Court the bad guys."

"This is conspiracy before the fact," I said.

"No, it's not. We won't do anything to lure him here or set him up; he will come on his own, because he won't want anyone, not even you, to outshine him, Meredith. His ego is too big to stay away."

"It could take months for him to finally break down and come here," I said.

"It could, but we'll be getting paid pretty handsomely the whole time, and maybe Maeve can stay home with Liam, so that he starts thinking of her as mommy, not just his mother."

"Oh, don't go and spoil it now," Andais said.

"Spoil what?" Galen asked.

"You had a lovely plan to kill the king, and now instead of fear or revenge, your motive is all love and sunshine; please, just let me have a few more moments of thinking that there is an Unseelie heart trapped in that overgrown pixie body."

The smile left his face, and he looked . . . cold. "Trust me, my queen, I am Unseelie." And just as Andais had accused me of my words being mild but my tone being insulting, so now Galen's words were fine, but the tone was . . . ominous, even threatening.

She looked at him, and there was something in her face I'd never seen before when she looked at Galen. She "saw" him, considered him in a way I don't believe she ever had before. Andais had a very binary way of looking at most men. They were either barely considered, victims of the moment, or potential lovers. He'd been her victim before, as had we all, and he'd been barely considered for most of his life, but now I watched that third choice cross through her eyes.

"If the genetic tests do not come back with your genetics listed, then perhaps I'll give you a night to prove just how Unseelie you are, Galen Greenknight."

He tensed, visibly, his newfound boldness stumbling. My heart was back in my throat, and I was clutching Doyle's hand a little. Mistral had actually moved a little apart from us, so that he was at Rhys's back, as if he thought she might try some violence, and in a way he was right, because she didn't have sex without violence. She was like the anti-vanilla, Auntie Vanilla, and once I thought of it, it was funny and I laughed.

I laughed and I couldn't stop laughing. I laughed so hard it began to ache in places that even sex hadn't bothered. I laughed until tears ran down my face, and I heard other laughter. Galen came to stand by my chair, taking my hand and joining me in helpless laughter, but we were the only ones. Everyone else stayed silent, and when I could wipe the tears away enough to look at the mirror I saw why: The queen was not amused.

She was on her feet with Eamon far enough behind her that she, or maybe he, was out of reach. Her tricolored eyes sparked like lightning behind gray clouds. *The storm isn't overhead, but it's coming.*

"I will not be laughed at, Meredith, not by anyone." Her voice had crawled down into that low purr that should have meant sex but usually meant torment for someone.

I managed to say, "You are the least vanilla person I know, Auntie Andais; you are anti-vanilla, Auntie Vanilla, get it?"

Rhys gave a small snort as he tried not to laugh. Even Mistral made a small noise; only Doyle stayed impervious to my dangerous silliness.

"No," she said coldly, "I do not 'get it.'"

Guards spilled into the room, some sidhe and some Red Caps. They had begun to train together, working on battle strategies that played to their mixed strengths. The goblins had fought like shock troops for the Unseelie sidhe for centuries, but never shoulder to shoulder with them.

Goblins had been used as cannon fodder, never truly as another warrior to fight beside. Now they spread out in front of us, sidhe and goblin, side by side. They stacked themselves around us in a move that was obviously practiced, making themselves a shield of flesh between their "queen" and her "kings." I hated that they might have to sacrifice themselves for us, but that was what it meant to be bodyguards, especially royal guards. Once it had been Doyle and the rest who were the sacrifice for Andais, and the female guards in front of me scattered among the men had been expected to do the same for Prince Cel.

"I allowed you to flee to the Western Lands and my niece's more tender care, but do not let it go to your heads, my guards. None of you are would-be kings. If I call you back to the court, you are oath-bound to answer and return to me." I couldn't see her through the bodies of our guards, but hearing the tone was enough to steal away the last bit of my laughter, even with happy tears still wet on my face.

Galen took my hand in his; he looked grim. Doyle, Mistral, and Rhys had all moved up around my chair, but they were still behind the wall of guards. In a real battle we might lead from the front, but in moments like this princes and kings did not stand in front of their bodyguards. I had spent months learning this lesson as I watched the men I loved risk themselves again and again to keep me and the unborn children safe. Now, they were having to learn the lesson. I looked at my three warriors standing so certain, so ready, and hidden from the threat. I knew that it would chafe on them more than it had on me, because a year ago they would have stood between the danger and Queen Andais; now they stood beside me.

A voice even lower than Doyle's came from that tall wall of guards. "We are goblin; you cannot call us back to your side, Queen Andais, for that has never been our place." It was Jonty, the leader of the Red Caps. He was smallish for his people, only a little over eight feet tall; some of the men in the line were closer to thirteen feet, like small giants, or average-sized ogres. Their skin color ranged through every shade of gray, yellow, and two golds that were almost brown. The sidhe warriors, so tall and commanding, looked small interspersed between them.

"You are Kurag the Goblin King's problem, not mine, but the men and women you stand beside—they are mine." Her voice went down another note to a purring, sexual depth, but it didn't excite any of us who were sidhe, because we knew that it promised violence, not sex, at least for us. I'd begun to realize that violence was a kind of sex for my aunt. She was truly like one of those sexual predators who are wired so that images of violence hit the same centers of the brain that "normal" sex does for the rest of us.

I projected my voice to be heard. It would have been more impressive if I hadn't been hiding behind my guards, but it would have to do, because Andais wasn't the most stable person, and I wouldn't risk myself betting that, one, she couldn't do magic through the mirror, and two, she would remember that she valued my fertile womb, if nothing else.

"They are not yours, Aunt Andais, not anymore."

"Do not let your fertility go to your head, Meredith. It may keep you and your lovers safe, but the rest are on loan, nothing more. Until you sit on my throne, the Unseelie sidhe are mine."

"They are oathed to me now, Aunt Andais."

"They cannot be oathed twice, niece. That would make them foresworn."

"The Cranes, my father's female guards, were never asked to make oath to Prince Cel; you just ordered them to guard him, so they were free to make oath where they will."

"They were oathed to my son," she said.

"No, they were not," I said. I would have liked to see her face, but I trusted the guards to do their job and stared at their broad backs, Galen's hand still in mine.

"Cel gave them a choice and they swore oath to him."

"Who told you that?" This was from Cathbodua, who stood at the end of the line that shielded us.

"Cel and the captain of the Cranes, Siobhan."

"They lied, then," Cathbodua said.

"Why would they have lied about that?"

"His reasons were his own, always, Queen Andais, but I swear to you that no one standing here today ever took oath to Prince Cel."

"I neglected much where my son was concerned, and I regret that."

Cathbodua went to one knee. "I am honored to hear you say that, Queen Andais."

One guard taking a knee was often a sign for all, but no one else knelt, and after a time Cathbodua got to her feet and joined her fellow guards again.

"I will grant that the female guards are free to be with you, Princess Meredith, but the men are mine."

"They took oath to me, as well, Aunt Andais," I said.

"Yes, remind me of our blood ties, Meredith, because you do grow tiresome so quickly."

"As do these moments between us, for me, auntie."

"Do not call me auntie."

"As you wish," I said. My voice was as neutral as I could make it.

"I will call all my Ravens home to roost, Meredith, and they will come."

"No, we won't." This from Usna, who stood beside Cathbodua. His normal joking voice, as if nothing were really serious, was missing. It was a very grim cat that stepped from the line.

"How dare you tell me 'no' and 'won't.' I will carve those words into your flesh."

"We all made oath to Merry; we are no longer your Ravens. You cannot call us home, and we are no longer yours to torture at your will," he said, and his voice sounded sad now. I realized that he did not believe that anything would keep him safe from Andais. Usna spoke bravely, but he didn't believe in that safety.

"Then you are all foresworn." She almost yelled it.

I spoke then, standing up as if that would help. Galen squeezed my hand tight as if afraid of what I would do. "They are oathed to me, which does make them foresworn."

"Then they will be punished for breaking their oath," she said.

"By exile from faerie? Isn't that the usual punishment for being foresworn?" I said.

"No!" She yelled it.

"Yes," I said, clearly, calmly.

"You can't all have chosen exile from faerie," she said, and her voice held shock.

"We are exiled from the Unseelie Court," Usna said, "but we are not exiled from faerie, for wherever Princess Meredith goes, faerie follows."

"That is not possible," Andais said.

"You have seen it yourself, Queen Andais," Cathbodua said. "She brought the gardens of the Unseelie Court back to life. Faerie is alive and spreading for the first time in over a thousand years."

Doyle spoke then. "The night itself must have told you that faerie is alive again."

"My power has whispered rumors to me," she said, and her voice was growing calmer. That could be a good thing or a bad thing; one can never tell with psychopaths.

"Then you know that faerie has come to the Western Lands and we are no longer exiles, but pioneers on the frontier of new fairylands," Doyle said.

"I cannot let anyone defy me like this, Darkness; you know that I am only as powerful as my threat."

"I am sorry for that, my queen."

"I must call one home and make his punishment terrible enough to prevent any others from joining your quiet rebellion."

"I do not know what to say to that, my queen; it is almost reasonable, and for you very reasonable."

"Send Usna to me, and I will leave the rest in place," she said.

I watched Usna reach out and take Cathbodua's hand. I was about to say something in their defense, but she spoke first. "I am pregnant with Usna's child."

"You are lying to save him," Andais said, voice certain.

"The little stick says I am with child, and the only man I have lain with is Usna."

"Little stick, what little stick can tell you you are pregnant?"

I said, "Cathbodua, do you mean a home pregnancy test?"

She looked behind to find me, and nodded.

"When did you find out?" I asked.

"Just before this meeting."

I'd had enough. I stepped forward with Galen's hand in mine. The Red Caps and sidhe in front of us glanced at each other, and then the sidhe looked to Doyle, and the Red Caps looked to me. Whatever they saw on both our faces, it made them move aside so we could come forward and face Andais.

"We have another fertile couple among the sidhe; it is something to celebrate, Aunt Andais, not punish."

She stared at me, and there was a look on her face that I couldn't understand, but it looked almost pained. On anyone else, I might have said it looked afraid, but Andais feared no one, least of all me.

"It is love that has made them fertile," Galen said. I glanced up at him, but he looked only at the queen. He looked handsome, commanding standing there, as if something had stripped away the last bits of childhood and brought him into the man he was always meant to be.

"The crow and the cat do not love each other; it is lust that has made a child." Her voice was thick with disdain.

"I didn't mean their love for one another, but Meredith's love for them."

"Are you saying they, too, are her lovers? Is no one safe from your lusts, Meredith?"

Rhys stepped forward. "Meredith loves them as a ruler is supposed to love her subjects."

"You cannot rule by love," she said, and her beautiful face was creased with angry lines, as if the monster inside her were starting to peer out.

Galen said, "But they oathed themselves to Meredith because she has shown them love and caring, the way Prince Essus did to his guards."

"Do not wave my brother's memory at me and think it will make me relent. Meredith has brought it up too often of late."

Doyle came to stand on the other side of Galen. "Prince Essus stood between you and those you would harm more than once. I don't think any of us understood what a good and strong influence he was on you until we lost him."

"I would allow Essus liberties that no one else dared."

"You loved your brother," Doyle said.

"Yes, yes, I loved my brother, but he is dead and gone."

"But his daughter stands before you; his grandchildren are in the other room waiting to see their great-aunt Andais. Meredith is truly NicEssus, the daughter of Essus, for she has shown the same nobility, kindness, intelligence, and love that he did. He would have made a fine and generous king."

Her eyes were wide, and I realized that the shine in them now wasn't magic, but unshed tears. "But for a few years of time he would have been eldest and king."

"Yes, King Essus," Doyle said.

One lone tear trailed from her eye. "You have made me cry twice, Meredith, daughter of my brother, mother of my nieces and nephew, bringer of life to the sidhe, creator of new fairylands, and they tell me you do all this by love. Is that true, niece of mine? Are you all sunshine and love? Are you all Seelie sidhe and there is none of the Unseelie's blackness inside you?"

"I do my best to rule through fairness and love, but I am also the wielder of flesh and blood; those are not Seelie powers, my queen."

"I saw what your hand of blood can do when you killed my son."

"I did not flinch when Cel tried to kill me; that was my father's mistake. If he had not loved Cel, he would not have hesitated in his own defense and my father would be here to see his grandchildren."

"Do you not think I have thought of that, Meredith, since I learned of my son's treachery?"

"You ask if I am all sunshine and love, and I tell you this, aunt, I do not rule by love and fairness alone."

"What then, kindness?" She made it an insult.

"Ruthlessness. I am more ruthless than my father. You can take credit for that, Aunt Andais, for you allowed sidhe after sidhe to challenge me to duels when I had no magic to defend myself. I had to become ruthless to survive, because you would not protect me. You would not acknowledge that the duels were attempts to assassinate me, attempts done either on Cel's orders or to curry favor from him. If you had only reached out to me, protected me, if not for myself, then for your brother's memory, but you did not. Essus taught me kindness, honor, love, fairness, justice, but you, dear aunt, you taught me ruthlessness—and hate."

She smiled then, and nothing she could have done in that moment would have frightened me more. It caught my breath in my throat and made my skin run cold. Galen moved closer to me, folding me in his arms.

"Then perhaps Essus and I have forged a fit ruler for the sidhe, at last. Perhaps it is Taranis who should fear you, Meredith."

"I do not understand, Aunt Andais."

"I will let it be known that my Ravens, and Cel's Cranes, have oathed to you out of love and loyalty the way rulers gathered followers thousands of years ago. I will let it be known that sidhe among your guards that have not been in your bed are with child. I will make certain that the Seelie know we have a new goddess of love and ruthlessness, for it was not only I who taught you that last lesson, Meredith. Your mother's neglect and Taranis's madness helped forge you into the ruler you are today."

I hugged Galen closer and nodded. "I will agree with that, Aunt Andais."

"I will make certain Taranis knows that." She gave a short, abrupt laugh. "You may be right after all, Galen Greenknight; perhaps love is frightening enough all on its own without any torture needed."

She laughed again, and then just walked out of sight of the mirror. It was Eamon who came forward, reaching to blank the glass. He spoke to me before he did it. "Princess Meredith, Prince Galen." And we were staring at our own startled reflections before I could give him his title in return.

CHAPTER

TWENTY-FIVE

M aeve Reed stalked around the main bedroom in a pair of cream slacks, cut wide so they swung enough to give glimpses of the pale taupe stiletto boots underneath. The boots matched her tailored suit jacket, the dress shirt buttoned up to her neck was almost pure white, and her thin man-style tie was metallic gold and cream to pick up the gold of her chain-link belt. The chain was tied into a loose knot to trail across her hip, swinging to cross her groin as she moved, more like jewelry for the waist than an actual belt.

"You look wonderful in this outfit," I said.

She stopped stalking the white carpet and turned to look at me. "You think so?" She trailed long, slender hands down the chain links, which drew the eye down to her groin again. It wasn't accidental, but it wasn't exactly flirting with me either. Maeve had made her living in Hollywood for decades; sex appeal had been one of the commodities that had helped her stay at the top, especially back in the fifties, when she'd have been considered too tall, too thin, and not curvy enough to be a sex symbol. Now she was very chic and very in, but then Maeve Reed, the Golden Goddess of Hollywood, had been one of the reasons the fashion had changed from curvy to a thinness that was almost impossible for a human woman to duplicate without starving herself. The sidhe were built differently, like fashion models with a bit more body fat so they still had breasts and ass, but they could eat a Thanksgiving feast every day and not gain weight. Humans couldn't, and yet they tried.

"I had to go into the studio today. I'm a movie star; people expect an effort."

"You don't have to explain it to me. You could have just dressed to be around the house. It's your clothes, your house, wear what you want."

She looked at me, blue eyes narrowing. She was using glamour to appear more human, hiding her very inhuman eyes with their tricolor blue and copper and gold lines that went out like miniature lightning bolts, changing her golden skin to a human tan, and even making her straight waist-length hair more yellow than her natural white-blond. I never understood why she darkened her hair; it was within human bounds either way. The skin and eyes she'd had to make more human, but the hair could have stayed.

"Why do you make your hair more yellow-blond than it is naturally? Humans have hair both colors."

"The yellow-blond looks better on camera," she said.

"Oh, that makes sense." I sat on the edge of the bed, swinging my feet, because I was far too short to sit and reach the ground. I was still wearing the purple dress, though I'd changed to a pair of black low-heeled pumps. I might get back into the stilettos in a few weeks, but right now having to fight my body on heels that high and thin just took too much effort. I'd lost most of my weight in an almost magically short time, but I still wasn't quite myself. The extra cup size in my breasts alone made me feel unbalanced. I'd been generously endowed before, but now it was a true embarrassment of riches.

"I'm sorry that you disagree about hiring lesser fey to work in the house, Meredith, but I just don't see the point in it. There are plenty of humans in L.A. needing jobs. If we hire only fey, then the media will accuse us of racism."

"Really?" I asked.

Maeve nodded. "Trust me on that."

"I do trust you, but we can't have human nannies around the triplets, or more specifically around Bryluen. Her ability to fascinate seems auto-matic; until she's old enough for us to teach her to control it, humans are nearly helpless around her."

"She's a baby, it can't be that bad."

"Come to the nursery and see for yourself. Perhaps your more pure sidhe blood will keep you proof against Bryluen's glamour."

"I'm not just sidhe, Meredith; I was a goddess and I'm still wor-shipped in a way as a celebrity, so if your babe cannot bespell me it's not really a good test."

"But if she can, then it's a very good test," I said.

Maeve looked thoughtful and then said, "Good point. Who is taking care of her besides you?"

"Kitto . . ."

"A goblin has no resistance to sidhe magic; of course he would be ensnared by her."

"Kitto is also half sidhe and has come into his hand of power."

She waved it away. "He was raised goblin; he will never be as sidhe as he is goblin."

"Why should that make a difference to his magic resistance?" I asked.

"You were taught certain skills from childhood, skills that your little man was not."

I slid to my feet, settling the skirt in place. "Don't call him a lit-tle man."

"Why not? He is the smallest of your men."

"If you were sidhe, yes, but you've lived with the humans long enough to understand it's an insult."

"What do you mean, if I were sidhe?"

"If Kitto's goblin upbringing undermines his ability to be sidhe, then a similar argument can be made that your centuries of exile out among the humans have made you more human than you would have been had you stayed in faerie as a member of the Seelie Court."

"I was the goddess Conchenn; how dare you compare me to some sidhe-sided goblin?"

"The goblins are every bit as fey as any sidhe, and this attitude of looking down on them because they have no magic, when it is the sidhe that stole their magic in the first place, really *is* racist, and arrogant. It's like an abusive spouse who blames his wife for not being able to walk gracefully, when he's the one who broke her leg."

"That is not a fair comparison, Meredith. The goblins and the sidhe were at war; they would have won had we not done the spell that took their magic."

"So I'm told by both sides, but that was a very long time ago, Maeve, a very long time ago."

"You weren't there, Meredith; you didn't see your friends die at their hands."

"No, but I have seen that the sidhe-sided goblins do fine magic once they're brought into their power."

"Your goblin twin lovers, Holly and Ash, are quite frightening. That you've armed them with your hand of flesh and blood respectively makes them very dangerous."

"I did not share my hands of power with them, it just happened to be their latent magic."

"Are you sure of that?" she asked, and gave me a very direct look out of those famous blue eyes.

"Kitto's hand of power isn't one of mine."

"He can bring people through a mirror even against their will; that is almost useless as a hand of power."

"It helped him and Rhys kill the goblin who tormented both of them," I said.

"His hand of power is so useless there is no name for it."

"It's incredibly rare, but it has a name: the hand of reaching," I said.

"The hand of reaching allowed small armies to be brought through a reflective surface. Your goblin cannot do that."

"Perhaps not, but the name is for the ability, not the degree of power."

"It needs a new name, something grand," she said.

I shrugged.

She frowned at me. She frowned a lot, actually; if she'd been human she'd have had frown lines by now, but she was sidhe and would never truly wrinkle. She could get some lines here and there, but she'd never have the lines of her unhappiness carved into her face like most people would.

"It's not just me who thinks the twins have only inherited your own magic, Meredith, nor am I the only one who thinks Kitto's hand of power is weak."

"I know that," I said, "but the others don't say it to my face as much."

"You are their ruler; they dare not speak their minds to you."

"And you are Maeve Reed, the Golden Goddess of Hollywood, and you don't plan on going back to faerie, even if Taranis lifted your exile."

She looked startled for a second, and then smiled. "How did you know that? I wasn't even certain myself until recently."

"I may not be your ruler, but I try to be your friend, and friends notice things."

She looked embarrassed then. "I am sorry, Meredith; I've been rude by human standards, and you're right. I've been exiled long enough that human culture is more natural to me than any in faerie, so my apologies."

"Please don't treat Kitto as less than the others anymore. He is my lover and maybe one of the fathers of my children. I would ask that you respect him for that, if for no other reason."

She gave a nod that was almost a bow, but not quite. "If you wish the goblins to be thought better of, then you do need to bring one into a power that isn't one of yours, and is more impressive than mirror-whatever."

"I've been discussing that with Doyle, Rhys, and the others. When I am able to have sex again, I will try to do just that."

Maeve shuddered. "I honestly don't know how you can have sex with Holly and Ash. Kitto, I sort of understand, he's like this beautiful miniature man, and he's kind to the point I'm amazed he survived among such a savage race, but the twins . . . they are savages, Meredith."

"What they are, or are not, is my business. I'm not asking you to compromise your racial purity."

She sighed and rolled her eyes. "I didn't mean it like that, Meredith. You seem determined to take insult."

"And you seem determined to give it."

We stood there looking at each other, almost glaring at each other. I was tired of Maeve's attitude issues. She hadn't been like this before she went to Europe to make the last movie. I didn't know if something had happened on the trip, or if it was something that had happened here, but something had changed, and not for the better.

"I do not mean to give offense," she said.

"I'd believe that if you didn't keep doing it. What happened in Europe, Maeve? Or what did you find here when you came home to make you angry with me, and my men?"

"My son treats you and your men as his parents, more than me. That hurts, Meredith."

"I am sorry for that, and we are willing to take the reality show offer to help you afford to stay home more."

"I told you at the hospital what I made on my last film, Meredith; there is no way that a reality TV contract will come close to that. We will be giving up our privacy for nothing. If anything, the cameras will record that Liam doesn't think of me as his mommy except as an empty word. Do you think I want to be humiliated like that on national television?"

"You're making it sound like Liam is dumping you for someone else. He's a baby, he doesn't understand."

"I am Maeve Reed, the Golden Goddess of Hollywood; I can't be seen as losing to anyone, not even the first American-born faerie princess."

"You aren't talking about Liam now, are you?"

"I've been a sex symbol since the early sixties, Meredith, and yet you have all the attention of the most desirable men in the household. I understand why, but my image is everything for my job. My agent and my publicist think that a reality show here could harm the image that I've built up over decades. I'm one of the most desirable, and desired, women in Hollywood, but I can't compare to you in my own home."

"Is that your agent and publicist talking, or just you?"

"All three of us."

"Are you serious?"

"Yes, Meredith, perception is everything in this town. If people believe that someone like you is this much more desirable than me, it will hurt my earning power, and maybe my box office draw."

"What do you mean, 'someone like me'?"

She blinked those big, beautiful eyes at me and did an expression I'd seen her do in a dozen films. I'd learned that was one of the ways she hid her true feelings in the real world. I didn't know if other actors did it, but she did; she acted to hide. It was her version of a cop face: actor face.

"Answer me, Maeve; what did you mean, 'someone like me'?"

"Someone who isn't a movie sex symbol," she said.

I shook my head. "That's not what you meant."

"Now you're telling me what I mean, as if I don't know my own mind?"

"Do you think the reason that Bryluen can bespell my mind so easily is because I'm not pure enough sidhe, just like Kitto?"

"I did not say that."

"And that is you avoiding answering the question; very sidhe of you, because we don't lie outright. We just prevaricate until the listener reads into our words whatever they want to hear, and we let them believe it."

"You're overthinking this, Meredith."

"Am I?"

"Yes, and that was a clear answer," she said.

"The one you just gave, yes, it was, but it's not the answer to my question, is it?"

"Drop this, Meredith, please. I'm sorry if I implied anything."

"What if I don't drop it?"

"What is wrong with you today, Meredith?"

"I could ask you the same thing."

"I had a meeting at the studio and they're already trying to pressure me to go right back to filming. I told them I wanted some time with my son, but I'm one of their solid moneymakers and any year without a Maeve Reed film hits their profits."

"You haven't been home a week yet," I said.

"If I leave again, Liam is going to just forget who I am."

I went to her then and touched her arm. "Can you say no?"

"I can always say no."

"Will it hurt your career, or put you in breach of a contract?"

She smiled and put her hand over mine where I was touching her arm. "You understand more than most people do about what really goes on at this level of 'stardom.'" She raised her hand to do one set of quote marks.

"I've watched what you've been through in the last year. I'm amazed at how badly you get treated sometimes."

"I have true power in this town; imagine what happens to actors who don't."

"It must be brutal," I said.

"Hollywood will eat you, if you let it."

"I wonder if reality TV stars have as big a challenge?"

"I don't know, honestly; I only meet them after they've become stars and then it's about their publicists trying to keep them in the news. I don't know how different it is in the beginning, but you wouldn't be like most reality stars. You're already famous."

"And that fame, like all my noble titles, doesn't pay the bills."

"You could go back to being a private detective."

"That won't help you say no to the studio. For that, we need more money than a detective makes."

"Thirty million dollars, Meredith; that is what I made for my last film. Nothing you can do will bring that kind of money in. I'm sorry, but it just won't."

"We have offers for a million here, a few hundred thousand there."

"What's the million dollars for?"

"They've been after me for a while to be a centerfold."

"No, no, because I know some of your publicity offers are from family-oriented things. You can be the sexy young thing, or the beautiful mother with babies, but you can't do both in the media, not in this country anyway."

"I'd appreciate your advice on the offers coming in, then, because I'm tempted to go for the most money. I hadn't thought about building an image."

"I'd be happy to help, but you will have to choose what kind of image you want to project."

I laughed. "Isn't it a little late for me to be the perfect mother since I've just given birth to triplets out of wedlock?"

"It's not that making the mother image hard to sell, it's the multiple fathers, and the fact that rumor has it that Frost and Doyle are lovers, too, that has really hurt their image in the mainstream media."

"Very homophobic," I said.

"Yes, it is, but it's still the truth."

"Can I be the sexy young thing having just given birth to triplets?" I asked.

It was her turn to laugh. "I don't know; I've never seen anyone recover their figure as fast as you who wasn't full-blooded sidhe. You're built human, but you're certainly getting your figure back more like a sidhe."

"Especially with triplets," I said.

She laughed again. "Yes, especially with triplets. The human media will want to know your secret for postbaby weight loss."

"There's no secret; apparently it's just good genetics."

"They won't want to hear that, Meredith. They want some exercise plan, or better yet some magic food, or pill, that will make them all pre-baby thin without any effort on their part."

"I'm getting my figure back without much effort, but every other good thing in my life has come with a lot of effort."

Her face sobered, and she hugged me. "I know that, and I'm sorry that I've been taking my mood out on you."

I hugged her back. "Now I'm supposed to say, 'That's all right,' but it's not. I will never again be anyone's whipping girl for their issues." I hugged her tighter and looked up into the face that had launched a thousand blockbuster movies. "Not even the most beautiful movie star in Hollywood."

"Do you really think so?" she asked, looking down from all that six-plus feet height in her high heels.

I smiled. "Of course I do."

She leaned down, and I went up on tiptoe to meet her kiss. It was a chaste kiss by fey standards, though if some paparazzi had gotten a picture they'd have sold it for a bundle, and the rumor would have been that Maeve and I were lovers. We had made wonderful magical love once, but it wasn't what we were to each other. I wasn't sure if we were extended family, or if she was a member of my inner circle of courtiers. Once such things had been more formalized, and they still were at the Seelie Court, but less so at the Unseelie, and if this was a court then it was the most informal of all.

She smiled down at me, her pinkish lipstick slightly smeared. I wasn't wearing lipstick, just not bothering with glamour so my lips looked red. Humans would assume I was wearing something, but the proof was in the kissing, and the only lipstick smeared was hers.

I pulled out of the embrace with a smile.

"I appreciate you letting me choose lovers from among the new sidhe guards," she said.

"They are free to choose and so are you."

"It's been a long time since I was surrounded by people who truly felt that way. Among humans and the Seelie there is always a price to pay, or strings attached."

"The Unseelie who are not under the queen's direct control are more like the rest of the fey. Sex is another need, like food."

"Yes, but your steak doesn't have feelings and emotional baggage; people, even the sidhe, do."

I nodded. "I can't argue that. The lesser fey treat it more sensibly."

"I think you'll find, Princess, that the lesser fey treat sex with the sidhe sensibly, because they expect it to be a onetime thing, or a fling. Very few non-sidhe ever become a marrying match for the sidhe."

"My grandmother did," I said.

"Your grandfather wanted to end his curse, and only willing marriage to another fey would do that."

"At least the curse didn't demand a love match. My grandfather wasn't called Uar the Cruel for nothing; he'd have never found someone to love him."

"How are his sons, your uncles?"

"They've seen modern doctors and nothing seems to be able to stop the venom from dripping out of the pores of their fingers, but modern plastic gloves have helped. They don't accidentally poison people now."

"Good, they did nothing to earn their curse. I always thought it was unfair that Uar's curse manifested in all his children being born with that birth defect," she said.

"Agreed, but then are curses ever fair? I mean, most of the fairy tales have a grain of truth, and so many of them talk about a curse on the prince, or princess, spreading to everyone in the castle, or kingdom."

"I've never actually known that to happen. I think the human fairy tales were supposed to be a warning to rulers to be fair and just, or their kingdom suffered, but most kings didn't see themselves in such stories."

"Really, so there's no truth to 'Sleeping Beauty,' or 'Beauty and the Beast'?"

"'Sleeping Beauty' is the old sleeping warrior idea, and that's real enough, but 'Beauty and the Beast' isn't based on anything that I'm aware of."

"There are Raven warriors asleep under the Tower of London," I said.

She looked at me, eyes narrowing. "How do you know that? The queen did not tell you, and I know Taranis didn't. She felt it unjust that only her people were used, and he was too cowardly to offer up his own guard as sacrifice at the end of the last great human and fey war."

"The Goddess showed me in a vision that some of the Queen's Ravens sleep an enchanted rest underneath the human tower. They're the ravens the legend refers to, not the birds."

"When the last Raven leaves the tower, then England will fall," Maeve said.

I nodded.

"If England is ever in danger of truly being conquered, then the Ravens are to wake and defend the country, that's really what it means."

"Why didn't they wake during World War Two?"

"If the Germans had touched English soil they might have."

"Who is trapped under there?"

"You mean names?"

"Yes."

She shook her head and all her smiles were gone as she looked at nothing, her eyes full of remembering. "We do not speak their names, and will not until they rise again to fulfill a bargain that should have been shared between the two high courts of faerie. That our king refused to sacrifice any of his golden throng should have told us all what kind of man he was. Instead the story was put about that the warriors sealed up were all monsters that even the dark court was happy to be rid of, when in truth they were some of the best warriors among the sidhe, and no worse men than the rest."

"But you will not speak their names?"

"I will not, for Taranis made all of us at the Seelie Court vow never to speak their names until they rise to complete the treaty between human and fey."

"Was it very hard to pretend to be a starlet back in the fifties when you had all those centuries behind you, inside you?"

She gave me a look, a considering look, and let me glimpse the fine burning intelligence that she usually hid. She didn't pretend to be stupid, but she didn't show everything either.

"That is a very good question. One that in all the decades of inter-views I've never been asked."

"I found it hard to pretend I wasn't Princess Meredith when I came to L.A. Even I found all my secrets hard to keep, hard not to share with someone."

"I told some of my secrets to Gordon. I wish he'd lived to see Liam. I think he's going to grow up to look like that handsome man I first met."

By the time I'd met Maeve's late husband he'd been riddled with the cancer that would claim his life, and the man who had been young in the sixties wasn't young three, almost four decades later. He had been a dying shell of the handsome director who had won Maeve's heart, but her dearest wish had been to have his child. Galen and I had done a fertility rite and the Goddess had blessed us with the energy to give Maeve and Gordon Reed their last wish as a couple. He'd died months before Liam was born, but he'd gotten to hear the heartbeat, see sonograms, and know for certain he had a son.

"I'm sorry that you lost Gordon."

"You gave us our son, Meredith; you have nothing to be sorry for."

"Shall we visit the nursery and the children?"

She smiled. "Yes, let's. If I'm going to remind Liam that I'm Mommy, I need to see him more."

"Am I supposed to apologize again for Liam's behavior?"

"If you had been raised in faerie courts and never left them, you would never have said that."

"Not apologized, or not felt like I should apologize for something that isn't my fault?" I asked.

"Both," she said, and smiled softly, but it was sad around the edges and left her eyes almost haunted.

I took her hand in mine, squeezed it. "I am sorry that you have had to spend so much time away from your son."

"If you hadn't said that, and meant it, I probably wouldn't say this: The movie I just finished filming is an amazing chance for me to stretch myself as an actress. If you and the others hadn't been here for Liam I wouldn't have taken it, or I might have tried to take him and a nanny with me, but he was better here at his home with his family. I just need to figure out how to be a bigger part of that family."

"I am very glad you think of us as family, Maeve."

"You have brought me back to faerie, or brought faerie back to me, after centuries of thinking I had lost it forever."

"I can't imagine losing it for so long. Three years of exile was hard enough for me," I said.

"But you truly are an American faerie princess, Meredith, so very American in your ideals. Like letting your guards have a choice when it comes to their lovers."

"I think that was what my father hoped when he sent me to public school and encouraged me to have friends outside the fey community."

"I never really knew Prince Essus, but he seems very wise. Not a single guard will say a bad thing about him."

"Have you tried to get them to?" I asked.

She made a waffling gesture halfway between a nod and a shrug. "A bit. I wanted to see if they were just speaking nicely for his daughter, but it seems as if he truly was as good as his press."

"Why would you care if my father was as good as he seemed?"

"Honestly?" she asked.

"Yes."

"Your uncle on your grandfather's side beat me and exiled me for refusing to marry him. Your grandfather was Uar the Cruel, and he earned that name. Your mother is narcissistic to the point of being delusional, and your uncle is the same. Your aunt on your father's side is a sexual sadist and a sociopath, or maybe even a psychopath; her son, your first cousin, was worse than his mother. He'd have been a sexual serial killer if the women of his bodyguards hadn't been immortal and able to heal nearly any injury. I've taken more lovers from among them than you have, and they hate the late Prince Cel with a fine and burning passion."

"We all knew that Andais was tormenting her guards and others of the court. She was very public about most of it, but I didn't know what Cel was doing with his guards. He was much more private about it."

"I think he hid it from his mother."

"She enjoys torturing people," I said.

"I've had more pillow talk about some of the horrors he did to the women, and I believe he was discreet because Andais might have stepped in and interfered with his fun."

"What's sauce for the goose is sauce for the gander," I said.

She shook her head. "No, Meredith, what Cel did to some of his private harem . . . I'm so glad you've found them a therapist."

"I'm glad they were willing to go."

"They didn't think they had a choice when they started."

"What?"

She smiled. "They thought you ordered them to go to therapy, and by the time they realized you hadn't meant it that way, most of them were benefiting from it, so they kept going."

"I would never order someone to go to therapy. I mean, you can order them to go the appointment, but you can't make them actually work their issues."

"You ordered them to talk to the therapist, and after what Cel did to them if they disobeyed him, or Andais did to anyone who disobeyed her, they worked their therapy as if their lives depended on it."

I shook my head and sighed. "They are all so much more damaged than I knew. Wait, is that why some of the female guards stopped going to therapy a few weeks ago?"

"Yes, they finally realized that you hadn't meant it as an order. A few of them tested to see if you meant it as a suggestion and when you didn't get angry about it, a few more stopped going."

"Most of them haven't stopped going," I said.

"As I said, Meredith, they worked hard at their therapy for fear of what you'd do to them if they didn't, and it worked strangely well for many of them."

"I didn't think you could force someone to do therapy like that."

"Neither did I, but it seems to be working for them."

I frowned, puzzling, and finally shook my head. "If it's working, it's working."

"You are surprisingly practical about very impractical things."

"Do I say thank you, or is that a problem?"

She smiled. "Neither, but the same guards who speak of Cel in hate-filled tones say wonderful things about your father. I think most of them are still in love with him, both as a good leader and as a man."

"I was actually thinking earlier that my family has more crazy than sane in it. Though you forgot that my grandmother was wonderful and caring, as were her parents, my great-grandmother and -grandfather."

"You're right, I did forget. Because your grandmother was half human and half brownie I counted her as less, but I shouldn't have, because it seems like the insanity comes from the sidhe side of things."

"We're not the most stable people," I said.

"I think it's living for so long, Meredith. Our bodies don't age, but maybe our minds do."

"Are you saying that Taranis and Andais have a version of dementia?"

"Maybe, though Cel wasn't that old by sidhe standards."

"I think Cel was always weak and twisted, but his mother indulged him, let him think he could do no wrong, and that cemented his crazy."

She studied me again as if looking for a flaw, or a hint, or something I couldn't guess at. "You are your father's daughter, and that is a good thing."

"I am my grandmother's, too, and that's a good thing as well."

"Yes, yes it is." She brushed off her hands as if brushing the topic away. "Let's go see the newest babies—though with Nicca and Biddy's daughter, Kadyi, and Liam, there are a lot of babies."

"Did you hear that Cathbodua and Usna are expecting?"

She looked startled, and then she laughed again. "No, I hadn't heard; that's wonderful and just fun, that the cat and the bird are having a baby."

"Andais said something similar, the cat and the crow."

Maeve's face sobered. "I would not be compared to the Queen of Air and Darkness in any way."

"I didn't mean to upset you."

She shivered, rubbing her hands up and down her arms. "It's all right, you didn't . . . it's just so many of us seem to go mad as the centuries pass, it makes me worry."

"Worry about what?" I asked.

"About my own sanity, I suppose."

"You have never shown any sign of the madness that haunts some of the noble lines of faerie."

"Oh, it's not just the noble lines, Meredith; some of the lesser fey are just as unpredictable, they just don't have the power of life and death to indulge their insanity."

It was my turn to study her. "What makes you say that?"

"The Fear Dearg, for one; you know we have one of them living here in Los Angeles."

"I've met him," I said.

She shuddered. "I remember the wars against them. It was like their entire race was as bad as Andais, Taranis, and Cel combined. It's why we took their magic away."

"The Fir Dhaeg said the sidhe also took their females, so though they live forever they're dead as a race."

She nodded, rubbing her arms again. "We could not work a spell to kill them, or destroy their evil entirely, but we destroyed what we could of them."

"The Fir Dhaeg said that I could give him back his name. That the curse the sidhe placed upon them could be cured by a royal chosen by Goddess and faerie."

"I do not know the details of the curse, but all curses must have a cure; it's part of the balance. Nothing is truly forever, nothing is that is made cannot be unmade, and that which is unmade has the possibility of being reborn."

"What happened to the Fir Dhaeg females? Doyle would not tell me details after we met the one here in L.A."

"We could not destroy them, Meredith, for they were as much a part of faerie as the sidhe, but we were able to kill them at a price."

"What price?" I asked.

"That we would take in their essence, absorb them. We would tie the Fir Dhaeg to the sidhe forever, so that if they reincarnated they would come back as one of us. The hope was that our bright blessings from the Goddess and Her Consort would cleanse their evil, but I wonder sometimes if the opposite happened."

"What do you mean?" I asked.

"I wonder sometimes if the Fir Dhaeg contaminated the sidhe with their darkness."

"Taranis and Andais were already king and queen by then; you can't blame their evil on the Fir Dhaeg."

"I suppose not, but I remember the day that it was done. The females didn't die; they faded and the energy went somewhere, Meredith. What if it went not into the land, or sky, or plants, or water, but into the ones that did the cursing? Andais was part of that spell; your father was not."

"You're saying that in cursing the Fir Dhaeg, Andais may have . . . what, become one herself?"

Maeve shrugged. "Maybe, or maybe she was mad even then and we just hadn't realized it."

"Faerie chose her to be queen of the Unseelie Court, so she was fit to rule once," I said.

"She was a great war leader, so yes, she was fit once."

"Have you discussed your theory with anyone else?"

"No, by the time I thought of it I was in exile. I had a lot of time to think upon old things while I was alone."

"I'll share your theory with Doyle and see what he thinks."

"Remember that he was a part of the spell, too."

"Doyle is not evil," I said.

"I didn't say he was, but being around evil changes a person, even if you're killing it on the battlefield."

I tried to read her face and couldn't. "Why tell me this?"

"I don't know; perhaps I've wanted to tell someone my idea for a very long time."

"You lived in the high court of faerie for centuries, Maeve, and then in Hollywood for decades; you don't say things without understanding how it will affect people, or how you hope it will affect people, so what's your point? Why tell me? Why now?"

"I don't know, and that is the honest answer; it just seemed time."

I shook my head. "I wish I believed that."

"I would never mean to make you doubt Doyle."

I laughed then. "I don't doubt Doyle; nothing you could say would make me do that."

She controlled her face, but for just a moment I saw she was unhappy. Why would she want to divide me from Doyle? Out loud I said, "Do you have an old grudge against Doyle?"

"Why would you say that?"

"He's been the left hand of the queen for centuries, and their court was often at war with yours, so just answer the question. Do you have a grudge against him?"

"If I had to choose a king to follow I would prefer the energy of sunlight and life, not darkness and death."

"Doyle was who faerie crowned as my king."

"Your Unseelie king," she said.

I nodded. "And faerie crowned me Sholto's Queen of the Sluagh."

She couldn't hide her distaste. "They are the stuff of nightmares."

"True, but the Goddess saw fit to make me their queen all the same."

"I would wonder who faerie would choose for you if it were the Seelie throne you were sitting upon, or a new throne of faerie. Who would be that king for you, Meredith?"

"Since we gave up the crowns that faerie offered us, and I can't go back to visit Sholto's kingdom for fear of Taranis, I don't think it matters. I think I've turned down too many thrones for the Goddess to offer me another."

The first pink rose petal fell from empty air and floated down between us. We watched it fall slowly to the floor.

"You are surrounded by miracles, Meredith."

"The Goddess blesses me with Her presence."

"I think She's happy to have someone worth blessing again."

Rose petals began to fall like a flurry of candy-colored snow. I stood in the center of it holding my hands up, raising my face toward the fall of petals. I thanked the Goddess for Her attention and Her blessing, and the rose petals fell faster until it was a blizzard of cotton candy petals.

Maeve Reed, the Golden Goddess of Hollywood, once the goddess Conchenn, fell to her knees and began to weep.

TWENTY-SIX

By the time Maeve recovered herself, the rose petals had almost stopped falling. Only a few of them trailed me to the nursery, like pink snow flurries. Two of the new Diplomatic Security Services, or DSS, guards had trailed us from outside Maeve's bedroom to here; now they stood at the door in bodyguard pose, one hand holding a wrist, or just arms free, but strangely at attention. They were on duty while all the rest of the guards were at blade and hand-to-hand training. The human guards had tried to participate, but the difference in strength and speed had made it . . . awkward. Though some of the humans had persisted.

It also meant that the only people left to tend the babies were human. Liam came running to us as we entered the triplets' nursery. "Mommy! Come see, babies!" he yelled, and grabbed Maeve's finger so he could drag her farther into the room.

Her whole face lit up, not with magic, but with happiness that he'd run to her, not me. She'd been spending as much time with him as she could in the last few days, and just like that, he was running to her more. A tightness I hadn't realized was there eased as I watched him pull her forward.

One nanny was diapering Gwenwyfar on the changing table. Alastair was in his crib with most of the dogs crowded around it, and him. Liam's nanny, Rita, was in one of the two rocking chairs, holding Bryluen, and that was where the little boy led Maeve. Rita's dark head was bent low, giving only a glimpse of her smile, as she gazed down at the baby. Rita was short for Margarita, and she was a pretty, dark, older woman, very shy. She rarely spoke and when she did, she didn't like to hold eye contact. I wasn't sure if she was just naturally that shy, or if it was being in the presence of Hollywood stars and princes and princesses of faerie. Danika, the second nanny, was as tall as Maeve with thick blond hair that fell to the tops of her shoulders. She did a serious yoga workout every day, and used the weights when the guards weren't in the room. She hadn't bulked up, just made her curves more firm. She moved with a physicality that reminded me of the guards. Apparently she'd gone through college on an athletic scholarship, and the habit of it hadn't left her. Rita was only a few inches taller than me, in her early forties, and had given up the fight for the gym a few years ago, so she was just comfortably round. She'd been a nanny when she was Danika's age, but a divorce had forced her out to work again. It had also made her interested in live-in positions like this one.

How did I know all this? Galen had told me; he'd apparently won her confidence with all his time in the nursery. She'd never seen a man who loved his children so much, and she'd informed me I was a lucky woman.

Danika glanced up and said, with a smile, "Ms. Reed, Princess Meredith."

"Hello, Danika. Hello, Rita," I said.

Maeve said, "Rita, are you all right?"

I walked farther into the room so I could see Rita more clearly around Maeve's tall form. Rita kept smiling and rocking Bryluen but never looked up at Maeve. In fact, she didn't react at all, as if she hadn't noticed us come into the room.

"Rita, Rita!" Maeve raised her voice a little.

"Bree likes 'ita to rock her," Liam said.

Maeve waved her hand between Rita's face and Bryluen's gaze. The nanny didn't react. Maeve kept her hand above the baby's face, completely blocking them both from looking at each other.

"Rita, can you hear us?" I asked.

Danika walked toward us holding Gwenwyfar. "What's wrong with her?"

"Rita!" Maeve said sharply, her hand still held between them.

Rita startled, almost as if she'd been asleep, her arms starting to unfold as if to drop Bryluen, but she recovered instantly and held the baby closer. The baby started to fuss.

"What's wrong? Did I doze off? I'm so sorry, Ms. Reed, I've never done that before."

Maeve straightened up. "It's okay, Rita, I know . . . it's not your fault."

"But I fell asleep with the baby in my arms." She looked at me. "I am so sorry, Princess, so sorry, I would never . . ."

"It's okay, Rita, honestly," I said.

She was completely beside herself, thinking she'd nearly dropped Bryluen because she fell asleep. I waited for Maeve to explain, but she didn't, and I didn't either. I wasn't sure how to explain it, and I definitely didn't want the media to know that one of the triplets was already so magically powerful that she could bespell people with her gaze. No, that bit of information was not something I wanted in the tabloids.

Maeve told Danika to take Rita to her room and make her take a short nap. Maeve took Bryluen from her. I took Gwenwyfar from her, so she could escort the still-apologizing Rita away.

Liam said, "Bree likes 'ita."

We looked down at the little boy. "Does Bryluen like Rita better than Danika?" I asked.

He nodded.

"Why does she like her better?"

He looked very serious, as if he were thinking hard, then said, "'ita plays."

"Rita plays more than Danika," I said.

He nodded, smiling.

"Do you and Bryluen tell Rita what to play?"

"Bree does," he said, smiling.

"And does Rita always play the way Bree wants?"

He nodded solemnly.

Maeve looked down at the baby in her arms. "Her gaze has a weight to it, Meredith."

"What do you mean?"

"I can resist it, but she just seems such a beautiful child. It's peaceful to look at her."

"It's a compulsion, isn't it?"

Maeve nodded, face very serious, as she looked at me. "We'll interview some nonhuman nannies. I'll call the agency and see if they have any available. If they don't have any, then we should ask in the larger fey community."

"Agreed, and until we find someone, Rita shouldn't help take care of the triplets anymore," I said.

Bryluen started to fuss, and Maeve rocked her back and forth. The baby quieted almost immediately, big eyes growing sleepy. "None of the humans should be around her much, Meredith."

"How did you know that Bryluen likes to be rocked that way, side to side, not up and down?"

Maeve stared down at the tiny baby. "I . . . I don't know. I just knew that's what she wanted."

"Can you stop rocking her?" I asked.

Maeve stopped, and Bree started to fuss; more rocking and the fussing stopped again. "She cries every time I stop."

"Try stopping anyway," I said.

Maeve tried, but eventually she started again. "No, I can't stop, not for long."

We stared at each other and for the first time I was afraid of Bryluen, because magic usually gets more powerful with age. She was only a week old; what would she be like in a few years?

"Maybe none of us should take care of Bree by ourselves," I said, softly.

Maeve went to the crib with the most pink on it. It had been purchased while I was in the hospital, and Kitto had let the clerk talk him into pink ribbons and little lambs. She was able to lay Bree down, but the moment she started fussing Maeve moved to pick her up.

"Don't pick her up," I said, and I held Gwenwyfar closer to me.

Maeve turned away, but the baby began to cry and she turned back.

Liam was at the crib now. "Pick her up, Mommy, she wants up."

Maeve picked Liam up and held him so he could see into the crib better. She was able to walk away with the toddler in her arms, but he wasn't happy.

"Mommy, pick Bree up, not me!" He started to push to be put down. She let him down and he ran to the crying baby. She turned to go in that direction, too.

"Pick Alastair up," I said.

She went to my quietly sleeping son and lifted him slowly. He slept through it, though the dogs began to whine around her feet, especially his puppy.

Maeve turned to me. "I can resist her demands now."

Liam had his tiny hand through the crib bars and had her hand in his. "Up, Bree. Up, Mommy!"

Maeve and I looked at each other. "She's only a week old, Meredith."

"I know."

"If it gets worse, stronger . . ."

"I know," I said.

"Why does holding the other babies act as charm against it?" she asked.

"I don't know."

"There have been stories of some being so beautiful from babyhood on that all that saw them were entranced, but I thought that was an exaggeration; now I'm not so sure."

"Do we have anyone here who was that compelling, this young?"

She held Alastair close, and thought. "Aisling. Stories tell how people loved him even as a baby."

"I saw one of our women claw her own eyes out, so he couldn't control her with his beauty."

"A human woman?"

"No."

"Lesser fey?"

"No, sidhe."

Maeve shivered, so violently that Alastair protested with a small cry. His puppy came and whimpered at her feet. "Did it work?" she asked.

"Did what work?"

"Did scratching out her own eyes stop him from having power over her?"

"She was able to stop answering questions truthfully, but she was still besotted with him, still magically infatuated. He told her the last sight she would ever see, ever remember, was his face, and she wept. She wept into her hands all blood and gore." I raised Gwenwyfar so I could smell the top of her head, that clean, pure smell that seemed to make everything all right.

"He was forbidden to use his charms in battle; it was deemed too horrible to make your enemy love you," Maeve said.

"I didn't really understand what his power was. I mean, I knew the stories, why he was veiled, but I didn't really understand until it was too late. I agree, some things are too terrible to use."

"You wield the hands of flesh and blood, Meredith. They are two of the most horrifying powers the sidhe have ever commanded. How can it be more terrible than that?"

"It's not lust, but love, obsession that he causes. She screamed when she saw him, when they kissed, as if it were the most horrible sight in the world. I never want to order anything done that causes that sound from another person."

"She was part of a group that was trying to kill you and the men you love, Meredith; you had no choice."

"It's pretty to think so, but in the end there are always choices, Maeve. People decide what lines they will not cross, I just found another one, that's all."

"You look haunted, Meredith."

I nodded. "I don't feel bad about much that I've done, or had others do, but that one bothers me."

Maeve came and used one arm to hug me to her, so that she encircled the babies and me in her arms. "I am sorry for that then, Meredith, truly sorry."

I realized I was crying, and wasn't sure why; maybe it was postbaby hormones, or maybe the thought that my wonderful babies, my children, might have frightening magic hadn't occurred to me. Most magic didn't manifest in the sidhe until puberty, but both girls had already shown power. Gwenwyfar with her lightning birthmark that actually caused a sort of static shock sometimes, and Bree with this, whatever this was. I held Gwenwyfar and pressed my head against the sweetness of Alastair's dark hair, and wept while Maeve Reed, the Golden Goddess of Hollywood, held me. In the end, faerie princess or box office queen didn't matter as much as being two women, two mothers, two friends. Maeve joined me in the tears, and I doubted she could have said why she was crying either.

TWENTY-SEVEN

left Maeve in the nursery to make sure Bryluen didn't bespell the nannies, and went in search of the fathers who were doing the most baby duty. I wanted to know if they'd had any problems, or noticed that Rita was being manipulated by our baby daughter. The guards were doing weights, weapons practice, and hand-to-hand, in separate groups, so I went to the weight room first. It was easier to ask questions there.

I had two guards with me, because I went nowhere without them since Taranis had kidnapped me. I couldn't complain about the extra security, but it meant that some of the guard had to miss the workouts at times. Saraid and Dogmaela paced just behind me and to each side. Saraid's hair was as glitteringly gold as Frost's hair was silver; her eyes were blue with a white starburst around the pupil, as if someone had drawn a shining white star in the middle of the blue of her iris. Dogmaela's more ordinary yellow hair seemed pale compared to the glittering braids that Saraid could boast, and her eyes, three rings of green and gray, seemed almost human-normal, but they were both tall and slender with fine muscles showing in their bare arms. Saraid was six feet even, and Dogmaela two inches shorter at five-ten. Her yellow hair flowed free, held back from her face by a metal helmet that was so not modern, but if no one made her wear modern equipment Dogmaela had a habit of reverting back to more familiar things. She did keep her sidearm, a modern Beretta .45, and according to Doyle she was one of the most accurate with a pistol. She liked her helmet and her familiar sword at her side, but she'd embraced the modern weapons wholeheartedly. Except for the color of her hair and eyes, Saraid looked like a very modern Hollywood model/actress in skinny jeans tucked into knee-high boots, and a tailored mannish suit jacket that didn't quite hide the sword she had strapped to her back, but distracted the eye from the two guns and extra ammunition that fit along her long, slender torso.

The women stayed outside the door, as the other guards had stayed outside the nursery. Rhys and other guards were inside the weight room, and that meant that the workout areas were one of the safest places in the house and grounds.

There was a big sign over the door to the weight room. It read, *IF YOU DON'T KNOW HOW TO USE A MACHINE, ASK FOR HELP. DO NOT BREAK THE MACHINES! THIS MEANS EVERYONE: SIDHE, RED CAPS, GOBLINS, DEMI-FEY, EVERYONE!*

I knew Rhys had made the sign after one of the Red Caps had stripped all the cables out of one machine, and one of the newer sidhe guards had damaged another, all in the same week. I could hear his voice without even going through the doorway, not the words he was speaking, but the rhythm of his voice. The room had been a ballroom back in the day when houses had them, because it was the only room with ceilings tall enough for the Red Caps, since they averaged between seven and thirteen feet tall. Maeve had let us buy what Rhys felt was needed for training the guards, so the once-elegant ballroom was filled with state-of-the-art padding, enough free weights to make Mr. Universe happy, and a forest of machines. The latter were mostly mysterious to me, because they'd been purchased after I got pregnant. I'd never spent a lot of time with weights, but I'd been forbidden to use anything but the lightest hand weights for so long that it was like a foreign land to me now. The machines were all taller than me, with interchangeable handles, pulleys, and attachables, and I had no idea what most of them did. I wasn't the only one overwhelmed by Rhys's fully equipped room.

"How can you use all this cold iron?" a woman's voice protested. I could glimpse Rhys through the maze of machines, but the woman was sitting down and I couldn't tell from her voice who it was, over the machines' mechanical clatter and the clink of the weights.

I nodded to the guards as I walked past. I'd learned that etiquette in the weight room meant you didn't say hello when someone was lifting, unless they spoke first. If they were into the zone of their workout, just having to talk too much could throw them out of it. Rhys had explained all this to me. I'd never lifted weights seriously enough to experience a "zone," but I trusted Rhys to know what he was talking about.

Most of the guards in the room were the newer ones who had only come from faerie in the last few months, but they were all tall and slender, with a play of muscles under their mostly pale arms, long legs moving the leg press machine easily. I didn't usually still feel like the short ugly duckling, but seeing them in the tank tops and shorts, or even just sports bras for some of the women, I suddenly felt far too round, and much too short, and just awkward as I walked across the special padded floor in my three-inch heels. I'd felt pretty good about myself until that moment, and then it was as if all the childhood years of being told I wasn't sidhe enough came spilling back. No one had said anything, or even lifted an eyebrow at me; sometimes it's just the inside of your own head that is the problem.

I squared my shoulders, made sure my posture was perfect, and kept walking toward Rhys with a smile on my face. My insecurities in that moment were my own.

Of course, I wasn't the only one who didn't look like everyone else. There were three Red Caps in the room, too. They were all between seven feet, short for a Red Cap, and thirteen feet, which was almost as tall as they got. The tallest and the shortest were shades of gray, but the middle one was the yellow of aged ivory. I wasn't close enough to see their true red eyes, but they were Red Caps; the eyes would be scarlet. The yellow-skinned one was Clesek, but I couldn't recall the names of the other two. They all wore the short, round caps that gave them their name, but right now the caps weren't red, more brown, the color of dried blood. They were all stuffed into sweat suits that strained to fit over their bodies. It was like trying to find workout clothes for the Incredible Hulk. They'd originally worked out in their undergarments, but Maeve had too many humans working in the house and they were uncomfortable with nearly nude giants striding through the hallways. They were in the far corner using the special free-weight bars that we'd had to get, so they could carry more weight than regular barbells without breaking; I hadn't even known that there were special bars to hold weights once you got up to four to five hundred pounds and more. The fact that human beings with no fey ancestry needed special bars like that amazed me a little, and made me feel even weaker. I was so not the strongest person in this room, not in any way.

I heard Rhys say, "The metal makes us have to work harder, because not all our magic works."

The woman's voice: "It's harder than I thought it would be."

"Good," he said.

The Red Caps saw me and dropped their weights with a clang that vibrated the room as they went down on one knee. They didn't have to do that during exercise, I'd told them all that, but the Red Caps were very devoted.

I stopped and called out to them. "It's all right, you don't have to bow in the weight room, remember?"

"You are our queen, we must show proper respect," Clesek said. He gave a narrow-eyed stare at the sidhe. "They should show it, too."

"It's dangerous in the weight room, Clesek; we discussed this," I said.

"Which of you dropped it?" Rhys yelled it, as he came striding through the machines wearing midthigh-length compression shorts and a tank top that was more straps than shirt so that the muscled beauty of his upper body was more revealed than hidden by it. The shorts showed off assets, too, but in the gym you were supposed to be paying attention to other things. His hair was back in a ponytail held by multiple hair ties spaced a few inches apart along its length so that it was almost a braid, but not quite.

Since he was six inches taller than me, I didn't think of him as short, but as he went for the Red Caps, he looked small. It made me wonder how tiny I looked standing next to the biggest of the goblins.

His voice boomed out, filling the room. One of the visiting human soldiers had called it a drill sergeant voice. "You do not drop the weights! If you have to drop the weights, then it's too heavy for you, and you do what?" He was pressed nearly into the Red Cap's chest, but his voice thundered through the suddenly quiet room. Everyone had stopped exercising to see someone else get dressed down.

The Red Cap mumbled something.

Rhys did that big voice again. "I can't hear you!"

"Lower the weights. But it wasn't too heavy for me. We needed to show respect to Queen Meredith," the Red Cap said. He looked sullen. His scarlet eyes narrowed in an unfriendly manner, though part of it was the color. Bloodred eyes with no whites in them could make the Red Caps look angry, or at least unfriendly, easily and often.

"But the humans on TV just let the heaviest barbells drop," one of the other Red Caps said. This one was a gray so pale that he was almost white. He also had one of the most human of faces, not exactly handsome, but not the frightening fanged expression that most of them had once had.

Rhys turned and got up in the face of the second Red Cap. It was almost funny to see the huge Red Cap's shoulders slump, head ducking, shame-faced at the much smaller man's angry rant.

I heard one of the sidhe closest to me say, "She's not our queen yet."

I turned and found one of the very newest refugees from faerie. Our policy had been to take in any fey who wanted to leave faerie and come to the Western Lands, but a few of the recent sidhe were making me doubt the wisdom of that.

Fenella was just a fraction under six feet tall, with hair that fell like a gold and yellow cloak to her ankles when it was unbound; now it was in two long braids that had been looped back in upon themselves so they glittered as she moved, one moment more gold, the next like sunshine spun into rope, with the beauty of her face shining through the light and jewel-bright glory of her hair. She wasn't called Fenella of the Shining

Hair for nothing. She blinked her tricolored eyes at me. At first you thought her eyes were white with two circles of yellow shades, until you realized that the white around her pupil was actually an incredibly light yellow like winter sunlight, then butter, and the brighter yellow autumn leaves. I'd always thought that her eyes would have looked better with less spectacular hair, or that she needed eyes that were as amazing as the hair.

"Do you have something to say to me, Fenella?" I asked.

"No, Princess, I do not."

"If you will not say it to my face, then please refrain from saying it behind my back."

She startled, as if too caught off guard to hide it under centuries of courtly manners, or maybe I wasn't worth the effort.

"Will you not allow us any privacy, even to our own thoughts?"

"Your thoughts are your own, but when they spill out your lips and I can hear, they are no longer private."

"Very well, Princess Meredith. I find it disquieting that the goblins bow to you and call you queen when you are not a queen . . . yet."

"I am not the official goblin queen, that is true, but I am Queen of the Sluagh."

A look of distaste flitted across her face. "There was a rumor that you were Shadowspawn's queen, but those of us in the Seelie Court had not believed it."

"First, never call King Sholto by that name again; you know it is an insult. Second, why not believe it?"

"You are of the same bloodline as our king. It is a pure sidhe line, and even your mother's lineage speaks to the light, but I suppose you cannot help the corruption of your father's blood."

"Are you trying to be insulting?" I asked.

She looked surprised, and I was almost certain it was genuine. She just didn't understand the insult. "I have given offense; I am sorry, Princess, but your mother speaks endlessly of the corruption and vileness of your father, so I assumed that you felt the same."

"And if I did, then why would I have stayed at my father's vile and corrupt court, when I could have been with my mother at the Seelie Court?"

Fenella seemed to think about that, and watching her eyes while she did it, I realized something I hadn't before. She wasn't that bright, not stupid by any means, but not a deep thinker. Sometimes I thought that Taranis wasn't that deep a thinker either; maybe his court reflected that?

Then a smooth voice came from the other side of the tall machine. "Most of us never blamed you for preferring to rule in hell, rather than serve in heaven, Princess."

Trancer was inches above six feet, maybe six-five, and thin, even by sidhe standards, as if he'd been stretched just a little too much. His arms looked firm, but not muscled. If he'd been human you could have taken it to mean he wasn't very strong, but among the fey, even the sidhe, what you saw was not what you got.

"My father loved me, my mother didn't; a child goes where she's loved," I said.

"Love. What do the Unseelie know about love?" Fenella said.

Trancer touched her arm, and I watched her think about why he'd just cautioned her with that touch. I looked up into his tri-blue eyes. His hair was a more ordinary golden brown, waving just below his shoulders. The Seelie men let the women have the longer hair.

How many times had Trancer had to save his wife from speaking out of turn, or too boldly? How many centuries had he minded her, protected her from herself? I spoke to him, as I said, "Love is very important to most of us, don't you agree, Lord Trancer?"

He gave me a long look. "Yes, Princess Meredith, we do."

"I just don't see why we have to exercise," Fenella said, and there was a childish whine to her voice that went along with the lack of understanding I'd seen in her eyes.

Rhys said, "Because all of the guards exercise, that's the rule."

"But we were never guards," she protested.

"Now, dearest," Trancer said, "you know that we have to find a way to be useful."

"I can set a fine table, and host a banquet, but I don't think I will be very good at guarding anyone with strength of arms. Magic has always been enough in the past."

Secretly I agreed with her, but I was letting Rhys and Doyle handle what to do with the fey who were seeking refuge with us. We had so many now that we did need them to pull their weight, but I doubted sincerely if I would ever trust Fenella to guard me or mine from anything. I would reserve judgment on Trancer, but . . . I wondered how well Fenella had done at weapons practice. What do you do with immortal beings whose major talents were being beautiful courtiers and toadies? What use were they in modern Los Angeles? I suppose that there were Hollywood equivalents of the job description, but Lady Fenella and Lord Trancer wouldn't know the modern world enough to adapt, and I wasn't a big one for sycophants, maybe because I'd never been powerful enough to have any, and now I didn't trust them.

"Then think of it as getting into practice for losing the baby weight."

"I won't need that," Fenella said.

"I thought you came into exile in the Western Lands so that you could get pregnant," Rhys said. He put an arm across my shoulders, drawing me in against his body. I slid my arm around his waist automatically, and just holding and being held helped me feel less short, less round, less bad about the changes in my body since the babies. The circle of Rhys's arms eased most of the anxiety that had started. Was it baby hormones still? It wasn't like me to allow anyone to make me feel that unhappy with myself.

"We did," Trancer said, beginning to rub his hand in small circles on his wife's back.

"Then getting a habit of exercise will help her get her girlish figure back afterward," Rhys said, smiling.

"But I will not need to exercise to lose my weight. It will just go."

"I may have lost my weight faster than most human women, but I'll still have to exercise when the doctor clears me for it."

"But you're much shorter than me, and I'm told that makes it much harder to lose weight."

"I don't think it's just about height," a voice said. It was Biddy just coming into the gym. She was six feet of broad shoulders and muscles, even after having her baby only two months ahead of my triplets. She was built more like a very tall human, and she put on muscle better than most of the sidhe, even the men, but then she was half human. Her hair was cut very short in a mass of brown curls. She'd chosen to cut it when she refused the late Prince Cel, and had been warrior enough and willing to do enough damage to make her *no* stick. She'd told me she'd keep her hair short to remind herself that she was stronger than she knew, and that no one would ever hurt her again.

"I'm having to work to get back to my fighting weight. I guess after three hundred years the metabolism slows down," she said with a grin.

"You're half human; I'm not," Fenella said.

"You know, Fenella, I'm beginning to wonder why you left faerie," I said.

Those yellow eyes narrowed. "I came here to get with child, not to sweat and guard . . . you."

Trancer's hand stopped moving in those small useless circles on her back. His smile looked frozen. "Now, dearest . . ."

"Merry had triplets. The last set of triplets among the sidhe was at least eight hundred years ago," Biddy said. Her solid brown eyes, so very human, were darkening with the beginnings of anger. She would get angry for me.

"Yes, triplets, like a litter of dogs," Fenella said.

Biddy said, "Bitch."

"Exactly," Fenella said.

Rhys made a small movement forward, but I held him tighter around the waist.

I didn't need to be protected; I had the power to do it myself now. "You know, Fenella, if you don't want to be one of my guard, that's fine; I don't think you're suited to the position."

"I can stop lifting these things?" She motioned at the weights.

"Yes, and in fact pack your bags and go back to the beach house."

"There is no fairyland at the beach house. It's just ordinary land."

"Princess Meredith, my wife didn't mean . . ." Trancer began.

I held up a hand and stopped him midsentence. "The beach house is lovely all year round, and maybe going back there will remind your wife that all the fairyland around this house is here because of me."

"The Goddess returned Her blessing to us," Fenella said.

"No," Biddy said, "the Goddess returned Her blessing to Merry, and Merry shares it with the rest of us." She stood very tall, looking down at the other woman from where she still sat on the front of the weight machine.

Fenella opened her mouth again, but Trancer actually put a fingertip against her lower lip. "My love, we will go to the beach house, as the princess bids. She is, after all, the ruler here in the Western Lands."

Fenella pouted with her lips still against his finger, but she didn't try to talk again, which was a relief at this point. She was the perfect example of exactly why I hadn't tried to stay at the Seelie Court. Yes, she was less astute than some of the nobles, but her attitude was about average. I wasn't pure enough, sidhe enough, and more than the Unseelie, the Seelie put great stock in physical purity.

"Pack and go, now," Rhys said, voice low. His skin began to hum with power, and about the time I noticed that, I could see the white glow of his power sliding almost cloudlike under his skin. I glanced upward and saw that the three circles of blue had begun to swirl, as his magic began to unsheathe itself.

"We will, my lord," Trancer said. He got his wife to her feet and began to ease out from among the machines and us. I realized that "us" didn't just include Biddy. The three Red Caps were looming behind us like the mountains were on our side, my side. I reached my free hand out and touched the closest Red Cap, who happened to be Clesek. I wanted them to know how much I valued them, and had since the night they risked themselves in battle to help me save the men I loved.

Clesek's cap was suddenly a bright scarlet instead of the dried brown it had been. The first thin trickle of blood began to drip down the side of his face from his round skullcap. The Red Caps had once dipped their caps in fresh blood often enough to keep them scarlet, but random slaughter for dipping purposes had been forbidden since the fey immigrated to America. I'd known that to be a war leader among them you had to have enough magic to cause your cap to bleed on its own, but what I hadn't known was that a sidhe with the hand of blood could give them back that ability and make all their caps bleed. That was why they called me their queen, and why they bowed, and why they had risked everything to help me, and had joined me in exile here.

Fenella hissed, "Unclean, Unseelie magic that."

I stopped touching Clesek, because I didn't want him to bleed enough to get the new padded floor bloody, but I'd had enough of the Seelie for today. "Yes, yes it is Unseelie magic, Fenella, and you might want to remember that the next time you insult me."

"Are you threatening me?"

Trancer tried to pull her toward the door, saying, "Hush, my dearest."

"Yes, yes, I think I am. I can come to you as a goddess of fertility and joy, or I can come as the dark goddess who brings the winter and kills the crops. That was the face of the goddess that the Seelie brought down upon themselves, centuries ago. You have learned nothing." And that last sentence echoed in the room in a way that human voices did not. Pink and white rose petals began to fall from thin air around me, Rhys, Biddy, and the Red Caps, but the fall of flowers stopped short of the two Seelie nobles.

Their eyes went wide and I saw fear on their faces. "She meant nothing by it, Princess, please."

"She meant everything by it, Trancer." My voice was almost mine, just the faintest echo of the Goddess around the edges of my words.

"We will pack and we will go to the edge of the sea, and await your pleasure to bid us return to this new bit of faerie," he said, pulling his wife backward toward the doorway.

"You do that," I said. The petals were thick as a snowstorm, but spring warm, so that I watched their frightened faces leave through a pink snowfall.

"It is not our place to say so, but they do not deserve your blessing," Clesek said.

Rhys hugged me. "I love you, our Merry, just as you are." And just like that, I started to cry again; stupid baby hormones. The rose petals fell so fast it was like being inside some magical snow globe that had been shaken by a giant. What did the Christians say—if God be with me, then who can be against me? That was true, but it still hurt to know that no matter how many wonders I performed, I would always and forever be too short, too human, too Unseelie for the most of the Golden Court to ever accept me. But then hadn't six out of sixteen of the Unseelie noble houses been against me the last time I stood in open court there, too? If the Goddess herself could not make them see their own bigotry, then there was no cure for it.

There was a soft kiss on my cheek. I looked up and found that Rhys's face was pressed to the top of my hair, and no one else was close. The Goddess had kissed my tears like my own mother never had. I whispered my thanks, and the petals began to slow. I was almost ankle deep in petals now; that was enough.

CHAPTER

TWENTY-EIGHT

Rhys and Biddy both offered to escort me to the outdoor area where Doyle was conducting the hand-to-hand training, but I told Rhys to stay and supervise the weight training. Biddy wasn't on full duty yet, and she helped run the household along with her husband, Nicca. I didn't want to put her back on guard duty; it wasn't where she was best used. Both of them were content when they realized Saraid and Dogmaela were just outside the door.

Rhys kissed me good-bye and gave me over to the two female guards. I'd already asked him my question, and he'd had no problem with Bryluen, and the two human nannies weren't needed when he, Galen, and Kitto were on duty, so he hadn't seen them with the littlest of our babes. It was interesting that Maeve and I both felt Bryluen's magic, but Rhys didn't. He was a death deity, and Maeve and I were both fertility, sex, and love. If that made us more susceptible to my daughter's glamour, then Galen would also have an issue, but Doyle and Frost might not. Come to think of it, Galen was the only one of the fathers who was spring and fertility, though he wasn't as close to Maeve's and my magic as a couple of the other guards. Adair and Amatheon weren't fathers, or my lovers anymore, but their magic was closest; I might see how they fared babysitting if Galen had more issues than the other fathers. If he didn't, then

I might ask one of the female sidhe and see if Bryluen had more power over women, though I couldn't think why she should.

"If you don't mind me saying so, Princess Meredith, you seem unusually solemn," Saraid said.

I glanced at her and smiled. "I don't mind, Saraid."

"You have everything any woman could want, and more; what do you have to be so sad about?" Dogmaela said.

"Dogmaela," Saraid said, making a caution of the other woman's name.

"No, it's all right, Saraid, truly. I may not answer the question, but you can all ask me anything."

"That is a most democratic attitude, Princess," Saraid said.

"I may be a faerie princess, but I'm also American. We tend to like democracy."

"I've been following your politicians in the media," Dogmaela said, "and I do not find all of them very democratic. In fact, many of them seem as if they would be happy to have a dictatorship if they could be in charge."

I laughed. "Very accurate of some of them, I grant you that."

"Well, you laughed, so that's a good thing," Dogmaela said, and she smiled. She was one of the guards who had gone to therapy with the same work ethic she'd applied to learning to shoot modern firearms.

Saraid had been one of the women who stopped going to therapy when she found out it wasn't mandatory.

"Is Uther coming over this week for movie night?" I asked.

Saraid ducked her head and grinned, that special stupid-faced, almost drunkenly happy grin. I loved seeing it on that angelically beautiful face, because Uther had been my friend back in the days when I'd been hiding as just plain Merry Gentry, a human with some fey ancestry. He'd been one of my coworkers at the Grey Detective Agency for three lonely years while I hid in L.A. on the shores of the Western Sea to keep my cousin, Cel, and his friends from killing me. Uther Squarefoot was the legal name on his license, and he was thirteen feet tall, with magnificent curling tusks, and a face that was almost more wild boar than human. He was a Jack-in-Irons, one of the solitary faeries, but still of the Unseelie Court, because the Seelie Court wouldn't touch any fey who was ugly. But Saraid had found in Uther the first gentleness she'd known in a man for centuries. He had found in her the wonderment of being loved by a truly beautiful woman. There were only two Jacks-in-Irons in the entire United States, and no one had ever seen a female one, so Uther had been lonely in a way that mere friendship couldn't fix. When he'd found out I was sidhe, he'd very politely asked me to help him break his fast for female companionship, but I was mortal and not sure I could survive his attentions. I wasn't sure what Saraid and he did together on their dates, but whatever it was satisfied them both, and they'd been a couple for almost six months.

"He is, my lady."

"Good," I said.

She gave me a shy smile, those star eyes full of a contentment that I had feared I might never see in the faces of the women who had been abused by my cousin. It made me smile back.

"You are truly pleased when the people around you are happy, aren't you, Princess?" Dogmaela said.

I glanced back at her. "Yes, I am."

She shook her head. "You are your father's daughter, Meredith, and it is a blessing for us all."

I touched her arm. "If I had known that none of you had been given a choice to go from serving my father to serving Cel, I would have tried to free you sooner."

Dogmaela looked frightened. "Oh, Meredith, no, the evil bastard was already trying to kill you through his toadies; if you had tried to take us away from him years ago, he would have seen you dead, or worse." She patted my shoulder. "No, things happened as they were meant to, and now we are here and you are the ruler your father hoped you would be."

I stopped walking, so they did, too. I looked at both of them. They'd been part of my father's personal guard, the Prince's Cranes, for centuries, and certainly through my childhood, but it had never occurred to me that they would know something I'd wanted to ask my father.

"People keep asking me why my father trained me to be a ruler when it seemed I would never wear a crown. I had no answer, but you were there. You were his guard, his confidants—did he intend me to take the throne, do you know?"

Dogmaela shook her head. "I was not a close favorite of Prince Essus, so I do not know what was in his heart."

Saraid was very quiet, face careful and empty.

"You know something; please tell me."

"He raised you the only way he knew, and that was to be a ruler, Princess Meredith, but he did not plan on assassinating his sister, your aunt, or her son, his nephew, to put you on the throne."

"What did he intend for me then?"

"I was closer to him, but he did not confide in me about you, except to worry for your safety. He spoke of you getting your doctorate in biology of some kind and being the first American-fey doctor; that thought pleased him."

I smiled, and nodded. "He wanted me to be a doctor at one point, a medical doctor."

"I believe that course of study takes many years by human standards; that seems to imply he did not plan on you vying for the throne."

I nodded. "I think you're right, but he told his sister that I would be a better queen than Cel would ever be a king."

"I heard him tell her that," Dogmaela said, "and she was furious with him. Had it been anyone but Prince Essus, he would have been tortured for such talk."

"She always did have a soft spot for her brother," Saraid said.

"She was afraid of him," Dogmaela said.

"No," Saraid said.

"She feared his power, Saraid. She knew he was one of the few in the courts strong enough to take the throne from her."

"To kill her, you mean," Saraid said.

"Yes, that is what I mean."

"My father loved his sister, and she loved her brother," I said.

They looked at me.

"They were devoted to each other, in their own ways," Saraid said. We all just agreed.

"If only he hadn't loved his nephew," Dogmaela said.

"He might still be alive to see his grandchildren," I said, and the thought made my chest tight, my eyes hot.

"But if our prince, your father, had lived, these would not be the grandchildren he would see," Dogmaela said.

I looked at her.

"You speak nonsense, Dogmaela."

"No, Saraid, if Prince Essus had lived, then Meredith would never have had to hide in the Western Lands, and the queen would never have sent Doyle to find her. He would never have brought her back to be guarded and bedded by the Queen's Ravens, so she would never have had sex with them, or fallen in love with Frost and Galen, and well, all of them. For that matter, if she'd gone on to be a doctor, would she have been able to bring the Goddess's blessing back to us, or would we all still be slowly fading as a people?"

Saraid and I stared at her. I wanted to say, *Dogmaela, you're a deep, philosophical thinker; I didn't know that.* But that seemed vaguely insulting, as if I'd thought her stupid before, and I hadn't, but . . . "Are you saying that my father had to die for me to help bring life back to faerie?"

"It's something I've talked to the therapist about, and yes, I think so. I would never have traded our prince, your father, for anything, but it is a way I've made sense of his death and everything that came after. If it was all so that you would save us, Meredith, bring our people and faerie itself back to life, then that makes all the pain worth something, don't you see?"

"That's just talk," Saraid said. "If it makes you feel better, then believe it, but Prince Essus did not martyr himself so that Meredith could bring the Goddess back to us and save the sidhe from themselves."

"I never said that our prince agreed to die to save us, Saraid, but it is a way at looking at all the pain and horror, and having some sense from it."

Saraid shook her head. "And this is why I stopped going to the therapist."

I wasn't sure how I felt about Dogmaela's comforting therapy reasoning. I wasn't even sure I thought it was comforting to me, but if it gave Dogmaela peace of mind, then I didn't want to argue with it.

"I'm sorry, Princess Meredith, I didn't mean to upset you. I have been thoughtless."

"I encouraged you to go to the therapist, Dogmaela; what you take from it has to work for you, not me."

She looked at me, seemed to study me. "If I may be so bold, Princess, perhaps taking your own advice might not be a bad idea."

"What do you mean?"

Saraid said, "No, no, you are not going to tell the princess she needs therapy. We are going to escort her to Captain Doyle and anywhere else she needs to go, and that is that."

Dogmaela dropped to one knee as the Red Cap had done in the weight room. "I beg your pardon, our princess."

"Oh, get up, you did nothing wrong, Dogmaela, and neither did you, Saraid. You're allowed to be different people and deal with your traumas differently. Right now I just need to talk to Doyle and Aisling."

"Aisling, why do you seek him?" Saraid asked.

"That is my business."

Saraid dropped to her knee beside Dogmaela. "We have offended you."

"Oh, get up." And with that I started down the hallway as fast as my high heels could take me. I made them jog a little to catch up with me, and then they dropped back to their bodyguard position half a pace behind and to each side. That was how we walked through the sliding glass doors and out into the Southern California sunshine, where Doyle was teaching hand-to-hand combat, and all I wanted to do was run to him and wrap the strength of his arms around me. I didn't, because it might have undermined his authority, but it took more control than a would-be queen likes to admit.

CHAPTER

TWENTY-NINE

Doyle stood under the shade of a huge eucalyptus tree that rose at least thirty feet high and spread out like a canopy. Most eucalyptus didn't have such a magnificent top, but this one was simply one of the prettiest ones I'd ever seen. Doyle had paced off a circle months ago that started under its shade and then spread out into the bright California sun. That circle of shade and light had become the unarmed combat practice area, because the Red Caps who practiced with the guard were too big to be thrown around inside any room the house could boast, so they got thrown around outside where they couldn't break things. Though, honestly, most of the guards who practiced with the Red Caps couldn't throw them around; it was more getting thrown around. The sidhe were quicker and more agile than the biggest of the goblins, but they weren't stronger.

The white, oversized tank top made a startling contrast with Doyle's skin, but the fitted exercise shorts were black so that it was almost hard to see them against his long legs. He was dressed like a hundred personal trainers in L.A., but the clothes were the only thing that was ordinary. No other trainer was going to have skin the color of night with purple and blue highlights when the sunlight hit it just right, and the pointed ears and ankle-length braid made him look like some elven prince from a fairy tale trying to blend into a modern gym. If Doyle wasn't different enough, the circle around him was full of the towering figures of Red Caps.

There were actually more Red Caps than sidhe standing and sitting around the circle. It was a first; the sidhe always outnumbered anyone else. Then one of the sidhe got up from where he'd been sitting on the ground, and the sunlight sparkled across his bare upper body as if he'd been sprinkled with gold dust. I knew that he had yellow and gold blond hair braided tight to his head, because he'd shoved it all up under a thin face mask that covered him from the chin up, leaving only holes for his eyes and mouth. It was far too hot even for the thinnest mask they'd been able to find, but it was the best solution we'd found so far to make sure Aisling's face wasn't exposed. He was why there were so few of the sidhe here. The Red Caps feared nothing, so they said, which meant they couldn't admit to worrying that Aisling's beauty would bespell them.

Dogmaela and Saraid moved in front of me, turning their backs on the practice and blocking my view entirely. "Princess, you should not be here; none of us should," Dogmaela said.

"Aisling is one of the people I need to speak with; please move aside."

"None of the female guard will risk seeing him bare of face, Princess Meredith, and we would be poor bodyguards if we let him bespell you," Saraid said.

"True love protects from his magic," I said. "I think you and I will both be safe, Saraid."

It took her a moment to understand what I'd implied, and then she blushed, which was not something you saw much among the fey. It made me laugh, not at her, but just happy for her and for Uther. He was like the ugly stepsister who had won the beautiful prince, and it couldn't have happened to a nicer guy.

"We are not certain that anything protects from Aisling's beauty, and he seems to have grown in power since he helped bring the dead gardens back to life," Dogmaela said.

I remembered that night. Galen and several of the sidhe who had once been vegetative deities had been absorbed into the very trees, rocks, and earth. When they came back out, they'd gained in power, or regained old powers once lost. But Aisling's sacrifice had been the most spectacular. A tree limb had pierced him through the chest, and he'd hung there. I'd thought he was dead, and then his body had exploded not into flesh, bone, and blood, but into a flock of songbirds that flew out into the garden to be lost in the dead trees. Their songs had been the first life heard in that lost place in centuries. Later Galen and all the rest appeared, melting out of the very walls and floor of the Hallway of Mortality, the queen's personal torture chamber. The hallway's cells had opened, and some had dissolved, and there were flowers and trees growing there now.

Aisling had survived all that and come back into more of his powers, or so some of the women believed. Since none of us could risk gazing on his face, I'm not sure any of us knew for certain whether Aisling had gained from his own sacrifice, or if everyone assumed it, because it was so true of the other men that had been taken by faerie and returned to us that night.

"I've seen Aisling with his shirt off before, and it hasn't affected me."

The two women glanced at each other, and then Dogmaela said, "I would not risk staring at any part of his body without a covering."

"Hafwen told us what happened when he revealed his face to Melangell."

I looked down at the dry grass. "I was there, I remember."

"Melangell clawed her own eyes out, so she would no longer be able to see him," Dogmaela said.

"I was there," I snapped at her.

She dropped to one knee, head bowed. "My apologies, Princess Meredith, I did not mean to offend."

"Get up, Dogmaela; I don't want any of you to abase yourself like that."

Saraid said, "Prince Cel expected that and more from us, so forgive us if we still fall back into decades of habit."

"I forgive you, but Dogmaela, please stand up."

"I angered you," she said, head still bowed.

"I regret what happened to Melangell. I didn't understand what I was asking when I told Aisling to use his magic on her, and a leader should know what a weapon does before using it."

They both looked at me, Dogmaela still on the ground. They exchanged another glance. It was Saraid who said, "Melangell meant to kill Galen that night. You were within your rights to do what was needed to find out the plan to assassinate you and your consorts."

"You did nothing wrong," Dogmaela said. "I just don't wish to suffer Melangell's fate by accident."

"I would not willingly use Aisling's beauty against anyone ever again."

"Why not?" Dogmaela asked.

"Because it wasn't lust that he filled Melangell with, it was love, as if she were forced to be in true love with him all at once, even though they hated each other." I hugged my arms tight trying to hold myself.

"You feel guilty," Saraid said, voice full of a soft awe.

"It was a terrible thing to do; why shouldn't I feel bad?"

They exchanged another look.

"Stop that," I said.

"Stop what?" they both asked.

"That look, just talk to me. I am not my aunt, or my dead cousin, I am not even my narcissistic mother, or egomaniac great-uncle, or my grandfather, Uar the Cruel; just talk to me, please, and for the love of Goddess, Dogmaela, stand up."

She got to her feet, started to glance at Saraid again, and then looked at me instead. "Regret is not an emotion we are accustomed to seeing in the royal family."

"No, they usually enjoy their cruelty," I said.

"We would never say that to you," Saraid said.

"I'm saying it, about my own family, but I am not them. I know a few months here doesn't erase decades of abuse, but I swear to you that I do not take pleasure from causing other people pain, or humiliating them."

"We believe you mean what you say," Saraid said.

I smiled, but it wasn't a happy smile. "You believe I mean it now, but you're wondering when I'll go crazy like my relatives and change my mind, is that it?"

"Time has taught us caution, Princess, that is all," Saraid said.

Dogmaela put her hands on her hips and then said, "I fell back into old, unhealthy habits, and I'm sorry for that, Princess Meredith. You deserve better than that, because you have shown yourself to be fair and sane, and . . . I am sorry."

I smiled at her. "It's all right, we're all learning as we go."

"That is true," she said.

"I still don't want to see Aisling's bare skin," Saraid said.

"Nor I," Dogmaela said.

"Then stand where you can't see him, but I'm going to speak with Doyle and eventually with Aisling. If you don't want to guard me while I do that, then you need to find guards to replace you."

They exchanged another look, and then Dogmaela looked embarrassed and said, "I'm sorry, Princess, it is a very old habit. The other Cranes were the only beings we could look to for help once the queen gave us to her son."

I thought the phrase was interesting: *gave*, like you'd give away a possession, or a puppy. You didn't give people away. It just wasn't supposed to work that way.

I had to go up on tiptoe to hug her. She stiffened, and didn't hug me back at first, and then patted my back awkwardly. "I'm so sorry, so very sorry."

She hugged me back then, and whispered, "Thank you for saving us."

I drew back with tears threatening in my eyes again. I didn't like this new emotional me, and really hoped that the hormones would even out and I'd regain more control, but the look on Dogmaela's face was worth a happy tear or two.

Galen came up to us smiling. He was shirtless, showing his flat stomach and the compact muscle that was underneath every bit of him. He didn't lift as seriously as Rhys did, and he didn't do the more extreme nutrition, so his body looked less defined, but wearing only a loose pair of shorts there was no way for him to hide the muscles that were inside all that smooth, pale green skin. Maybe it was being surrounded by so much grass, trees, and plants, but his curls looked very green, that one tiny braid still the only memory of when his hair was almost to his knees.

"Is everything all right?" he asked, reaching his hand out toward me. It was as natural as breathing to take his hand and stand at his side.

"We're fine," I said, and leaned into him, going up on tiptoe to meet his kiss.

Dogmaela mumbled, "Fine," and turned away to hide her own emotions, I think.

"We don't think it's safe that the princess be here with Aisling," Saraid said.

Galen grinned then. "She's safe enough."

"I think it's careless," Saraid said.

"If you're in love, really in love, then Aisling's magic has no power over you," Galen said.

"The princess told us the old wives' tale about true love keeping you safe from him," Saraid said.

"Meredith said that Saraid, you, and she would be safe," Dogmaela said. She'd wiped quickly at her face, and turned a stony, unreadable face to us, though she was as careful as Saraid not to look toward the practice area.

Galen drew me into his arms, grinning wider. "Then the three of us are safe as houses, but Dogmaela might want to go somewhere else."

She nodded. "I will, with Meredith's permission. I have not even an old wives' tale to keep me safe from the Terrible Beauty of him."

Aisling had once been called Terrible Beauty, though the Gaelic equivalent of it, and since I didn't know what country Aisling had started out in, I didn't know what his original Gaelic name had been. Saying *Gaelic* was almost like saying *Romance language*; some were so different from each other.

"You may go, Dogmaela; I think I'm safe enough." I knew I was smiling, and it was my own version of that stupid-faced, I'm-so-in-love smile.

She darted a glance at Galen, me, and then finally at Saraid. "Are you sure you want to stay?"

Saraid shook her head. "No, I'm not, I . . ." She glanced at me and then back to her sister guard. There was something close to pain on her face.

"Go, Saraid," I said. "Go if being near Aisling makes you this uncomfortable."

"It's okay," Galen said, his face sober, worried even. "Merry is in good hands." He hugged me closer to him, and I wrapped my arms around the slim smoothness of his waist.

"I just don't want you to think I hold my personal safety above that of the princess. I would lay down my life for her."

"I believe that, Saraid," Galen said. "We both do, but this is not life and death."

"You're dismissed, Saraid, Dogmaela; now go with my blessing," I said.

"And mine, if it matters," Galen said.

"It matters," Dogmaela said, smiling, a little sadly.

She and Saraid exchanged another glance; then they bowed, arms crossing their chests so their hands rested over their hearts, turned, and left.

"Why do they do that, touching their hearts, do you know?" I asked.

"It was Cel's idea, to show that he owned not just their bodies but their hearts."

I looked up at him and must have looked as horrified as I felt.

He hugged me tight against the front of his body, and I pressed my cheek against the warmth of his chest and wrapped my arms tight around his waist, holding on.

"I'm so glad you killed Cel," Galen whispered against my hair.

"So am I," I said, breathing in the scent of his skin and the slight dew of sweat, but it wasn't a masculine smell, it was almost like sweet cut grass.

"Now if you could just kill a few more of your relatives, we could live in peace."

"The queen is behaving herself," I said.

"All right, just one of your relatives then," he said.

I drew back enough to look up into his face. "Since when did you get so bloodthirsty?"

He smiled, but his green eyes were empty of it. "When he hurt you, and then when he tried to sue for visitation rights with our babies. He needs to be dead."

I hugged him as tight as I could, gazing up at him, studying his face. I didn't know why, but I was suddenly frightened for him. "Promise me you won't do anything foolish, Galen."

"I'm your bodyguard; it's my job to keep you safe. I'm the father of your children, and a husband in all but name; that gives me all the right I need to do anything to protect or avenge you, my Merry."

"If the king tries to kidnap me again, then do whatever you can, or want, but just promise me you won't go off and try to beard the tyrant in his lair, so to speak?"

He kissed me, and I kissed him back, but I studied his face as he drew back from it. "Galen, promise me."

He smiled at me, fingers tracing the edge of my cheek. "I can't."

"Don't get hurt, or worse, please, Galen. I've lost enough people in my life, all right?"

He hugged me tight again, and gave me a little shake. "I love you, Merry, and I love our children. I want to be here for you and them."

"Then don't do anything stupid, okay?"

"Me, stupid?" He gave me that look that was charming and self-deprecating, and in that moment I didn't trust it at all. I was suddenly so afraid for him that my chest was tight with it, as if I couldn't breathe past it.

"Remember, I don't want you to die for me, Galen; I want you to live for me."

He grinned. "I already live for you."

I would have pushed it, but Doyle yelled a warning, and Galen took me to the ground with him on top of me. I got a glimpse as I was falling backward of one of the Red Caps flying over us, tumbling through the air, before Galen's chest blocked my view of everything.

could feel Galen's heart pounding underneath my hand where it was trapped against his bare chest, as his arms wrapped me close, pressing me between his body and the rough grass, his body a shield to protect me. I knew it was his job, but in that moment all I could think was, if he actually gave his life for mine, I wasn't sure I'd ever recover from the loss.

His chest filled my vision; I could see nothing but the edges of grass and sun haloing us. I felt him move and knew he was looking around. What was happening?

I heard voices yelling, "Is she all right? Merry! Is she hurt?" I felt and heard people running toward us. Funny how much you could feel vibrating through the ground when you were lying on it.

A deep rumbling voice said, "Don't worry about me, I'm fine."

Galen got to his feet and helped me stand. There were enough Red Caps standing around that they put us in the shade as if a grove of small trees had magically sprung up around us. Doyle was there, taking my other arm, while Galen still held me.

"Are you hurt?"

"No, startled, that's all." I looked at him, knew something was different, and then realized the white tank top had been badly ripped down the front, so that it flapped around him as he moved.

"No one gives a tinker's damn if a goblin gets hurt, it's all about the sidhe." It was the Red Cap that I'd seen go overhead. He was only about nine feet tall, with skin a deep charcoal gray setting off the scarlet of his eyes like rubies. His face was smooth and strangely pleasant, and though his mouth was almost lipless, it wasn't a bad mouth. Considering all the Red Caps had once had a mouth full of jagged teeth, or even fangs, it was a very good mouth indeed. His round skullcap was almost black.

"Hello, Talan," I said.

His brilliant red eyes narrowed. "I would not have been thrown so, before your magic changed me."

Doyle let go of my arm, taking a half step in front of me. "Do not blame Merry for your lack of prowess on the battlefield," he said in a voice that held an edge of growl to it. It wasn't his dog form coming out, just that first rush of testosterone, before the real fight began.

Talan started forward, but another figure was already there, moving between Doyle and the Red Cap. Jonty's skin had been the color of dust when I met him; now it was a nearly silver gray, shining almost metallic in the sunlight. He was shorter than Talan, but broader through shoulders and back. His biceps were as round as medium tree trunks; the weight lifting that Doyle had insisted on for all of them had made Jonty lean and filled him out at the same time, so that he was even bigger than he'd started, but now you could see the muscles with no extra flesh to hide them, and he was simply massive. The cap on his head was fresh scarlet and bleeding. His cap bled whether I was around or not, which was one of the reasons he was the leader of the Red Caps.

"Apologize to Merry," Jonty growled.

"I will not apologize for the truth."

"Merry didn't make you a whining bitch, Talan; you were always that." I saw Jonty plant his back foot.

Doyle motioned and Galen was moving me back. I didn't argue; if the two Red Caps were going to actually fight I didn't want to be standing less than ten feet behind them. Twenty feet would be about minimum safe distance. Galen seemed to agree with me, because he kept moving me back until we were near where the fight had started at the practice circle.

Only Aisling was left kneeling in the center of the circle. His hands were held up to his face as he rocked forward, those glittering shoulders hunched as if he huddled around some great pain. He was hurt, badly hurt, because the warriors of faerie do not show pain unless it is too great to bear.

Galen and I went hand in hand to him. There was blood in a spatter of glittering crimson on the grass in front of him. He must have heard us, because he folded in upon himself, burying his face against his knees.

"Aisling, how badly hurt are you?" Galen asked.

"Don't look at me!" He yelled it, voice high with fear and pain.

Galen dropped my hand and moved toward the other man. "Talan couldn't have done anything to mar your beauty, Aisling, not without a weapon. Even a Red Cap can't hit one of the sidhe that hard," Galen said, and he put a note of joking in his voice.

Aisling's voice came muffled. "You're half right, Galen. He didn't mar my beauty, but he hit me hard enough to do harm."

"Aisling, how hurt are you?" Galen touched one of those bare shoulders.

Aisling screamed, and scuttled away on knees and one hand. "Don't touch me! Goddess help me, don't touch my bare skin."

"True love is proof against your magic, Aisling. Let me see how hurt you are; you will not bespell me."

Aisling thrust one hand back as if to ward off a blow, and the other hand stayed at his face. I realized that he was covering his face, and that I could see the complicated braids that held all that yellow and gold hair tight to the back of his head. The mask that had been covering his hair and his face was gone. A thrill of something close to fear went through me from the bottoms of my feet to the top of my head. Galen might have been sure that true love would protect him, but he was immortal, and I wasn't. I knew that the immortal sidhe were not proof against Aisling's power, but he wasn't allowed to show his face to any human, no matter how in love they might be. Mortal blood just didn't protect against magic as well as immortal.

Galen reached out and grabbed Aisling's outflung hand. "Let me help you, Aisling." Galen's voice held pain; he could never stand to see someone so distressed without wanting to make it better.

Aisling's hand made a fist, and he went very still. "You are a good man, Galen; do not let me hurt you by accident."

"Let me see what is bleeding on you." Galen knelt beside the other man, his hand still holding his arm.

Aisling cried out and jerked free of him, crawling away from Galen, using both hands to scramble faster, and looked directly at me. He hadn't realized I was standing just behind them.

CHAPTER

THIRTY-ONE

We had a long, frozen moment of staring at each other. I waited to be bespelled, but though his skin was what the sidhe called sun-kissed as mine was moonlit, and though his face, like the rest of him, seemed to be sprinkled with gold dust, still there were others in faerie whose skin was more beautiful to me. The blue of his eyes was the color of a late-spring sky, but then part of Rhys's eyes were a similar color. Aisling did have spirals in his eyes, as if someone had tattooed them on his irises, so that the spirals took attention away from the sky blue, but again there were others in faerie with more unusual eyes. I don't think I would have been so critical if I hadn't grown up being told he was so beautiful that to gaze upon his bare face was to fall in instant, irresistable lust, if not actual love. I tried to see the lines of his face and found him beautiful, but I thought Frost was fairer of face. Maybe I was prejudiced, but though Aisling was amazing, his was not the most amazing face I had ever seen. I had my father to compare him to, as well, and I still thought my father was one of the most handsome men I'd ever known. Maybe I was prejudiced, but then isn't that what love, all kinds of love, is supposed to do?

I smiled, and Aisling let out a wail of despair and hid his face behind both of his hands.

Galen said, "Merry."

I smiled at him, that face that I had loved since I was fourteen. "I'm fine."

Doyle called out, "Merry!"

I turned and watched that tall, dark body stride toward us. He was moving so fast that his long braid bounced and I could see the flash of it as he stepped. The torn white shirt looked like some prop in a strip club, artfully ripped to give glimpses of his chest and stomach. The sunlight glittered off the silver earrings in the high, graceful points of his ears and caught the glint of the nipple ring on the left side. I just watched him and enjoyed the view, and the fact that he was mine, and I was his.

I turned back to Aisling, who still had one hand held up in front of his lower face like some movie harem girl, so that only those blue eyes with their spiral shapes showed. I smiled at him, and he closed his eyes as if in pain. He raised his other hand and hid even his eyes from view.

I realized he was saying, "No, no, no," over and over again.

Doyle grabbed me and whirled me round to face him. He searched my face with nearly frantic eyes, and whatever he saw there calmed him, because he smiled. We wrapped our arms around each other and kissed. We kissed long and thoroughly, until I could wrap the sun-warmed feel of his body around me like a perfume made of flesh and warmth and love.

We broke the kiss and came away from each other's lips smiling. "I love you, my Merry."

"And I love you, my Darkness."

His smile widened, and he ran his hand along the edge of my hair. "Let us comfort our fallen man."

I nodded.

We went to him still holding hands. "Aisling," Doyle said, "Merry is not bespelled by you."

He just shook his head, hands still covering almost every bit of his face.

Doyle knelt beside him. "I saw your face when Talan struck you and ripped your mask off, and I was not bespelled either."

"You saw what happened to Melangell," he murmured through the shield of his hands.

Doyle touched his arm, and Aisling jerked away from the touch. Doyle touched him again.

"Don't touch me!"

Doyle grabbed both his upper arms and held him tight when the other man tried to flinch away. "Your skin is just skin to me, Aisling, no more or less beautiful than all the sidhe."

Aisling just kept shaking his head, hiding behind his hands, and whispering, "No, no, no."

I knelt beside Doyle and touched Aisling's shoulder. He tried to move away, but Doyle's grip was too firm. If he wanted to escape from Darkness he would have to fight.

I petted his shoulder the way you'd comfort a friend. "It's all right, Aisling; I've looked into your face and I'm not befuddled, I swear."

"Look at me," Doyle said.

"No."

"Aisling, look at me."

He lowered the one hand just enough to gaze over it at Doyle. "You have not harmed me, Aisling."

He closed his eyes and whispered, "You don't understand."

Doyle put a hand on either side of Aisling's face and gave him all the concentration out of those black eyes. "Drop your hands, Aisling, drop them."

Those spiral eyes were too wide, almost wild like a horse that is about to bolt, but he slowly let the other hand fall away. Doyle held his face between those two, big, dark hands and gazed directly into his face. "You do not have to hide from us, my friend."

I touched his arm and said, "You don't have to hide anymore, Aisling, not from us."

Aisling started to tremble, and then to shake as if he were freezing cold instead of kneeling in the warm sunshine. One single silver tear trailed down from the corner of his eye, and then another, until the tears seemed to be racing down his face. Doyle rose high on his knees and kissed him on the forehead.

Galen came to kneel on the other side of Doyle, and when he moved his hands from Aisling's face, Galen kissed his forehead, too. "You're safe," he said.

I hugged Aisling. "You are safe with us."

His shoulders started to shake, and then he started to cry almost hysterically. His arm came around me and around Galen on the other side, so that he held all three of us with Doyle in the middle, and we held each other and we held him, and let him cry.

The Red Caps and sidhe who had been about to have a fight all trooped back into the house quietly, faces averted for the most part. Only Jonty risked a look; he nodded at me, and I nodded back. We were left alone in the warm sunlight, with the smell of eucalyptus filling the dream of eternal summer with a crisp, healing scent. We laid everyone's discarded shirts underneath the shade of the big tree, so we wouldn't be lying on the scratchy, dry grass, and put Aisling in the center of us, so that we could all touch his bare upper body. We petted and stroked him, not as lovers do, but just to fill the terrible skin hunger that he'd had to deny for so long. Babies who don't get enough touch will fail to thrive and die, even if they are well fed and otherwise well cared for; touch is so much more important than most people want to admit.

We touched his back and shoulders at first, and then he rolled over and we ran our hands over his chest and stomach. The three of us gazed into the spiral of his eyes, traced his face with our fingertips. I got within inches of him until I could see that the black spiral lines were formed of tiny birds all flying out of his eyes. I remembered that moment in the dead gardens when his body seemed to have exploded into tiny song-birds. I traced the line of his cheek and said, "Have the spirals always been tiny birds?"

"Not in a very long time," he said, softly.

Galen peeked over the top of his head, so that he was staring at him upside down from inches away. "I don't remember them ever being tiny birds."

Aisling laughed, and it filled his face with a joy that I had never seen there; even behind his veil he had been a solemn man.

"It has been longer than your lifetime, Galen, since Aisling had birds in his eyes," Doyle said.

The happy glow faded around the edges, and then without looking at any of us, he said, "Would you unbind my hair and . . . touch it, please?"

I glanced at Doyle and Galen. They both nodded, and Galen smiled. We had Aisling sit up so that we could take out the pins that held all those small braids tight to his head. Even with three of us doing it, it took a while to undo all the braids. We ran our fingers through the gold and blond of his hair. It didn't shine with its own light the way Fenella's hair did, but it gleamed, catching every bit of light that filtered through the leaves above us.

His hair fell in ankle-length waves, thick and warm, not as soft as Galen's, or Frost's, or even Rhys's, closer to Doyle's texture. Aisling lay down on his stomach and let us pet and play with all that shining hair until we made a cloak of it fanning out around him.

He gave a deep, contented sigh and rose up on his elbows. "Some of the nobles of the Seelie Court contacted me. They offered me the throne."

"When?" Doyle asked.

"A few days ago."

"Why did you wait to tell us?" Galen asked.

"Because I thought you would cast me out, and I have nowhere left to go."

I smoothed his hair back, piling it into my lap like a pet, until I could see the side of his face. "I would not cast you out for the machinations of other nobles. You have no more control over the different factions within the courts than I do."

He glanced at me. "You aren't angry?"

"No," I said.

"You have two factions within the Seelie Court that want you on the throne."

"Sir Hugh's contingent and the king himself, but I know that there are Seelie nobles as there are Unseelie nobles who see me as unfit for either throne."

"They fear that your mortal blood will steal away their immortality as it did on the dueling grounds."

"I know that, and honestly for all I know they may be right."

Aisling looked at me, obviously surprised. "You're worried about it, too, then."

"Yes."

"Will you take the throne then?"

"The Goddess and faerie itself crowned Doyle and me as rulers of the Unseelie Court, but the Seelie sithen did not recognize me when I entered it."

"You were part of the wild hunt, Merry; you can't be queen of any court and lead the hunt," Doyle said.

"You mean ever?" I asked.

He smiled and shook his head. "No. When you ride with the hunt, especially if you are the huntsman, it is your only title. You lay the crown aside to lead it, and pick it back up only if you give up being the huntsman."

"You were the huntsman once, I remember you said so."

"I was, but not of the same wild hunt that you and Sholto led."

"I never saw more than one wild hunt and that was the sluagh," Galen said.

"As there were once many more faerie mounds, so with the wild hunts," Doyle said.

"I remember when Darkness led his own wild hunt and was the huntsman for our queen," Aisling said.

Doyle stroked a hand through the other man's hair. "You are older than I am, my friend; you would remember."

"What did you tell the nobles who offered to make you king?" I asked.

"I told them I would not betray you, or Doyle."

"What did they say to that?" I asked.

"They told me to think upon it before answering."

"If you want the throne, Aisling, take it," I said.

He looked startled. Doyle said, "Merry!"

I stroked the hair so gold and warm in my lap. "No, Doyle, you've seen how some of the Seelie nobles treat me. They've come here in hopes that I can help them get with child, and many of them still treat me like some mongrel. People follow you for only three reasons; love, fear, or loyalty. No one at the Seelie Court loves me, or fears me, and I'm not certain there's much loyalty to anything there except whatever, or whoever, will further their own pursuit of power."

"Lord Hugh wants a baby with his lady," Doyle said.

"But he also wants to be close to the throne, and if he put me on it, he would be," I said.

"There has never been a welcome for Merry and me at the Seelie Court," Galen said.

"Are you both serious that Merry should just give up the golden throne?" Doyle asked. He was looking from one to the other of us.

We both nodded. "Besides, Doyle, the Seelie sithen recognized Aisling when the Seelie first came to this country. Taranis exiled him; because of that his own sithen wanted to crown a new king. The sithen has already chosen Aisling as king; let it stand."

"What if the sithen has changed its mind after over two hundred years?" Aisling asked.

"Then you will be welcome back here in the Western Lands," I said.

"Aren't we forgetting something?" Galen said.

"What?" I asked.

"The king would have to be dead for Aisling to take this throne."

"That works for me," I said.

"Me, too," he said.

"Me, three," Doyle said.

"If I agree, it seems like a plot," Aisling said.

"I've wanted him dead since he took Merry," Galen said.

"Oh, yes," Doyle said.

"For hurting Merry I would happily slay him, too," Aisling said.

"If the sithen still wants you as its king, then be the king of the Seelie, Aisling. The sithens will let a hereditary monarchy rule, but the start of every lineage is chosen by each kingdom. I believe that when we stopped letting the land choose its own ruler, that was the beginning of our decline as a people."

"When the Irish stopped letting the great stone choose their kings, that was the beginning of their undoing, as well," Doyle said.

I stroked his arm, because I knew that his people had been among the Irish and he still felt for how much they'd suffered at the hands of the English, though I'd only learned his feelings on it in the last year. Doyle had been such a mystery, not just to me but to most of the court. He had been the captain of the guard, and the Queen's Darkness, her left hand, her assassin, but it was as if all that had kept him from having feelings, or being entirely real. In his own way, Doyle had been as lonely as Aisling.

"You would truly let me take the golden throne, when you could unite the two thrones of the sidhe for the first time in centuries?"

"It's a pretty thought that I could unite us, but I think there is too much fear and hatred between the Darkling throng and the golden one. Oh, Aisling, six of the noble houses declared themselves against me. I'm not certain I can safely rule even the Unseelie throne, but I know that the Seelie throne is too dangerous for me and the babies, and the men I love. I would not risk all that I hold dear for any throne, so be king if you can; the sithen has chosen you and that should stand."

He studied my face and finally said, "You really are the most extraordinary person, Merry."

"I am a practical person in this, or a selfish one. I do not wish to lose any more of the people I love, not just for power."

"That's right, you and Doyle both gave up the Unseelie crowns given to you by faerie itself to save Frost's life."

We smiled at each other, and we reached out at the same time to take each other's hands, which made us smile more. "What is more important than love?" Galen said.

We looked at him, and I held my other hand out to him. He took it with a smile. "Nothing," I said.

"I'll disagree," Aisling said.

We all looked down at him where he still lay propped up on his elbows. "What's more important than love?" I asked.

"Safety," he said.

We were all silent for a moment, and then we all nodded. "The power to keep that which you love safe," Doyle said.

"It always comes back to power," Aisling said. "It has to, because without power you can't protect what's yours."

"I can't argue with you," Galen said, "but damn, that was a mood killer."

We laughed, even Aisling. "You are charming, Green Knight."

"It's part of my magic."

Aisling looked up at him. "Truly?"

Galen nodded. "Apparently."

"To be charming in a friendly way, not a romantic way?" Aisling asked.

"Yes." He smiled, and shrugged. "I think it's what helped me not get killed in a duel years ago. People just liked me, even when I was a political disaster and didn't have enough powerful friends to protect me."

I drew Galen down to me so we could kiss, and said, "I'm so glad you're magically likable; I would have missed you."

He grinned. "I love you, our Merry."

"And I love you, too, my Galen."

"I'm jealous," Aisling said.

We all looked at him. He added hastily, "I don't mean of Merry in particular, but of your being in love, and being able to lie with a woman. I haven't dared break my long fast for fear of bespelling some poor woman."

"I guess it is ironic that to be safe to have sex with anyone, you'd need the woman to already be in love with someone else."

"Something like that," he said, and gave a half laugh, but it was more bitter than happy.

Doyle patted his back. "I'm sorry, my friend."

I remembered why I'd wanted to talk to Aisling. I told him about Bryluen's effect on Rita the nanny. He sat up, spilling his hair all around him, face serious as he listened. "It is highly unusual for one so young to exhibit such powers."

"So you didn't have to worry about hiding your face when you were a baby?"

"No, not until I reached my teens, and then the year that I grew six inches, my shoulders filled out, and I suddenly looked more my age, and that was the beginning of this. I thought I was just very good with women, and then I started attracting women I didn't want to attract, and we began to figure out what was wrong."

"Your power is the closest to what Bryluen is doing; can you see if you sense anything?" I asked.

"I will happily look at the baby, but I'm not sure what I can tell you; as I said, my powers didn't manifest until I was in my teens. It's very unusual that both your daughters would be displaying powers almost from birth."

"They are going to be very powerful," Doyle said.

"I believe you are right," Aisling said. He began to gather his hair back from us, and to braid it almost absentmindedly. "I will need a covering for my face before I go to the nursery."

We finally used the remains of Doyle's shirt to make a mask that went around his lower face and tied securely enough to make Aisling happy with it. He left his hair in two long, thick braids. It reminded me of the way Saraid had worn her hair, though his was longer and seemed thicker. I hadn't petted her hair, so I wasn't sure on the thickness. We walked toward the house with Doyle and Galen holding my hands. Galen held out his hand to Aisling. I couldn't be certain, but I thought he was smiling under the white mask when he took the offered hand. We walked four abreast out of the practice circle, and as soon as we left the magical spell that kept the reporters from seeing inside it, we heard a yell of, "Hey, Princess!"

I looked, and I knew better, but they'd have pictures of me with the three men wearing nothing but exercise shorts—well, pants for Aisling, but either way three mostly nude men and we were all holding hands. There'd be rumors about Galen and Aisling being more than friends soon, because no one in America could understand that men could hold hands and just be friends. I loved my country, but it was a weird culture when it came to touching.

CHAPTER

THIRTY-TWO

Aisling sat in the nursery rocking chair holding Bryluen. He'd gone back to his room to change, so that he wore his usual gauzy veil wrapped around his head; only his eyes showed bare to the world. The veil was layers of nearly transparent gold cloth so that you could see that all that hair was in multiple braids snugged tight to the back of his head. He wore a silk T-shirt that was only a few shades lighter gold than the veil, and then the dress slacks were a darker gold. Just seeing the outfit let me know that Maeve had picked it out. She liked layers of gold and cream. I'd have put him in blue to see if it would bring out the color in his eyes. In the gold his eyes looked grayer than I knew they were.

I knew that Maeve was helping a lot of the sidhe shop for modern clothes; one, because she enjoyed shopping, and two, because she would often use the shopping trip as a way of getting to know them and seeing if she wanted to sleep with them. That hadn't been an option with Aisling for her, because Maeve was still grieving for her dead husband; that would not keep her safe from his magic.

She stood across the nursery watching him as he rocked Bryluen. The look on Maeve's face was speculative, and the look was enough; she would have pursued him as a lover if she could have done it safely.

She caught me watching her, and smiled brilliantly at me. It was her public smile, beautiful, vibrantly sincere, and it was her version of a "blank cop face." She could hide any emotion behind that shining smile. I knew it, and she knew I knew it, so either she didn't care, or her emotions were so strong about Aisling that she couldn't hide it any better from me. Or maybe I just knew Maeve that well now?

Little Liam was playing near her feet, rolling a ball along the floor for the dogs to chase. The terriers chased it in a happy, barking, snarling pack. No dogs were allowed in the exercise room, so when Rhys was there his terriers had started coming to the nursery, or following Liam around, or Galen, or me. Minnie and Mungo, my own pair of greyhounds, were pressed to my side, so I could play with their ears and stroke their heads. They usually didn't press like this unless they sensed I was nervous. Why was I nervous? Because watching Aisling made me wonder if we were going to have to veil our daughter like Aisling. The thought of having to hide her sweet face from the world, so we could save the world from her, was somehow horribly sad.

Maeve came to me and touched my shoulder. "Your face, so sad; what did you just think to take the light from your eyes?"

I looked up at her and shook my head. How could I say in front of Aisling that the thought of Bryluen sharing his fate of having to hide his face for all his life seemed awful?

Maeve looked where I was looking and her eyes showed that maybe she knew me as well as I knew her now. She drew me into a hug and whispered, "We will not have to hide her cute little face."

I didn't so much return her hug as hold on to her. What was wrong with me today?

Aisling stood up with Bryluen in his arms and came to stand next to us. "Merry, why the tears? She is lovely and powerful, but no reason for such sorrow."

I heard myself saying my fears out loud, while the crying grew. Aisling helped Maeve hold me while I cried. Bryluen stared up at me with those big, solemn eyes and I realized that there were distinct lines in her irises; they were still blue, but it was as if someone had drawn faint lines that were dividing the color up. Was this how a tricolored iris started to change? I realized that I'd never seen a baby with triple irises. I was the last baby born to the sidhe in America, so I didn't know if Bryluen's eyes were just going to be blue with pale circles like Aisling's spirals of birds, or whether this was the beginning of her irises separating out into different colors. For some reason that made me cry harder, as if the fact that I didn't know what it meant for her eye color was just another symptom of me not knowing about her magical powers, or Gwenwyfar's for that matter. How was I supposed to raise them if I didn't know the answers?

Maeve took Bryluen and let Aisling hold me while I wept. It was close to the way he'd cried earlier in the garden, but there I'd had Doyle and Galen to help me comfort him; here a man who had never been my lover, or even a close friend, held me tight while I cried so hard my legs gave out and he was left holding all my weight as if I were fainting. Part of me knew it wasn't logical, and stood aside in a sort of horror that I would show such weakness to someone who didn't even love me, but the rest of me was consumed with a near-hysterical grief.

I just had no idea what I was grieving about.

CHAPTER THIRTY-THREE

Then there were other arms holding me from behind, helping Aisling hold me, and it was Galen, dressed and showered from practice. "Merry, what's wrong? What's happened?"

I shook my head, too lost in my hysterics to answer, and honestly I had no good answer.

Aisling was trying to explain when another set of arms reached in and took me from between both of them, lifting me so I could curl against his chest, as he held me. Doyle's hair was damp from the shower, loose of its braid so it could dry faster. I wrapped my arms around his neck and buried my face against his shoulder and neck. I breathed in the scent of his skin, the soap and shampoo and the fresh smell of the clean shirt, so that it all mingled together to make him smell so good and fresh and real, and . . . just the scent of him began to calm me, as if I could breathe easier when he held me close.

"Let us go visit our Killing Frost," he said in that deep, rumbling voice of his, that seemed to vibrate through my body as if the deep, thick sound of it could fill me up and leave no room for anything else.

He walked out of the room and down the hallway, moving effortlessly toward the room where Frost was still resting, healing from the last time Taranis had tried to kill my Darkness, or force him to kill us.

Taranis was mad, insane in a very real way; how do you keep yourself safe from someone who can enter your dreams and turn them into nightmares?

Doyle was so strong, and I felt so safe as he carried me down the hallway, but it was an illusion, because no matter how good you were with a sword or gun, or how much magic you had, death could still come, could still carry you away. I could not protect anyone, not really, and by that same thought, they couldn't protect me. Eventually, we all lost.

I kept my face buried against Doyle. I breathed in the scent of him, and didn't look up as he adjusted his hold on me and opened the door to our bedroom. He kicked the door closed behind us, and I heard Frost say, "What has happened now?"

What *had* happened now? It wasn't just me. We were all getting . . . battle fatigue, hadn't they called it once? Doyle started to explain what little he knew, and I just let their voices wash over me. It didn't matter, nothing mattered, because no matter how hard I tried, or what I did, I couldn't defeat all our enemies, I couldn't find us a safe haven in the midst of it all. Even here in the Western Lands, as far from my family as I could travel, they would not leave us in peace.

Doyle laid me on the bed between the two of them, my favoritest place in the world to be, and for once I felt nothing but a dim numbness, like trying to sense the world while wrapped carefully in cotton and put away somewhere so I wouldn't break.

Frost was above me, propped up on one arm. He touched my face, traced the still-wet track of my tears, and said, "Merry, our Merry, what has happened to make you weep so?"

I stared up into that heartbreakingly handsome face, those gray eyes, and I saw again that image that sometimes showed in them, like the inside of some magical miniature snow globe. It was a winter-barren tree on a hillside with snow all around it, but for the first time there was a mist of pink buds, the promise of blossoms to come. For no reason that I could name, the sight of that promising pink blush of life made me start to cry again.

I wept as if my heart would break and spill out of my eyes in shattered pieces on the sheets, and their hands tried to comfort me and save the pieces I was crying away. The light and the dark hands touching me, caressing, their voices saying all the things you say when the people you love are in pain. I started to yell at them, tell them that they were wrong, that it wouldn't be all right, that it would never be all right. I told them they were lying to themselves if they believed it would be all right. I screamed and cried and fought, and it wasn't them I was fighting, it was everything else, but as so often happens it's your nearest and dearest who take the brunt of your rage.

Arms found me that wouldn't let go, that held me so tight that I couldn't push them away or struggle free. I was pressed against a chest, held in arms so strong that it felt as if nothing could move them or tear them from me. Strength like that could have made me panic, but when Taranis had done what he did, he hadn't held me tight; the injury had done that for him. He was a man who didn't know how to hold on to anything, or anyone, but himself. The man who held me now knew how to hold and keep and protect, and I gave myself over to that strength. I collapsed into the dark solidity of his arms, my head pressed against his chest, arms limp at my sides as I let myself cry in a way I hadn't allowed myself yet. I cried until there were no more tears, and I felt empty like a seashell that held only echoes of what it had once been.

I ended up lying on top of him, my head on his chest so I could hear the sure beat of his heart, while one arm held me close and the other stroked my hair. Doyle's deep voice rumbled up through his chest as he whispered, "Merry, Merry, Merry."

The bed moved and I knew it was Frost; then his hand stroked my back, and he said, "I would do anything to take this pain from you."

I turned my head so that my other cheek lay on Doyle's chest while I looked at Frost. He lay on his side beside us, his hand still laid gently on me. Tears shone on his face, his eyes looking darker gray than usual like clouds before it rains, heavy and dark, or maybe that was just how I felt.

"I know that," I said, and my voice was still thick with tears.

He lay down beside Doyle, who moved his arm from holding me to let Frost slip into the circle of his arm, and put his arm across me and hold me against Doyle's body. Frost's head lay on Doyle's shoulder, one long leg going over Doyle's legs, so we lay entwined, the three of us. I loved seeing two such big, physical men hold each other, and hold me like this. It made me feel safer and more complete than anything ever had.

Yet even here with them, the fear wasn't gone. It was pushed back, but it was like a battle; being here with them meant I was safe and happy for now, but the next wave of invaders was coming. Maybe that was always true of life? I'd had a professor in college who said we were all temporarily able-bodied; at the time I hadn't understood, but I did now. Were we all just temporarily happy? Or were we all just temporarily sad? I guess it depended on how you looked at things.

I reached out and traced the tracks of tears on Frost's cheek. "Why are you crying?" I asked.

"Because you are, and I love you," he said.

I laid my hand against his cheek, and my hand was so small that I couldn't cover the whole side of his face even with my fingertips spread.

"I do not love you less because I do not cry," Doyle said.

I moved my head enough so I could see his face. "I know that," I said.

"We both know that," Frost said, and moved his head just enough so he could meet the other man's eyes, so that we were both gazing up at Doyle.

He looked down at both of us, from inches away, and suddenly he smiled bright and glorious in the darkness of his face. "I had given up such dreams as this."

"As what?" I asked.

He hugged both of us with the arm he had around each of us. "This, the two of you in my arms, gazing at me like that. It is more than I ever hoped to have again, one person to love and be loved by, but to have both of you is such riches as no man would ever expect in one lifetime."

I smiled at him, and I knew that Frost was, too, but I glanced to see that smile, those gray eyes gazing up at our tall, dark, and handsome man.

"I, too, had no thought of ever being this happy again," Frost said.

"I've never been this happy," I said.

They both looked at me. "Not even when you were in love with Griffin?" Frost asked.

"I wasn't in love with Griffin when my father made him my fiancé, but he was handsome and sidhe, and my father's choice."

"So it was a political coupling, not a love match?" Doyle asked.

I nodded, my chin resting on his chest.

"We all envied him," Frost said.

I turned to look at him. "You and the other guards talked about it?"

"No," he said, and seemed to think about it, and finally said, "I can only say, I envied him."

"I didn't think you even liked me," I said.

He smiled. "I will admit that it wasn't you, our Merry, but more any woman at that point, but when I saw you look at him with your face shining with love, then I envied him you."

I sighed. "I did grow to love him, but looking back at all of it I don't think he ever loved me. If he'd gotten me pregnant we would have married, and I'm not sure when I would have figured out how little he valued me."

Doyle raised his hand from my body to touch my hair, and Frost laid a kiss on my shoulder. "We love you," Frost said.

"I know that, and I love you, but it is true love, not some infatuation made up of sex and magic. It is loving you that's let me look back at his behavior and realize that he must never have truly loved me."

Frost laid his face against mine, and Doyle kissed the top of my head. Doyle lay back down and cuddled us both tighter in his arms. "Whatever comes, we can see it through together. For all the blessings that we have in our lives right now, there is nothing I would not do to defend us, and our children." He smiled again, that bright surprise of a smile.

"The babies are a wonder to me," Frost said, softly.

Doyle rose so that he could lay a quick kiss on his lips, and then I rose so he could share that kiss between us. "I've never been in love with someone I called friend before, Frost; it is everything we were as friends and now all this, and to be fathers together"—he hugged us again—"I am happier than I can remember."

Frost got that almost-shy smile that he only seemed to get when the three of us were alone, and it was usually from something that Doyle said, not me. I wasn't sure why it worked that way, but I knew it did.

He turned to me that pale handsome face, those serious gray eyes. "Whatever comes, Merry, we will face it together, with the other fathers at our side. Never has such might been joined in one purpose among us; we will prevail against all that stand against us. We can do this."

"How can you be so certain?" I asked.

He smiled. "Because such love as ours cannot be without purpose, and if it were wasted by death or tragedy this soon, it would be without purpose, and I do not believe the Goddess and the Consort so cruel as that."

The first pale, pink rose petal fell from empty air to land on Doyle's shoulder. A second joined it as I said, "I am sorry that I lost faith for a moment. I love you both more than I have words to say; you are my hearts, and I will not despair again if the two of you are with me." I touched Frost's face again and gazed into those eyes. "I am blessed by Goddess and the Consort in so many ways; how dare I give in to sorrow."

The petals kept falling, as if we were inside an invisible snow globe that was full of summer warmth instead of winter cold.

"The Goddess and Consort are with us, Merry, with us in a way that they have not been in centuries," Doyle said.

"But magic is returning to our enemies, too," I said, and I felt that hard knot in my stomach again. I realized that I was afraid of Taranis, truly afraid.

The rose petals began to slow, but the scent of a summer meadow with the wild roses sweet and thick-smelling in the heat was stronger.

"There is a purpose to that, as well, I think," Doyle said.

I knew he was right, so why couldn't I let go of my fear?

"In another few days I will be completely healed, and then the three of us can celebrate our happiness again," Frost said.

"Does it sound odd to say that I've missed you both terribly when we've spent most of the last year sleeping next to each other?" I asked.

"No," they said together, and then they laughed, a wonderful deep, shared masculine sound that I loved.

"You are meeting Sholto two days from now at the beach house, correct?" Doyle asked.

"Yes."

"Then it's our turn," Frost said.

I looked from one to the other of them, and felt a deep, happy shiver run through my body that finally spilled out enough to make me writhe.

Doyle laughed again, "Oh, don't do that again; my self-control is only so good."

Frost sat up, pulling away from us. "You and Merry can have sex now, and in a day or so we can all be together."

Doyle caught hold of his wrist and held him beside us. "No, my friend, we will break our fast together."

"You do not have to wait for me," Frost said.

"If I loved only Merry, then there would be no point to waiting, but I love you both, and that is worth waiting for," Doyle said. His face was fierce as he said it.

Frost gave that shy smile and then looked down, his silver hair spilling forward to hide his face. "You shall make me cry again, Darkness."

Doyle smiled, not fierce this time, but gentle. "That you both cry for love of me delights me."

We both looked at him, and I didn't have to see Frost's face to know we were giving our Darkness almost the same look from both our faces. We loved him. He loved us. I loved Frost. Frost loved me. It was all more wonderful than I had ever dreamed. Doyle was right; as long as we were together, nothing would stop us. I believed that, I honestly did, but . . . but I was still afraid. I was beginning to wonder if Dogmaela was right. Maybe I did need a therapist. My father had taken me to one as a child, because I'd had flashback nightmares about Aunt Andais drowning me, or trying to drown me. She'd done it because no sidhe could die by drowning. Her reasoning had been that if she could drown me, then I wasn't truly sidhe, and so I would be no loss. The therapist had helped me process it all; maybe the right one could help me again.

I gazed at the two men in my bed. They were worth fighting for, even if that fight was against the issues in my own head. I knew Maeve had seen someone after her husband died of cancer, and the therapist had helped her deal with the grief. I had everything I could ever want and more, but I felt like I was grieving something; maybe it was time to find out what.

I kissed them both, long and thoroughly, then went to find Maeve and apologize to Aisling for falling apart all over him. He would tell me not to worry about it, that it was his honor or something, but he wasn't my lover, or my love, so I'd apologize, because that level of care should come with love attached to it somewhere.

CHAPTER

THIRTY-FOUR

The three of us, and then the five of us, talked for hours about everything that was worrying me. Doyle, Frost, Galen, Rhys, and Mistral had all had different points of view that helped me think and helped us all plan. Maeve had joined us in interviewing lesser fey for nanny duty. We thought we'd found some possible candidates. We'd done what we could to plan about the babies, especially about Bryluen's powers. Aisling had helped reassure us that we did not need to veil her; he said her power did not come from her face. So she was still a concern, but that particular fear was gone. We'd gone back to the days when I had no hand of power and kept bags of antinightmare herbs tucked into our pillows; so far either it was working, or Taranis had not tried to invade anyone else's dreams. It was odd that we really couldn't know if the herbs worked, only if they didn't. I realized that having real sidhe magic had made me arrogant like the rest of the nobles, and I'd thrown out almost all the anti-fey practices I'd used for years to keep me safer around my relatives. It seemed odd that I, of all people, would forget that there are so many more kinds of magic than just sidhe, but I had. I was part human and part lesser fey through my brownie heritage. I needed to remember all the parts of myself, not just one.

We planned, we talked to Sholto via mirror about our plans, and then two days later I was standing on a windswept beach waiting for him. One of his titles was Lord of That Which Passes Between, and that was why we were at the edge of the sea where the water met the sand in swirling, whooshing waves. The edge of the surf is one of the between places, neither dry land nor water, but both, and neither. The edge of a woods that bordered a meadow or a plowed field would probably be where he started, hundreds of miles away in Illinois, because that was a place that was neither wild nor tame, a place between. He was also able to control the recently dead, animating them until their bodies were well and truly dead, and he could call a taxi out of nowhere, or any kind of transport that spent its time going between places.

The wind was cold off the water—not winter cold, it was L.A., but still plenty cold as it whipped my short skirt around my thighs. I was happy for the thigh-high hose with their lace edges, because it was at least something between my legs and the wind. I was standing on the next-to-last step on the long stairs that led from the house on the cliff above to the pale sand. The high-heeled pumps would look awesome as I walked back up the stairs, but they weren't meant for protection from the elements. I'd dressed for cute and sexy, not standing beside the ocean in the early-morning chill. Even in June, Southern California could have mornings that felt more like Midwestern fall.

"Princess Meredith, please take my jacket." Becket, one of the human DSS guards, held out his suit jacket, which left most of his arsenal of weapons very visible against his white dress shirt. His tie was like a black stripe down his chest, held in place against the wind with a tie bar, so generic I wondered if it had come standard government issue. He was broad through the shoulders, and without the jacket on, the shirt sleeves seemed to strain just a touch over the muscles of his arms, which meant his jacket was going to be huge on me.

His partner, Cooper, said, "Let her have mine, Becket; yours will swallow her."

Cooper was a few inches taller, a few years younger, and a lot more slender. If I hadn't had so many sidhe to compare him to I'd have used words like *willowy* and *graceful* to describe Cooper, but he was only human, and that put more bulk on his thin frame, and meant that he'd never have the speed or dancing grace of the nonhuman guards. His hair was truly black, and he had the skin tone to match. Becket was one of those blonds with a ruddy complexion as if he'd burned years ago and never been able to get rid of all of it. He had his pale hair cut so close to his head that it was as if he had started to shave himself bald, but stopped most of the way through. Coop's hair was thick, and longer on top than any of the other diplomatic specialists assigned to us. I wondered if he put hair gel in it and went out to clubs in his spare time.

He helped me slip into the jacket. It was still warm from his body, and smelled faintly of nice aftershave. I was betting he fought to keep his hair long enough to style. I didn't blame him, but it was just interesting. He was also one of the few of the men who weren't married or in a serious relationship.

Becket and most of the others had been eager to have a diplomatic assignment in the States so they could be with their loved ones more. It was hard to maintain a relationship from halfway around the world, and usually in a place too dangerous to bring your family. Los Angeles was dangerous, but not in the same way as Pakistan.

"We really appreciate you asking for us this morning, Princess Meredith," Coop said.

"You're welcome, Agent Cooper, Agent Becket." I wrapped his jacket around me. It covered me to midcalf, as if I'd borrowed my father's coat to wear, but I was warmer, and that seemed more important than looking sexy, for now.

"Not to look a gift horse in the mouth," Becket said, "but why us?"

I smiled at him, because I'd already learned that he could never quite leave well enough alone. He had to ask that one more question, take that one more small chance. Cooper would never have asked.

"I saw you practicing with the other guards."

He looked embarrassed, rubbing his big blunt-fingered hands down his sides. "Yeah, that wasn't such a great idea."

"I told you that before we did it," Cooper said.

Becket shrugged those big shoulders. "Hey, how do we tell the princess here that we can take care of her, if we don't know how we stack up against her main guards?"

"That was the reasoning that made me agree to it," Cooper said, but he didn't look happy about it.

"You both acquitted yourselves well," I said.

"Acquitted ourselves well; if that means got our asses handed to us, then I'll agree," Becket said.

I laughed, and a distant flight of seagulls seemed to laugh back at me, as they arched their wings and let the wind carry them closer to us.

"Yeah, it was pretty embarrassing," Cooper said.

"Becket's turn of phrase was what made me laugh. You both did well in practice—Doyle said as much, and he never gives praise unless it's earned."

"Yeah, your . . . main . . . person," Becket stopped and looked across me at his partner.

Cooper said, "Captain Doyle is reserved about a lot of things when we're around."

"And by 'we,' he means humans," Becket said.

Cooper frowned at him. "I said what I meant, Beck."

Becket shrugged. "We're the odd people out here, Cooper. The princess knows that; why not say so?"

I smiled again and let the banter go on around me. Doyle hadn't liked me coming out to the beach house without him or Frost, but our shared man was still healing, and I'd felt that we needed to use the human guards more, at least the ones who had braved hand-to-hand practice with Doyle and the others. I had brought Saraid and Dogmaela with me, but they were inside the house. One of the other female guards needed a word with them. The shared abuse had made many of the guards more comfortable talking to each other, so I'd let them handle it. I'd also reminded Doyle that there were other sidhe guards at the beach house. We'd started putting anyone we weren't sure was entirely trustworthy here first. The main estate was building more rooms, but there were still more sidhe than rooms. The other sidhe had been very insulted that I'd come down to the beach with only the human guards, until I'd asked them if they thought humans were lesser beings, bearing in mind that I was part human. To that they'd said the only thing they could—"Of course not," which was a lie, but a political lie. When everybody knows it's a lie, it isn't like lying at all, just doing what I wanted them to do, and we could all live with that. The sidhe had been impressed that Becket and Cooper had joined practice at the main house. That the men had even tried to hold their own with the fey had earned them points with me and with Doyle. He'd said, "They aren't bad, and for humans they are really quite good." If Becket only knew what high praise that was from him, he'd have been happier about it.

"It's okay, Agent Cooper, you and the rest of the human guards are the outsiders at the house."

"See, told you so," Becket said.

"But it's not just because you're human, it's because you're new. We don't know you yet, and you don't know us; that makes you all the odd people out. There's a learning curve when new sidhe join the guards, too," I said.

"You usually give very good eye contact, but you're staring at the horizon while we're talking. What are you looking for, Princess Meredith?" Cooper asked.

"King Sholto."

"What?"

"You asked what I was looking for, and I answered the question."

"I thought his title was Lord Sholto," Becket said.

"He's the only sidhe noble with a different title in another court," I said.

"Is Lord, or King, Sholto coming in by boat?" Cooper asked.

"No," I said.

"Then why are you looking out at the ocean for him?"

"He is coming from the ocean, just not by boat," I said.

"Okay, I'll bite; if he's not coming by boat, how is he getting here?" Becket asked.

"He'll walk," I said.

"Princess, you don't do this often, but when you do, it's like pulling teeth to get you to answer a straight question."

I turned and looked at Cooper, and thought about it. "I'm sorry, you're right. I've spent the last few months with just other fey, and we aren't always known for straightforward information sharing."

Becket gave a snorting laugh. "That's an understatement."

"Becket," Cooper said, voice sharp.

"It's all right, Agent Cooper, truth is truth."

"All right, then if King Sholto isn't coming by boat, how is he going to walk here?"

"Magic," I said, and went back to staring at the edge of the water.

"Can you elaborate, please?"

I smiled, and thought about it. "Do you know what his title is as lord among the sidhe?"

"He's the Lord of That Which Passes Between," Cooper said.

"Exactly," I said.

"What does that mean, Princess?" Becket asked, and he sounded impatient now.

I sighed, and shivered for a minute even in the borrowed jacket. "The edge of sea and shore is a place between, which means he can use it to travel to me."

"You said he was going to walk; do you mean he's going to walk onto the beach like magic?" Cooper asked.

"Not *like* magic, it *is* magic."

"You mean literally 'oooh' magic?" Becket said, making a finger-waving gesture when he said "oooh."

"Exactly," I said, smiling. I liked Becket. He made me remember that I missed being around people who weren't sidhe, or fey, or familiar with the high courts. It was a more formal world, and I'd been surrounded by people who had lived in it for centuries, and it had made me lose some sense of myself that wasn't sidhe, or even brownie. I'd forgotten that being human could be fun, and that though I'd hated being exiled to Los Angeles without any way to interact with another sidhe, and losing all of faerie had been like a living death, I'd found a part of my humanity that had gotten lost at the Unseelie Court. I'd grown up with a house full of sidhe and other fey, but I'd gone to school with humans—American humans—and our neighbors had been the same. I hadn't realized until this last year that being raised outside faerie had given me more of a connection to my human grandfather's culture, and having the ambassador and his men in the house had made me realize I'd gotten sucked right back into the culture of the courts. It was a different culture than either the Seelie or Unseelie, but it was still not a human way of looking at things. The soldiers who had visited hadn't helped me understand that, because they'd come more as priests and priestesses seeking answers. That hadn't been normal enough to make me realize that I was in danger of losing something important. My human great-grandfather had been a good man, from every story I'd ever heard. He'd been a Scottish farmer who had been special enough to fall in love with the family brownie, not a type of fey known for their beauty. I didn't want to lose that part of my heritage again. I'd actually begun to wonder if I needed to work at the Grey and Hart Detective Agency just to remember that I was more than a faerie princess. I was a person, I was Merry Gentry, or had been for three years until the queen had sent Doyle to these Western Lands to find me and bring me home. Now I had sidhe lovers, and faerie had come to us. I had almost everything I'd been homesick for, plus three children, and the magic of the Goddess returned, but in all that wonder I didn't want to forget that I was part human, too, and part brownie. I wanted to find a way to honor all those parts of me, and share that with our children.

"You look very serious all of a sudden, Princess; what ya thinkin' about?"

I glanced at Becket and smiled. "That I'm part human, not just sidhe, and I need to be reminded of that."

"I don't understand," he said.

"Are you saying we remind you what it's like to be human?" Cooper asked.

"No, you remind me that I *am* human."

He gave me a look, one dark eyebrow rising. "Forgive me, princess, but you aren't exactly human."

"My great-grandfather was."

"And your grandfather is Uar the Cruel, one of the high nobles of the Seelie Court, who is mentioned in myth and folklore going back hundreds of years."

"My great-grandmother was a brownie."

"And your father was Essus, Prince of Flesh and Fire. He was worshipped as a god before the Romans conquered Britain."

"Agent Cooper, are you saying that the noble side of my heritage is more important than the non-noble side?"

He looked startled. "I wouldn't say that. I mean, I didn't . . . I didn't mean that."

"She so got you, Coop," Becket said.

"I didn't mean to insult you, Princess, but you can't just say you're human with the pedigree you have."

"I didn't say I'm just human, but I'm not just sidhe either, and I want my children to understand that they're more than just sidhe. Through me they're brownie, and through Galen they're pixie, and Doyle gives them phouka. I want them to understand that they are more than just sidhe of either court. I want them to value all parts of their heritage."

"It sounds like you've been thinking about this," Cooper said.

I nodded. "For a few days, yes."

"So you want your kids to grow up being more human?" Becket asked.

"Yes," I said. A shimmering caught my eye at the edge of the sea. One moment it was just the waves and the sand, and the next Sholto just stepped out of nowhere and started walking up the beach toward us.

"Holy shit!" Becket said.

Cooper had started to reach for his gun, and then forced himself to relax, or at least pretend.

The wind caught Sholto's hair, streaming it out around him in a pale blond halo that intermingled with the black of his cloak, so that he strode toward me in a cloud of silken hair and dark cloth. The three yellow rings of his eyes had already begun to shine as if they were carved of gold, citrine, and topaz. It almost distracted from the beauty of his face, the broad shoulders, the sheer physicality of him as he strode toward me.

"You can try to be human, Princess, but that's not human," Becket said.

"Oh, Agent Becket, you have no idea how not human he is." Then Sholto was there, sweeping me into his arms, kissing me as if he hadn't seen me in months, instead of just days. I wrapped myself around him, and he put his hands under my ass and started up the stairs, his mouth still married to mine. He climbed smoothly, easily, as if he could keep kissing me forever, whether he was climbing a set of stairs, or a mountain.

Becket called after us, "I don't know, Princess, I think the glowing eyes give it away."

I broke from the kissing long enough to look over Sholto's shoulder and let the men see that my own eyes had started to burn.

They looked startled, but it didn't stop Becket from saying, "Humans don't glow, just so you know."

I might have said something pithy back, but Sholto ran his hand through my hair and kissed me again, and nothing seemed more important than giving all my attention to the man in my arms.

THIRTY-FIVE

We passed the sidhe in a hurried rush. Some of them looked astonished, others . . . *hungry* was the only word I had for it. They all watched us pass, though; Unseelie culture didn't demand that they look away. In fact, in all fey culture, if someone was trying to be attractive or sexy and you didn't pay attention, it was an insult; no one insulted us.

Sholto and I made it to the bedroom before the clothes began to come off, but barely. In fey culture we could have been nude in front of the guards and it would have been taken in stride. Nudity taboos were more human, and both the Seelie and Unseelie courts were closer to the rest of the fey; nudity meant just without clothes on, neither good nor bad.

I did toss Cooper's jacket off to one side so it wouldn't be in danger of getting messy. If I'd been thinking more clearly I'd have thrown it back to him before we got to the bedroom, but I wasn't thinking clearly about anything. It was all hands, and mouths, and the weight of Sholto above me as he pressed me to the bed. It wasn't a time for thinking, it was a time for feeling his smooth skin under my fingertips, his muscles under my hands, him pulling my top over my head in one eager motion so he could stare down at my breasts in the lacy bra I'd chosen for him.

"Your breasts were magnificent before, but now they are beyond amazing," he said in a voice that was low and almost hushed, the way people talk in museums around works of art.

"Hopefully they won't stay this big," I said, gazing down at more mounding creamy goodness than I'd ever thought possible on my own body.

He shook his head, all that pale hair sliding around the blackness of his clothes. "No, Meredith, they are beautiful, you are beautiful."

"I'm just not used to them this big. I pass a mirror and it startles me. The belly is gone, but the breasts are still out to here." I laughed.

He drew his gaze up to look into my eyes. The glow in his eyes was just a faint shine now, like a fire banked for the night, hot just near the center of the wood.

"Whether your breasts stay this magnificent size, or become the beautiful, pale mounds that they were, they, and you, will still be as desirable."

I hadn't realized until that moment just how much the body changes were still bothering me. You want to be able to breast-feed, especially when you have a baby like Bryluen who might not be able to take formula. I'd expressed milk for her before I came on this little booty call. The others could have formula in a pinch, but Bree couldn't. It wasn't all natural, and only that was safe for her.

"Such a serious face, Meredith; what are you thinking about that steals the light from your eyes?"

I sighed. "The babies, Bryluen in particular." I looked up at him, touching his arms where they were tented on each side of my body, while the rest of him sat sideways on the bed, most of his long legs still off the side of it.

"I'm sorry, Sholto, you deserve better than a distracted me. Would it be odd to say, this is the longest I've been away from the triplets, and I'm both excited for the time away and weirdly missing them. That doesn't make any sense at all, does it?"

He smiled, and it was gentle. I wondered if I was the only one who got to see that particular smile. "It means you will be a good mother, are

a good mother. You are, what's the phrase, wired right for motherhood."
He suddenly looked very serious, almost sad.

I stroked my hands up and down his bare arms; he'd taken off his
near-medieval-looking tunic but was still wearing a very modern black
undershirt. It was one of those designed more for working out than just
wearing, but the stretchable material fitted his muscular upper body like
a glove, tucked into the top of black breeches that matched the tunic that
was now on the floor.

"Now why is your face all serious?" I asked.

He looked at me, smiling, but it was tinged with something not
happy. "To another female in my bed I might lie, but that is not our rule."

"No," I said, "honesty between us, always."

"As my queen commands," he said, smiling more now.

I smiled back. "As my king requests," I said.

We smiled at each other with that special happy softness that couples
have when they use one of their endearments that they use with no one
else.

"Then I will speak honestly to my queen. I had feared that perhaps
you would not be wired to be a mother."

I studied his face, trying to read more of his thoughts. "Why would
you think that?"

"Your own mother is not the most maternal of women. Your aunt
was devoted to her son, but cruel and horrible to almost everyone else.
Your uncle, the king, is little better. Your grandfather is Uar the Cruel."
He shrugged, and raised a hand so he could take my hand in his.

"You were worried that my family is mostly crazy, so would I be
crazier than I seem, too?"

He began to rub his thumb over my knuckles. "Have I said too much
honesty to you, my queen?"

I smiled up at him and squeezed his hand. "No, I was thinking the
very same thing earlier this week, but not about me, about the babies."

I sat up and shared my fears with him. It might have been more logical to share them with Doyle, or Frost, or one of the fathers who actually
lived with me, but sometimes it's not about logic in relationships, it's

about the people, and in that moment Sholto gave me an opening to talk that no other man in my life had managed. I'd noticed that it worked that way a lot; the man you thought would be perfect for this or that wasn't always the one who worked best for it.

He wrapped his arms around me, pressed me to the slickness of the modern undershirt, my hands trailing a little lower as I hugged him back, so I felt the nearly velvet texture of his leather trousers, still tucked into the knee-high boots. I pressed the side of my face against the firm strength of his chest. I could hear his heartbeat against my cheek. It was a good, steady sound, the kind of sound you could plan your life around if you were looking for a center to your world. Sometimes I felt I had too many centers to my world, and the triplets had just amplified the sense of too many people pulling me in too many directions.

His voice vibrated up through his chest against my face as we held each other. "Your idea of raising them with more non-sidhe and humans is sound, and they will already be visiting my court. That will certainly expose them to a wider world of faerie than the high courts can offer."

I leaned back enough to see his face, sorry that I couldn't keep the beat of his heart in my ear, but my desire to see his face was greater.

"In a few days, or weeks, we'll know which of the babies is yours; don't you mean that child will visit your court?"

He looked down at me, his face arrogant and almost heartrendingly handsome. It was the face he wore when he was hiding his emotions. Why did he feel that he needed to hide from me about this?

"Do you want only my genetic child to visit the sluagh?"

"No, I want them all to understand just how diverse their world is, but I hadn't talked to you about it, and I didn't want to assume."

Some tension went out of his arms, his shoulders, and that release traveled through my arms, where I held him. His face went from arrogant and model perfect to smiling broadly at me. He looked so joyous that it made me smile back.

"Only one babe may be mine genetically, but they are all a part of you, Meredith, and I love you." He touched my lips with a fingertip, as if

I'd made some motion to speak. "I know you are not in love with me, nor I with you, not yet, but I do love you more than any woman before you."

I kissed his hand and used mine to move him so I could speak. "I am honored to have such a place in your heart, Sholto."

"This sounds like the beginning of a 'let's just be friends' speech."

I laughed then, and he looked puzzled.

"Oh, Sholto, no, I do not want to friendzone you. I love what we have together. I love that we do things in the bedroom that no one else can do with me, because no one else has the diversity of your equipment."

He laughed then, joyous and somehow masculine, that sound. I liked the tones of men laughing when they were happy enough not to worry how it sounded, or who heard them. Good that I did, since I was likely to be surrounded by men for the rest of my days.

"That you list my extras as part of what you love about me makes me love you even more."

"Good, because I love that you want to take all the babies to see your kingdom. I love that you spend more time in the nursery helping with them than half the other men, even though you don't live at the house all the time. I love watching your face when we're alone and how many different expressions I get to see that I'd never seen at court, or when other people are with us. I love the look on your face when you hold the babies. I love how your arms feel when you hold me, and the sound of your heart when I press my cheek against your chest."

"And this would be when Rhys or Galen says, 'But you aren't in love with me.'"

"But you aren't in love with me, either," I said.

"True," he said, and he pulled me close again. "And they are, and it is always hard to love more than you are loved."

I snuggled up against his body and said, "That sounds like experience talking."

"It is. I had many a serious crush on noble ladies of both courts, but I was the Queen's Perverse Creature, as Doyle was her Darkness, and Frost her Killing Frost. I feared someday that she would say, 'Where is my Creature, bring me my Creature,' when she wanted to send the sluagh out to frighten or kill her enemies." He held me tight and said, "Before you came to me, Meredith, I feared I would simply become the Queen's Creature."

"Doyle is the Queen's Darkness," I said, softly.

"Yes, but it is frightening and romantic for the Queen to say, 'Where is my Darkness, bring me my Darkness,' and someone would bleed or die at his hand."

"You and your host have made men lose their minds at the sight of all of you in full strength, and bled many, killed many."

"What is that old children's rhyme, 'Sticks and stones may break my bones, but words will never hurt me'? Anyone who says that doesn't understand the power of words. They can cut deeper than any knife, hit harder than any fist, touch parts of you that nothing physical will ever reach, and the wounds that some words leave never heal, because each time the word is thrown at you, labeled on you, you bleed afresh from it. It's more like a whip that cuts every time, until you feel it must flay the very skin from your bones, and yet outwardly there is no wound to show the world, so they think you are not hurt, when inside part of you dies every time."

I hugged him as tight as I could. "I love you, Sholto, King of the Sluagh, Lord of That Which Passes Between, Lord of Shadows, I love all of you, and would not have you any other way than you are."

"Oh, Meredith, Meredith, Meredith, I do love you more and more."

"I cannot offer you to make love yet, but I want to touch and be touched by you. I want to feel all those wonderful extras do the amazing things that only you can do. I want all of you, touching as much of me as possible."

The shine in his tri-gold eyes brightened as if someone had set a match, and the golden-yellow flame was coming alive again. "Whatever my queen desires," he said, and took me in his arms again, but this time the skintight shirt wasn't flat against his body. Bumps and bulges stretched the fabric and began to move, pulsing and writhing under the shirt. It was still tucked into his pants so they couldn't escape, and then the edge of the shirt appeared from his pants, and I realized that his extras were pulling the shirt loose from the inside. The first tentacle peeked out of the cloth, wriggling free like a snake spilled out of a bag. Once analogies like snakes in a bag had frightened me, made me not want to touch Sholto. Now, just the sight of the tentacles beginning to appear at the edge of his shirt and pants tightened things low in my body, anticipating the pleasure to come.

He let the thinner, lower tentacles roll the shirt up slowly, exposing his stomach below the belly button, which was smooth and showed that he'd been working out with the rest of my warriors, but above that round indentation that I'd licked more times than I could count now was the first fringe of thin tentacles that were as pearl white as the rest of his skin, but with darker red tips. I knew that those tips had tiny, delicate suction cups on them. The thought of what Sholto could do with them made me shiver with anticipation.

The shirt rolled up a little more to reveal the first grouping of longer, thinner tentacles that grew in groupings around his ribs and upper stomach. I knew that they were a hundred times more sensitive and flexible than any fingers. They helped roll the shirt up, but it was the larger, heavier tentacles at the far edge of his chest that did most of the lifting. The medium tentacles rolled the cloth, while the thicker ones lifted that roll upward, until they themselves were revealed in all their glory, thick and white with a marbling of gold along their lengths. They sat just below his nipples, thick and heavy like leprosy-pale pythons, except they stretched and grew in size more like other body parts that were very sidhe, very human male. Once the tentacles had always been this real, and only his ability to use glamour and illusion had hidden them, but now unless he willed it they were like a very realistic tattoo. The Goddess and God, returning their grace to us, had manifested for each of us according to what we most needed, or what was most useful to them.

"The look on your face as I revealed them, Meredith, it is a look I have waited all my life to see on another sidhe's face."

I reached out, and one of the thickest tentacles wrapped around my hand and wrist. The image may have brought snakes to mind, but these felt almost rubbery, like petting a dolphin, except not wet. I squeezed where the tentacle wrapped around my hand, holding "hands."

"Now that you have the tattoo you might be able to find another sidhe lover," I said, gazing down the length of the undulating tentacles, like a bed of exotic sea creatures waving in the current, except this current was his body, his muscles, his thoughts.

"But they would only love me with the tattoo in place hiding my extras." He ran his hands through both sides of the graceful movements of those other body parts.

My gaze followed his hands down through all that potential until he came to the band of his pants, where he caressed his hands over the only bulge that was still hidden behind cloth. I let out a shuddering sigh, because I knew that the promise of that bulge was everything a woman could want.

"The heat in your eyes never flinches, just sharpens as you see things you like more, but there is nothing on me that you do not enjoy in some way." He started drawing me closer with the tentacle I was holding "hands" with.

I half crawled and half let him pull me across the bed toward him where he stood beside it. My heart was racing, my body already wet, though right now that was a mixed blessing, a messy mixed blessing.

"I am so sorry that I had any issues at first," I said.

He smiled and wrapped another tentacle around my other wrist. He wasn't holding hands this time; he wrapped around my wrist like a rope, or a chain made of muscle and skin. The one I'd been holding twisted in my grip and he suddenly had both my wrists bound. It caught my breath in my throat, sped my pulse even more.

"Just as I need someone who sees all of me as desirable, you need bondage."

"We can't be rough yet," I said, but my voice was already lower, almost choked, just from him holding my arms out to my sides, and feeling the unbelievable strength as he held me. I knew I couldn't get away if he didn't want me to, and that was part of the thrill, but I also knew that if I asked he would let me go instantly, and that was one of the reasons I trusted him to do bondage with me. It was all about trust and desire, and understanding yourself and your lover.

"I'll never be rough compared to Mistral, but you wouldn't want that rough every night." He pulled me over the bed, my body sliding help-lessly toward him. There was nothing I could do to stop that muscled strength. Luckily I didn't want to escape; I so wanted to be caught.

He smiled, and it filled his eyes with that darkness that wasn't fey, or human, but just male. It made me shiver, but not with fear.

"No," I whispered.

"How long has it been since you had any bondage?" he asked, pulling me close enough that some of the smaller tentacles could trace across my skin in teasing lines.

"You know how long," I said, my voice a little hoarse.

"Do I? As you said, I don't live with the rest of you; how do I know what you are doing?" He made it light, teasing, but sometimes when we tease there is a truth to it.

"Do you want to live with us?"

"It is not want, Meredith. I cannot leave my kingdom and move to yours." He forced my hands straight out to my sides, until it was almost uncomfortable. His tentacles stretched effortlessly outward to hold me, while the smaller ones traced teasing lines, careful not to go inside my bra or panties.

I found my voice and said, "I have no kingdom of my own."

"Perhaps not, but you have a court of faerie, and more magic gathers to you every day."

I didn't know what to say to that, so I said nothing and just gave myself over to the sensation of him touching me, and being held so ter-ribly, wonderfully tight. I began to pull. I knew I couldn't break his grip by just struggling, but sometimes struggling is the best part, or the best part until the man pins you and makes the struggling impossible.

I closed my eyes and pulled harder.

"You can't get away," he said, voice full of that arrogance that big, athletic men can have.

"I know," I said.

"Then why try?"

I opened my eyes and let him see that my eyes had started to shine, just from this. "Because I like to struggle, and you like to feel me struggle."

"True," he said, and it was almost a whisper. One of the thinner tentacles trailed the edge of my bra, and another the band of my panties.

"Please," I whispered.

"Please what?" he asked, but the look on his face said he knew exactly what I wanted.

But I played the game and said, "Slide inside my bra and panties, touch me, suck me, make me come."

"And what do I get out of it?"

"I'll return the favor," I said.

He grinned, and then it turned into a smile that was full of as much lust and eagerness as anyone could have wished for, and I did wish for it.

"Ladies first," he said.

It took me a second to realize what he meant, and then he slipped those long, thin pieces of himself inside my clothing and began to caress and tease along my breasts, and at the top edge of my panties, not really sliding inside them, but only playing just inside the band, when I knew he could go so much farther down.

He began to suck on my breasts, a small suction "mouth" wrapping around my nipples. Other parts of him slid a little farther inside my panties, tickling and caressing and finally sliding lower to tease, caress, and begin to bring that near-magical pleasure that usually takes someone's mouth, but Goddess had shaped Sholto so that his mouth could be kissing mine, while other parts of him kissed me, so much lower down.

He drew back from my lips, his eyes glowing brighter, the circle of yellow around his pupil beginning to glitter like molten gold, the amber circle gleaming, and that last circle of pale yellow like elm leaves in autumn shimmering in rich, golden sunlight. His hair spread out around him like a cloak of new snow with just a hint of yellow, like snow reflecting the light of the rising sun. His skin began to blaze as if the moon were rising inside him to shine a cold, cool light that played out the tips of the smallest tentacles like shining rubies, and the largest ones that held me so tight were marbled with colored lightning, soft red, softer violet, bands of gold like the colors of his eyes. He was a thing carved of light, and color, and magic. It vibrated down his body, so that his skin hummed against mine, and the weight of pleasure began to build between my legs, and my breasts. It quickened my breath, and those shining ruby tips sucked harder, deeper, and that heaviness between my legs burst into pleasure and power, spilling through my body in a wash of light that decorated the room in the twin shines of our moon-bright skin, and when I threw my head back to scream my orgasm, my hair shone like spun rubies and garnets woven in cool fire across my face.

He didn't stop with my screams of pleasure, but kept sucking, stroking, until one orgasm followed another, and I could see the spark of power from my own eyes like emerald and melting gold, until I was blinded by the colored fire of my own magic.

Sholto brought me until I was a quivering, shaking thing, and only the pull of his body held me upright. He laid me down on my side, on the bed. I lay there shivering with happy aftershocks, my eyelids quivering so hard that I couldn't open my eyes and was literally blind with pleasure.

I sensed the bed moving like a distant thought, but I couldn't think what it might mean. I couldn't do anything but lie there and let the aftershocks of pleasure have their way with me. The light in my eyes and hair had faded enough that I could see the colors of the actual room in bits and pieces, when a hand smoothed my hair back from my face. I blinked and tried to focus, to see; I knew it was Sholto, but in that instant he was a pale blur of movement and colors seen through the fluttering of my eyelids.

He leaned in and kissed me, soft, but there was still magic in him, so that the kiss vibrated and tickled across my lips. It brought a soft moan from me, and then he lifted my head and put a pillow ever so gently underneath. He stroked fingers down my cheek, and I was able to turn toward his touch. Parts of me were beginning to work again, but the languorous edge of orgasm still held most of me delightfully immobile.

He ran a fingertip across my lower lip, and I opened my mouth. I wasn't sure if I meant to kiss him or just to touch more of him, but he took it as invitation, finger sliding between my lips. I closed my mouth around him, and the movement was so much like sucking on other things that it was almost a shock to feel the bone and hardness of finger, when part of me had already started to think about other, bigger things that had no bones, but only round, solid, flesh.

He pulled his finger almost out of my mouth and then slid it back in until his knuckle met my mouth, and then he pulled out again, and began to slide in and out, and then two fingers for me to suck and lick, and then three. He had to be careful with his fingernails not to cut me as he began to plunge his fingers in faster, and then four and he couldn't go in deep now, because he was too wide and the fingernails were harder to be careful with. I rolled my eyes up to him, and found him nude and eager. The tentacles were like a dream painted across his skin, a tattoo of exquisite detail, but his body was lean and solid, and human looking. I'd asked before, so I knew that the tentacles got in the way of his view when I was in certain positions, and he liked to watch me while we made love.

Now he knelt above me, his body as muscled and sculpted as any sidhe in my bed. He folded his thumb in with his fingers and shoved all of it into my mouth. I opened as wide as I could, and still he could only push in to the second knuckle of his hand; there was just no way to go deeper when he was that wide. He started to back out, but I grabbed his wrist and urged him to push in farther. His eyes widened, but he didn't argue, just kept pushing his hand into my mouth, pushed, pushed, until my mouth was impossibly wide and it was uncomfortable, but there was something about that discomfort that I enjoyed. He finally shoved his hand as hard and far into my mouth as he'd ever gotten it, and I finally had to tap his arm and let him know that I was done, I could take no more.

He drew his hand carefully out of my mouth, and before I could completely catch my breath, the hand that had been so deep in my mouth was wrapped around that long, solid, quiveringly eager part of him, and the rounded head was against my lips like an invitation.

I opened my mouth for him, because after that much of his fist inside me, I wanted as much of the rest of him inside me as possible. I mounded the pillow up so that my mouth was like an offering to that long, hard piece of him. It felt so much better than just fingers; it seemed to complete something in me to feel him slide between my lips, across my tongue, and then not too deep, before he pulled out, but I grabbed his ass and started pushing him in and out faster and harder than he and I usually preferred, but Sholto had said it earlier—it had been a long time for me. Months of not daring to risk an orgasm throwing me into labor, months of having to be so careful, so safe. I didn't want to be either today.

He followed my urgings and begin to slide himself deep into my throat, pushing until he buried himself as deep against my mouth as he could, and I had to fight my body, force my throat to relax around all that hard flesh. I urged him on with my hands on his body, with the shining that began in my skin and eyes, that set my hair blazing like spun rubies around the edges of my vision. The tattoo across the moonlit white of his skin glowed with the colors I'd seen on them so that his human shape ran with colors in a pale rainbow play of red, violet, shades of gold that mirrored his eyes that stared down at me as he plunged himself fast and faster into my mouth and down my throat.

I began to have to time my breathing for the top of his stroke, grab a quick breath and then he was down, plunging inside me, gagging me almost, and then pushing past even that, cutting off my air. He found a rhythm that was deep and slow, which gave me more time to breathe at the top of his stroke, but also meant he was deeper, longer down my throat, so that I began to have to fight my body not to panic at the lack of air, and even that filled a need, so that I wrapped my hands around the tightness of his ass and held him tight with him plunged so deep inside me that my mouth was sealed against the front of his body and I fought my body not to gag, not to panic, as it asked to breathe, and all the time our bodies shone bright and brighter, painting the room in shadows and light.

He vibrated across my tongue, down my throat so that the deep, plunging thrum of him seemed to calm the panic and just make me want to hold him inside me as long as I could. Then between one downstroke and the next, the orgasm hit me, one made up of the feel of him inside my mouth; all that thick, vibrating flesh brought me almost as if he had been shoved between my legs. It made me set my nails into his body as my body writhed around him; when he drew out enough for me to breathe, I screamed my orgasm around him.

He cried out above me, and then he shoved himself down my throat one last time. I felt the involuntary movement as his body pulsed and he spilled himself down my throat so far back I couldn't taste him but only felt the sensation of warmth. So far down that I didn't so much swallow as he poured himself down my throat, while I rode my own orgasm, nails digging into his ass, the rest of my body almost convulsing around him, helpless and eager for him.

When he was done, he drew himself out enough for me to breathe in a gasping rush of air. He collapsed over me on all fours, arms on the other side of my head and the pillow I rested on. His head hung down, his hair spilled around us both like a shining, silken tent. He pulled himself out of my mouth as I let my head roll farther down the pillow.

He found his words first and said in a voice that was still breathless with effort, "Oh, my God and Goddess, that was amazing."

"Yes," I said, "yes, it was."

He moved his head enough so we could look at each other, so he was looking at me almost upside down as he said, "I love you, Meredith."

I smiled up at him and said the only answer there ever was for such a moment: "I love you, too, Sholto." Rhys and Galen would argue that I didn't love them as much as I loved Doyle and Frost, and that was true, but in moments like this I did love the man I was with, maybe not always in the way he would wish, or want, but it was true: still real, still love.

Sholto moved so that he could lie beside me. I curled into the mound of his chest, the curve of his arm, the hollow of his shoulder, and was content.

CHAPTER

THIRTY-SIX

We slept, and I dreamed, but I wasn't alone in this dream. Sholto walked beside me, his bigger hand clasped in mine. We had to hold hands, because the rose vine tattoos on our forearms were real again, alive again, binding us together with the vine that moved like something much more alive than any normal rose. Its thorns bit into our flesh, and bound us with flesh and blood and life. Sholto was crowned once more with a wreath of living herbs and tiny white, pink, and lavender flowers. I felt the crown on my own hair and knew it was mistletoe and white roses. I was dressed in a flowing white dress, and Sholto in white tunic and breeches, tucked into silver-gray boots. I wondered, *Why am I still barefoot?*, and between one step and the next I felt flat sandals on my feet. Apparently, I'd just needed to ask.

"Meredith," Sholto said softly, "where are we?"

We stood in the middle of a flat plain with short, scrubby grass and harsh, dry weeds. The ground that showed between the plants was pale and dry tannish brown; there wasn't much water on this ground, but it wasn't the barren sand and rock I'd seen before. In fact, when I looked up there was a small house in the distance. It looked old and weather-beaten, but "normal," or maybe *American Midwest* was a better phrase.

"There's a road with power lines behind us," Sholto said.

I glanced back and found he was correct. It was drier and more desolate, but it felt like Midwestern farmland, and indeed there were distant houses scattered around more cultivated fields. The land around this house was barren and the barn near it was literally falling down around the wrecks of farm equipment peeking out from the vines that seemed to be both destroying the wood and holding it together.

"I think we're somewhere in the United States, maybe the Midwest, but it's drier than Missouri or Illinois, different vegetation, too."

"I thought you only appeared in the desert where your soldiers were fighting."

"I did, until now," I said. The sun was bright overhead. If a car came down the road we'd be exposed to view. Up to this point only the soldiers and those fighting with them had been able to see me, as far as I knew, but someone getting pictures with their phone of us standing here like this would be on the Internet in minutes. I pushed the thought away and tried to "feel" who had called me, us, and why? Always before, people's lives had been in danger. What was dangerous here, and who was in danger?

"I thought only you traveled in dream at the Goddess's bidding?" Sholto said.

"That was true, until now." I stared at the house with its ramshackle barn. I thought that was our goal, but I wasn't sure. Appearing here and not in some faraway country had thrown me, and having Sholto with me like this puzzled me more.

"I am the first of your men that the Goddess has drawn with you?" he asked.

"Yes," I said.

He smiled then, and said, "I am honored." The scent of herbs and roses grew stronger as if we walked in a garden surrounded by a bank of wild roses, instead of the barren yard that smelled of sunbaked grass and some bitter weed baking in the heat. It wasn't as hot as some of the deserts I'd been in, but it was still much hotter than Los Angeles.

I smiled at the fact that he was happy to be with me even here, not knowing why, or where. I squeezed his hand a little tighter, which made the vines squeeze a little tighter as if they were happy with us. It should have hurt, but it didn't; as before when we were handfasted by Goddess, it was more pressure than anything, though the blood dripped a little more. The dry ground soaked up the blood eagerly; moisture was moisture to the earth and plants.

"Why are we joined as a couple?"

"I don't know," I said, softly; we weren't whispering, but our voices were hushed the way you did in human churches sometimes, as if you knew God was near.

"Does your crown always manifest in dream and vision?"

"No, almost never."

"Is your soldier in the house?"

"I think so," I said, but I was . . . distracted and puzzled that Sholto had come with me. I'd been asleep and touching a lot of the other men, but they'd never been transported with me. Why Sholto? Why now? Why in our "wedding" finery? I tried to let the questions go so I could hear Goddess's message. If you let your thoughts get too loud, then you can't hear God, or Goddess.

I took in a deep breath, closed my eyes, and stilled my thoughts, but the warmth and solidity of Sholto's hand in mine was a part of that stillness. The wind touched my face, and I raised my head, eyes still closed, and knew that the house was where we needed to go. I couldn't have explained it in words, but "knew" in the same way that the flower knows which way the sun is rising; it is just that simple, and that complicated. I started walking toward the house, leading Sholto by the hand. He didn't question, just came with me, and that was a kind of faith. I wasn't sure if it was faith in the Goddess, or faith in me, or both, but I walked forward believing, and he came beside me the same way. Our blood decorated the ground as we walked, and began to decorate our white clothes as the dry, hot wind whipped my dress around us. It spattered our blood across the white like a Jackson Pollock painting.

Most of the paint had peeled off the house, leaving it shades of weathered gray, the wood pitted and marked as if it had been beaten by small, sharp objects, but I knew that it was just the elements of wind, rain, heat, and time. Houses need love and care just like animals and people; without it, our dwellings begin to fade and die just like we do. No one had loved this house in a long time.

We stepped up on the warped, uneven boards of the porch and I reached out to the screen door. It had been torn long enough that the edges had begun to discolor, the screen going almost brittle with heat and neglect.

The inner wood door was peeling and had warped so badly that I couldn't push it open easily. Sholto put his hand on it and together we opened it. It should have made a horrible racket of breaking wood and scraping metal, but it didn't. The door opened as soundlessly as if it had been recently oiled and opened only moments before, though I knew it had to have been weeks since the door was used. With the silence of the door came a more profound quiet, as if the world were holding its breath. I saw the living room under a layer of gray dust, the floor littered with mail as if months' worth had just been thrown on the floor. There was a couch sagging under a pile of knitted afghans, and a pillow. A small gray cat was curled up on the pillow, blinking huge yellow eyes at us. I wondered if it could see us.

As if in answer to my thought it hopped down from the couch in one graceful arc, padding toward the only hallway that led to the left. It turned and looked back at us, and gave a plaintive meow, tail twitching.

"It wants something," I said.

"I'm more interested in what Goddess wants," Sholto said.

The cat gave him an unfriendly look, then looked at me, dismissing him, or that was how it seemed to me. The scent of roses and herbs grew stronger.

"It's like standing in a sun-warmed garden full of herbs and roses; the scent of everything is stronger. Why?"

"The cat knows where we need to go," I said, and led us toward the waiting cat.

I think he opened his mouth to protest, but in the end he simply followed where I led. He followed me better than almost any of the men, considering he was a king in his own right; it was impressive.

The gray cat walked ahead of us, tail held high, tip twitching slightly. She stopped in front of the first closed door in the short hallway. There was another screen door at the end of the hallway. I wondered if that was the door people came in through, or if no one ever came into the house, or ever left it. No, the cat was too much a pet, too well cared for; it hadn't been alone for months.

The cat put a delicate paw up against the door and looked at me with those intense yellow eyes. It gave another plaintive meow.

A man's voice called out. "Stop it, Cleo, stop wailing outside the door. I left a message for Josh, he'll take care of you."

The cat meowed again and scratched at the door.

"Stop it!" he called out.

I thought I knew the voice. "Brennan," I said, softly.

"Who's there!" His voice sounded strident, almost panicked.

"Brennan, it's Meredith."

"Meredith, you can't be here. I am crazy."

The cat pawed at the door again. I used my free hand to touch the doorknob and open it. The cat slid inside as soon as there was an opening big enough for her slender body. We had to open the door wider for Sholto and me to step through.

The cat was already rubbing back and forth on his boots when he finally saw us. The dark of his desert tan had lightened, but his large brown eyes and short dark hair were the same. The hair was a little longer, but I knew that face now. One hand was around his necklace, and the other was holding a gun. It looked like a Glock, but I wasn't an expert on guns. I recognized ones I'd shot, or the people around me used frequently.

He blinked up at us, confused, as if he weren't sure what he was seeing. "Meredith, you don't look . . . is there someone with you? Are you holding someone's hand?"

"Why can't he see me?" Sholto asked, softly.

I didn't know, but out loud I said, "Yes, I have Sholto with me."

"Why can't I see him clearly?"

"What do you see?" I asked.

"It's like heat in the desert, the air wavering until you start thinking you see things that aren't there in the pattern of it."

I tugged on our bound hands and drew Sholto a step farther into the room. From the look on Brennan's face, Sholto must have simply appeared—one moment a wavering in the air, the next fully formed, solid, and real.

"What the hell!" Brennan exclaimed. He startled enough that the cat backed away from him, hissing, as if his foot had hit her accidentally.

"I'm sorry, Cleo, you okay?" He offered her the hand that had been tight around the charm around his neck, though perhaps *charm* wasn't the right word. It was a long, dark nail, with a leather cord bound around the top of it so that it hung point down just at that small depression at the base of the neck. It still looked discolored as if my blood might still have been on it. It had been part of the shrapnel used in a bomb. Every nail that had bled me had fallen out as I healed people that night, and each soldier who had been healed and gained a nail had kept it as a sort of talisman. I think it had started as superstition for having survived, but it had become more. It had become their cross, their holy item that gave them a direct link to Deity. But somehow, I was that deity. Their prayers that involved that bit of metal went to me, if the need was dire enough, but this was no desert battlefield.

I looked at the gun still in his hand as he tried to persuade the cat to come closer to him. I remembered that he'd said someone else would look after the cat, and I suddenly knew that there were battles being fought in this room.

"You called me, Brennan," I said.

He stopped trying to coax the cat and shook his head. "I didn't call you with blood, metal, and magic this time, Meredith. I got no wounds." He held his hand up as if to show it healed and whole.

"Not every wound leaves blood behind," Sholto said.

Brennan glanced at him. "I remember you from when I visited Meredith in Los Angeles, but I don't remember you with a crown, either of you." He started to motion with his gun, stopped himself in midmotion, and used his free hand. "What's with all this?"

"What were you thinking just a few minutes ago?" I asked.

He shook his head. "It doesn't matter."

"Brennan, you wrapped your hand around the symbol at your neck and you prayed. You prayed for something important enough to call me to your side and bring King Sholto with me. What was it?"

He shook his head again. "No."

"Brennan, you prayed to the Goddess and I'm here; tell me."

He glanced at us both again. "Why are your hands bound together?"

"It's how faerie and the Goddess handfasted us," I said.

"What does that mean, handfasted?"

"It means we are married, but with no official legalities."

"The Goddess herself has wed us," Sholto said. "It is the way all marriages were once between our kings and queens."

I smiled at him and went up on tiptoe to offer him a kiss.

"Oh God," Brennan said, and the sound was almost a sob.

I turned back to him. "What, what is it? What do you need so badly that you were about to shoot yourself?"

He looked at the gun in his hand as if he'd almost forgotten it. "It sounds too pathetic."

"You brought us all the way from L.A.—the least you could do is tell us why," I said.

He nodded as if that made sense to him. "Okay, okay, that's fair." He wrapped both hands around the gun, not like he was going to use it, but more like he was holding on to it as a sort of comfort object. He talked without looking at us.

"Jen is dating someone and it's serious. He's got money, a nice house, great career, hell, even his ex-wife says good things about him. They had a little girl and they seem to share the custody without getting all ugly the way most people do. Jen deserves someone that good. Someone who can give her all the things I can't. Someone who isn't crazy. Someone who doesn't wake up in a cold sweat reaching for his gun."

He looked at us then, and there was anguish in his face. "I could hurt her, by accident. I have flashbacks, nightmares. What if I lash out during one of them? I couldn't stand it if I hurt her. I'd rather die than risk that."

It was Sholto who moved forward and drew me with him. "So you've decided to kill yourself instead of telling this woman that you love her?"

Brennan looked startled, eyes too wide, and then he said, "No, she knows I love her. I told her, but I told her I was no good for her. I'm not good for anyone right now, not like this."

"Did you find a counselor like we talked about when you visited us?" I asked.

"There's a waiting list at the VA and I can't afford it any other way. The farm is dying. My dad must be rolling in his grave seeing how Josh neglected this place."

"Who's Josh?" I asked.

"My brother, kid brother, he was supposed to hire people to work the land after Dad died, but he didn't do anything. He finished his degree and got a good job, beautiful wife, baby. It's like he's turned against everything Dad taught us, or doesn't want to be reminded where we came from. This land has been in our family for nearly four generations, and now we're going to lose it to the bank, because my baby brother couldn't be bothered to take care of it. He lied to me in his letters, on the phone, looking at his face over Skype, and he fucking lied to me, said it was handled. He was handling it."

He laughed, but it was one of those laughs that was so bitter it needed a different word. "How can I drag Jen down with me? I'm about to lose everything. I can't do that to her."

"Does she have a job?" I asked.

"Her family owns a hardware store and a restaurant. She manages the store and helps out weekends in the restaurant."

"How's business?" I asked.

"Good, they're doing good."

"So, how would you drag her down with you? You're not endangering her job or her family's businesses, are you?" I asked.

"No, I mean her family are good people. Her dad offered me a job, but I know she made him do it."

"Is it a job you can do?" Sholto asked.

Brennan looked at him, and then nodded. "Yeah, I mean I worked in their hardware store all through high school. I know the business."

"Then maybe they need the help," I said.

He seemed to think about that. He looked at the gun in his hand, and then at us, and finally at me. "I was about to shoot myself, you're right, because I can't save the family farm. I left a message on my brother's phone telling him to take care of Cleo, the cat, and that I didn't want to see the farm go to the bank."

"You wanted to make sure he felt guilty and knew it was his fault," I said.

"I guess I did. Goddess, that is pathetic." He laid the gun on the side table. He looked up at us. "I guess I'm not going to kill myself today."

I didn't like the "today," but one battle at a time. We'd worry about winning the war later.

"You going to help me save the family farm?" he asked.

I said, "I don't think so. You weren't thinking about money when you were praying just now."

"The hell I wasn't, I was thinking how to get enough money to save the farm."

"Not when you prayed to me," I said.

He frowned and touched the nail again, wrapped his hand around it in a familiar gesture. "I was thinking about Jen, and how much I loved her."

"You called me with love, metal, and magic," I said, smiling.

"Love, not blood, but love."

The scent of roses and herbs was sweet and intense again. "Yes, Brennan, you called me, us, with love."

"I smell roses and . . . a garden."

"Take the job that Jen's father offered you," I said.

"I can't do that to them. Jen is getting serious with a really great guy."

"Better than you?" I asked.

"Not better than me, but better for her."

"Is he stronger than you?" Sholto asked.

"No."

"A better warrior?"

Brennan laughed again, but this time he was amused. "No."

"Is he more attractive than you are?" I asked.

Brennan had to think about that one, but finally said, "We're different, but he's not bad looking. He's handsome in a soft sort of way, if that
makes sense?"

"It does," I said.

"So you're stronger, a better warrior, and both of you are equally
handsome; how is he the better man?" Sholto asked.

"He's got more money, a better career, and he's not crazy."

"Does she need his money?" I asked.

"No, Jen isn't like that, and I told you her family is doing good. She's
practically running the hardware store on her own. That's why her dad
wanted me to come work with her; they can't find good help."

"Is she impressed with his career?" I asked.

He smiled. "No, not really. She says he's too ambitious for her. He'll
want to move away and not stay, and she can't leave her parents. She loves
the store and the town, always has."

"So, the only reason not to take the job, declare your love, and marry
the woman is because you are crazy and the other man is not?" Sholto
asked.

Brennan seemed to think about it again. "I guess so, but seriously I'm
not safe."

"Have you hurt anyone?" I asked.

"No, not yet."

It was Sholto who said, "One of your soldier friends hurt someone."

"How did you know?"

"So you have PTSD," I said. "So do I, so do a lot of us, but we don't
all hurt people. We get therapy, we talk to our friends, our family, other
soldiers, other survivors, and we heal. We find love." I smiled up at
Sholto.

There was a knock on the door, no, a pounding on the door, as if it had shut behind us as tightly as when we tried to open it. We heard someone running around the house, and then the screen door we'd seen at the end of the hallway banged open, and whoever it was came running down the hallway. I thought at first it would be the brother, but then a woman's voice yelled, "Brennan, damn it, you better not be dead, or I am so going to kill you!"

Brennan stood up. "It's Jen."

Sholto and I stood there as a woman with short brunette hair came rushing into the room. She saw him, the gun on the table, and ran at him slapping his chest, finally slapping his face hard enough to rock him.

"Your good-for-nothing brother told me the message you left. I left him in charge of the store and told him if anyone stole anything I'd see him in jail. Josh always was useless."

Brennan just stared at her, too surprised to speak, I think. He glanced back at us, but she either hadn't seen us or couldn't see us.

"Jen . . ." he started.

"Don't you Jen me, Brian Fitzgerald Brennan. You are not going to kill yourself; you are not going to leave me just because you're losing the family farm. It's just land, just a house." She grabbed his arms and shook him. "I'm here, I'm real, and I love you. Don't leave me to marry Tommy."

He was holding her arms, to keep her from shaking him more. "I thought you loved Tommy."

"No, he's nice enough, but he's so boring. I hate to be bored, you know that."

He laughed. "I remember."

"You never bore me, Brian, never. You're the only man who never bored me, even when we were kids."

"I love you, Jen. I'm sorry."

"Sorry you love me, or sorry you almost did something stupid and ruined it all?" She motioned at the gun.

"That last part, because Jennifer Alice Wells"—he dropped to one knee—"if you'll have me, I will do my best to never be boring for the rest of our long and interesting lives."

She started to cry, and so did I.

"I will, I do, you stupid man, yes, I will."

Brennan picked her up around the waist and lifted her off her feet. The gray cat, Cleo, sat on the floor and purred. He put Jen down and said, "Thank you."

"You're welcome," she said, laughing and crying.

"She can't see us," Sholto said, softly.

I shook my head. I thought we'd have to walk out of the house to break the dream, but the room started to fade. The last thing we saw was the two of them kissing. Sholto and I woke naked on the edge of the Western Sea in a bed covered in white rose petals, and sprigs of thyme and rosemary, all covered in the delicate blossoms that still decorated his crown.

Sholto turned to me, smiling. Our hands were no longer bound, but the matching tattoos of the rose vines on our arms shone blue. He raised his arm up so he could watch it glimmer, and then laid his arm next to the glow of mine. "They pray to you for protection and fertility, but what am I?"

"Love, apparently," I said.

"Love?" he said.

I nodded. "You were there, Sholto. She was his true love, and he hers, maybe marriage."

"King of the Sluagh, King of Nightmares, the Queen's Perverse Creature, Lord of Shadows, and behind my back, Shadowspawn, and now you're telling me I'm a deity of love and marriage?"

"Yes," I said.

He smiled, then grinned, and said, "Me, a god of love and marriage," and he threw his head back and laughed until the sound of it danced around the room. Then distant from outside the house came the singing of a mockingbird. It was loud, clear, and sweet, falling from one song to another, and I remembered that it had been a mockingbird that welcomed us back to L.A. the night that Sholto had brought us all back to the edge of the sea. He laughed, the bird sang, and tiny multicolored flowers and white rose petals started falling from thin air.

CHAPTER

THIRTY-SEVEN

Sholto and I got dressed, him back in his mix of modern and museumworthy fashion, the black making his skin whiter, and strangely bringing out more of the yellow in his mostly white-blond hair.

"I always like you in royal purple; it makes your hair even more scarlet, and only green makes your eyes more brilliant." He touched my hair as he said it, gazing down at me as if to drink in the sight of me in one of his favorite colors.

I smiled up at him, putting my hand over his so I could rest my cheek in his open palm. He felt safe and warm, his hands large enough that he could cradle the entire side of my face.

"Why do you think I wore it today?"

His smile lit up his face, not with magic, but with happiness. "I have never had anyone pay as much attention to my preferences as you do, Meredith."

He was over three hundred years old; the thought that I was the first person to ever pay the attention that all lovers deserve made me sad, but I didn't say it out loud, because I didn't want to take the happiness off that handsome face.

I let my smile quirk at the edges and put into my eyes the heat I felt for him.

"We just finished," he said, laughing.

"I am never finished with the pleasure you can give me, Sholto."

His face sobered, his gold-on-gold eyes gazing down at me with a tenderness that was almost frightening, because I only aimed such looks at other men. I loved Sholto, but I was not in love with him, though that might come. I'd learned that my heart was big enough for more than just one great love of my life; maybe it could hold more than two someday?

I let him see the hope on my face, not the worry, and he leaned down to lay another kiss on my lips. I melted into his arms, getting as close as our now-clothed bodies could manage. It felt almost odd to not feel his extras. I must have stiffened, because he pulled back.

"What's wrong?" he asked.

"It feels different without your extra bits," I said.

He looked down at me, and I could see him thinking. "Different good, or bad?"

I frowned. "Just different, but"—I hugged him tighter—"I do sort of miss them when they're not touchable."

He laughed and hugged me close, folding his upper body over me, so my head was pressed into his chest not in a romantic way, but almost in a childlike way. I could forget how much taller almost all of my lovers were, but every once in a while they would do something and I would be forcibly reminded that I was tiny. I didn't feel that tiny, but it was as if Sholto could have folded himself around me twice. His hair fell around our bodies like a pale curtain.

I pushed at him enough to make him rise up so I could see his face. "What is so funny?"

"You're not horrified by the tentacles; you miss them when they're gone. Do you know what a wonder that is to me?"

I touched his face, still bent so close, and smiled. "I have some idea, yes."

The laughter died around the edges and left his eyes haunted. "I would have given anything not to have them when I was younger. It wasn't until the Seelie cut them off and I thought I would never have them again that I realized they were a part of me, as much as my arms and legs."

I held his face between my hands, gazed into those golden eyes, and said, "I'm so sorry they hurt you, and so happy that the Goddess and Consort made you whole again."

"That's just it, Meredith; I didn't realize until they were lost that I wasn't whole without them."

"Sometimes you have to lose a thing to value it," I said, softly.

He nodded, but his face was serious now, the laughter gone as if it were a dream. He stood back up all straight and tall and every inch the sidhe warrior and king. He pulled his dignity around him like a familiar piece of clothing, or a well-used shield. I wrapped my arms around his waist, happy that I got to see inside that shield.

He smiled down at me and hugged me back but stayed standing this time, so it was just his arms across my back. "Well, I value you without having to lose you, my queen."

I smiled, and said, "And I value you, my king, so much."

"I had given up having a sidhe for my queen."

"Would you have taken someone from among your sluagh?"

"I would have had no choice, would I?"

I thought about it. "Humans can be driven mad seeing some of your people, and goblins are, well, goblins. I cannot imagine you happy with one of their women, though Kitto is very dear to me, and if you could have found a female similar in nature to him she might have been quite lovely, and there might be lesser fey who would have been willing."

"I mention it in passing, and you think seriously about it."

"I'm sure you thought seriously about it," I said.

"Not as hard as you might think, my queen. Remember, my throne is the only one in faerie that is not normally an inherited one."

"The goblin throne isn't inherited either," I said.

"True, but they kill the old king and the victor takes the crown. I may retire from my job, and help my people vote another in my place."

"Has any King of the Sluagh ever stepped down voluntarily?"

He laughed again. "Well, no, but we can step down; the goblins do not give their rulers that choice."

"No, they do not."

"Now you look worried; what is wrong?"

"Holly and Ash," I said.

"The goblin twins who are your visiting lovers. You fear they will kill their king, Kurag."

I nodded. "They mean to, eventually, I think."

"It is the goblin way."

"Yes, but I have no treaty with Holly and Ash. I have one with Kurag."

"You brought them into their hands of power, and turned them from sidhe-sided goblins to true sidhe. They must be grateful for that."

"They are both thrilled with the power, but grateful enough to stay bound in treaty to me, knowing that I have enemies at both sidhe courts." I shook my head. "I don't know if they're that grateful."

"Have you not won them over with the pleasures of your body, as you won the rest of us?"

"I might have, but I haven't been able to have sex with anyone for months. The goblin twins weren't tamed enough before I had to stop entertaining them."

"Then as soon as you are able, Meredith, you must invite them to visit you."

I studied his face. "You aren't bothered by me sleeping with them?"

"I always find that euphemism for sex confusing, because the last thing you do with the two of them is sleep."

I smiled. "Fair enough, but my question remains."

"It is politically expedient to keep the goblins as your allies, and that means Holly and Ash must want to be on your side, because you are correct, they will be the next rulers of the goblins."

"I've been wondering how they'll divide up the throne. They can't both be king," I said.

"I think Ash will take the crown, but they will rule the goblins as they have done everything in their lives."

"They will rule together," I said.

"Yes."

"Ash is the more dominant personality, but up to the point where they disagree they are a unit."

"And then Holly lets Ash win the disagreement?" Sholto asked.

I nodded.

"I wonder what would happen if Holly wouldn't give way to his brother?"

"I don't know. I don't think either of them would have survived without the other. Sidhe-sided goblins are physically weaker than most goblins."

"Like your Kitto."

"Kitto is weaker than most," I said.

"You have given him a refuge and a home, Meredith; it is good to see."

"I didn't think you cared for Kitto one way or another."

"I did not know him, but I knew the fate of the sidhe-sided among the goblins and I would not wish that upon anyone."

"You are much kinder than your reputation among the fey."

"The King of the Sluagh needs a fierce reputation to keep his kingdom and people safe."

"That may be true of all rulers in faerie," I said.

He touched my face. "Now you look too serious."

"I am not respected, or feared, enough to keep us safe."

"The Goddess walks with you, Meredith. You have brought back the magic that we lost, and the sidhe are having children once more; those are all things worthy of much respect."

"Many of the sidhe still see me as a mortal abomination, the first sidhe ever born who was mortal and could be killed by normal means."

"You and I are both abominations to them. You with your human mortality, and I showing that the humanoid bias of the sidhe no longer wins genetically. We are both living proof that the sidhe are fading as pure people."

"They do hate us both for that," I said.

"Let them hate us, we know our worth," he whispered, and leaned down to kiss me again. I kissed him back eagerly, because he was right. We knew our worth now. Those who hated us for physical traits we could not change could go hang themselves. Racists are always evil, whether it's the color of your skin they hate, or how many limbs you have, or how fragile you are; it's all hatred and it's all just fear. They hated us because they saw us and thought, *There but for the grace of Goddess go I, or my children*. Sholto and I were the bogeyman in the mirror, and yet he was a king and I was a princess, and those who hated us most were neither. I wondered, did they hate us more because we were different, or because we were different and ruled in faerie and they with their pure, perfect, sidhe bodies did not?

CHAPTER

THIRTY-EIGHT

left my hose off so that I could walk barefoot through the sand to kiss Sholto good-bye at the edge of the surf. He'd protested, "The sand is chilly, and the surf cold."

"I would kiss you as often as I can, before you go. If that means getting my feet a little cold in the edge of the sea, so be it."

The pleased look on his face was totally worth padding barefoot through the sand and letting the chill wind have its way with my bare legs. Sholto had given me his jacket this time, so at least my upper body was warm enough. I'd protested, "I'll have to give it back to you at the water's edge, and then I'll be even colder walking back to the house."

"No, keep it until I return. I have other jackets and I love the idea of you wearing mine. Give it back to me smelling of your skin, and I will be content."

What could I say to that but yes, and, "You are a terrible romantic, my king."

He had grinned at me, that grin that made him look younger and carefree, as if no sorrow had ever touched him. I loved that I could get that smile from him.

"I thought I was a very good romantic, my queen," he said.

I'd agreed and there had been more kissing. Now, we stopped just short of the waves where they spilled along the sand, and kissed again. An energetic wave found my feet and I startled from the cold. He laughed and picked me up, holding me around the waist effortlessly, my arms around his neck and my bare feet suddenly kicking in empty air while I laughed with him.

I didn't hear the shot; I felt it spin him around and suddenly we were in the waves, the sea like ice water pouring over us. He was on top of me, pinning me, as the waves drew back and left me gasping.

Saraid and Dogmaela were there, bending over us. Saraid yelled, "Princess! Princess, are you hurt?"

"Lord Sholto!"

The next wave came, leaving me spitting water, and coughing. Sholto never moved. I said his name, but I knew. If he could have, he would have been helping Saraid and Dogmaela. He would have been up protecting me, but he just lay there as the next waves came and Saraid dragged me out of the water.

Beck and Cooper were there, guns drawn, looking outward for someone to shoot. Dogmaela had grabbed Sholto and was pulling him farther up on the sand. Saraid had pinned me underneath her on the sand, using her body as a shield, and yelling for reinforcements from the house.

They came, the sidhe, armed, helping shield me from danger, but all I could see was Sholto. Dogmaela rolled him onto his back and I could see the wound that came out a few inches below his right arm. The hole looked big enough to put my fist through. Exit wound, I thought, and then, could he heal it? Could King Sholto, Lord of the Sluagh, heal a high-powered rifle round that might have gone straight through his heart?

Dogmaela was trying to hold pressure on the bullet hole on the entry wound. Someone else knelt and started trying to hold pressure from the other side. I saw them look at each other, and then Dogmaela looked not at me, but at Saraid.

I screamed, "No! Sholto! No!"

Far off I heard seagulls calling in their rough, complaining voices, but there was no mockingbird to sing sweet music. The wind from the sea was cold, and the sea was colder.

CHAPTER

THIRTY-NINE

I sat at the hospital with Galen on one side of me and Frost on the other. He was still hurt, but as he said when he came through the door, "I am well enough for this."

I hadn't let the nurses and doctors take the jacket or the clothes I was wearing, because the jacket was Sholto's and it, and my dress, were covered in his blood. When they all gave up on the beach, I'd gone to him and held him, and he'd bled on me. He'd still been warm, neither death nor the sea had stolen him that far away, so that he still felt like he should open his eyes and smile up at me. But he'd lain in my lap with that stillness that nothing mimics, not sleep, not illness, nothing but the warm dead feel—so alive and at the same time they move in your arms as you hold them, nerveless, flopping like some great doll, so that you know, you know even while life still warms their skin, you know, oh Gods, you know, that it is the last warmth that their skin will ever hold, and the only thing left is the cold, the terrible cold.

Galen held my hand, and Frost had his arm around my shoulders and it helped, but . . . I had prayed to Goddess and the Consort, but the petals that had fallen from the sky had been all white, no pink, just white, and I'd known that there would be no help even from Her.

I was starting to shiver and couldn't seem to stop. A nurse came and kneeled in front of me so she could look into my face, because I seemed to be staring at the floor. "Princess Meredith, please let us take your clothes and get you in something warmer. You're in shock and the cold, wet clothes aren't helping."

I just shook my head.

She pushed a strand of hair back behind her ear to try to get it to stay in the ponytail she'd started her shift with, but she needed to take it out and redo the ponytail, just shoving it back behind her ear wasn't going to fix her hair. I almost told her that, and then realized concentrating on her hair I'd stopped listening to what she was saying.

"I'm sorry, but I didn't hear any of that," I said.

"We have to get you warm, honey, or we'll be admitting you next."

"Can we just take her home?" Galen asked.

"We'd like to get her warm and dry, and have a doctor look at her."

Frost asked, "I thought you did all that before we arrived."

The nurse smiled, sort of an unhappy or maybe frustrated smile. "The Princess wouldn't go into a private area, she just kept insisting she was all right."

Frost hugged me with the one arm across my shoulders and spoke low with his face against my hair. "Merry, you need to let the doctors look at you."

"I'm all right," I said, and even to me it felt automatic.

Galen raised my hand that he was holding up so that he could lay a kiss on the back of it, but I pulled back at the last second. "I have blood on my hands."

"There's no blood on the back of your hand." He held it up so I could look at it. "See, all clean."

I just shook my head, over and over again, and shivered harder. My teeth started to chatter.

"We have to get her dry and warm," the nurse said, her voice sounding like there was no more arguing about it.

"I'm fine," I managed to say between chattering, and even as I said it, I knew it wasn't true. I had no idea why I didn't want to let them help me, except that I hadn't been shot. Sholto had been shot. Sholto was dead, not me. I realized that part of me seemed to think that if I just didn't let them help me, they'd be able to help him more. It made no sense, but that was finally the thought I dragged up into the front of my head, from where it had been hiding in the back of my thoughts, so I was acting on it, but didn't know why.

"Merry," Frost said, "you are not fine. Where does she need to go for a doctor to look at her?"

"Follow me," the nurse said, obviously happier now that someone was being reasonable.

I didn't want to be reasonable. I wanted to be totally unreasonable. I wanted to scream at her, lash out at Frost, scream at the world, and the only thing that kept me from it was that voice in my head saying, "That makes no sense."

I was a princess, a queen actually, Sholto's queen, which meant I had to do better. The last thing I could do for him was to remember I was his wife—funny, but I'd never thought the word *wife* much about Sholto and me, but we had been married by the very magic of fairie and Goddess, and that was about as blessed a union as you could get.

I thought of something I hadn't before. I looked at Frost. "Has anyone told the sluagh that their king is dead?"

"They know," he said.

"Are you sure?" I asked.

He nodded. "Yes." He helped me stand, but the high heels that hadn't seemed that high turned underneath me, and he had to catch me or I would have fallen. A small pain sound escaped him, and I remembered he was hurt, too.

"Frost, you're hurt. I'm so sorry, so sorry . . ." I pushed away from him, but he wouldn't let me go. I pushed against his chest, trying to force him to let me go, but he flinched and I realized I was pushing against his wounds. I started to cry again. "Everyone keeps getting hurt."

Galen picked me up, and Frost let him. "I'm not hurt," he said with a smile.

"Not yet," I said, as I curled my arms around his neck and buried my face against the side of his neck. The tears stopped and I was suddenly exhausted. I started shivering again, trembling in his arms as if I would shake myself apart.

I felt him walking and lifted my head enough to see we were following the nurse and that Frost was behind us. The guards that had been waiting outside the little alcove seating area closed in on either side of us. Usna and Cathbodua were there, her raven feather cloak had morphed into a fitted black leather trenchcoat, but I knew it was partly illusion. I wasn't sure how I felt about her still being on guard duty now that I knew she was pregnant, but it was too hard for me to think about, so I let it go for now. Uniformed police came in at the front and back of the knot of security. They'd given me the breathing room I asked for, but my guards both sidhe and human DSS had been doubled, and the police were determined that I didn't get killed on their watch.

"Where's Doyle?" I asked.

"He's tearing Saraid and Dogmaela a new one," Galen said.

"It wasn't their fault," I said.

"He's really mad at himself, but he's going to take it out on them."

"Why is he mad at himself?"

Frost spoke from just behind us. "Because we both believe if we'd been with you this wouldn't have happened."

I shook my head, fought to talk around my chattering teeth, and said, "That's not true. I don't think that's true."

I tried to think, was there a moment when someone could have done something? Would Doyle and Frost have made the difference? Would that have been much better than Saraid and Dogmaela? Frost had been hurt; he couldn't have been there today, but Doyle . . . would Doyle being there have made the difference, or would he have died, too? That thought was too awful. I pushed it back and started to shake until I could barely keep hold of Galen. He held me closer, tighter, as if trying to share his warmth.

The nurse, whose name was Nancy, yes, Nurse Nancy, led us to a private room. One thing being a faerie princess had always gotten me was a better room at the hospital. Being a princess didn't keep me out of the hospital; in fact, it seemed to put me in more often than if I hadn't been one, but I did usually get a private room. It was the only way to control the media and the gawkers. I'd been newsworthy all my life, and right at that minute I would have traded all of it for Sholto to walk through the door alive.

The police wanted to secure the room, so did the men and one woman of the diplomatic service, but the sidhe pointed out that none of them could look for magical dangers. It was like trying to get a rugby huddle into one room, no one wanted to be left outside, and each branch of guard wanted to search the room.

Nurse Nancy settled it all. "We've got to get the princess out of her wet clothes, so unless you've already seen her naked in person, you have to get out."

All the humans, both goverment issue and police issue, went in an embarrassed mass for the door. There were enough of them that they had a traffic jam at the door. One of the cops stepped back and asked, "Are you sure that just the two fathers are enough protection for her once we leave the room? She had four guards at the beach."

It was Cathbodua who said, "Only Usna and I are leaving of our seven guards. I think five Raven guard should be enough."

"She had four at the beach, remember?" he said.

"Nothing personal, but two of the four were human. This is five of the Raven guard."

Galen sat me on the bed where the nurse told him to, and then she produced a large plastic bag. "We can put your clothes in here, Princess, if the police don't need them for evidence. Then they can go home with you."

I touched the jacket, cold with seawater and wet with blood, and didn't want to take it off. In some part of my mind I knew it made no sense, but it felt as if once I took it off that Sholto would be more lost to me. Stupid, but it was his jacket, he'd put it on me himself, and it was his blood on it—it was his in a way nothing else would ever be again.

Galen bent over and held my chin in his hand, made me look into his eyes. "Merry, you have to get warm, and for that the clothes have to come off. No one's going to take the jacket away."

I nodded, because I was shivering too hard to talk.

Nurse Nancy touched my face. "She's cold and clammy to the touch. We have to get her out of these clothes now."

"We will," Galen said. He sat beside me on the bed and began to slide the jacket off one arm. I let him take it, because it was Galen, and I trusted him to help me keep it.

Frost stood beside me and helped take the other sleeve off, but when he bent a certain way, he hesitated in midmotion as if something hurt.

I grabbed his hand in mine and just looked at him as I sat there shivering in the short skirt and tiny top. Funny how sexy outfits are never good emergency clothing.

Nicca came forward, his knee-length deep brown hair was back in a braid. He'd started wearing it back once Kadyi got old enough to grab hair. Nicca's skin was still the rich brown of autumn leaves, and I knew underneath his very modern-looking clothes were huge moth wings, but like Sholto's tentacles, his wings could be just an incredibly vivid tattoo if he wished. Just that thought made my mind skip a beat, like I'd almost thought too much about it, and now I had to stop thinking altogether.

"Let me help her undress, Frost, please?"

"It doesn't do any good for you to be here if you reopen a wound," Galen said.

Frost frowned like he'd pout, which he'd done a lot once upon a time, but then he found the room's only chair and sat gingerly on the edge of it. Was his back hurt, too? I didn't remember any of the scratches being there, but I was having trouble remembering everything that happened in the last hour, and that was days ago. How could I remember something that far back?

Cathbodua had shooed everyone else out and closed the door behind her. It was then that Nurse Nancy seemed to figure out that five of the men were staying and helping her undress me. "OK, gentlemen, the rest of you can go on out with the rest of them," she said.

Ivi said, "You said we could stay."

"No, I said only the people that had seen her nude could stay."

"Well, then we can all stay," Ivi said. He wasted a smile on her and flipped his nearly ankle-length hair so that the pattern of ivy leaves that climbed all that paler green hair showed clearer. Humans were always thinking that Ivi had somehow decorated his hair with the pattern of ivy vines and leaves, but it was natural, an outward sign of his inner nature.

But Nurse Nancy was made of sterner stuff than some and didn't respond to the flirting. "I know the fey are more comfortable with nudity than most humans, but I didn't just mean that. I meant . . ." The nurse seemed lost for words. She was ignoring the flirting, but her discomfort was real.

Brioc moved where I could see him and where he could help Ivi flirt and intimidate the nurse. Brioc was as tall, slender, and muscled as Ivi, but Brioc's hair was a bright yellow blond, his skin a pale grayish white like some of the Red Caps had, but Brioc was pure sidhe. His skin was the color of cherry tree bark, just like the incredible red of his full lips wasn't due to lipstick of any kind. He was the cherry tree made flesh and blood, as Ivi was for his namesake. Vegetative deities were always interesting. Brioc said, "You meant her lovers could stay."

"Yes, that is what I meant," the nurse said.

"We assumed that is what you meant," Ivi said.

I couldn't see the nurse's face, but I heard her silence, even through my shivering and chattering teeth. "Are you saying that you're all . . . lovers?"

"Yes," Ivi said.

"Ex-lovers," Brioc said, "but yes, so we can guard the princess no matter her state of undress."

Galen and Nicca had peeled off the wet top and the bra. For some reason my bare breasts seemed to galvanize Nurse Nancy. "The hospital gown is on the bed, it closes in the back, just open the door when she's dressed . . . undressed . . . redressed." She fled. Apparently, five lovers was a few too many over the nurse's comfort zone. Under other circumstances it might have been amusing; now it just seemed like another reminder that I would never completely understand human culture.

I was in shock, as in the kind of shock that needed a bedsize heating pad under me, warm blankets, and an IV to give me fluids. I felt fragile and very human ending up in a hospital bed just from shock. There was nothing wrong with me; I hadn't been the one who got shot. I didn't have a scratch on me, though they'd probably been aiming at me. Had the bullet been for me, and Sholto just got in the way? No one wanted to kill Sholto, but plenty of people wanted to kill me.

The bed was warm, I was warm, and I was suddenly so tired. Frost sat beside the bed, his hand in mine, and my eyes were fluttering shut. I managed to ask, "Did they give me something?"

"What do you mean, give you something?" Frost asked.

"To sleep. Did they give me something to make me sleep?"

Galen came to stand on the other side of me, stroking his hand across my forehead. "Yes."

"I'm not hurt. I don't need to sleep."

"We agreed with the doctor," Galen said, voice soft.

"Damn it," I managed to say as my eyes fluttered closed again.

He leaned down to lay a soft kiss on my lips. "I love you, Merry."

"I love you, too," and that was the last thing I remembered, before sleep came and I could not fight it.

CHAPTER

FORTY

The dream began innocently enough, but like all innocence it could not last. I stood in the high, round room of a tower that I had never seen before. There were beautiful tapestries on the walls, rugs bright as stained glass on the floor, and through the room's two windows the sunshine was golden and thick like honey for the eyes. It was beautiful, peaceful, so why was I afraid?

A man's voice came from behind me, "I can keep you safe, Meredith, you and our children."

My throat closed tight, and I couldn't breathe for a second, because I knew that voice. I turned as one does in a horror movie, slowly, unwilling, because you know the monster is right there—behind you.

Taranis stood in a bright swath of sunlight, most of him lost in the light, so that he seemed to be forming from the light itself as he stepped farther into the room. He held his hand out to me, a smile curling his lips, and it was as if that smile were some happy jewel set between the red-gold of his mustache and beard. His hair flowed in matching curls and waves as if his hair couldn't decide how curly it wanted to be. I didn't think I'd ever seen him when his hair wasn't perfectly styled. This careless play was somehow more pleasing, and more real. His eyes looked just a brilliant green rather than the green of many flower petals in every shade of green known under the sky, and those more human eyes smiled kindly at me.

I actually took a step toward him, but I stumbled on the edge of my floor-length skirt. I looked down and found myself in a dress that matched the tower room. I was dressed like some fairy-tale princess waiting to be rescued. My heart climbed into my throat, so that I was choking on it.

"Meredith." And the moment he said my name, the fear receded. I gazed up at him and found this new, more human Taranis comforting. Part of me knew that was wrong, that he wasn't comforting, but it was as if I couldn't think the thought all the way through.

He crossed the room and touched my cheek, ever so gently, with the back of his hand. "Come to me, Meredith, come and be my queen and I will keep you safe from all that would harm you."

His tone was sweet, but his words jarred me, because they did not ring true with my own memories. I moved my face back from that touch and said, "You're part of what I need to be protected from."

He looked puzzled, as if my words made no sense. "Meredith, I would never hurt you."

I looked up into that handsome face and thought, *He would never hurt me, of course he would never hurt me.* I said, "No," not because I believed it in that moment, but as a place to start. No, he was wrong somehow. No, I shouldn't be here. No, just no.

"Oh, Meredith, I want to take care of you, you and our children."

I shook my head. "No . . . not . . ." Not what, I thought? What was he not? What was not true? That was it, something he'd just said wasn't true, but what was it? Why couldn't I think?

He touched my face again, and I started to rub my face against his hand, but stopped in midmotion, because there was nothing familiar about his hand on my face. I had so many men who touched my face, who held me, who kept me safe, but this hand wasn't one of them. This man wasn't one of them. Who was he then, what was he to me? Why couldn't I think?

I shook my head hard enough that he had to move his hand. I tried to back away from him but tripped over the hem of the dress, falling to the floor hard enough that it jarred me, and I tasted blood, from biting my tongue. A single pink rose petal drifted down into my lap, and a tiny drop of blood began to fall from my lip, and it was as if time stretched forever as that drop fell in slow motion down, down, to finally land on that pink petal.

It was as if time, sound, reality all resumed with a rush that should have had a sound to it like the Doppler shift of a car speeding past me in the dark, so near that its wind ruffles my hair, tugs at my clothing, and leaves me gasping at the nearness of it.

I looked up at him, and said, "I know who you are."

He knelt beside me, smiling. "Of course you know me, I am your beloved."

"You are Taranis, King of Light and Illusion; you beat me and you raped me, and everything else is a lie."

His smile faded around the edges; that pleasant face flickered, like a TV set that wasn't quite on one station, so you got the ghost of other images, and then he was back to pleasant, smiling, handsome, but harmless. I could change my physical appearance using glamour, but I couldn't add an emotion to it and make someone feel things they didn't actually feel. Was that all that his illusions were, just personal glamour with the addition of being able to project thoughts and feelings?

"Meredith, Meredith, see how much I love you."

I looked into his face and saw . . . love. He loved me, of course he loved me. He had always loved me . . . and the moment I thought that, I knew it was wrong. I remembered him beating me as a child. I remembered how terrified I had been of him. I remembered reaching out to my mother and she had turned away. It had been my grandmother, her mother, who had saved me from the king's anger.

I shook my head. "It's a spell, it's just a spell, it's not real."

"I want you, Meredith, I need you, that is true. I swear it by any oath you ask of me." He reached out to touch my face again.

I flinched away from his hand, but that put me almost prone on the floor, and I knew that was a bad idea, so I tried to stand, but I got tangled in the long skirts and fell back to my knees.

His hands closed on my upper arms, and he pulled me against his chest. He was so much bigger than I was, as tall as any of my lovers, and broader through the chest and shoulders than anyone but Mistral. He would be stronger than me even if he'd been human, but he wasn't human, he was sidhe, and once had been a god. He held me against his body as we knelt on the floor of the tower and I was happy for how full my skirts were, because I could only feel his chest and stomach against my back; the skirts protected me from feeling anything lower on his body.

I was so scared I couldn't breathe, as if the fear were squeezing my chest too tight for me to draw a complete breath of air.

He whispered my name, "Meredith, Meredith, Meredith," and with each repetition of my name my fear began to fade, until by the time he'd said it a dozen times I melted in against his body, letting his arms wrap around me, so that his big hand held my lower arms and then wrapped my arms and his across my body, so that I was held so close, so safe.

"I need you, Meredith," he whispered; his breath was warm against my hair and face as he bent over me and planted a kiss on my neck. His lips were so warm.

"But give me a willing kiss, Meredith, and then you will be mine."

It seemed so reasonable. I began to turn my head back toward him, and then what he'd actually said came to me. "Willing," I said.

He laid another warm kiss along my neck. "Yes, Meredith, willing. I want you always to be willing, so there are no more misunderstandings between us."

"Misunderstandings," I said.

"Yes, Meredith," he said, and kissed higher on my neck, just under the line of my jaw. His lips were so warm, almost hot against my skin, as if he were fevered. I didn't remember his skin being hot like this last time, and just thinking about that last time made me remember coming to with him on top of me. I remembered the fear, and the pain of the concussion from where he'd hit me. He hit me. He raped me. He did not love me, had never, ever loved me. I wasn't sure King Taranis could love anyone but himself.

I tensed in his arms, because the fear was back, screaming through every nerve in my being. I wanted him to stop touching me. I spoke around the pulse in my throat and it made my voice have to squeeze out around the fear, "Stop, please, stop touching me."

"Meredith, you don't want me to stop."

My name from his lips began to calm the fear again, but him telling me that I didn't want him to stop pissed me off. I knew my own mind, and I did not want him to touch me, ever again.

I remembered coming to with him on top of me. I remembered him naked, and on top of me, and I hated him. I hated him with a fine, burning hatred. "You have hurt me too much and too often, Taranis. Your spell will not work, because I keep remembering how much I hate you and what you have done to me."

His weight was just suddenly more, pinning me harder to the rugs, hard enough that I could feel the hardness of the stones underneath. My fear washed over me so that my skin ran cold with it.

"Will you forgive nothing, Meredith, and remember only the bad?"

"What good memories do I have of you, Uncle Taranis?"

"Meredith, Meredith, hear me, feel me, and know that I love you."

Even with his weight pressing me into the floor, and my fear almost choking me again, that unnatural calmness started to take me over again. It was magic, it wasn't real!

"Is this how you seduced them all, Taranis, through trickery and lies? Are you not the great lover, but just a great liar?"

He squeezed his hands around my wrists until I thought he meant to crush them, and then he slid his knee between my thighs, and the fear robbed me of everything. I couldn't think past the fear as he began to try to worm his way between my legs.

"Stop!"

He leaned his face close, his voice ugly with his rage. "Shadowspawn is already dead. His sluagh will not hunt or protect you now, Meredith.

Your Darkness and your false storm lord will be dead soon, and I do not fear the rest of your would-be suitors."

I knew he meant Doyle, but it took me a second to realize that the third death was Mistral. I was suddenly less afraid, because my anger helped chase it back. "You had Sholto killed. You ordered it."

"He led his wild hunt into the heart of my sithen. I could not allow that to happen again, Meredith."

"Stop saying my name!" I yelled it, holding my anger to me, because even now when he said my name, I could feel the compulsion in it, to just give in, to believe him. But he had me pinned to the floor, his weight on me, and that helped me not to believe he loved me.

"If you but kiss me once, Meredith, you will enjoy the rest, I promise you that."

I kept my face turned away from him. "A kiss, or a willing kiss, uncle?"

"Do not call me that," he said.

"You are my uncle. You are my grandfather's brother. Nothing you do will change that."

"I have never acted as an uncle to you, Meredith."

"No, you tried to beat me to death when I was a child, and you almost beat me to death less than a year ago, and you raped me after you had beaten me unconscious. A good uncle would do none of these things, I suppose."

He used his body weight to keep my body pinned to the floor, and wrapped his big hand around both my wrists where they were still pinned under me. He was freeing up one of his hands; nothing good would come of it. I struggled to free the wrist that he was trying to hold with one hand, and felt his fingers begin to slide. His free hand grabbed a handful of my hair and pulled my head back.

I spoke through gritted teeth as I fought to keep my face down. "A stolen kiss will not win you my affections, not even by your magic. You said it yourself, it must be willing."

"I could have made this pleasant for you, Meredith. I meant it to be, but you are always so difficult!"

"Yes, I am difficult, uncle; you will not win me."

He pulled my hair tight enough that it hurt and growled his anger in my ear. "I will have you, Meredith. You can enjoy it, or you can fight me and I will take my pleasure and not worry about yours."

"Are you saying that I can either enjoy my rape, or not enjoy it?"

His grip in my hair loosened slightly, and some tension went from him, as if by hearing it spoken so bluntly, even he heard that it made no sense.

His voice was calmer when he said, "I can leave this dream now, Meredith. I can free us both of this dream, and call back the assassins that are going to kill Doyle and Mistral, if you will but kiss me here and now."

"I trust Doyle to kill anyone you send against him, and you must fear Mistral very much to target him, so you know what he is capable of; they are not easy to kill."

"Sholto shouldn't have been easy to kill either, Meredith, but he was; think upon that as the minutes tick away. Think upon that and decide whether you would rather your Darkness and your Storm be alive but parted from you, or dead and parted from you forever?"

Fear poured over me again, and the fresh memories of holding Sholto's body on the beach. I didn't think I could bear seeing Doyle dead. I admitted to myself that I would not grieve Mistral as much, but I remembered the moment on the battlefield when I'd thought my cousin Cel had killed Doyle. If I left them, then Doyle would still have Frost; they would not be alone, but I would be. I would be worse than alone.

"One kiss, Meredith, one willing kiss, for the lives of two of your lovers, is that so much to ask?"

"No, not if it were just one kiss, but if I give you a kiss, uncle dearest, then what happens next?"

"I kiss you back, of course."

"I am not stupid, uncle; if I kiss you willingly, what does the spell do?"

"You will no longer be afraid; you will be safe and happy in my arms."

"But for it to work you must win a kiss from me." I laughed, I couldn't help it. "You need to 'Kiss the Girl,'" I said.

"Yes, I suppose I do need to kiss the girl."

"No, uncle, I'm quoting a movie that you've never seen."

"I do not know what you are talking about, Meredith. The assassins are even now in place, and I promise you they will strike, as they did this morning for your shadow lord."

"You don't even know there was a movie of 'The Little Mermaid,' do you?"

"I have read the story by Hans Christian Andersen, if that's what you mean."

"Yes, that is what I mean. I forgot the Seelie Court enjoys reading fairy tales, and laughing at how wrong the humans get things."

"It would be a shame if you kissed me too late to save them, Meredith. I can only offer their safety for a little while, and then the assassins will do their jobs and it will be too late."

"They made a movie of the story. They made a movie of 'The Little Mermaid,' and there was a song in it called 'Kiss the Girl.'"

"What does it matter, Meredith? Why this delay, do you want them dead?"

"You don't understand. By killing Sholto you put them all on alert, and I trust my men, and the human guards, and the human police, to fight."

"It will not be a fight, Meredith, any more than Sholto had a chance to fight."

"What of my babies? What happens to them if I let you bespell me?"

He settled his weight more firmly against me, one knee between my legs. "They are our babies, Meredith. They will come with you to the Seelie Court. They will be princesses and prince here with us."

"You'll never take them to a Disney movie, or read them a fairy tale without showing your disdain for the human who wrote it. You won't love them."

"I will love them, as I love you, Meredith."

"You don't love me!" I yelled it at the floor, the echo of my own voice strident in my ears.

"I love you, Meredith."

"Swear it, swear that you love me truly, swear it by the Darkness That Eats All Things; swear that oath, uncle, and I may give you your willing kiss."

"That is an Unseelie oath, and I will not utter it."

"It is an oath that will hunt you down and destroy you if you break it. The only reason not to take such an oath is that you know you do not love me."

"You will love me, Meredith. You will adore me. Our children will see us as a devoted couple."

"You are not their father! The genetic tests will come back in a few weeks and that will prove that I was pregnant before you forced yourself on me. The tests will prove that you are a rapist, a liar, and infertile, and I will do everything I can to get you convicted of my rape. I will plaster it across the human media, that the great King of the Seelie is so insecure that he has to beat and rape rather than seduce."

"You won't; you will drop the charges against me, Meredith. You will tell everyone that you came to me willingly, Meredith."

Of course I would; he was right, of course.

"You will tell the newspapers and the television that the Unseelie kept you prisoner and it was only when Shadowspawn, Darkness, and Storm were dead that you felt safe enough to escape to the Seelie Court with your babies."

"You always go too far, uncle," I said. "You almost have me under your spell, and then you say something that is so outrageous that even your magic can't make me believe it. You are evil, uncle, did you know that?"

He got both of his legs inside mine, and only the dress with all its layers of petticoats kept him from pressing closer, but even through all the clothing I could feel him against me. I had to swallow past the lump in my throat. I prayed to Goddess that he would not touch me again.

"Do you feel that, Meredith?"

"I don't know what you mean, uncle." It was a lie, but I was not going to play along.

He ground himself in against my ass. "Do you feel me now, Meredith?"

"Yes," I whispered.

"I dressed you for this dream, Meredith; I can just as easily undress you with a thought."

"Don't."

"Kiss me, Meredith, and then you will want me to, and it will not be rape."

"Lust magic is the same as date-rape drugs in human courts, Uncle Taranis. Even if you bespell me, humans have forensic wizards who specialize in understanding spells like this; I have too many friends among the human police. They won't believe that I was willing. Even if you win this moment, the police will free me of your spell eventually, and when they do, you will be jailed, or exiled from this country."

"At worst they would limit me to the Seelie Court, Meredith, and that is where I stay anyway."

"No, uncle dearest, you had a king of another kingdom assassinated; that is an act of war, and that is the one thing that will get you kicked out of this country."

"Only you know what I did, Meredith, and once we kiss, you won't tell."

"You don't believe the human wizards will free me once you have me under your spell?"

"No, Meredith, I don't. Human magic has never been a match for mine. Now, about that dress."

"No," I said.

My clothes vanished and I was suddenly naked against the rugs and the stone. He was still pressed against my ass, but now he felt bigger and harder, eager for his conquest.

"NO!" I pulled my hand free, and I prayed as never before, *Let this work, let my hand of power be real here!* Taranis made his clothes vanish. I had a moment of feeling him naked on top of me, pinning me to the floor, and then his hips began to shift, to hunt for an angle that would let

354 LAURELL K. HAMILTON

him enter me, and I shoved my hand against his bare arm. The same arm that I had twisted in the last nightmare he'd given me.

His arm began to fold in upon itself. He let me go, and it was his turn to scream, "NO!"

I turned and saw him on his knees, naked, and maybe he was handsome, but all I could see was the monster he was, and his left arm was a curling, deformed thing. I waited for it to reach the main part of his body and turn him inside out so that he wouldn't be able to hide the monster inside, behind the handsome façade. I would make him into the truth of himself, and pull the horror out so all the world could see it.

"Meredith! Help me, Meredith, help me!"

I said, "No."

He vanished, and a second later I woke in the hospital with Doyle bending over me. He wasn't dead. I wasn't trapped with Taranis, and he hadn't bespelled me, and maybe, just maybe, the damage I'd done to him in dream would be real when he woke. Now, all we had to do was stop the assassins from killing Doyle and Mistral the way they'd killed Sholto.

CHAPTER

FORTY-ONE

A sound in the darkened room had frightened me at first, and then I'd seen the nightflyers plastered to the wall around the window, and my heart had lifted, because only Sholto could have brought them to L.A. He wasn't dead? Had it been another dream? No, it had been real. I held Doyle's hand in mine and looked around the room for Sholto.

Galen was on the other side of the bed. "I told you what she'd think when she saw the nightflyers. I'm sorry, Merry, but Sholto is still dead."

"How did they get to L.A. without him?"

"Kitto brought them," Doyle said.

I looked from one to the other of them. "Am I still dreaming?"

Galen smiled. "I could pinch you to prove we're real."

It made me smile a little. I tried to reach for his hand, but I was still hooked to an IV, so he took my hand instead. "No pinching necessary," I said, "but how did Kitto bring the sluagh across the country?"

Doyle answered, "He used his hand of power."

"The hand of reaching only lets him bring someone through a mirror during a call." I looked at the mass of nightflyers covering the far wall and clinging to part of the ceiling. There had to be at least two dozen of them, though the way their flat bodies overlapped it was hard to get an accurate count, but still . . . "It would take hours to bring through this many of the sluagh. How long was I trapped in dream?"

My heart was pounding in my throat again, because though Doyle was here safe beside me, Mistral was not.

"You have only been asleep a short time, Merry; it has not been hours," Doyle said.

"Where is Mistral?" I asked.

"At the main house, in charge of seeing that no harm comes to the babies. A hate group had claimed responsibility for trying to assassinate you, so I made Mistral stay at the house and see to the defenses there. He made me swear I would explain that only duty to our children would keep him from your side."

"Doyle, you and Mistral are in terrible danger. Taranis means to have you both killed, as he killed Sholto. He fears the three of you the most of my men, and he intends to strip me of you, and then try to claim me for himself."

Doyle touched my face, looking very hard into my eyes, as if trying to tell if I was telling the truth, or mad, or still dream befuddled.

"It was not just a nightmare, Doyle. Taranis was in my dreams again."

Galen cursed softly. "Damn it, we let them put you to bed without the herbs in your pillow. I am so sorry, Merry; I should have thought of it."

"We know that it is not a human hate group, but traitors among the sidhe themselves," Doyle said.

"How do you know? Did Taranis invade someone else's dreams?"

"No, but Rhys and Barinthus went to the beach house to make certain the sidhe there cooperated with the police, and forced them all to let the police take their fingerprints."

"Are you saying one of the sidhe at the beach killed . . . shot Sholto?"

"Rhys and the police both quickly realized that the angle of the shot meant it could not have come from the hillside, but had to come from one of the upper windows of the house itself."

"A lot of them didn't want to cooperate with the police," Galen said.

"I understand the murderer not wanting to cooperate with the police, but why did the rest refuse?"

Doyle and Galen exchanged a look, and it was Doyle who said, "They felt that the human authorities had no sway over them. I sent Rhys and Barinthus to convince them that they were mistaken." There was something ominous in the way he said the last; at another time I might have asked how harsh the methods of persuasion had been, but frankly, I didn't care. How dare they not want to help solve Sholto's . . . murder.

"They refused to help when they thought that I'd been the attempted target?"

"They said that Sholto was not their king, and that he died so easily proved he was either not sidhe or contaminated by your mortality."

I just stared at him for a few seconds. "What?"

They exchanged another look between them.

"What was that look just now? You've mentioned almost everybody but Frost; where is he?"

"He's with a doctor," Doyle said.

I started to sit up, and he held me down with one hand on my shoulder. "He is all right, or as all right as when he entered the hospital," Doyle said.

"What does that mean?" I asked, and it was as if the fear from the dream had just been waiting below the surface, because it came bubbling up now. I fought the panic, and knew it was at least partly the nightmare and Taranis, but . . . sometimes there was so much that I felt as if I'd been on the edge of panic for months.

As if talking about him had conjured him, the door opened and Frost was there, looking tall and unbelievably handsome. His hair glinted in the dim light of the room the way the Christmas tree had looked on Christmas Eve when I was little, all gleaming and beautiful as my father turned out the lights because Santa wouldn't come if the lights were on. We celebrated Yule and the winter solstice as a religious holiday, but he wanted me to have a more American holiday when I was very small, and had even been willing for me to go to Christian church with some of my school friends, and to temple with my friends who were Jewish. My father had wanted me to understand my country, not just our people. Frost's hair looked like that long-ago Christmas tree tinsel, and the Christmas mornings I'd seen on television, but that never quite happened to me. I'd so wanted brothers and sisters, and family holidays that hadn't been full of political debate, or photo opportunities for the press. Frost coming through that door made me feel like Christmas morning was supposed to feel, and never had.

Whatever he saw on my face made him smile, that bright, too-wide one that made his face both less model perfect and more amazing all at the same time. Galen moved back so Frost could take my hand and lean in to kiss me. He hesitated somewhere in the middle of standing back up, as if something in the middle of his body had caught, or hurt.

"What did the doctor say?" Doyle asked.

"He gave me some antibiotics and told me not to do anything physically taxing for at least three more days."

"Wait, are you saying that the dog scratches are infected?" I asked.

"It would seem so," he said; he held my hand in his, and smiled down at me.

"You can't get infection from a wound, except through poison, or an evil spell. None of the fey can just get an infection."

"Nonetheless, it is why I am not healing as I should."

"Frost, you . . . I've seen you heal bullet wounds in less time than these scratches. They were deep, but not that deep."

"The doctor assures me that these are natural antibiotics, not man-made, so I should not have an allergic reaction to them, and because I have never had antibiotics before, the infection shouldn't be immune to it, as it might be if I had had more modern medical care."

"Frost, are you saying you're healing human-slow, as slowly as I might heal?"

Frost wouldn't look at me. I looked at Doyle and Galen at the foot of the bed. "Someone talk to me, now," I said.

"Some of the newer sidhe were not happy that Frost isn't healing as he did before he left faerie," Doyle said.

"Before he was with me, you mean," I said. I held both their hands in mine, squeezed them tight.

"It doesn't matter what caused it," Frost said, and his face was still serene, peaceful, even happy.

"You were immortal and unaging. You would have been this beautiful and amazing forever, and loving me has stolen that from you. How? How did just being my lover damage your immortality?"

He raised my hand and rubbed his lips along my knuckles. It felt wonderful, but all I could think was that he would age now. That in loving him I'd killed him.

"We do not know why or how it happened," Doyle said.

"So Sholto dying is my fault; that he couldn't heal it like a nightflyer might, or a sidhe might, is because he loved me? How can that be?"

I wasn't panicked now, I was horrified.

There was a hissing from the nightflyers and one of them slid to the floor and rose upward as if a manta ray could stand. It spoke with the flat, lipless mouth on its underside, gesturing with its tentacles that were so like Sholto's.

"Our queen, it was a fearsome wound; even we might have died of it."

There was a hissing, sibilant chorus from the others.

"Do not blame yourself, and if your mortality did spread to our king, he was still the happiest we had ever seen him."

One of the others peeled itself back enough from the wall to say, "So young and so sad, until you came."

The one that was standing, swaying like a fleshy carpet, was able to walk forward. "We will see you safe, and the killer punished. Your little goblin shamed us into coming to protect you and the babes; it is the last duty we can do the best king in all of faerie."

All the nightflyers were very old, so saying *thank you* was potentially an insult, but I wanted to say something. "What is your name?" I asked.

"Barra, my queen."

"Sholto was the best of rulers in all of faerie, and a good man. I am honored that you, Barra, and so many of the nightflyers have traveled so far to help keep me and Sholto's children safe."

He bowed, and it was clumsy, because among the sluagh they weren't expected to do something that worked so awkwardly for their anatomy.

"The bow is much appreciated, but I know that among your own people that is not a gesture expected of you, and I will not expect it either."

He looked at me with huge dark eyes. "You are wise in our ways."

"I am your queen until you elect another king; I will do my best by you all, until that time."

It was as if the mantle of his body flowed, or waved from top to bottom. "It was voted on; we will elect no new king until we have avenged King Sholto."

"That might be months," I said. "Won't you need a ruler before that?"

"You are our ruler until we have a new king."

I said the only thing I could say. "I am honored, and I will do my best to rule as Sholto would have wished."

Doyle put his hand over his heart and bowed to all the nightflyers. "We are all honored by your presence here, but I do not think it will be months before Sholto is avenged."

We all looked at him. "Rhys's last phone call said that they had linked a fingerprint to one of the sidhe at the beach. Rhys and Barinthus and some of the Red Caps have taken the suspect to the police station."

"Is he the one who shot Sholto, or did he just load the rifle?" I asked.

Doyle looked down at me, and it was an approving look. "Sometimes in these months of you being pregnant I have forgotten that you were a detective here in the Western Lands before I found you."

"Sometimes I feel like I've been pregnant forever, and never anything else, but being a mother doesn't make me not Merry Gentry, private detective."

"We do not know if he pulled the trigger, or if he was part of a conspiracy. Until we are certain we have no other traitors among the sidhe, we will surround you with guards we are certain of, like all in this room."

"We appreciate the trust you show us," Barra said.

"The sluagh have more honor than most of the guard of any court," Doyle said.

Barra gave another of those strangely graceless, graceful bows.

"We need to know everything the suspect knows," I said.

"He is not wanting to talk."

"I'm assuming he's claiming diplomatic immunity as a noble of the court," I said.

"Of course," Doyle said.

"Good," I said.

He looked at me. "Good, Merry? That means the police cannot question him at all."

"It also means that the sidhe has put himself firmly in the hands of faerie, and I am a queen of faerie. We will treat our traitor as a noble of the faerie courts, and he will tell us everything we want to know."

"If you torture him, the police will likely stop you."

I smiled and could feel that it wasn't a pleasant smile. "I don't think we'll have to resort to traditional torture."

"What are you planning?" Galen asked, and he sounded suspicious.

"How much of the sluagh is here in the Western Lands? Is it just nightflyers?"

"No, our queen, we are many. Your goblin sidhe brought many of us through the mirror."

"Even better," I said.

"Merry," Galen said, "what are you planning to do?"

"I am the Queen of the Sluagh, and he's slain my king; I am within my rights to use the sluagh to question him."

"Some of the sluagh seen without magic to protect the mind can cause madness," Doyle said.

"I think he'll talk before that happens," I said.

"Ruthless, and practical," Barra said. "We approve."

There was another hissing sound like a Greek chorus from some Lovecraftian nightmare. It made me smile, because it would likely scare the hell out of our traitor.

"I brought you fresh clothes," Galen said.

I smiled at him. "Then let's get me dressed and go help Rhys question our prisoner."

"Let the doctor say you are well enough to go, first," Doyle said.

"I am well enough."

"Galen, fetch the doctor."

Galen turned without a word and went for the door. One of the nightflyers slithered across the ceiling, poured like thick water down the wall, and crawled sideways out the door. Galen held the door without being asked, as if he expected it.

"There are more guards outside the door, both human and fey. It has been decided that none of your lovers go anywhere without extra guard."

"I agree," I said.

"We will lose no more princes of faerie to this plot," Barra said.

I let go of Doyle's hand so I could hold Frost's with both of mine. "But we will lose this prince of faerie, eventually. I am so sorry, Frost."

Frost smiled down at me. "We will grow old together, my Merry. What could be better than that?"

Doyle leaned in and put his dark hand over our clasped ones. I realized he was crying, the tears gleaming in the lights. "Do not leave me all alone, not both of you, I do not think I could bear it. I would rather age and fade with the two of you than live the rest of eternity without either of you."

We opened our arms and the Darkness laid himself across the bed so we could hold him while he cried, because we would age and he would not.

CHAPTER

FORTY-TWO

Trancer's handcuffs were fastened through the metal ring on the metal table in the interrogation room. His feet were chained to a ring in the floor. His long brown hair was disheveled, but since he couldn't raise his hands to smooth it into place, there was nothing he could do about it. I knew how vain the men of the courts were about their appearance, so it bothered him more than it would have most men, but there were probably things about his physical appearance that bothered him more right now. One tricolored eye was swelling shut, the cheek underneath it was swollen, and his mouth had blood drying at the corner of the opposite side from the other damage, as if someone had hit him on one side, then backhanded him and hit him again. For all I knew that was exactly what happened, but honestly, I didn't care. I hoped it hurt, hoped he was hurting. If he had pulled the trigger and killed Sholto, I planned on him hurting, a lot.

I was strangely calm as I sat across the table from him. I felt icy calm, as if something in me had gone cold and would never be warm again. It was still a type of shock, emotional shock, and I knew that, but thanks to being in shock, I didn't care about that either. It would help me think; it would help me question the man sitting chained across from me without losing my temper. The police hadn't wanted me in here, and as Merry

Gentry, private detective, I wouldn't have been, but I was sitting here as Queen Meredith of the Sluagh, and Trancer was still invoking his rights as a citizen of faerie, so being a queen trumped my PI license all to hell.

No matter what you see on television, interrogation rooms are small, so with Rhys and Doyle standing behind me, and Detective Lucy Tate standing in the far corner along with one local detective it was . . . cozy. Lucy was here as a courtesy since she was L.A. homicide, not Malibu, which was where the beach house was located, but the Los Angeles County Sheriff's department was like most police departments, they both fiercely protected their turf and wanted desperately to avoid blame in high-profile cases. There was always that mix of wanting to be the hero and not wanting to be the scapegoat for a mediaworthy case like this one. It was a thin line to walk, and they were willing to let me help them walk it, for now.

"You told me you and your wife wanted me to help give you a baby; was that a lie?"

I had a moment to see him surprised by the question, before he schooled his face to polite blankness. It didn't work as well with the bruises and blood, but he did his best. He was a noble of the Seelie Court; he knew how to hide his feelings.

"Answer her," Doyle said in a growling deep voice.

"I don't have to answer her," Trancer said.

Detective Ivan stepped away from the wall, running a hand through his short, dark hair. He looked exotic, almost Asian, but not quite. "You don't have to talk to us, local cops, or even Detective Tate here, because your diplomatic immunity means we have no authority over you."

"See, I don't have to answer any of your questions." He sounded far too satisfied when he said it.

"You don't have to answer our questions," Lucy said, "but you do have to answer to your own people."

"The princess is not one of my people."

"Technically, I am a princess of both courts, but I'm not here as a princess."

He actually sneered at me. "What then, as a private detective?"

I smiled, not pleasantly. I clenched my hands together in front of me, because if I lost control of my temper I didn't want to hurt him by accident. No, if I hurt him, I wanted it to be on purpose.

"No, as Queen Meredith."

"Queen of what?" And again he made it disdainful.

"Queen of the Sluagh, married and crowned by faerie itself to King Sholto."

A flicker of uncertainty crossed through the one eye I could read well, but his arrogance climbed back into place almost instantly. "The sluagh are already electing a new king, and then you will be nothing to them. They are not a hereditary monarchy, so even if your babies are Sholto's they gain no hold on the crown of the dark host."

"The sluagh have voted to elect no new ruler until King Sholto's murderer is punished. Until then, I am Queen Meredith the First, of the Sluagh."

I saw the first hint of fear, but he conquered it quickly and was back to arrogance. "I don't believe you."

"It is unprecedented in all their long history, so I can understand you not believing it, but you don't have to take my word for it." I looked back over my shoulder and said, "Doyle, could you ask Barra to come inside, please?"

He went to the door without a word, spoke low, and held the door open. Barra didn't walk in; he crawled sideways around the wall of the door frame and flowed up to hang on the ceiling above me, which put him above the table, and our prisoner—who stared up at the nightflyer with undisguised fear on his face. Good.

But Trancer was made of stern stuff, and though he couldn't quite control his face, his voice was unconcerned. "Almost every type of fey has been exiled at one time or another. One nightflyer in the Western Lands proves nothing."

"Oh, is that all," I said. "Doyle, if you please."

He opened the door again and the nightflyers flowed inside like writhing, fleshy water, until they covered the ceiling and most of the walls.

I spared a glance for Lucy and Detective Ivan; they had both been introduced to the nightflyers and knew the plan. One of the reasons Detective Ivan was the local policeman in the room was that he was the one who had had the least amount of discomfort interacting with them. Lucy had visited with us at the main house, so she knew that fey came in many shapes and sizes.

Trancer wasn't pale, he was gray from fear. He had to lick his lips twice before he said in a strained voice, "They could not have traveled here this quickly."

"You thought that once Sholto was dead no one else could open the way for his sluagh, didn't you, Trancer?"

He just stared at them; the skin near his one good eye had started to twitch. "This is not possible."

"Who is the Queen of the Sluagh?" I asked.

They answered in a hissing chorus, "You are, Queen Meredith." The last syllable of my name hissed nicely in echoes around the room.

"Are you expecting Taranis to rescue you, Lord Trancer?" I asked.

There was the barest flicker of confirmation in his face, quickly hidden between a mixture of ongoing fear and the last bit of arrogance he could muster. "He is the only king I acknowledge."

"But there, you see, Trancer, we have a problem."

"I have no problem, for I am a noble of the Seelie Court and neither the humans nor you have authority over me."

"Actually, we contacted the Seelie Court and they don't give a damn what we do with you. In fact, the various factions seem to be very busy disavowing all knowledge of your actions."

He frowned. "What are you babbling about? The factions all bow to our one true king."

"If you mean Taranis, he is no longer King of the Seelie, or of anyone anywhere for that matter," I said.

"Your lies will not trick me," he said.

"It is true that Taranis was the absolute ruler of his court, and once given the throne it's for life, which means in his case forever."

"Your own words prove that you are lying," Trancer said.

"There are only two things that could dethrone a King of the Seelie," I said.

He blinked at me, and I could see him thinking. "The king is father of at least one of your brats, proving that he is not infertile."

"Ironic, isn't it," I said.

He was recovering himself, burying his fear under centuries of court manners. "King Taranis knows who is loyal to him."

I smiled a little wider. "Perhaps, but since he is no longer king, his loyalty is of absolutely no help to you."

"What are you babbling about, girl?"

The nightflyers moved restlessly and it was as if the ceiling and walls breathed and flexed. It was unsettling even to me, and they were on my side.

"Neither my subjects nor I like you very much, Trancer. I'd try to play nicer with us, if I were you."

He swallowed hard enough that I could hear it, and then said in a much milder tone, "What do you mean that Taranis is no longer king?"

"I told you, there are two reasons that a Seelie ruler will lose their right to rule. One is infertility, but there is one other. It hasn't been invoked in a very long time, but it's still irrevocably tied to rulership of the Seelie Court. Do you remember what it is? Because I do. I remembered it when Taranis invaded my dreams at the hospital."

"He is still physically perfect; his arm was not deformed in reality, only in the dream. He said that he saw it twisted from the corner of his eye, but none of the rest of the court could see it, because it was not real."

"Not the first time, no," I said.

"You are lying now; no one can cause true harm in dream. That power was lost to us long ago."

"Taranis was able to make this dream much more real. I couldn't break free of it. Maybe it was the drugs the hospital gave me to help with the shock I went into after my king died in my arms, or maybe Taranis recovered more of his own power over dreams. I suppose we'll never know, but as he made the dream much more real, and much more frightening, I was able to make my magic much more real, too."

"You didn't . . . you couldn't have."

"I could, and I did. Whatever power, or favor, Taranis offered you to assassinate Sholto, he can't pay it now, because as an ex-king he has no access to the treasury, and no ability to make political appointments or give out noble titles. All he can offer now is his friendship. Is that enough, Lord Trancer? Is the friendship of a fallen king payment enough for you to have assassinated a king?"

"You are just trying to manipulate me into a confession of some sort."

"I do want to know who else is involved in the plot to assassinate King Sholto, Prince Doyle, and Prince Mistral, that is true."

His arrogance slipped away and what color he'd regained went with it, so that he wasn't just gray, but pasty gray, as if he were suddenly ill.

"You're wondering who told me exactly which of my men was being targeted? I could pretend that someone else involved has talked, but the truth is so much better. Taranis himself told me. He confessed everything like a villain in a superhero movie, because he thought he would use a love spell and I would forget everything he told me, or be so besotted with him that I wouldn't care."

My anger rose, and with it my magic, so that my skin began to shine, just a little. It was hard to see in the fluorescent light, but Trancer saw it, because the fear made his one good eye flash white, like a horse about to bolt. I took long, even breaths to control my anger and the power. I glanced at the two police in the corner. Lucy gave the smallest shake of her head, telling me to calm down. Detective Ivan was wide-eyed, his hand going to a gun that wasn't at his hip, because you weren't allowed to bring guns into an interrogation room. Their reaction let me know that my eyes had started to glow, and maybe even my hair was starting to do that ruby luminescence. I worked until I could swallow most of that magic down, and then did my best to speak calmly.

"Taranis would have had me like some drug addict with him as my addiction. He meant to control me and gain control of my children, and for that evil plan he has paid with two of the things he values most in the world: his beauty, and his kingship."

I stood up and leaned a little across the table. "Be careful, Lord Trancer, that you do not pay with the things you hold most dear."

"What do you . . . mean?"

"If you will not name a conspirator, then I have to assume that your wife, Lady Fenella, was an active participant in the murder of my husband."

"She knows nothing, I swear it."

"Make me believe that, Lord Trancer."

He made me believe it, because he really did love his wife. He bargained for her safety, and never tried to bargain for his own, because he knew there was no point. I'd looked into his eyes and seen that he loved his wife, and he'd looked into mine and seen his own death. We were both right.

CHAPTER

FORTY-THREE

We had enough from Trancer's confession to get the human authorities to limit Taranis to the Seelie Court's sithen, not just faerie, but inside the Seelie Court's mound only. They actually made it part of the National Guard unit that was still assigned to keep watch in Cahokia in case another battle broke out, to report if Taranis stepped outside the sithen. He had been the King of Light and Illusion, but his hand of power was twisted in upon itself so he could no longer use light as a weapon. He could still make illusions with his other hand, so that you'd believe almost anything he conjured on himself, or that's what our friends among the Seelie report, but they also report that he can't change the arm I damaged. No matter how perfect the rest of his illusion is, the arm remains deformed, foreshortened, with the hand half swallowed up somewhere close to his elbow. He had been able to stop my hand of flesh from turning him completely inside out, but from the elbow down he was a walking example of what my magic could do to even the most powerful among the sidhe. Everyone's been much more respectful. Andais said it: People will follow you for love, respect, or fear. I preferred love, but fear would do.

Andais has continued to be the perfect aunt, until we finally allowed her and Eamon to visit in person. We made it a media event for the

Queen of the Unseelie Court to visit her nieces and nephew. It was some of the best press that our court has had in, well, ever. Perhaps she behaved herself better because the cameras were watching everything she did, but the tears she shed when she held Alastair were real enough. He looks more like my father every day, so she says. His full name is Alastair Essus Dolson Winter after my father and his two genetic fathers, Doyle and Frost. Wynne, Gwenwyfar Joy Tempest Garland, actually seems to look like Rhys and Galen had a love child, but her magic is all Mistral's. Her first name was the oldest Welsh spelling of Guinevere, Rhys's choice. Then Joy to reflect my nickname, so that we're Merry and Joy, and yes that was Galen's idea, but he and Rhys also chose Garland, both because it's a wreath of flowers and you wear it to celebrate victories and special occasions, but also for Judy Garland, because of Rhys's love of old movies. For Mistral it was either Windy, Storm, or Tempest, and he chose his favorite of the three. We've all been doing our best to teach our budding storm princess how to control her temper and her powers. They seem to be more intense if she's outside where she can see the sky; so far she's only been able to call some clouds and a few raindrops if she throws a tantrum outside, but since Mistral's rage can call tornadoes we're working with a child psychologist to help teach the girls how to control their magic. Alastair seems to be the most normal baby of the three, so far. Our last baby is Tegan Bryluen Mary Katherine. Tegan was Sholto's grandmother's name on his father's side, and Royal is happy with Bryluen because it means "rose" in Cornish and plant names are traditional among the demi-fey. Then Mary for me, and Kitto chose Katherine for his daughter because it could be shortened to Kitty, which looked like his own name. We've actually started calling her Tegan Rose, as if it's one name. She's learning to control her powers, too. Maeve's son, Liam, is still insisting that Rose is his, the way you'd claim a puppy, but I have to wonder if her ability to fascinate might have had a lasting impression on the little boy. We shall see.

I've made it clear that I have no desire to sit on Taranis's vacated throne. The many factions inside the Seelie Court scrambled to try to put their candidates on the throne, but through our friends among their nobles we suggested they let the sithen choose, as of old. Their faerie mound sang with joy when Aisling was finally allowed back through its doors, because now that Taranis was no longer king, all those that he exiled have a chance to return home.

Maeve Reed has no plans to visit, just yet. She's still afraid of Taranis, and rumor has it that he's convinced that he may find a cure for his arm, as the long-ago Lugh of the Silverhand did when he lost his hand in battle and had to give up the throne because of his lack of perfection, until a magical hand of silver was formed and he was made whole again. I think Taranis is lying to himself, but as long as he stays inside faerie and away from us we will let it lie. Do I want him dead for what he did to Sholto? Yes, but I want peace in faerie more. We'll see how Taranis reacts as Aisling's coronation gets closer; it's going to be the first-ever faerie coronation to be televised live.

Andais would still step down and let Doyle and me have her throne, but we still don't trust our safety inside either court, light or dark. I am content ruling the growing Western Lands of faerie, because it is spreading, and more enchanted land keeps appearing, here and there around L.A. They say that Hollywood is magic; they've never been more right.

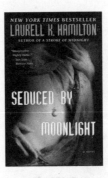

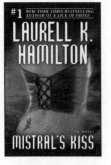

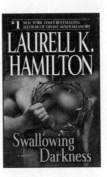